MW00617245

# BEATSPLOITATION

Today we would call the sensationalizing of the cultural phenomenon known as the beat generation to sell books and movies, Beatsploitation. What you won't be reading in this volume are lost or overlooked classics of Beat Lit. Don't expect to find books the caliber of On the Road, Go, Junky or Last Exit to Brooklyn. The books herein were written to cash in on the beat movement...

Although the writers of these books never achieved any literary grandeur, it shouldn't be inferred that they didn't have beatnik cred. Indeed, all three of the authors lived in that milieu—Coons and Golightly in Greenwich Village and Geis in Venice, California. These books don't have any literary pretension of defining what the beat movement was, but rather they reflect the places and period in which beatniks were prevalent.

This fact doesn't make these books any less worth the attention of the student of the beat generation. Indeed more can be learned about the reaction of the public to the beatniks than by reading the entire oeuvre of authors such as Kerouac or Ginsberg...

—from "How JFK Killed the Beatniks" by Jeff Vorzimmer

# A Beatnik Trio

Like Crazy, Man
by Richard E. Geis

The Far-Out Ones
by Dell Holland

Beat Girl
by Holly Golightly

STARK
HOUSE
**Stark House Press • Eureka California**
**www.starkhousepress.com**

A BEATNIK TRIO: LIKE CRAZY, MAN / THE FAR-OUT ONES / BEAT GIRL

Published by Stark House Press
1315 H Street
Eureka, CA 95501, USA
griffinskye3@sbcglobal.net
www.starkhousepress.com

LIKE CRAZY, MAN ©1960 by Richard E. Geis and originally published by Newsstand Library, Chicago. Reprinted as *The Beatniks* by Dollar Book, Chicago, 1960.

THE FAR-OUT ONES ©1963 by Neva Paperback, Inc. and originally published by Neva Paperbacks, Las Vegas.

BEAT GIRL ©1959 by Bonnie Golightly and originally published by Avon Books, New York.

This compilation copyright ©2020 by Stark House Press. All rights reserved under International and Pan-American Copyright Conventions.

"How JFK Killed the Beatniks" copyright ©2020 by Jeff Vorzimmer

Cover photo of Ted Joans at Café Bizarre ©1959 by Burt Glinn/Magnum Photos. Used with permission of Magnum Photos.

ISBN: 978-1-951473-13-6

Book design by ¡caliente!design, Austin, Texas

PUBLISHER'S NOTE
This is a work of fiction. Names, characters, places and incidents are either the products of the author's imagination or used fictionally, and any resemblance to actual persons, living or dead, events or locales, is entirely coincidental.

Without limiting the rights under copyright reserved above, no part of this publication may be reproduced, stored, or introduced into a retrieval system or transmitted in any form or by any means (electronic, mechanical, photocopying, recording or otherwise) without the prior written permission of both the copyright owner and the above publisher of the book.

First Stark House Press Edition: November 2020

# How JFK Killed the Beatniks
## Jeff Vorzimmer

An article in the November 1963 edition of *Ace* men's magazine tried to answer the claim of its title "How JFK killed the Beatniks." Aside from the bad timing of being on the newsstand the month Kennedy was assassinated, it didn't propound a cogent argument about how, indeed, Kennedy had killed the beatniks. The argument, albeit tongue in cheek, was that, though he was the youngest president we'd ever had, he had nothing in common with the beatniks, nor any sympathy for their lifestyle. Their points were 1) Kennedy bathed regularly, 2) He was "conspicuously married" and 3) Only "square" artists, musicians and writers such as Igor Stravinsky, Leonard Bernstein, Pablo Casals and Arthur Miller had been invited to the White House. The likes of Jack Kerouac, Allen Ginsberg, William Burroughs and Norman Mailer had yet to darken the door there, nor did it seem likely that an invitation would be forthcoming.

This was the gist of the article and, although weak, it didn't mean that a stronger argument couldn't have been made to support such a claim. It should be noted, though, that beatnik culture was already waning by 1960, satirized on television, in film and magazine parodies as well as being absorbed into mainstream American culture. All over America young men were sporting goatees and writing bad poetry, while librarians modeled their mode of dress after Audrey Hepburn in movies such as *Funny Face* and *Breakfast at Tiffany's*. A photographer named Fred McDarrah was running a rent-a-beatnik service out of the *Village Voice* in the early 60s that would rent out real live beatniks to read poetry at your party.

Kennedy did indeed put the nail in the coffin of beat culture, starting with his inaugural address in January 1961. "The torch has been passed to a new generation of Americans," he said and it was clear by the end of the speech that he was speaking particularly to the country's youth. It was to them he said, "Ask not what your country can do for you—ask what you can do for your country."

This was Kennedy speaking directly to the country's disaffected youth in attempt to get them out of the dark basement coffee houses into which they huddled and into public service. He made good on his election promises to make the youth of America part of the process by creating agencies such as the Peace Corps and instituting the President's Council on Physical Fitness.

The Beatnik scene was all about jazz and the improvisational and abstract in music, art and literature, but by the late 50s, there were other factors taking hold of the psyche of America's youth that would ultimately eclipse beatnik culture, most notably, the revival of folk music. Recitals of free form poetry, jazz music and comedians such as Lenny Bruce and Mort

Sahl, were being replaced in the coffee houses of North Beach, Venice and Greenwich Village by folk troubadours such as Glenn Yarborough and The Kingston Trio.

The rise of folk music went hand in hand with the rise in political consciousness among the country's youth, which was in stark contrast to the beatnik ethos of dropping out of "square" society and being separate from it rather than of changing society from within or through protest. The youth were coming out of the cafés and jazz clubs and into the light of Washington Square Park and the beach in Carmel.

To be clear the hippies were a younger generation rejecting the hipster culture that preceded it. The black and white geometric op-art of the late 50s/early 1960s by artists such as Bridget Riley and Victor Vasarely was replaced by the pop-art of Andy Warhol silkscreens, Roy Lichtenstein's comic strip panels and the psychedelic colors of Peter Max.

The year 1965 marked an explosion of color in print, television and film. That year the number of color televisions sold surpassed black & white sets. By the start of the 1965-66 season, most television shows had made the switch to color. Clothing was becoming more colorful than it had ever been, especially for men and tie-dyed clothing in psychedelic colors become popular. All this color was in stark contrast to the black clothing favored by Beatniks.

What ultimately killed the beatniks, though, was parody in magazines, movies and television shows, which made beatniks appear ridiculous in the extreme. It had started as early as 1960 when Alfred E. Newman appeared as a beatnik on the cover of the *Mad* Reader, *Like, Mad* and Jerry Lewis lampooned beatnik coffeehouse denizens in the film version of Gore Vidal's *Visit to a Small Planet* (which, incidentally, features in Geis' book *Like, Crazy*).

The ultimate ignominy came with two back-to-back episodes of *The Beverly Hillbillies* in April of 1965, with Jethro playing at being a beatnik and even convincing Uncle Jed to finance a coffeehouse when the owners couldn't make the rent. What they didn't know was that the building was owned by Uncle Jed's banker, Mr. Drysdale, who was about to evict the troublesome tenants.

Today we would call the sensationalizing of the cultural phenomenon known as the beat generation to sell books and movies, Beatsploitation. What you won't be reading in this volume are lost or overlooked classics of beat lit. Don't expect to find books the caliber of *On the Road, Go, Junky or Last Exit to Brooklyn*. The books herein were written to cash in on the beat movement for readers who might be intrigued, curious, or even repelled by the whole Beatnik lifestyle.

Although the writers of these books never achieved any literary grandeur, it shouldn't be inferred that they didn't have beatnik cred. Indeed, all three of the authors lived in that milieu—Coons and Golightly in Greenwich Village and Geis in Venice, California. These books don't have any literary pretension of defining what the beat movement was, but rather the books merely reflect the places and period in which beatniks were prevalent. They were not *of* the movement, but *about* the characters and environment of the movement.

This fact doesn't make these books any less worth the attention of the student of the beat generation. Indeed more can be learned about the reaction of the public to the beatniks than by reading the entire oeuvre of authors such as Kerouac or Ginsberg.

## Richard E. Geis

Richard Geis knew from the age of ten that he wanted to be a writer while reading a copy of *Astonishing Stories* one day at the beach. He started by writing sci-fi fanzines. After a series of starts and stops and many disappointments along his chis chosen career path, he found himself living in Venice, California in the late 1950s. He was starting to have some success selling his own science fiction stories and decided to write a novel, not a science fiction novel, but a novel set in the midst of the beat scene in Venice.

He sent this first novel, *Like Crazy, Man* to a small publisher of soft-core erotica in Chicago called Newsstand Library, which published it immediately. Geis claims to have only received $100 in royalties for the book, but his career, as a novelist was underway. He would write one other book for Newsstand before moving on to other soft-core publishers, such as Brandon House and Midwood, where he wrote under the pseudonym of Peggy Swenson.

If Geis' books are largely forgotten today—not a single one of his books remain in print—he earned a footnote in the history of twentieth century American literature. On October 21, 1964, he was indicted, along with 14 other people for "conspiring to publish and distribute obscene literature." A few days before, Geis was arrested at his home in Portland, Oregon and brought before a judge who told him there was a fugitive warrant out on him in the state of California. He was ultimately extradited to California, where he was booked in the L.A. County Jail and eventually released on bail put up by lawyers for his publisher Milton Luros.

Milton Luros, the publisher of Brandon House Books and various nudist magazines, dubbed by the media "the king of the girlie magazines" or "the king of smut" and his fourteen "co-conspirators" would spend much of next three and a half years fighting state and, ultimately, federal charges. Among the fifteen were Luros' wife Beatrice, writers, photographers, various editors and the circulation manager of Brandon House Books and London Press, the parent company of the magazines, as well as the companies that printed the books and magazines.

The fifteen were brought before Judge Joseph Wapner, later of *The People's Court* fame in the 1980s, where bail and a court date were set. Geis recalled years later that the state prosecutor objected to his "small" bail amount of $5,000 (the equivalent of $40,000 today), adding, "God knows what other sex crimes this man has committed in the past." It was decided that the case would go before Judge Harold Collins on November 2, 1964.

After several delays, a new trial date was set for February 23, 1965, charges against 10 of the 15 defendants, including Geis and Luros' wife, were dropped. Federal prosecutors knew that if they brought a federal case against Luros, they would not likely get a conviction in a California district court, so they were already planning on prosecuting the case in Iowa. A 1958 statue allowed for the prosecution of obscene materials in any state to which the materials were shipped.

A 25-count federal indictment included 12 people, most of whom had been party to the California indictment, but dropped some authors and added two more, as well as another editor for Brandon House. Richard Geis was named in the federal indictment just one month after charges against him had been dropped in California. In all, four authors were indicted, including Sam Merwin, Victor Banis and Wayne Vance. Two photographers, already well known, were indicted: Elmer Batters, the fetish photographer, and Bernie Abramson, famed photo chronicler of the Rat Pack. Also mentioned in both the California and federal indictment were the books *Three Way Apartment*, written by Geis under the pseudonym of Peggy Swenson and *Two Women in Love*, written by Sam Merwin under the pseudonym of Stanley Curson.

The 12 defendants were arraigned on April 20, 1965 and all pled "not guilty." In an interesting side note, one of the authors, Wayne Vance, was never found and charges against him were eventually dropped, at least temporarily.

The defense attorneys asked for a dismissal on the grounds that the charges were in violation of their defendants' first amendment rights and of their intention of filing motions to dismiss the case and/or ask for a change of venue to Southern California and for the return of all property seized from the defendants. The motions were filed on May 17 and on June 29, 1965 two of the motions were denied and the third, return of the property was postponed. A trial date was set for July 19, 1965, but the defense attorneys challenged Judge William Hanson's refusal to dismiss charges in an appeal to the Eighth District Court. A new trial date of October 18 was set.

Meanwhile the case in California had been dismissed by Judge Joseph Sprankle on June 14, 1965, contending that the books listed in the indictment didn't go as far in description of sexual acts as *Tropic of Cancer* (Henry Miller) did, a book that the Supreme Court had ruled as not being obscene.

When the trial opened on October 18, 1965, the defense attorneys again sought to have the case moved to California and to delay the case. Both motions were denied. The next tactic was to have the case dismissed on charges of entrapment. The defense claimed that defendants were set up by Los Angeles Postal Inspector Donald Schoof who had several Iowa postmaster subscribe under assumed names to nudist magazines from London Press to be able to try the case there. That motion was also dismissed and it later came out in the trial during the testimony of one the London Press employees that, in fact, over 29,000 publications had been shipped to Iowa in the year 1964.

As part of their case, the prosecutors ordered the jury members to read the seven books in question as well as review 29 issues of the nudist magazines cited in the indictment. The books were *Three Way Apartment* by Peggy Swenson (Richard Geis); *The Affairs of Gloria* by Victor Jay [Banis]; *Two Women in Love, Lesbian Alley* and *Lesbian Sin Song* by Stanley Curson (Sam Merwin); and *Pleasure House* by Wayne Vance (Morton Feinberg). On December 17 after nine weeks, the prosecution rested its case and the judged dismissed everybody for a two-week recess over the Christmas holiday.

When the trial resumed on Tuesday, January 4, 1966, Judge Hanson once again denied motions for acquittal, but also dropped the charges related to the nudist magazines and against two of the writers, Victor J. Banis—the only openly-gay defendant—and "Wayne C. Vance" who was thought to be traveling in Europe, unaware of his indictment.

In a surprise move, the defense called no witnesses and completed summation of their case by Monday, January 10. By Tuesday afternoon, the trial went to the jury and after four days of deliberation, the jury came back late Friday night, January 14, with a guilty verdict on all 147 of the remaining charges. Richard Geis was charged on one count of obscenity for *Three-Way Apartment* and Sam Merwin was charged on one count for each of his three books. Although *Pleasure House* by Wayne C. Vance was found to be obscene by the jury, it was decided that the author would be tried separately. By then he had been tracked down and identified as the well-known novelist Morton Cooper [Feinberg], who the following year would have a best-seller, *The King*.

By mid-January of 1967, several other obscenity cases, concerning the publication of the 18th century novel *Fanny Hill* and Ralph Ginzburg's *Eros* magazine, had reached the U.S. Supreme Court, so Judge Hanson granted a stay on further court proceedings until those cases had been decided and some kind of precedent set. An interesting note is that a Brandon House edition of *Fanny Hill* was also listed in the original California indictment of Milton Luros, but ultimately dropped when it was learned that an obscenity case had already been brought against another edition of the book.

In a split decision on March 21, the Supreme Court ruled that the State of Massachusetts was wrong in banning *Fanny Hill* but upheld the lower court's decision on the magazine *Eros* as obscene. On the basis of the *Fanny Hill* decision, Milton Luros' attorneys petitioned Judge Hanson to vacate his prior ruling. On November 4, Judge Hanson did vacate charges against all the defendants except Luros and the four companies, including Luros' wife, Beatrice, the two authors and the photographer Elmer Batters. Bernie Abramson had been dismissed from the case before the end of the trial due to ill health.

Richard Geis was finally free from prosecution after a two-year long ordeal that included a three-month trial in the dead of winter in Iowa, but on January 6, 1967, Milton Luros was sentenced to five-years in prison and $25,000 (the equivalent of about $200,000 today).

On January 13, Luros' attorneys appealed the decision to The Eight Circuit Court of Appeals. On February 7, 1968, The Appeals Court overturned Judge Hanson's decision on the grounds that it violated First Amendment rights. In its written decision, the three-judge panel noted that the lesbian novels "can be described as distasteful, cheap and tawdry. Yet these facts alone do not constitute a crime."

## William R. Coons

Bill Coons never intended to a writer, but two factors in his life thrust that life upon him. The first was his college friend, Donald Westlake, the second was a stint at Attica.

Authors Lawrence Block and Donald Westlake got their start writing the soft-core porn that was the subject of so many of obscenity cases of the 1960s. They had met while working as fee-readers for Scott Meredith and eventually both left to pursue full-time careers as writers. They remained life-long friends and even collaborated on two sex novels in 1960 under the pseudonym of Andrew Shaw (They would write a third Andrew Shaw novel together in 1962).

Both were making good money for these books, with advances as much as $1,200 ($10,000 in today's dollars) per book. Anybody could write these books, they reasoned, and Block and Westlake had somewhat higher aspirations. They didn't want to give up the money, just the writing.

That's when they got the idea that they could get someone—almost anyone—to ghostwrite these Andrew Shaw novels for publisher Bill Hamling at Nightstand Books. They could recruit writers to write the books and keep a percentage of the advance and royalties. Larry asked Don if he knew anybody who could write these books. Don thought of a friend of his, Bill Coons, who he knew from Binghamton University.

Don introduced Bill to Larry Block and together they initiated Bill Coons into the craft of writing sex books for Nightstand. They gave him a quick training on plots, length, deadlines and even on the little inside jokes they made such as referencing the title *The Sound of Distant Drums*, which the worked into the stories or character names that were anagrams of their real names. There is an example of this in Coon's *The Far-Out Ones*, included in this volume, in which a character sees in a jukebox "a recording of 'Sinfully Yours' by John Dexter's band." This is a reference to the title of a book Coons had written the year before under the John Dexter byline.

Since Coons included these references in the books he wrote as Andrew Shaw and as Dell Holland, it had the unintended consequences of being red herrings for future scholars of mid-century erotica trying to pin down authorship of these books fifty years hence.

The problem was that Bill Coons consistently missed his deadlines. He was always late with some excuse. Once he said he parked near the publisher's office to deliver a manuscript, which was already more than a week late, but instead of bringing it right up, he decided to leave it in the car while he ducked into a nearby bar for a quick drink. When he returned to fetch the manuscript, he found the car had been broken into and the manuscript stolen. Or so he claimed.

Once Lawrence Block was writing one of his own sex books and felt the plot was going nowhere and the writing was terrible. Rather than just putting it aside, he decided to take it to Bill Coons to see if he would write a few chapters and maybe collaborate on the rest of it.

When he got to Coons' apartment in Washington Heights and proposed the idea, the first thing Bill wanted to do was go out for a drink, so Block put the manuscript down on the coffee table and went out. When they came back, Bill's wife Cammy (Nappi) was sitting on the couch reading it. She looked up and said, "I think you're really getting better," she told Bill. "This is far and away the best thing you've ever done."

The book was eventually published as *Man for Rent* and was submitted to Hamling under the joint byline of Andrew Shaw and Dell Holland, the latter being Coons' own pseudonym for which he was trying to get some name recognition. Unfortunately, the book came out as by John Dexter, one of Hamling's often-used house names.

By 1963, Coons had had enough of writing sex books and decided to pursue a Master's Degree and was accepted at Cornell and by the fall of 1964 he had a acquired a teaching position at Skidmore College. By then his New York City friends had lost touch with him and didn't hear much about until July of 1969.

It was on July 3, 1969 that Coons was arrested with another man, William J. Gay, and charged with criminal possession of a controlled substance, specifically 200 capsules of LSD, described by a local newspaper as "the largest supply of LSD ever confiscated in upstate New York."

Coons was eventually tried and convicted on "third degree possession of a dangerous drug" and "third degree selling of a dangerous drug." He was sentenced to three years in Attica, of which he served 15 months, getting out just three months before the infamous Attica Uprising of September 1971. While in prison his wife Cammy served him with divorce papers.

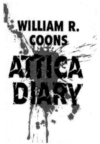

After getting out of Attica, Coons wrote an article for *The New York Times* titled "An Attica Graduate Tells His Story" on the tensions that lead to the Uprising. At the time he was already at work on a book about his time served there. The *Times* article led to a book deal with Stern & Day, which, it should be noted, was not negotiated by Coons' agent at the time and the book was not promoted by the publisher as much as it should have been.

*Attica Diary* would be Coons' last book and the only book to appear under his own name, but would earn Coons a place in the pantheon of prison literature. Unfortunately, as with all of his books, it is no longer in print.

## Bonnie Golightly

As with the other authors in this volume, none of Bonnie Golightly's books remain in print and, as with Geis and Coons, she has been reduced to a footnote in history. In 1959 Golightly sued Truman Capote, *Esquire* and Random House for libel and invasion of privacy claiming that the character of Holly Golightly in Capote's book *Breakfast at Tiffany's* published the year before was based on her.

After the Capote's novella appeared in the November 1958 issue of *Esquire*, several of Capote's friends came forward to claim that they were the real Holly Golightly and the game, Capote called the "Holly Golightly Sweepstakes" was afoot.

Bonnie Golightly owned a bookstore in Greenwich Village and had already published her first novel when she first heard about Capote's story. A friend of hers told her that he had attended a reading at which Capote read an early draft of *Breakfast at Tiffany's*, which featured a character named *Connie* Golightly. Bonnie had apparently told this friend, who supposedly knew Capote to tell him not to use a name so close to hers.

When the story came out in *Esquire* the character had been renamed *Holly* Golightly, but Bonnie felt as though she had even more in common with the character than just her last name. Like Holly, Bonnie was originally from the South, had lived in a brownstone on Manhattan's east side, just around the corner from a bar that featured folk music and a lot of theater actors as patrons, as well as being a cat lover. There was enough evidence to convince a lawyer to take the case and file suit on her behalf, asking for $800,000 (the equivalent of $7 million today) in damages.

When told of the lawsuit Capote replied in his inimitable fashion: "It's ridiculous for her to claim she is my Holly," he said. "I understand she's a large girl nearly forty years old. Why, it's sort of like Joan Crawford saying she's Lolita." Indeed, contemporary newspaper accounts referred to Bonnie as "full-figured" and as a "twice-divorced blonde built along dinner-at-Schrafft's lines"—quite different from the petite brunette of the book and later as portrayed by Audrey Hepburn in the movie made the following year.

When no decisive link could be found between Bonnie Golightly and Truman Capote, nor that it could be proved that he even knew of her existence prior to writing the novella, her lawyer dropped the case. In actual fact all that Capote likely borrowed from Golightly was her name. It would be hard to believe that Capote wouldn't have seen Golightly's name on her first back paperback novel, *The Wild One*, which was in bookstores, drugstores and on newsstands all over New York City at the time he was writing the story, the cover of which featured a petite brunette. Capote would dismiss the coincidence of the name Golightly by claiming it was not an uncommon name in the South.

Bonnie found that she had been stigmatized by bringing the lawsuit, a feeling that would stay with her for the rest of her life. She talked about it in an interview she did less than two weeks before her death. "It semi-ruined my writing life," she claimed. "I'm not kidding you . . . I was advised to change my name. I had become a figment of [Capote's] imagination. It was very discouraging."

Despite the publicity, Golightly managed to write a sequel to *The Wild One* called *Beat Girl*, the title of which had likely been changed by the publisher to cash in on the burgeoning beat scene of 1959.

# LIKE CRAZY, MAN
## by Richard E. Geis

# Chapter One

I looked up at the words "HIGH WATER—BEER" flashing red neon in the cold misty ocean side night. Booming bass notes from a loud juke box leaked out through the plate glass door and windows. Behind me across the wide Venice beach the Pacific battered idly at the sand.

I glanced at my watch. Ten o'clock. I swallowed and forced a deep breath. Hell, Ackerman, I thought, get on with it. If she's in there that's why you flew nine hundred miles. If she isn't, you wait.

I'd discovered an hour ago that she and her "lover" had moved from the address Ed been given, but were known to hang out in this beer joint.

I opened the door and went in, flinching at the blast of sound. To my left three women in slacks and shirts looked up from a small billiard table. Mannish female heads swiveled at the long bar. Their eyes turned cold with hostility. For a second all talk ceased and the Wurlitzer blared uncontested.

Goddamned lesbians. Hadn't they ever seen a real man before? I closed the door and walked down the narrow room to an empty stool, glancing at the women as I went. No luck. I'd have to stick around.

A handsome early fortyish woman in man's clothes was tending bar. A jaunty yachting cap set off her short wavy black hair. She wiped the bar in front of me. I could see suspicion in her eyes.

"Hamm's," I said. She silently served the beer and made change from the buck I threw on the bar. I took a deep swallow of the cold brew and looked around more closely.

The walls were blue murals of undersea life . . . mostly busty mermaids. The ceiling was too high for a tavern so an imitation thatched roof had been built out over the bar. Very cozy. The light was dim, coming mostly from a shaded bulb over the coin operated billiard table up front.

A small ugly woman sitting next to me raised her glass and drained it. She had a close mannish haircut. "Sonovabitch," she said loudly to herself. "Why do these half-assed squares always butt in where they're not wanted?"

She looked at me with mean dark eyes. In the dim light she looked as much a man as I. The floral sport shirt betrayed nothing of her breasts if she had any. Her grey slacks hung loose from slender hips. Except for the high voice she could have fooled anybody.

"Why the hell don't you get out?" she said.

"What's the matter, don't you like sitting next to the real thing?"

I'd thrown salt into an open wound. Her eyes flared and she drew back a small fist. I partly slid off the stool and turned to face her.

A woman, a real woman of perfume and white flesh in a tight red knit dress came between us. "Take it easy, Hank. Easy, baby. You don't want any trouble. I'll take care of him."

The fisty lesbian looked at her, then me. "Okay, Shirley, but get the jerk out quick or there'll be trouble. I mean it." She picked up her bottle and glass and moved up to the front where she sat by the window and glared at me.

The woman was solidly built, thick-waisted, with long brown hair framing a round face. Her breasts were big and heavy under the clinging red material. She sat on the vacated stool and smiled a lopsided warm smile.

How old was she? Thirty ... thirty-five? There were tiny age lines radiating from her eyes giving the impression of wisdom, humor and wry self-knowledge.

"What's your name, baby?" She gave my slim six-four frame a quick once-over.

"Jeff." I examined well fleshed thighs outlined by the tight skirt bunched under her by the leather topped stool. The perfume was devastating. It surrounded her with a magnet-like field of sexual attraction. I put out my hand. "I'm glad to meet you, Shirley."

Her smile broadened. It was an inviting smile. Her hand touched mine and its soft womanliness sent a wave of sudden hot desire flooding through me. I'd been too long without a woman. I'd been trying to forget Dawn by work, hoping she'd come back, holding onto my end of the marriage vows even if she had cut loose hers.

Now I looked into Shirley's warm brown eyes and wanted those big breasts mashed against me. I wanted to fill my hands with her flesh and press deep into her. It must have shown in my eyes. Her hand squeezed mine and then brushed against my thigh.

"Big boy," she said, "I like you. But you're in the wrong place. How did you come to walk in here? You a tourist?" She patted my arm and ran her fingers over the expensive tweed of my sports coat.

"No, I know I'm in a lez bar. I'm waiting for somebody to show up."

She laughed. "Who?"

The door opened up front. I lifted my beer to my lips and glanced along the shiny enameled bar that led like an arrow to the newcomers. My heart lurched.

There she was, using her maiden name of Dawn Hunter, but still my wife. With a lesbian: a husky young man-dressed, man-talking lesbian!

I slipped off the stool and started toward them. A few of the bar sitters and the billiard players were crowding around the two shouting greetings over the still thumping bass and screaming brass of the hi-fi juke.

Shirley tried to hold my arm. "Hey, Jeff . . ." But I shook her off, hardly aware of anything except the barely visible top of Dawn's golden hair. I pushed a barrel-bottomed lez out of the way and stood before Dawn, looking down at her breathtaking body. Imagine a spectacular girl six feet tall with a Marilyn Monroe face, golden yellow hair and deep blue eyes. Now take the head off and squeeze that body, compact it, until it is only five feet tall. Now replace the head. That describes Dawn.

She was unzipping a loose mink collared jacket when she saw me. Yellow silk capri pants clung to her prize winning legs. Some kind of tooled leather sandals were on her small delicate feet. I'd seen these things before; they were part of the ruinously expensive wardrobe I'd been forced to buy her to keep her happy.

Her eyes widened and shaded into the angry purple I knew too well. She sought the hand of the powerful lesbian beside her. I knew this must be Tex.

Tex looked at me, frowning. "What the hell do you want, bud?"

I started to fry inside. "I want to talk to my wife for a minute if you don't mind."

Dawn's lips pouted in childish anger. "We did all our talking in Portland. Why can't you leave me alone? Who told you I was here in Venice?"

"Jack Grimes, a private detective. How else could I find out? What did you expect me to do when you left me flat with only a short three line goodbye note? My God, Dawn, I love you. We're married—"

"No you don't love me!" Anger caused her to jerk her body sideways. The jacket swung open and revealed her bust. She wore a yellow silk blouse that was stretched tight by the big round swollen breasts that I knew jostled each other for room on her chest.

My throat went tight. Instantly I remembered long nights, her posing naked before a special full length mirror in narcissistic admiration as I lay in bed watching, waiting. And I remember other things I wanted to forget, things that make a man hate.

"I've got to talk to you, Dawn. Give me at least a few minutes."

"Why should I? When did you ever think of me except when you wanted to show me off to your friends or when you wanted to go to bed?"

I could feel my shoulders tense with anger. Here it was, the beginning of another typical argument. The juke box had stopped. Our voices were all that filled the silence. I looked angrily around at the crowded interested faces.

I yelled back at Dawn. "Don't tell me you didn't like to strut around like a peacock because I know damned well you did. I had to pay for all those clothes! And I see you brought them all along with you, too!"

"They were mine! You gave them to me!"

"I'm glad you appreciate them. Just like you appreciated the fifteen hundred dollars in our checking account. I had to clean out the savings account to pay Grimes and come down here."

"I had to have *some* money, didn't I? You make plenty."

"Not that much! Dawn, you've had your fling. Come back with me. I've got a job to get back to."

"Oh, yes, that precious advertising job. It's always been more important to you than I am. You don't care a fig about me or my career. Everything has to center around Kingman's, that shriveled old boss of yours and advertising, advertising, advertising!"

"Yes, and that's the way it should be!" I grabbed for her arm. "Now come on. You've caused me enough embarrassment."

Tex came forward and shoved me away. "Get goin', fella. Dawn belongs to me now."

I looked full into the narrowed black eyes, then slowly looked her up and down. A bigger heavier version of the lez I'd had trouble with a moment ago at the bar. Close cut black hair, expensive men's clothes, men's shoes, masculine rings and watch. What had Grimes' report called her? A bull dyke. A roaring, tough, battling bull dyke who had fought or scared away all the others who were competing for Dawn's favors. I figured she weighed about what I did, one-eighty.

I sneered at her and imitated her woman's voice. "'Dawn belongs to me now.' Phooey! You perverts make me sick, trying to be something you're not. You can't get a man so you prey on women." I looked at Dawn. "What do you see in this twisted—"

I didn't finish. Tex's white shirt and western braid tie moved between us and the next thing I knew something hit me hard on the side of the head. I stood there, dazed, blinking like a silly fool, and watched Tex draw back a heavy tanned fist. This time she caught me on the chin.

I went backwards with a surprised look on my face. I stumbled awkwardly against the billiard table, flipped over it on my back and landed hard on the cement floor. A sharp excruciating pain lanced through my left knee. I thought I heard Dawn cry out my name.

I lay there shaking my head, trying to clear it of pain. The damned basketball injury had been renewed. The knee would puff up like a balloon. And Tex . . . she was standing over me. I could see her polished oxfords inches from my face. How could she hit so hard She hit like a Mack truck! Being a man was no casual thing with her . . . she'd been taking lessons.

I heard laughter from the crowd, jeers, congratulations for Tex. Then I felt her hands gripping me, trying to lift. My coat ripped at the shoulder seam. She got another grip and up I went. God, this lez was strong!

I braced on my good leg and tried to punch at her grinning face but my bad knee gave way and I lurched into her. I caught a whiff of after shave lotion before her fist clobbered me again and I kissed the floor. My head was filled with buzzing. My brain was rattling around in my skull with all its wires pulled loose. Tex pulled me up again and my nylon shirt ripped open.

I felt cold air. Tex crowed victoriously and shoved me out the door with all her strength. I took three agonized steps with my left leg and rolled off the promenade into cold dirty sand.

I raised my head weakly and spat the gritty stuff out of my mouth. I heard Dawn's voice. "Let me see if he's hurt."

"The hell with him," Tex said. "Come on back in here!" The door closed and a few seconds later the juke started up again.

"Strike three," I muttered and groaned my way upright. I walked, limping badly, gritting my teeth, to one of the cement benches that line the promenade. I sat in a pool of light from the arc lights above and massaged my knee.

So much for 180 pounds of Y.M.C.A. conditioned bone and muscle. Three years ago star forward for Slates Gill at Oregon State, now a crumpled wreck on the slum beach of southern California.

I'd spent three hundred dollars tracing Dawn to this crummy old resort town and then blown the whole bit in three minutes. What now? Back to Portland on the next plane to face the snide remarks and arch looks of our relatives? Back to face the low-voiced office gossip? What a rich mother lode of scandal those vultures had chewed over the last three weeks since Dawn had packed up and left me.

And what would they say when I returned from a trip, bruised, limping, and failed to bring her back with me? I cringed from the thought. I'd be a laughing stock: "Poor old Jeff . . . it just goes to show . . ." and knowing office politics and the unwritten laws of corporation policy, I could kiss goodbye any thought of advancement into the top level. With Dawn on my arm I was that bright young executive with a future at Kingman's department store. Without her, humiliated, I was nothing.

A blast of sound came from the High Water as the door opened. Shirley stepped out and locked around. She spotted me and walked over.

"How you feel, baby?"

"Fine. I've got a broken leg and a split head. It only hurts me when I laugh."

"I could have told you Tex was rough. Trying to get Dawn away like that wasn't very smart."

"You seem to know a lot about them."

"Sure, I know just about everybody around here. I'm everybody's friend."

I tried some weight on my knee and cursed as pain shot up my thigh. "How about helping me over to the parking lot? It looks like I sleep in my shiny new rented Caddy tonight."

"With that leg?" She put her arm around my waist as I leaned on her shoulder. "Baby, why don't you come up to my place and soak in a hot bath? I only live a short block away."

She was smiling invitingly. In spite of a developing headache and the shooting knee pain I felt a resurgence of my earlier desire for her. I had a yearning to kiss her lips, to taste them for softness and passion. Yes, God knows it had been a long time.

I nodded.

Her smile widened. "This way, honey."

"No, I've got to get some clothes out of the car first." I looked like a badly built scarecrow. My coat and shirt were torn and my pants leg was ripped.

"Get them tomorrow morning. You'll feel better then."

"Maybe you're right." It was two blocks along the promenade to the parking lot. I leaned more weight onto her and hobbled along at her side. Damn, my shoes were full of sand.

We tottered up a street and paused before crossing a narrow alley-like road that ran parallel to the beach. A pair of blinding headlights bore down on us. A low green convertible thundered past us full of high school kids, then squealed to a stop. The horn gave a blast and a young pony tail girl in a well filled sweater stood up in the back seat and yelled, "Hey, Shirley's got a customer! Screw him once for me, Shirley." There was a scream of hysterical laughter and then she was thrown down to the seat by the sudden jerk of acceleration as the car jumped ahead.

It simply hadn't occurred to me that Shirley was a prostitute. I hadn't thought of her as anything. It shocked me to have our relationship so baldly stated by a smart alecky kid. I resisted her guiding tug. I didn't want to cross that road yet.

I looked up at the street sign. "Why is this called Speedway?"

"C'mon, baby, don't mind what that damned Rosemary said. You come with me and we'll fix that knee up fine."

"You know that girl?"

"Oh, yeah, she's a dirty little slut who runs a small gang around here. They start 'em young in Venice." There was an uncomfortable short silence. Shirley reached up and smoothed the sandy hair out of my eyes. "Don't you like me, Jeff?"

"Yes, it's just . . . I've led a sheltered life." Stupid! God, that sounded stupid! "I mean . . . I never had to go with a . . . I always had plenty of girls of my own." I felt like a bastard.

"I'm just a woman. There doesn't have to be anything between us if you'd rather not. But you should soak that knee. You won't be able to walk for a week if you don't."

A week! My problem with Dawn and my job came rolling in on me. Nobody knew I was down here. I'd thought I could fly down Saturday morning, pick up Dawn and be back by Sunday night at the latest. There were advertising schedules to set up for Winter, a theme for the store Centennial to dream up, conferences with the old man about total advertising outlays for the coming year . . . God, if I wasn't at my desk on Monday . . .

I took a step across Speedway. That promised hot bath was now a matter of survival. I carefully put one foot before the other. A street light a block away cast long shadows. The patched roadway was salted with broken glass and cigarette butts. Shirley had to steer me around isolated piles of dog manure. We crossed the road and entered a narrow, darker alley. Here you couldn't see what you were stepping on. Every few feet a series of rusty oil drum garbage cans denoted a different shadowed end of a house.

We came to a looming apartment house and entered the back door. "Take it easy now, honey. It's only up to the second floor. One step at a time."

I had to gasp as we climbed the narrow flight of back stairs, but at last we reached the top and shuffled along the hall toward the front of the building.

Shirley whispered, "Here it is," and I leaned against the wall as she unlocked apartment number four.

## Chapter Two

I hopped in after her. "The bathroom is right there," she said, pointing to a door to the right of the entrance. There was a click and a single small bulb lit up in an old six-socket light fixture hanging from the ceiling.

We were in a dining room designed for the 1920's. Dirty Venetian blinds covered the windows. Dirty curtains. Dirty Mexican braided rug. A pair of sliding doors led into another room on the left.

"There should be lots of hot water." She helped me into the old fashioned bathroom. The tub crouched on the floor with short ugly animal legs. "That's about the only good thing you can say about the dump." She pushed down the toilet seat lid and let me ease myself down to it. "There's a clean towel on the rack."

She stooped to insert a worn rubber plug in the bathtub drain. Her big rump was outlined close to my face. She looked under her arm at me, her face split by an upside down smile. "Don't get any ideas . . . oh!"

I grinned and decided I liked the firm bounciness of her flesh. No girdle. "That's what I like. A good solid woman."

"Huh!" She turned the hot water handle. There was a sucking gurgle, then a jet of steaming water spurted from the faucet. She straightened up, still smiling. "Honey, you need any help getting undressed?" She bent over, her lips close. I inhaled the perfume and a slight musky animal smell. Her fingers played with my belt.

There was sweet sickness deep in my gut. I moved my head and kissed her. Soft warm lips. Then a bold searching tongue that brought a groan from me. My hands rose from my sides and sought her breasts. I mentally damned the heavy-duty bra she wore. For long seconds we held the pose.

She broke the kiss and backed away. "Take your bath, baby." She stood in the doorway. "Did you ever see *Hell's Angels?* Jean Harlow was in it."

I shook my head no and started unbuttoning my shirt. "Before my time."

"There's a scene where she's dressed in a real low cut dress, front and back. She's on a couch with this flyer. So she gets up and says, 'Excuse me, I'm going to change into something more comfortable.'" Shirley smiled the lopsided smile and winked. "I'll be back in a few minutes."

I was just slipping into a delicious foot of hot water, feeling the heat enclose my injured knee, when she reappeared in the doorway dressed in a sheer blue nylon robe. She held a tall tinkling glass in her hand.

"Here we are, to the rescue again. I hope you like gin."

"Love it."

She bent down to hand me the drink and I looked into the gaping neckline to the milky white of her naked breasts. They hung free and loose against the thin material, pressing dime size nipples into sharp relief.

Then came the jolting realization that I was totally exposed to her gaze. I followed her eyes and almost covered myself with a hand. I even blushed a little.

"Ummm," she said. "I hit the jackpot." She raised an eyebrow. "No wonder little Dawn left you . . . you're a big man."

I blushed more. "That wasn't the reason." I'd never heard a woman talk this way before. It didn't seem right, yet I liked it. I relaxed and the blush went away. I began to enjoy the situation. She was so natural and matter-of-fact about seeing me and letting me ogle her breasts that my embarrassment faded. It was a good feeling, a feeling of release from everyday morals and codes of conduct.

Here was a woman, a prostitute, who had seen and done everything. Nothing could shock her and certainly she would never put on the hypocritical false modesty act that ninety percent of the "respectable" girls used as a weapon.

With Shirley I relaxed as I never had before. I sipped at the drink and looked up at her appreciatively. Her legs were round and sturdy, solid columns of white barely visible through the blue nylon.

"Okay," she said, "then suppose you tell me what is the matter between you two?" She sat on the toilet lid.

"You heard what we were arguing about. Dawn isn't very mature. She's selfish. All she thinks about is taking. She never gives anything in return. She's only interested in herself."

"Why did you come down here after her then? I should think you'd be glad to get rid of her."

It was a question I didn't want to answer. "Hell . . . I love her. She's my wife." Even to me it didn't sound convincing. I did love Dawn, that was part of it, but . . . "Let's talk about you for a while, Shirley. How did you happen to . . . do this for a living?"

She shrugged and looked away. "Who can say? I'm from a well-to-do family and my father spoiled me. We lived in a nicey-nice neighborhood in Detroit. Maybe I had too much time with boys after school . . . or maybe I was just cut out for it. I was a hot-house girl. The boys were after me when I was eleven. And I liked it." She rubbed her eyes slowly.

"I remember the first time. It was a hot summer night and we were in the attic of my house. We were both giggling and playing some silly game up there. Who was he? I can't even remember his name. Bobby something. He was a tall gangling kid, a freshie in high school and I was a week past my 12th birthday. I remember it hurt like hell. After that I liked it." She met my eyes. "I liked it too much for my own good."

I felt like a bastard for having asked her. I raised my glass. "Why aren't you drinking too?"

The lopsided smile. "Would you believe it? I've got an ulcer."

"Definitely not what I'd think of as an occupational disease."

"Yeah, but I worry too much."

"What about?"

"Oh . . . things." There was a pause. "Baby, you ask too many questions. Around here that isn't good. You could wind up face down in the ocean if somebody gets the idea you're an informer or on the vice squad."

"Ahhh . . ."

"No, I mean it. It's dangerous." She stood up and gathered my clothes off the floor. "When you get through soaking come into the bedroom. I'll massage your leg for you."

"I think I'd like to do a little massaging of my own."

A slow smile. "I'll be waiting, baby."

I stayed in the tub ten minutes longer till the water cooled to lukewarm. A few minutes later I walked naked through the open sliding doors and found myself in a living room. My knee felt a lot better. Shirley's voice came from behind half closed louvered French doors on the left. "This way, baby. I'm waiting for you."

The quiet was ruptured my a measured thumping from the apartment above. I could hear the muted wail of a trumpet. God, another hi-fi. I listened a few seconds more. Jazz this time.

I padded into the bedroom. Shirley was lying on the bed, white and naked, barely visible in the darkness. My mouth got dry. I climbed in and lay beside her. My arm touched her warm hip.

"How's the knee?"

"A few twinges." Her musky animal smell was stronger. I put my face close to her skin and breathed deep. My hand touched her belly and slid upward.

"Not yet, baby." She sat up and straddled my leg. Her hands were strong and sure as they probed and kneaded the muscle and bone. My eyes adjusted to the faint dining room light that sifted in the doorway.

Her large breasts swayed and moved like huge hanging melons. I reached up and buried my fingers in them. They were warm skins of Jello with two stiff nipples set in dark round centers.

"You like big girls?" I could hear the smile in her voice.

"You know it."

"I like big boys."

The hi-fi above us increased in volume. "Somebody up there likes jazz."

"That's Zeke. He manages the building."

"Doesn't anybody ever complain about the noise?"

"Sometimes, but we're all Outsiders here. We don't have to worry about old crochety pensioners or squares. As long as Zeke keeps the place full and collects all the rents the owner doesn't care either."

"You don't have to rub my knee any more."

She chuckled deep in her throat. "I want to talk a little bit. You and Dawn have got me curious."

"I told you."

"No, not everything you didn't. I still don't know why she ran away from you and came down here."

I frowned and breathed out quickly in irritation. "Oh, hell. One of our neighbors was a lesbian. I guess she got to Dawn and told her about Venice. How many lesbians are there around here?"

"Hundreds. Go on."

"If you must know I caught them at it twice. Kissing and feeling each other on the couch. I got mad as hell the second time and beat them both up. I don't know what she sees in queer love."

"Maybe you didn't satisfy her."

"Huh! What a crock of sweet violets that is. It was the other way around. She couldn't satisfy me. All she could think of was her beautiful body and how it might get bruised. I'd try to squeeze her a little bit and she screamed about a blemish. I'd try to get into her and she'd say it hurt. So I'd get her so hot she was giving off steam and she'd go off before I did. Then what do you think she said?"

"What did she say, baby?"

"She said, 'Aren't you finished yet?' or 'What's taking you so long, you're heavy.' Good gosh! I got so mad some of the time I jumped off her, went into the bathroom and finished by hand. That's the kind of wife I've got!"

"When did you marry her?"

"I met her in my senior year . . . when she was a freshman. I swept her off her feet and married her. It was a mistake. I should have let her go through the college dramatics course until she found out she was no good. Now nothing will convince her."

Shirley stopped massaging my knee. "I still don't know why you're down here after her."

I squirmed on the bed. "I've got a good job, but it's no good unless I'm happily married . . . or it looks that way to the old man. He doesn't want bachelors or marriage failures in top spots. I'd be eased out in a year. And I do love her, damnit. It's not just the job!

"We had some terrific times together on our honeymoon and just after that for six months. She really loved me then. She'd told me she wasn't interested in a career anymore. But I guess she got bored or that damned mother of hers whispered in her ear about how she was wasting her talent. Suddenly I wasn't good for her any more!"

I stopped caressing Shirley's breasts. I took two handsfull and squeezed hard.

"Oww, stop that! Damnit, that hurts."

"Stop asking so many questions, then. What's it to you, anyway? What do you care?"

"I'm just curious. That's another of my faults." She gently rubbed her hurting flesh.

"I'm sorry."

"You don't sound sorry."

"I am! What do you want me to do?"

"Kiss them and make them well, baby. Kiss them."

I rose up on my elbows and met her leaning body with my lips. Her skin tasted slightly salty. Her hands were between her knees, running up my leg, seeking me.

Her hands were small, like a little girl's, and she used both. "Just a minute, baby," she said. "Just a minute. Nurse a little longer." Then her hands pressed my head closer, forcing my face into a soft breast. I could hear her breath rasping in her throat. "I like it," she said. "I like it too much . . ." Her hips slid forward and raised up.

On the outside Shirley was full and soft all over. And warm. Her body was soothing warmth. But then she lowered and I was enveloped by hot liquid flesh, surrounded by superb active muscles, grasping, tightening milking muscles.

I gasped and flopped back. She was a real professional. Her hips rose and fell in long deep strokes.

"Baby, baby, baby . . ." she said, her voice thick with lust.

I crossed my feet and pushed up at her. The thumping hi-fi above set our pace. Short minutes later her body quickened. Her fingers curled around my arms. I closed my eyes. The building split asunder, the sky poured into my brain and stars exploded and pinwheeled. I felt Shirley collapse onto my chest.

## Chapter Three

After long minutes of sighing, gentle appreciative kisses and quiet listening to our hearts slow down, Shirley began talking about a different world. We talked about art, writing, politics and psychology. It was a conversation that rambled through the spectrum of ideas like a curious donkey nibbling green grass on wide acreage.

She surprised me. The books say the common prostitute is below average in intelligence and comes from a low income group. To which I say crap. It may have been true fifty years ago, but no more. Shirley betrayed a keen mind and some formal higher education. As we talked I realized why some men marry women like her, knowing of their past but not caring.

I lay on the bed, tired, a fog of sleepiness slowly rising from my brain. "I don't think so," I said. "A lot of the so-called classics in literature are the singular property of college professors. They say thus and such a book written by an ancient geezer is a classic and that makes it a classic. Nobody cares one way or the other because nobody reads them except the professor and a few poor graduate students in English Lit. Let somebody outside their charmed incestuous circle disagree and they shout him down as an ignorant barbarian. So what happens? The . . ."

I let my voice trail into silence. There were steps on the front stairway leading up to the apartment. A mumble of voices. The steps and sounds of quiet words came closer and stopped. I heard a key inserted in the apartment door.

What was going on here? I looked quickly at Shirley. She was frowning. "It must be Lena. We share the apartment."

"What the hell am I supposed to do?" I felt betrayed. Here I was naked as a jaybird and a couple of people were coming into the place. I climbed under the covers.

Shirley put a small cool hand on my chest. "Take it easy. She told me she was staying all night with another model at Malibu. Don't get excited."

In the meantime the key turned in the lock and a second later the mumble became clear. A man's baritone voice was saying, ". . . matter, don't you trust me? All I want is a little drink."

"I thank you for the return, Craig, but I am tired." A young woman's voice, almost as deep as his. It was husky, sensuous, with a clear foreign accent I couldn't place. The voices moved into the dining room.

"Aw, c'mon, don't be that way, Lena. I didn't drive you all this way from Hollywood just for the ride. I'll only be a few minutes."

"I say no, I mean it. Please leave."

"I don't dig you, girl. You show up at the party dressed in that slinky outfit and then decide to go home when things get interesting. I put you onto Arnold Leppin and you freeze him into ice cubes. He's only the fair haired director at Grand Productions. Why didn't you play up to him?"

"He is a dirty old man. That kind of playing up I don't do."

"Well now look, kid, that kind of cooperation is necessary nowadays. He can help you a helluva lot. And as far as that goes, so can I. I made you a top model but I can break you, too. Who was it discovered you in this lousy slum? Who photographed you and put you over in 'Fling?' I did."

"I am grateful . . ."

"Sure, you're grateful. Why don't you show it once in a while? Everytime I want to get cozy you turn on the refrigerator. You think I can pose you for hours and not want to climb all over that terrific body? You like torturing me?"

"Please, Craig, it is no use talking. I will pose only as business. You promised no touching."

"God, I'm only human. Have a heart."

"I am sorry."

"What's the matter with me? Are you queer or something? Is that why you wanted out when Gloria didn't show tonight?"

"I am grateful to you—"

"Ohhh, she's grateful. Here we go with that again. The four word vocabulary." His voice hardened. "I'm tired of fooling around with you kid. I don't ask much. You've put me off too long as it is. You come across or the word'll get around that you're no good any more. You'll be on the *it* list. No more modeling, no more fifty bucks an hour jobs. You'll be back slinging hash down on the beach. You want that?"

"I don't care. I will pose, but—"

There was a scuffling of feet and her quick indrawn breath. He whispered loudly, *"Please!"* and there was the sound of ripping material, then a sharp cracking slap.

Shirley was up off the bed and into her robe. She charged out of the bedroom as he said, "Bitch! If that's the way you want it—"

Shirley burst in on them. "Okay, mister, that's it. Get the hell out!"

"What is this? Who're you?"

"I'm Lena's roommate. Now clear out before I call the cops!"

"Yeah? Her roommate, huh? You know what? I think you're both queer!"

*"Get out!"* yelled Lena.

"You bet your life. And you better forget about any more posing, kid." His voice changed quality as he moved into the hall. "I'd like to know just one thing. Which one of you is the butch?"

The door slammed. I heard him muttering to himself as he clumped down the stairs.

"You all right, baby?"

"Yes. It is these men. How I hate them." A short silence was ended by what sounded like a kiss and a long sigh. "What are those? Are those a man's clothes?"

Lena had spotted my stuff on the chair.

"Honey, I met a guy at the High Water tonight. He had a bum knee and was feeling low so I brought him home."

"Shirley, you promised me not to hustle. You promised if I paid the rent."

"Oh, baby, this is different. I didn't take any money."

"Let me see this man." She walked into the bedroom and turned on the overhead light. I blinked and stared at her. She was breathtaking.

I'd seen her incredible body in all the men's magazines. Public demand had provoked three and four page spreads for the last five months. *"Fling"* especially had featured her. Some of the picture story titles came back to me: "Hawaii's Hottest Hula Girl", "Sweeterina Lena", "Gift From The Islands." I remembered some other information. She was twenty-two, nearly six feet, an orphaned daughter of a Polynesian father and Eurasian mother. She never gave out her last name and was known simply as Lena. She was a "beautiful mystery woman from the exotic East."

She was dressed in a glittering silver metal-cloth ensemble of tight lounging slacks and matching top. Her blue-black hair was cut short in the current short Italian style. Her familiar narrow elfin face and full, almost negroid lips, were in open dislike. Her hard grey eyes had an oriental cast. They were cunningly accented by light green mascara and eye shadow.

"Another big one. Tall, you always like them tall." She swung around to confront Shirley who had followed and was biting her lower lip.

Lena was a terrific, jolting mammary wonder of a woman. She was tall and Junoesque, possessed of a staggering 44-27-37. I and millions of other men knew those magic figures by heart. Now I was seeing them in person. I swallowed and tried to mentally strip away the silver cloth. The low cut neck was ripped ever lower. I couldn't blame the photographer for feeling as he did.

Lena continued. "You think I will be away one night and right away you have a man. Is that your way?"

"Honey, I told you from the start I was convertible. Just because you pay the rent doesn't mean you own me."

Tears began to glitter in Lena's eyes. "Behind my back. Behind my back." She clutched Shirley in an embrace and kissed her.

I felt odd; shocked and mad at seeing two women kiss like that, yet curious and excited. Shirley was responding. Her fingers sought a gap in the back of the silver outfit and explored the revealed tan skin.

"You love me?" Lena kissed Shirley's white throat and caressed a big, slightly pendulous breast through the sheer nylon robe.

"Baby, you know I do." Shirley looked at me without expression, then winked.

I watched as the two women clung to each other. The sight of their busy hands was making me hot again.

Lena said to me, "Leave, go away."

"No, Lena, he hasn't any place to go. He's new in town and his clothes were ruined in a fight."

"The hell with it. I'll go." I sat there in bed, though, and didn't move. In fact I drew my knees up a little higher. I couldn't face walking past them, nude, in my aroused state. "Just get my clothes so I can dress."

"No, Jeff, that won't work. The cops run patrols down the Speedway every ten minutes at night during weekends. They'll spot you trying to get into your car and pull you in because of your clothes. You'll be in jail for days trying to explain that fight with Tex. I know those bastards. If you look like a bum, you *are* a bum." She sat on the bed. "Lena, let him sleep in the pull down bed in the dining room. We can close the sliding doors."

Lena looked at me closely. "Tex did this to him?" She smiled. "Yes, let him sleep there." She wriggled her shoulders. "I hate these clothes."

Shirley disappeared and came back with my shorts. Under the guns of their amused gaze I managed to slip them on under the covers. I still felt naked when I stood up and walked past Lena.

"Men!" she said, spitting the word. "Muscles and sex brains."

Shirley showed me that a wide mirrored panel in the dining room actually pulled out and around on a pivot. Standing upright on the reverse side was a pull down Murphy bed. I let it down easily amid a squeal of little used springs and counterweights.

Lena appeared in the wide doorway. She was nude to the waist! I gawked like a schoolboy. For just a second I couldn't breathe.

"Shirley called you Jeff. How do you like me, Jeff?" She stretched her arms up behind her head and took a deep breath.

Gosh! Her breasts were out of this world. They were cantaloupes, self-supporting and silky smooth, big and round and full. Her nipples were flat nubs surrounded by wide salmon pink circles that shaded into the natural tan of her skin.

I wanted to leap over that bed and touch her. I would have given a year of my life to run my hands over them, to kiss them. And she knew it! Damn her, but she knew it. She was gloating, reveling in my raw desire.

"You want more to see?" She began slipping off the silver slacks.

"Lena, cut it out." Shirley kissed her on the cheek. "Go to bed. I'll get him some bedding and be with you in a minute."

"No, let him see. Let him see what men cannot touch." She stepped out of the slacks and then the pink lace briefs. She struck the pose again. She moved her shoulders and her breasts swayed heavily.

I licked my lips. "You actually enjoy showing yourself to men, don't you? You torture them deliberately."

"Yes, yes, I do. I hate them. I hate you!"

"Just because I'm a man?"

"Yes!" A sudden intense burst of passion. "*I hate all men!* I like to see them suffer from want of me. I like to see their fingers move and their muscles strain to take a step they fear to take. Most are afraid." She studied me closely. "Not you. You would do it if Shirley were not here."

I looked at her long thighs, the wonderful S-curve of her waist and hip. I shook my head sadly. "What a waste. What a lousy criminal waste. You ought to screw every man in the world. It would give us all a small bit of heaven. Just a few minutes of impossible happiness. Then we could all die when our time came with that single bright flame of memory to console us."

She seemed to shrink into herself. Her magnificent body shuddered. "NO!" She darted into the bedroom.

Shirley moved close to me. "Take it easy, Jeff. Something terrible happened to her when she was young." She smiled and pecked me on the lips. "I'll get a blanket and some sheets. I'm sorry, we don't have an extra pillow."

A minute later she piled them onto the bare mattress, said goodnight, and closed the two sliding doors. I looked around the room and wondered how I'd ever gotten into this. If somebody had told me two days ago . . . Finally I set to work making up the bed.

Sleep was closing in on me. It had been a helluva long Saturday. Up at six that morning to catch the Western Airlines flight south. Now it was close to two in the morning in slum-by-the-sea, Venice, California. I ached pleasantly as I turned out the lights and climbed between the clean sheets.

But I could hear them talking in the bedroom. The sliding doors didn't keep out sound worth a damn. It looked like this was my night to overhear conversations. I couldn't restrain my curiosity.

I reversed my position on the bed and put my head near one of the doors. Their voices became clearer. Shirley was speaking.

". . . while he's in the apartment?"

"It is nothing to be ashamed. Take off your robe."

"Can't we wait till tomorrow, I'm pooped tonight."

"He tired you? No, now. You must prove you still love me."

"You know I do."

"No, leave the light on this time."

Shirley sighed. "You want an audience."

"Come."

Their bed complained. There were rustlings, heavy breathing, the sounds of kisses and the soft whisper of flesh against flesh.

Shirley whispered something.

"Yes, I want him to hear!"

"Am I better than he?"

I had to see it. Hell, Lena had invited me to look. I pulled one of the sliding doors open a few inches. By resting my head on the extreme end of the Murphy bed I could see into the living room and through their wide open bedroom doors.

Lena was kissing Shirley's breasts and her hands were seeking, probing. I could see Shirley's thigh muscles twitch. I could almost feel those fingers. Sweat broke out on my forehead. I was breathing hard just from watching.

Lena from any angle was a stirring sight. It came to me stronger than ever what a crime it was that she loved only women. I watched as she inched down Shirley's body.

Inexplicably I thought of Dawn. What was my wife doing? This same thing? Was she locked in the arms of that female bull? Were her naked hips jerking like Shirley's were doing now? Was Dawn holding her breath with Tex as she had with me when her shallow passion trickled through her? My fingers were digging into the blanket.

I watched it to the end and heard Shirley moan in ecstasy and press Lena's head closer with straining arms. Then I slid off the bed and went into the bathroom.

## Chapter Four

The doors sliding open wakened me in the morning. Shirley came into the room wearing a white terrycloth robe. "Sorry," she said, and went into the bathroom.

I looked at my watch. It was ten o'clock. The mid-morning sun was blasting through the windows. I stared at the badly painted ceiling. Sunday. Sometime today I had to get Dawn away from Tex. Yeah, if that was all there was to it. If only she were a prisoner and I a knight in shining armor. I felt a sick fear leaking into my gut. I couldn't see any way of changing her mind. My presence seemed to make her more determined.

The toilet flushed and Shirley came out of the bathroom. She sat on the edge of the bed. "Lena wants you out before she gets up."

I nodded.

She put a small restraining hand on my chest as I sat up. "Did you see us last night?"

"Yes."

She smiled the lopsided smile. "It must have been an education."

"C'mon, I'm not that square. Do you really like that kind of thing?"

"You mean, do I like it more than sex with a man? It's different. The kick isn't any stronger, but it's smoother." She shivered and grinned. "Lena has quite a technique."

"What about me?"

"I like you just as much." Her hand slid down under the covers and squeezed me once. "That's one place Lena can't match you." She rose and paused before going back through the doors. "Why don't you go up and rent a room from Zeke? 5A is empty, I think. You've got to stay somewhere, don't you?"

"I've got to take Dawn back with me tonight."

"Don't kid yourself. If you really want her you'll have to stick around and fight for her. It'll take time. If you don't think she's worth it, leave and forget her."

"I've got work that can't be put off!"

She shrugged. "It's your decision." And she went into the living room.

I crawled out of bed and put on my torn clothes. I had a sudden suspicious thought and hastily checked my wallet. It was all there, four hundred in cash. More than enough for plane tickets back to Portland . . . *if.*

I had to admit Shirley was right. It would take time to persuade Dawn. But time was my master.

I let myself out of the apartment and stood undecided in the hall. I could call Bob at his home in Portland and tell him I'd be away a few days. He could make some excuse to the old man. I could make it up to him later. He was my assistant, wasn't he? He could take on an added load for short time. This was an emergency.

I climbed the stairs to the third floor and realized my knee felt fine. Not a bit of pain. As I walked toward the front apartment I noticed a large section of the hall was taken up by a huge abstract painting. It covered the wall to the ceiling.

A plastic "Manager" plate rattled on loose nails when I knocked on the door. I could hear sophisticated jazz from inside half covering two angry male voices.

The door opened and I stared into a pair of wild green female eyes. I blinked and took in long unkempt wine colored hair, pale skin, and lips bare of coloring. She was slim, almost skinny, with a long beautiful neck. She wore a dirty zip-neck sweatshirt and black corduroy pedal pushers. No shoes.

Her eyes in turn traveled my body. She looked at me questioningly. In back of her I saw a balding middle-aged man in a business suit shouting down at some one out of sight. The jazz was louder.

". . . to have it repapered. It isn't even a painting, just . . . just *color!*"

"Yeah, man?" the girl said.

The out-of-sight man replied to the other. "Like I told you, I ran out of canvas. An artist has to paint. Don't flip, man. You got a Zeke Rowen on your walls. You're going to have squares digging the building as a museum. Charge admission."

"Shirley said you had a room empty I could rent."

"I'll charge *you* for new wallpaper and a gallon of pastel You hear me. Either that paint outside is covered up or I'll get another manager and throw you and all your beatnik friends out."

"Where'm I going to get the bread, man? I got no cash for wallpaper."

"Sure," she said, "fall in." She stepped aside.

"I don't care how you do it, but it had better be done or you'll be out on your ear! I'm warning you. Next week!" The man was red faced with anger. He brushed past me, stopped to stare with disgust at the wall, and stamped angrily away.

I went inside and entered a strange new world. I was in a pad.

The room was constructed exactly like the dining room in Shirley's apartment below, but there the resemblance ended. The double doors that led to the living room were locked shut. The walls were festooned with paintings, violently colored splashes of raw paint laid on straight from the tube. Only a few of these monstrosities boasted crude wooden frames.

Where the pivoting Murphy bed should have been was a gaping hole which had been fitted with unpainted plank shelves. Books, clothes and a hi-fi rig crowded the space. On the floor was a wide mattress covered with an old army blanket. Next to it were piles of L. P. records. Jazz, jazz, jazz.

Where in the apartment below by the windows there was a table and chairs, here an orange crate had been made into a crude altar supporting an incense burning Buddha. On either side of the box were pots of artist's brushes. In a corner was an easel and an open box of oils. All about were candles in empty wine bottles.

Dangling from the empty ceiling light fixture was an authentic hemp noose. Sitting in the noose was a papier-maché figure of a man with tape on his mouth, a blindfold on his eyes, and his hands pressed against his ears. The little figure sported an immense erection.

"Take it cool, man, your eyes are bugging." Zeke looked up at me from a cross-legged Buddha pose in the center of the mattress.

He was a short creature with uncombed hair, a handlebar mustache and an improbable three inch goatee. A pot belly strained an ancient pair of army pants. No shirt, no shoes. His bare chest was a splotched unhealthy combination of tanned and untanned skin.

I had to grin. "You are a bona-fide A-number-one dyed-in-the-wool beatnik. Right? Right!"

Zeke raised an eyebrow. "A square. Go away and file your edges."

"Shirley said you might have a room empty."

"Shirley? You said the magic word. What you want the room for? You trying to make the scene?"

"I'll only need it for a few days, but I'll pay for a week."

His eyes lit up. "The breadman cometh. Sit down." He extended his hand. "Lay it on me, man. Ten of the finest." He turned to the girl who held a similar pose beside him. "Make with the food. I'm empty."

I sat on the mattress, my legs extended awkwardly, aware of a bad odor; the combined smells of old food, old sweat, and hundreds of gallons of cockroach killer that had been sprayed and absorbed by the building over the years.

The girl had been staring at me. As she rose and went into the small kitchen I couldn't resist staring back. She had nice long legs.

What a weird place! What weird people! I felt like laughing. My God, what a way to live! I turned back to Zeke. "My name . . . my name is Jose Jimenez."

"You're putting me on. You're not Mex."

I grinned again. "Just a joke. My real handle is Jeff Ackerman."

He looked ill. "I'm Zeke. *Yonder* is Rill."

"Rill?" I looked into the kitchen but she was ignoring us. I did a double-take. She had her hands up under the sweatshirt and appeared to be fondling herself. Her head was thrown back and her eyes were closed.

I looked at Zeke. It was his turn to grin. "Don't get shook. Rill gets more kicks out of her tits than most girls get out of a good screw." He raised his voice. "Cut the swinging and make breakfast!"

She responded with, "Crap!" but a few seconds later I heard dishes rattle.

Zeke put out his hand again. "Like, cash, man."

I pulled out my wallet and gave him a ten dollar bill. He saw the thick sheaf of twenties and tens. His lips pursed in a soundless whistle. He looked pointedly at my ruined clothes. "What's the word if you don't mind saying?"

I told him I'd had a fight with a bull dyke and that Shirley had rescued me. "I've got some other clothes in the Caddy."

"Gilt-edged," Zeke muttered to himself. "What's your gig?"

"Gig?"

"Work, job, slavery. What pays you that kind of loot?"

I wondered what his reaction would be. "I'm Advertising Director for a department store."

"It figured. The squarest shuck of all."

"That's bad?"

He rolled his eyes to the ceiling. "A professional liar and he asks is it bad."

"There's nothing wrong with my job!"

"Come off it, Ackerman. I used to do commercial art by the ream for you boys . . . till I got sick of it. I'd take a chintzy three dollar dress and draw an ad that made it look like a twenty buck item. I made tinny tubs on wheels look like land yachts and cats like you wrote lies that sold them for three times their cost. I drug through that for three years."

"Look, advertising performs a necessary function in today's society. You can't deny that. If it weren't for us prices would be sky high."

"You guys created today's junk society. No wonder you're necessary."

Rill came out of the kitchen with a bowl of hot spaghetti and a gallon bottle of cheap red wine. She set them down beside Zeke and resumed staring at me. "Thanks, chick," he said and fondled a breast for a second. She slid a long white hand up his back and played with the long uncut hair on his neck.

He took a slug of wine. "I know the crap you feed each other about how civilization would collapse if the ad man died. Turn it off, please, I've heard it all before." He began spooning the steaming spaghetti into his mouth. "You want something to eat?"

"No, thanks." I looked at his paintings again, then the locked doors. "Don't you use the rest of the apartment?"

He shook his head no. His mouth was full and spaghetti trailed past his chin and colored his goatee. He swallowed, chewed twice, and swallowed again. "Storeroom."

I watched him for a moment. "Is that all you eat? You can't stay healthy on that stuff." I looked closely at him. His eyes were bloodshot, the skin around his nose was cheesy and there were cracking sores in the corners of his mouth.

"I keep alive," he said.

Then I noticed a sprinkling of tiny needle scars in his upper left arm. My God, I thought, gosh . . .

Rill got up and went into the kitchen again, looking sideways at me. Those green eyes were alive with disturbing shifting lights. She walked with a loose boneless grace.

Zeke sneered. "You'd say Rill was healthy, wouldn't you?"

I nodded. Her skin was flawless, not dry like his.

"Dig what she eats!"

Rill came back eating out of a can. There was a Mona Lisa smile on her lips. She held the can so I could see the label. She was eating dogfood!

"One can a day," Zeke continued. "And a little dago red to wash it down." He took a long slug of wine. "Where does that put your eggs and milk and steaks and salads and all the other high priced manure you're paid to push?"

I shrugged and smiled at her. "It's a good diet. They put everything in that can a dog needs to stay healthy. Same goes for humans. But I imagine it takes a lot of getting used to."

He made a face. "Like, you know it. I can't stand the stuff."

Rill's smile widened. "It makes living simple. I like things simple."

"Where are you from, Rill?"

She became wary. "Around. Just around."

I remembered Shirley's warning. "I'm sorry. I shouldn't ask personal questions. I'm always too curious for my own good."

She smoothed the front of her sweatshirt and I could see the outlines of low slung pointed breasts. "I dig. Maybe later I'll let you in."

Zeke sighed, finished the last of his spaghetti and rubbed his eyes. "I'm shot." He fished in his pants pocket and dropped a bunch of keys in Rill's lap. "Show him the cell, chick. I'm going to turn on."

She rose and padded to the still open door. I got up and followed her. Behind us the door closed and locked. We went down the stairs and along the second floor hall to the rear. About midway in the building she stopped in front of 5A. It had a padlock on it. A moment later I walked into a 1920 version of a bachelor apartment.

The walls were peeling not one but at least six layers of flowered wallpaper. The floor had been painted once and then covered with a print linoleum rug which was now worn through. The woodwork was a flaky evil brown. The ceiling was ten year old cracked-plaster white. The furniture consisted of a bed, a straight backed chair, a table, and a built-in dresser with mirror.

"Where's the bathroom?"

She opened a closet door, smiled at herself, and opened a door beside it. It had a slide lock and gave access to a cement floored bathroom painted battleship grey. A home-made shower stall stood next to an outside door.

"You have to share it with a writer cat in five and two gay boys in eight. They won't bother you . . . unless you *like* fairies."

"I'm a woman's man."

She closed in on me and began rubbing herself against my chest. "You're nice for a square. You want to make my scene?"

I put my hands on her flat buttocks and moved them up under the sweatshirt. Her back was smooth and muscular. No bra. Had she ever worn one? "Won't Zeke get mad?"

Her eyes were closed. "Oh, man, he's always too *tired.* Let's make it a three day piece of work for size."

"I might not be here three days." But a little voice in the back added: *It might be six days or forever.*

"Who cares?" She pressed her thighs forward and bent back at the waist. "Come on, use your hands. I've got handles in front."

I moved my hands around. She moaned when my fingers touched her big warm nipples.

"Go, go, go. Speak to me, lip me, tongue me." She pulled the sweatshirt up to her neck. Her pale ivory breasts swooped down and out, pointing wide with nipples at red alert.

I bent down and took one in my mouth. I liked doing it. Did that mean my mother weaned me too soon or fed me from a bottle? I didn't care about the reason. Women liked this. Dawn had liked it very much.

I switched from one to the other. She cooed to herself and mumbled disconnected phrases. "Crazzzzy . . . go, go . . . I'm flipping . . . way out across the big blue . . . send me off, take it cool . . ."

I put my hand between her thighs. "No joint needed now," she said, "no joint needed now . . . not now . . . keep with it . . . I'm faaar out . . . *I'm climbing the mountain . . . Haaaah!"* Her hands squeezed my wrist and pressed tight.

A minute later her eyes opened. She took a deep breath and let it out slowly. "Dad, you've got style." She pulled the sweatshirt down. "You going to want to eat in this place?"

For an instant I wasn't sure what she meant. But she was looking around the room. Hell, I was hot as a firecracker and she ignored me. Was she another Dawn? All take and no give? Screw you, I thought.

I looked at the hole-in-the-wall kitchen. "Is there a restaurant anywhere near?"

"Down on the corner. On the promenade."

I opened the old gas refrigerator. It stank. "I'll eat there."

She shrugged. "Okay." She clicked a key off the key ring. "Here's a key for the place. You want to rent some sheets and like that?"

"Yeah. How much?" I reached for my wallet.

"I'll bring them down later. Pay Zeke then. You going to get your stuff?"

"Yes."

"See you, daddy-o." She turned away.

I watched her leave, then called out, "Hey, Rill, do you know any lesbians around here?"

"Sure, man, they try to make me all the time."

"Do you know a Dawn Hunter?"

"Dawn? Sure. She lives in the penthouse."

"This penthouse? This building's penthouse?"

"Sure. She and Tex moved in a couple days ago."

A crazy elation filled me. I ran out of the room and made for the stairs.

## Chapter Five

It turned out that the back stairs were the only way up to the roof. They ended in a small two door entranceway. One door was partially open and led past the bulk of the penthouse to the clothesline strung roof. The other door was marked "10" in painted over old fashioned metal numbers.

Now I was scared. I raised my hand to knock and felt that bottomless gulf open up in my stomach. I set my jaw and banged on the door.

Nothing happened. I was about to knock again when I heard the inside lock click off. The door opened a few inches and Dawn stared sleepily at me. It took her a second to realize who it was.

"Jeff!" She automatically opened the door wider. There was pain in her voice and her eyes seemed to ask forgiveness when she saw my clothes and bruised face. For a fraction of an instant I thought she might throw herself into my arms. But the impulse died, if it ever existed, and we were suddenly strangers.

She was barely covered by a man's green striped pajama top. The sleeves were too long, but the half buttoned front was filled out by the partially revealed twin swells of her breasts. The thin cotton cloth ended tantalizingly just below the curve of her hips.

Her hair was tousled from bed. She looked no more than fifteen years old.

"Dawn . . ." Tears started in my eyes and I felt guiltily proud of them. "Can't we talk? Can't we give it another chance? I love you."

Her pretty little face twisted with conflicting emotions. "Jeff, I—"

Tex walked heavily into the room. She was wearing the bottom half of the pajama set and didn't seem to care if I saw her naked from the waist up.

She wasn't anything to look at. Her breasts sagged flat on her thick chest. They were marked by deep welts. In a flash of insight I knew what caused them: she'd bound her breasts tight for years to eliminate any disgusting hints of bulging femininity. She was a man in her view, and men didn't have breasts, nor did they mind if anyone saw their chests.

Her eyes narrowed. "What the hell do you want, buster? Another beating?"

I ignored her. "Dawn? We could leave right away."

She bit her lips and looked at the floor. Her fingers twisted the tail of the pajama. She said nothing.

Tex came forward and put her arm over Dawn's shoulders. Her hand slid down inside the pajama top and humped like a busy spider on one of the deep round breasts. "But Dawn doesn't want to leave, do you, Dawn?"

Dawn blushed and tried to shrug the arm away. "Please, stop it. I don't like you doing things in front of people."

"Oh, but Jeff here isn't people, he's your husband. You shouldn't mind him seeing how much we love each other." Tex's other hand brought Dawn around to face her. She looked at me triumphantly over Dawn's shoulder, then kissed her passionately, her hand now busy in another place.

Dawn's thighs shrank from the touch and she grabbed at the marauding hand. "Please!"

Tex laughed. Her hand returned.

These lesbians. They all want to show off their women in front of men. They're always trying to prove something.

And what about Dawn? Why *did I* want her back? Were our rare days of happiness enough to compensate for selfish immaturity? I knew in my mind I should have left her there in Tex's embrace. It was what she wanted, wasn't it? But something held me.

I got mad. Damnit, I was still married to her! She was still my wife! I stepped forward and ripped them apart. Dawn staggered backward against an old writing desk beside the door.

"*You goddamned queer,*" I yelled at Tex. "If she says stop it, you stop!"

Tex was surprised. She drew back that massive arm. I beat her to the punch, catching her with a short left to the stomach. She doubled forward, air whooshing out of her. I straightened her with a right uppercut, not putting too much power behind it. I still couldn't think of her as a man. I felt guilty hitting her.

She went down with a keening moan, trying to recapture her breath. She writhed on the threadbare rug.

Dawn stared down at her, wide-eyed, looked at me, then back at Tex.

I pushed her roughly toward the fallen woman. "Aren't you going to make over her? Aren't you going to sooth her wounded vanity?"

"Jeff, you hurt me!" She frowned and rubbed her shoulder. She slipped the pajama aside to look for marks. "That's all you know how to do is hurt me." She sank to her knees and bent over Tex. "Is it all right? Did he hurt you bad?"

Tex drew an agonized breath and spat a curse. She crawled into the bedroom. I stopped Dawn from following.

"What do you see in a woman like that? What can she offer you? Do you like living in this lousy town, in dumps like this?"

"You don't understand me. You never did. She's good and kind and gentle. And she wants to see me get ahead. In a few months we're moving to Hollywood. That's something you'd never do!"

"Dawn, you're a lousy actress and you know it. If you couldn't make it with the Portland Civic Theatre, how on earth—"

"They were all jealous of me! I can too act! I'll show you!"

"Why can't you be a happy housewife? What's the matter with that? You've got to get over what your parents have been telling you ever since you could understand words. They spoiled you rotten because they were ugly and you were a beautiful baby. They thought you were a gift from heaven and God meant you to be a movie star."

"I will be, I will!"

"You won't! You're a lousy actress, a fair dancer and a terrible singer."

"All you want me for is to decorate that expensive split level thing up on the hill. You want me to look pretty like a . . . a lamp while you get drunk night after night."

"What did you expect me to do when you wouldn't let me touch you? If I even looked at you you got frigid. Hell, I want you to be my mate! I want you to be a mother."

"Yes, you want me to get pregnant! Nothing would suit you better. I'd have to stay home then. I'd get big in the belly and my figure would be *ruined!*"

"Dawn—"

"I won't be that way. I won't!" She began to cry.

I felt helpless and confused. This was it, the same old gut wrenching, frustrating argument we'd had a hundred times before.

I tried to lift her up and kiss her the way she liked. It was a game. She would lock her legs around my waist and I'd kiss her lips and then work down to the lovely pink and red flowers at the tips of her breasts.

But she fought me and I turned her loose, the bitter acid taste of defeat in my mouth. "Do you really hate me that much?"

"Yes . . . no! I don't know. I just want you to leave."

"I can't leave you down here in the hands of . . . I can't let you—"

Tex appeared in the bedroom doorway, still gasping, holding onto the scaling white doorframe with one hand. In the other was a deadly looking revolver. The vicious black hole at the end of the blue steel barrel weaved back and forth at me.

"Get out of here!"

"Tex! Where did you get that gun?" Dawn was terrified.

She ignored Dawn and looked at me with murder in her eyes. "Get out of here or I'll gut shoot you. *I'll gut shoot you!*" Her eyes were black marbles of hate.

"Be careful. Put it away, *please!*"

She turned her head slightly toward Dawn. "Shut up!" To me: "God damn it to hell, *get out of here!*" She came forward, the gun extended, her finger tightening on the trigger.

I backed out of the apartment door. Dawn was staring at the gun. Tex stepped forward and slammed the door in my face.

I went down the stairs slowly. Midway between the first and second floors I sat on a step and began to tremble. My mouth got dry. I put my head in my hands. What now? Stay or go? Fly back to Portland alone and leave her to this life, or continue fighting? She was such a stubborn *child*. She was only twenty!

I went out into the ugly running sore of an alley, along the Speedway and into the parking lot. In my eyes the Caddy was big and satisfying in the sunshine, gleaming clean silver blue and chrome. If it was a status symbol, at least it was a gratifying one. I liked to see heads turn when I nosed it through traffic. Down here in L.A. it was just another Cadillac, and rented at that, but up in Portland I owned one just like this baby, free and clear, and it was *something* to drive up Broadway in it.

I stood for a moment and tried to enjoy the feel of the hot sun on my head. A sick feeling still lingered in my stomach.

I unlocked the car, dragged out my suitcase, and locked up again. Before I left the lot I paid the man his fee for three days. There was one important thing I had to do and then I was going to find a bar. I needed a drink bad.

Back in 5A I changed to the clean pants of my extra suit, (why had I packed it? Had I unconsciously known . . . ?) put on a clean white nylon shirt and went out.

To hell with wearing a tie and coat. This was the land of informal attire, wasn't it? I could probably take off the shirt and no one would squawk. Not here in Venice West, not in this human junkyard.

## Chapter Six

The front door of the building faced a wide sidewalk that ran from the Speedway inland up to Pacific Ace. It was a walkway. No cars could use it. The dirty alleys and an occasional through street were available for cars. Between the Speedway and the promenade was a street half a block long. Iron pipes set in the cement blocked it off from the beach.

I walked down to the promenade . . . Ocean Front Walk the street sign said. My apartment building was on Seaside Avenue . . . the walkway.

On my right was the restaurant Rill had mentioned. Ted's Place. A menu was hanging in the window. I realized I hadn't eaten since I'd gotten off the plane yesterday afternoon. But I wasn't hungry. Next to the restaurant was the High Water.

On the left side of the street was a small grocery huddled under the bulk of a big five floor plastered apartment house. Some of the plaster had come loose and fallen to the sidewalk. It looked like it had lain there a long time.

I entered the store and spotted a pay phone on the wall by the butcher's small refrigerated display case. This was a mama-papa store, and maybe Uncle Herman was the butcher.

I got three dollars' worth of change, dialed long distance and gave the operator Bob Snider's home number. A moment later I was feeding quarters into the slot. Clinkety-BONG, . . . clinkety-BONG . . . you know the sound. I could hear his phone ring. I hoped to hell he was home.

"Hello?" It was Karen, his wife, a sweet motherly type who was in fact five years older than he, and he was six years older than I.

"This is a long distance call from Venice, California, person to person, to Mr. Bob Snider."

"Long distance? Just a minute."

I could hear her calling him. As he came near her voice said, "Who do we know in Venice, California?"

"I don't know. Hello?"

"Hello, Bob, this is Jeff."

"Jeff? What the hell are you doing down in California?"

"I finally found out where Dawn was living. I flew down yesterday to get her."

"Oh . . . well, are you going to make it back by tomorrow?"

"That's why I called. I might have to stay down here a few more days."

I became aware of a silence behind me. I turned and saw mama and papa and uncle listening intently.

"Cripes, Jeff, that throws a helluva load on me. This week is the year's killer."

"I know. I'm sorry. I thought I'd be able to fly right back but . . . things didn't work out that way."

"The old man will be furious. He wants that Centennial campaign all mapped out this week. Hell, you promised him you'd have it off the pad ready for orbit."

"I know, I know." He was putting me on the defensive. I felt lousy enough without him piling it on. "Look, Bob, I can give you the general theme right now. You can work it up pretty well until I get back. Show a covered wagon with oxen pulling it. Behind it, rising into the air on a pillar of fire is a rocket. Work up about twenty titles like, 'A Hundred Years Of Progress For You'. You know what I mean."

"Sure, but it won't match your stuff. I can manage, though. I'll explain to the old man."

"Thanks, Bob. I'll be up as soon as I can."

"You know I'm for you a thousand percent, Jeff. I know the problem you have with Dawn. Don't worry about anything up here. I'll manage."

I was sure he would. Bob was ambitious even though he was a second rater. I was sure he'd manage to make it appear I was malingering, quitting under fire, unreliable. He wanted my job and the $20,000 salary plus bonuses that went with it. It would be quite a jump from his current $7,500.

I couldn't blame him. I was taking a big chance. I almost told him I was catching the next plane home.

"Fine, thanks, Bob. You're a *good* man."

"Oh, what's your number down there so I can call you if anything comes up?"

Did the apartment house have a phone? "I don't know yet. I'll let you know. It's the Seaside Apartments."

"Well . . . okay, I'll see you soon."

"It won't be long, Bob, count on it." A little warning not to get *too* eager.

"Swell. Goodbye." He hung up. Damn, he had hung up on me. *He* had ended the conversation!

The sick feeling, temporarily forgotten, came back. My temples throbbed with the beginnings of a headache. I couldn't afford to stay down here more than two days. Any longer and I'd be flirting with disaster.

I went out into the glaring sunshine. A slight breeze was blowing. I looked up and down the promenade. Where was the nearest bar that wasn't a lesbian hangout?

A brightly painted open sided tourist tram chugged along the promenade toward me, headed south. "10c To Ocean Park" its front said. I flagged the driver, an old geezer in a red cap and red striped shirt, paid him his dime and plopped into the seat beside him. The motor sat between us under a steel hood. It wheezed and stuttered like a refugee from a junked model-T.

"Any bars around here that don't serve lesbians?"

He scrutinized my face and cracked a smile. "You have a little trouble with them, did you? There's some places down on Windward where you won't find 'em."

"Where's that?"

"Right up here to the end of the line." He pointed. "See up there where it says St. Marks Hotel? That's Windward."

"Thanks." The motor pulled the tram along only a little faster than I could have walked. I began to get impatient and fidgety. Dawn . . . Dawn . . . Dawn . . . the problem I had to solve. What was my next move? Was there a next move? I kept seeing the gun in Tex's hand. Bob's words echoed, "The old man will be furious . . . furious . . . furious."

I gritted my teeth and hit my leg with a balled fist. The headache was worse. I had all the questions lined up and no answers I The goddamned tram was going into slow motion. I needed a DRINK!

We crept past a long empty bingo palace, a modern cardboard and plaster motel, a one-story apartment house, then past The Gas House, the much publicized beat hangout with its painted windows and displays. Two scrawny young men with beards were slumped in chairs outside its doors reading books.

At last! A block further and the tram stopped. I vaulted out and walked swiftly up the street past the hotel, crossed the Speedway and went into the first bar I came to.

It was a beer parlor, dim, the floor a continuation of the street, full of dirt, spit, cigarette stubs, odd papers and spilled liquid. I ordered a beer and drank it quick. It went down nicely, like it's supposed to in the TV commercials, down a sun parched throat, down to a nervous jumpy gut where it soothed and cooled.

I drank part of a second beer and looked around. It was still Sunday morning and the bodies which occupied the stools beside me looked like they'd been left over from the night before. One of them was a woman.

She was short and skinny. She looked frayed and faded, as if she'd been caught in an automatic washer for thirty years.

The beer hit me on an empty stomach. I felt disgusted. Two beers and I was whoozy. I felt sleepy. I spoke to the woman. "I hope you're not a lesbian."

She looked up from the glass she'd been nursing. "What kind of a girl do you think I am? I get the creeps when one of 'em even looks at me."

I didn't think she was a girl at all. More like the far side of thirty. I nodded sagely and ordered a beer for her and another for myself. "It isn't natural," I said. "They steal women away from their husbands. Oughta be in hospitals."

"They better not try stealing me. Thanks for the beer."

"S'all right."

"My old man don't give me nothing. Throws his salary away like it was water." She laughed. "Like it was water."

I scowled. I had an old man, too. Old man Kingman, owner of the store. Seventy-five years old and likely to live another seventy-five. A leather covered mummy with blue spotlight eyes. He paid good but he expected too much. The old bastard wanted you to *live* your job!

"What's your name?" I asked.

"Lillian."

"Lillian, do you know anything about these beatniks?"

"I never pay any attention to 'em."

"They never work. They don't *want* to work. They don't want Cadillacs. That's not natural. They're sick or something. Oughta be in hospitals."

"I sure wish *I* had a Cadillac."

Conversation died. Two more beers went by. I was getting drunk on the stuff. I was lonely. I wanted a woman, a real woman like Shirley, only . . . I looked at Lillian. "You like me?"

"Sure, I guess so."

"How about . . ." I struggled for words. My mind was like glue. She had to be like Shirley in one very important particular. Had to find that out first. "Do you have muscles?"

"Sure, who doesn't?"

"I mean muscles in your . . . between your legs."

"What? Say, what kind of a girl do you think I am, anyway? I'm a married woman! That's a fine way to talk to a married woman, you bastard!"

I blinked at her. She wasn't like Shirley. "I'm shorry . . . sorry."

"Of all the gawdamn nerve!"

Shirley was wonderful without Lena. A vision of Lena's incredible breasts took shape in my fogged brain. The vision closed like a camera shutter, opened, and I saw Dawn's breasts . . . then Shirley's . . . and Rill's. My life was a series of breasts. The world was a series of breasts. They were everywhere.

Open a paper . . . bra covered breasts; open a magazine . . . naked breasts; go to the movies . . . barely covered breasts. The breast culture. See, see, look, look, *but don't touch!* Naughty naughty dirty minded men for looking at breasts and wanting to touch. For that you had to pay. You had to pay with little pieces of your pride, your self-respect, your manhood . . . coin of the realm.

I shook my head from side to side and got off the stool. My head was spinning. I needed fresh air . . . fresh smog. I walked out the door as straight as I could. The sunlight hurt my eyes. I felt like a bat flying out of a cave.

Good old taverns . . . what would lonely time haunted men do without them? Dim, dark, warm, they were substitute wombs.

I glared at the ridiculous imitation of old world Venetian architecture that lined the sidewalk on both sides of the street: ugly scabby Corinthian pillars that were as useless as I was.

I walked back toward the ocean. A colored man was preaching on the edge of the promenade to bleary-eyed winos and tourists waiting for the next tram. "And uh I say to you uh that unless you accept GOD you uh will be DAMNED to uh an eternal life of TORMENT and uh the DEVIL will take your one and uh only everlasting SOUL." Two of the tourists snapped his picture.

The breeze cleared my head a little as I walked back toward Seaside Avenue. I passed the Gas House. One of the beards was still reading. The other was talking with two teen-age girls and a hulking boy, all wearing swim suits.

The skinny brown haired girl was vaguely familiar. She wore a tight one piece lastex suit under an unbuttoned man's shirt. She showed more breast than she had any right to. The other girl was shorter, still plump with baby fat. The boy was the same, big and fatty muscled. He watched me pass with black envious eyes.

Then I placed the girl: she was the one who had stood up in the convertible last night and yelled at Shirley and me. She was watching me pass, too. I wondered if part of those impressive twin bulges were sponge rubber. I wondered if *she* would be like Shirley.

I felt ashamed of myself. Crap. I was lusting after half-grown teen-age girls. What was doing this to me? Was there a disease in the air that corroded morals and rotted character? I'd never thought or acted this way before. I wanted Shirley, that much was sure. I walked faster.

Shirley answered my knock. She was still in the terrycloth robe. As I stood there the alcohol in my system took command again. I began to weave on my feet and steadied myself against the door frame.

"I thought of you, Shirley. I was drinking beer and I thought I'd like to see you. I'm sad. I've got trouble." I grinned foolishly.

"You're loaded."

"On beer. Stinking beer. Only half loaded. Half a load is better than none. That's an aphor . . . aphorism."

"I can't talk to you now."

"Don't want to talk. Want a re-run of last night. Want a kinescope . . . by popular demand."

"Go somewhere and sleep it off, huh? Lena's mad as hell about you."

I winked at her. "I rented 5A. I'll wait for you. You sneak over. We'll exercise your muscles."

"I can't, Jeff."

"Whatsa matter? I'll pay you. How much?"

"Just go on to your room. I wish to hell I hadn't gotten mixed up with you."

"Fine attitude. A fine attitude. My money's not goodnuff for you? You're a whore aren't you?"

"Shut up. Get away from here!"

The door slammed in my face. I staggered back. Everybody was slamming doors on me. Dawn . . . A knifelike sorrow cut through me and I pushed it back under the fuzzy alcoholic carpet of my mind.

All right, I'd show 'em. I conceived a deep hatred for Lena. What right had she to cut me off from Shirley? I vowed drunken revenge.

I'd noticed that the mama-papa store on the corner sold liquor. I was going to get royally stinking drunk. To hell with all of 'em. Bob could have my lousy job. Tex could have Dawn. Lena could have Shirley. I was going to get DRUNK!

## Chapter Seven

Ten minutes later I was staring stupidly at the lock on my door. Two bottles of whiskey clinked together in a bag I held close to my chest.

The padlock on the door was hanging on the hasp and the door was open a few inches. I frowned and kicked it open further. Rill was bending over the bed smoothing a sheet into place. She looked around when she heard me.

I walked in unsteadily. The damned beer was still with me. "Well, if it isn't little miss hot tits doing her good deed for the day."

She said nothing. I put the bottles on the table. She went about adding a blanket to the bed.

"You like Johnny Walker, Rill? Wanna drink?"

She finished tucking in the corners of the blanket and sat down. "You're high, man. What're you shooting?"

"No dope for me. I'm a dope already. Everybody says so." I noticed a small pile of clothes on the built-in dresser. Something black and a grey sweatshirt. There was a book on top. "These things yours?"

She nodded.

The stuff looked like a duplicate of the outfit she was wearing. I picked up the book. It had a ragged cream and green dust jacket. It was titled "How To" by Jack Woodford. A helluva title. How to what? I put it down and looked at her. "You moving in with me?"

She nodded again. Her green eyes flared.

"How about the rest of your stuff?"

"That's all."

"You mean, that's all there is?"

She nodded.

Damn, but she didn't say much. Except when somebody was sucking on her. Then she was a torrent on sound. "You think you're going to get a lot of free kicks, don't you?"

She cocked her head like a curious bird. "I don't dig."

"You like guys to service you but you won't do anything for them."

She still looked puzzled.

"Like this morning!"

She smiled and moved her hands up under the sweatshirt. "Yeah, man, you were good. Let's make that scene again."

I didn't move. "What about me?"

"Whatever you want, daddy-o, whatever you want."

I shut the door. She was pulling the sweatshirt over her head when I reached the bed. Her breasts pointed wide. She looked sexy as hell when she flung the sweatshirt to the floor. Her wine-red hair tumbled over her shoulders in waves that lapped at the beginnings of her breasts. It was beautiful against the ivory of her skin. And her eyes, her green eyes were signaling wild erotic messages to me.

She began unbuttoning my shirt as I unzipped her black pedal-pushers and slid them down her long pale thighs. I kicked off my shoes and seconds later was stripping off my shorts.

She wasn't watching me. Her eyes were closed and she was toying with herself. I lay beside her and began doing what she liked. The flow of words began.

"Oh, daddy-o, you are educated, you know how . . . you turn on the current. AC, DC, it's all the same to me . . . ohhh . . . like that . . . that's the scene. . . ."

It went on for long minutes this way, with her reaching climax after climax. I was about to quit when she flipped her eyes open and began moving her hips.

"Second stage," she whispered to herself. "Second stage wants it." Her hands fluttered down to her thighs and then over to me. "Time for a joint, daddy-o, time for your work."

Her eyes were open but she wasn't seeing anything. I felt her legs curl around me and then I moved. She gasped like a landed fish. Then the words came faster and louder than ever.

"Big joint, big joint, big joint, big joint . . . go go go . . . go to China . . . go to China . . . find your way down . . . down. . . ."

It went on and on, louder and louder until she was shouting when the big one came and shook her body and mine like a mountain shakes the ground before the top blows off and lava spews into the sky.

I collapsed beside her and slept.

When I awoke the sun was gone and the day was twilight prone. Rill was still beside me, staring up at the ceiling.

I climbed over her and went to the bathroom. I smiled. That woman in the bar must have thought I was nuts. She should have heard Rill.

In bed Rill shivered and climbed under the covers.

I started to get into my pants and shirt.

"Where?"

"I'm hungry."

"Want some of mine?"

I remembered her dogfood and shook my head. It was getting dark in the room but I could still see her hands moving under the blanket. Good God, you'd think she'd wear out those sensitive nerves. I went out and down the stairs. I wondered why she didn't get calluses on her nipples. The more I thought about it the funnier it got.

I ate two breaded veal cutlet dinners at the corner restaurant. The waitress thought I was nuts when I told her what I wanted and went off to the kitchen to giggle the order to an old Jewish woman. I had three cups of coffee, too. The food was pretty good.

When I returned to my room I found Rill still in bed. There was an empty dogfood can on the floor beside her with a spoon sticking up out of it.

I undressed quickly and slipped into bed beside her. I pushed one of her hands away and took up the good work.

"Full of square food, daddy-o? Got lots of energy?"

I wondered if her nipples ever got a chance to shrink to normal size.

"I'm working on it."

She sighed and stretched. "You're fine, real fine."

"Where you from, Rill?"

She was silent for a minute. "Ohio."

"What brought you out here? Why do you live like this?"

She looked at me and shrugged. I couldn't read a thing in her eyes.

"Don't you trust me?"

"Why do you want to know all that?"

"I'm just curious. I've always been interested in people. Ever since I was a kid. My mother said I should have been a writer, except there isn't any money in it."

"Jazz me slow and I'll tell you."

I hesitated and she impatiently grabbed my hand and pushed it down her body. Such smooth skin!

Her thighs jerked. "Easy. . . ."

"Sorry." A minute passed. "Why did you come out here to Venice?"

She sighed and for once put her hands behind her head. "I was married to a grooved square. He was a salesman. He sold new rain gutters for houses. All day he went and looked for houses with run down gutters and then he'd try to con the owners into new ones. And, like, we owed everybody. He borrowed money from everybody. He wanted all the new toys from Westinghouse and like that. The house was on time, the new chariot was on time and I wasn't. One month I missed."

She wriggled. "You got long fingers."

"Thanks. What happened then?"

"The bastard! He thought more of his new power-mower than he did of me. Right away he wanted me to get rid of it. He didn't want to owe a doctor and hospital, too."

I noticed her hands clenching into small delicate fists. "What did you do?"

"That smart sonovabitch, oh that smart sonovabitch! He had me using knitting needles. Then he had to try it." Her left cheek began to twitch. "Crap, I never knew anything could hurt like that. He scrambled my insides like that spaghetti Zeke eats. I started to bleed and we couldn't stop it. Then I really had to go to the hospital. When I got out a week later he wasn't around. He took the car and flaked off down the highway. I haven't seen or heard of him since."

"I'm sorry."

She laughed. It was the first time I'd heard her laugh. It was a cackle, weird and high, verging on the insane. "You think I should still be in that square house with that square jerk enjoying square TV while our square kids grow up to be j-d's."

I thought I could see tears in her eyes. Her hands unclenched slowly. "I got out of that bit. I'm free now. My folks send me twenty bucks a week to live on and I make it fine. No babies to worry about like a lot of the chicks. I can't have any. Not ever. And what a ball I'm having. Jimmy did me a favor. I think he did me a favor."

But I still saw the tears flowing and I understood why she grabbed me then and pulled me into her as deep as possible. I did my best, but I don't think anybody could ever again make her pregnant.

It was much later and we were both tired. Rill rolled out of bed, went to the bathroom, and came back.

"Time?" she asked.

"Nine-thirty."

"It's been a long time since I had a watch. Never had one like that with a luminous dial."

"They're nice to have."

"I've got so much time I don't have to measure it."

"Rill, you're a damned nice girl once a guy gets to know you. I'm proud you like me enough to stay with me a few days."

"Cut the slop, daddy-o. You wanted me for what I've got down here. You were going to kick me out unless I came across."

"No, look, I was drunk."

"What's that bit about wine making a man tell the truth? Don't put me on, man. I like you because you're not really too square. You've got bread and a soft bed. And you got style. That's all I want from a cat."

"You don't understand me."

She laughed that wild laugh again and changed the subject. "You want to live a little, daddy-o? You want to dig a real shooting party? You want to flip once in your honest john life?"

"What are you getting at?"

"Tomorrow night a swell chick in B.H. is laying it out. Zeke's going, I'm going, a couple others for color. You come too."

"I think I'd be a party pooper. What do they want with a square like me?"

"Zeke can get you in. He told me to invite you. He thinks you can be saved."

"You mean depraved. Okay, I'll dig the scene."

"He needs your car to get there."

I felt humiliated and angry. I was being used. I was a handy man with the money, with the car, with the hands and lips and . . . what did Rill call it . . . a joint. And Dawn had left me because I wasn't willing to be used as she wished. To hell with her. At least Rill gave something in return. At least Zeke was taking me along to the party.

I felt Rill stirring beside me. She was fishing in among her clothes on the floor. The room was totally black except for a thin line of light under the two doors that led to the hall and bathroom. The light in the bathroom was on all the time. It must have come on automatically with the hall lights.

Somebody walked along the hall, entered the bathroom, used it, flushed the toilet and left.

"Daddy-o, you want to try some pot?"

"Do you have some marijuana cigarettes?"

"Just a roach." She struck a match. It flared in front of her face. I watched as she lit a very small hand rolled stub of cigarette. She had to hold it with the tips of her fingernails. She sucked strongly on it to get it burning and held the smoke in her lungs for a second before letting it out slowly. She handed it to me as the match went out.

Holding it properly was difficult but I managed to suck on it as she had. The thing was very slim and scrawny, like a frayed bit of wire wrapped in roll-your-own paper. The smoke tasted funny. I held it in my lungs as she had, exhaled and handed it back to her. It didn't seem to affect me. Probably not enough of the weed in that tiny thing to hurt anybody.

We passed it back and forth twice more before it got too small to hold. Then Rill snuffed it out and put it away. I gathered you didn't leave marijuana stubs laying around no matter how small.

More light seemed to be coming in through the window. Rill's hair beside my head seemed exceptionally dark and rich in the dimness. Her contrasting skin was infinitely appealing. I had to touch it. Gently. I ran my fingers down to her breasts. She arched her back. I could hear slight sounds in the building.

"You like it?" she whispered.

"What?"

"Turning on."

"That little thing didn't affect me."

"Sure, it's your first time. It didn't take much. But I can tell by the way you touch me."

"I don't believe it."

She laughed high and wild and it hurt my ears. "C'mon, let's make it again." She pushed my head down to her waiting nipples.

## Chapter Eight

I woke up to bright sunlight with a headache, a thirst for water and an urgent desire to use the bathroom. I glanced at my wristwatch and yawned. Seven-thirty Monday morning.

I sat up in bed and stared down at Rill. I shook my head in wonder and slowly lifted the covers away from her upper body. Even in sleep her hands cradled her breasts. I could see her fingers move slightly. There was that Mona Lisa smile on her face. Was she dreaming two babies were suckling on her?

She wasn't putting on an act. Her breathing was regular and deep. That can be faked, but her eyes weren't moving under her eyelids as they do if someone is feigning sleep.

I slipped out of the bed and stretched. The three narrow windows gave a good view of the alley. I watched an old man in a faded plaid lumber jacket and blue pants scavenging among the garbage cans across the way.

Then I saw Tex, dressed neatly in slacks and blouse, walk past the old man away from the apartment house. I forgot my body's insistent demands. The day brightened for me. Tex was going to work. That meant Dawn was up in the penthouse all alone. And *that* meant I might have a fair chance of convincing her. We could catch a plane today!

I went into the bathroom and relieved myself. I caught a look at myself in the mirror. Was that me? Two days beard, a big purple bruise on the side of my head, and bloodshot eyes. "What do you say, gallant warrior?" I said to my reflection. "You better get cleaned up for the big interview."

I dug into my suitcase for my shaving kit, lotion and comb. I took a shower and had to stand dripping wet in the coolish morning air because I hadn't packed a towel.

Then the outer bathroom door opened and a guy with thinning blonde hair over rimless glasses peered in at me. "Hey, I'm sorry, I didn't know anybody was using it. Why didn't you use the lock?"

"I forgot."

"Oh. You just rented 5A, huh? I live right next to you in 5. I'm Phil Carling."

I nodded to him and wished he'd get lost. No such luck. He was one of the talkative kind, one of those gregarious extroverts who are only alive when they can commandeer someone's attention.

"I'm a writer. I've been writing novels since I was seventeen. Course I've done other things too, to keep alive till I get published, but I'm not worried. I'm aiming at quality, you know? Like Wolfe and Kafka and Joyce."

He stood there with his head inside the door and the rest of him outside. He was stocky and slightly paunchy. He looked about thirty-five.

"I'll be out in a minute."

"That's okay, take your time. Are you a writer, too?"

"In a way."

"You got any of your stuff with you? I'd like to read it."

"No. Look, Carling, would you mind leaving me alone? I can't shave when somebody's watching me."

"Oh. Okay. I'll see you later." He closed the door.

I made a face at myself in the mirror and finished shaving. I went into my room, locked my side of the bathroom and was pulling on my pants when there was a knock on the door. It was the writer again. He had a sheaf of typewritten pages in his hand.

"You got a minute? I'd like to read you something I wrote yesterday. It's really beautiful, you know? It has a flow."

"I thought you wanted to use the bathroom."

"Sure, but this is more important. I want your opinion on this." He stepped inside the room before I could do anything. His voice was pitched on a vibrant piercing level, and he always seemed to talk a little louder than necessary. He looked at Rill's exposed chest and grinned and winked at me. "Lucky man, lucky man. I heard you last night. Right through the wall." He looked longingly at her. "How did you get close to her so fast? I've been trying for three months."

Rill groaned and turned on her side away from the noise of his voice.

I sat down and began putting on my socks. "I've got something important to do so I can't stay and listen to your immortal prose."

"That's all right. It'll only take a minute. See how you like this. 'Herm and me stood mutely under the azure sky like two nails waiting on the road to hell, waiting for a tire of God to roll along so we could blow it out. But it wasn't to be. The sky purpled like a magnificent steak under ultra violet light and still no cars came along, and the desert wind was like the clean teeth of a saber toothed tiger on the prowl ten thousand years after his extinction.'"

He looked at me expectantly.

"Purple prose," I said and tied my shoe laces.

"What do you mean? Doesn't it have a flow, doesn't it make you see what I'm trying to say?"

"It flows all right, but so does crap. That stuff of yours is turgid, sophomoric and overwritten." I grinned up at him to soften the blow of my words.

"No, you can't deny the beauty of it, the sound. Wolfe wrote this way and he's considered a genius. Haven't you ever read his stuff?"

"Yeah." I stood up and reached for my shirt. "What's your story about? What's the plot?"

"Plot? I don't mess with a plot. I'm not writing a lot of commercial junk, I'm aiming for quality, immortality, you know? I never could write magazine stuff. I can't stand the taboos and rules for this and that. I just write what I feel like. Now this guy I'm writing about now, this novel, I'm sending him across the country to Venice West, here, and he's going to dig the scene and get to know a girl out here and then he'll lose her and commit suicide or die some way. I haven't decided."

"You should cut out a lot of those tortured metaphors."

"What have you been reading? Metaphor is the *soul* of good writing."

"Who told you that?"

"It's just the way I write. It's my style." He took off his glasses and rubbed his eyes. "I've got eleven novels done. Furst, the agent, has three of them now. He thinks they're good, too, but the market isn't ready for them yet."

I stood with my hand on the doorknob. "I've got to go now."

"Let me read you a little more. You'll change your mind then. You've got a minute."

"No, I haven't got a minute. Would you mind leaving?"

"C'mon, it can't be that important. Listen to this: 'Herm keeled over like a lobster boat without water and I tried to hold him but he took me with him to the sand like a piece of adhesive tape flapping on a sore thumb. We—'"

I opened the door and started out.

"Hey, don't you want to hear the rest of this?"

"Read it to Rill."

His eyes lit up. "Yeah, thanks, I will."

I closed the door behind me and walked down the hall toward the back stairs. Let Rill take care of him if she wants. She could sit in bed feeling herself and he could sit there reading his terrible prose. They'd both be happy.

## Chapter Nine

I knocked on the penthouse door. Nothing happened. I knocked again, louder, a vague fear forming in my mind.

I heard a door open inside, then Dawn's voice. "Who is it?" She sounded sleepy and cross.

"It's Jeff."

"Go away. Haven't you done enough?"

"Please, Dawn, let me in."

"Go away. I was sleeping."

"I've got to talk to you."

"No, not again. Besides, Tex made me promise."

"To hell with Tex! You open this door, Dawn, or I'll break it in!"

"Oh, all *right!* But it won't do you any good."

The lock clicked and she opened the door. She was dressed the same as the previous morning, hair tousled, eyes sleepy, the same green pajama top barely covering her. I could feel my heart picking up speed.

"Why do you keep coming up here? Why do you keep trying, Jeff?"

"You know why. I can't leave you. I can't get you out of my head. I saw Tex go to work this morning and I couldn't help hoping that maybe this time. . . ."

She pouted and refused to look at me. "I'm sorry you got hurt. But don't you see? I can't leave here now, not till I find out about Hollywood. I could get a start soon with a producer. It could happen just like that!" She snapped her fingers and her eyes flashed with excitement. "I could be a star."

"Dawn, you haven't got a chance. There must be thousands of girls in L.A. who feel that way. Come home with me. Please."

"Jeff, I *can't!* There's too much at stake."

"You know it. I'm the one who's putting it all on the line. All you have to lose is a little bit of ego."

"I don't know what you mean. My whole future is . . . is . . . hanging in the balance."

I fell to my knees before her. I felt tears filling my eyes. "Oh, God, Dawn, come back to me, *please!* I need you, I need you." I started blubbering words and drew her to me, my arms around her hips, my head pressed into her belly. The green cloth smelled faintly of her perfume and body.

"Jeff . . . Jeff . . . do you really love me that much? Do you?" Her fingers were running through my hair. "If I don't make it down here I'll come back to you. I promise I will. I really don't like Tex that much. We had an argument almost all last night about you. And I really do hate this place. It's so dirty."

She shuddered in my arms. I ran one hand up and down her legs. "Come back with me. Let's leave right now. I'll do anything you want only come back with me."

"You really love me, don't you? Oh, poor darling. Oh, Jeff, you shouldn't."

My hand was on the front of her thighs now, seeking. A minute passed.

"You're getting me all worked up." She swayed on her feet and she looked down at me, flushed, lips parted. She was breathing deeply.

"Do you really love me, Jeff? Treat me gentle like Tex does. Prove you love me. Prove it. . . ." She pulled the pajama top up and over my head like a tent. I was face to face with the softness of her inward curving belly. I filled my lungs with the rich aroma of her womanliness.

"Prove it, Jeff." Her hands pushed down on my head. Her lips thrust forward against my face. I kissed the white skin.

I jerked away and stood up. "What do you think I am?"

"There's nothing wrong with it."

"Maybe not, but I've never done it and I don't think I ever will. If you want that you'd better stay with your precious Tex. I don't want to be somebody you call in from the second squad . . . a substitute."

"I didn't—"

"The hell you didn't! I'm the ace down in the hole for you. Or so you think! If you don't make it in Hollywood you figure you can always come back to good-old-Jeff and his nice house and money. In the meantime good-old-Jeff can fill in for Tex because Tex got mad last night and didn't provide the nightly thrills."

"That's not fair."

"Huh! You know what I was doing last night? I was in my room, right downstairs in 5A, and I was screwin' my head off half the night. Yeah, and I had a woman Saturday night, too. And both of them were a lot better at it than you ever were! How do you like them apples?"

"*I think you're horrid!*" She screamed it at me and ran into the bedroom. She slammed the door and locked it.

I was left standing in the living room feeling humiliated, guilty, mad and confused. I looked around the room, picked up a big vase and threw it at the door. It smashed into fragments with a loud satisfying crash.

"What are you doing?" She sounded frightened. It made me feel better.

"I'm leaving! From now on you live your life and I'll live mine. I hope I never see or hear of you again!" I went out, leaving their apartment door open. As I clumped angrily down the steps I heard her yelling, "All right, all right, *all right!*"

I stopped before my door before going in. I heard voices inside: Carling and Rill.

"Flake off, man. Quit handling the goods."

"Aw, c'mon, Rill, be nice, let me feel you a little."

"Quit bugging me!"

"Please be a sport. I need the experience. I've got to live deeply, so I can write about it. You don't care who does it, do you? I've seen you diddling yourself lots of times up in Zeke's."

"Man, what a funk you are. Leave me."

I sighed and opened the door. Here I go, I thought, a knight in tarnished armor to rescue a Beat damsel in not-much-distress.

Rill was dressed in her black pedal pushers and sweatshirt again. Again? That's all she ever wore. She was bending over, making the bed. Phil Carling was at her side trying to feel her, one hand still clutching his precious manuscript. Every few seconds she'd push him away.

I felt warmly toward her then. At least she had *some* scruples and good taste. Carling was debasing himself, figuratively crawling on his knees, begging for the great privilege of touching her for a minute. It made me sick. A deep unreasoning anger rose in me.

I took two steps and spun him around. I'll never forget the astonished look on his face. Then I hit him, flat on the nose. I felt the cartilage give. He staggered back against Rill, but she made a face and pushed him away. His typewritten sheets fluttered to the floor. He squealed and brought his hand up to his nose. Blood was pouring out and down his mouth and chin, dripping onto his cheap white shirt and brown pants.

"You must be pretty hard up if you have to mooch around somebody else's woman!"

He didn't answer. He was sniveling. He dug a handkerchief out of his pocket and pressed it to his nose. "God . . . God . . . God. . . ."

I started to push him out the door but he twisted away with surprising strength. "No, I want—"

"OUT!" I swung at him again.

He ducked and went to his knees. *"I need my words!* Let me get my words!" He began to gather up his precious papers with one hand. Some drops of blood spattered on them. He got up and moved toward the door. "You didn't have to do that."

I knew it. I was sorry I'd slugged him. It was just that when I'd seen him begging Rill as I had begged Dawn. . . .

I made a spasmodic move toward him, meaning to apologize, but he backed away from me out of the room. "I won't forget this." His voice was muffled by the handkerchief. "I'll get even."

I followed him out. He retreated down the hall to his door. "Carling," I said, "think of the invaluable experience you've just had. It's priceless to a writer of your caliber. Sit right down and write it while it's still hot in your mind. You should thank me."

A thoughtful look came into his eyes and he went into his room without another word.

I heard steps on the front stairs and a small slim black haired young man came down from the third floor. His eyes widened when he saw me and he minced close in that funny-disgusting swish manner.

"Hel-lo. You're new, aren't you?" He had large pretty eyes. His fingernails were pale ovals, painted pink. "I'm Davey. Are you living alone?"

Then he spotted Rill behind me in the room and his eyes turned hard. "Rill, can't you leave any of the new men for us?"

I laughed at him. "You've got nothing I want."

"Oh no?" He licked his lips suggestively. "Try me sometime, big boy."

I couldn't think of anything to say. I went inside and slammed the door. I heard him go to the bathroom. From the left wall I heard a typewriter going in quick floor vibrating spurts. Carling was a speedy typist.

Rill was sitting on the bed, watching me with those green eyes. I stared back. There was an aching in my mind. A sick realization was coming home to me. My life was changed now and nothing could retrieve it. I was sinking into the hip world, turning my back on Portland and Dawn. I unbuckled my belt. "Take them off," I ordered.

A slow smile widened her lips. She was naked in ten seconds. "I feel like a bitch, daddy-o." She was on her hands and knees on the bed. "Make like a dog."

She was nuts but she was fun. Lots and lots of fun. I climbed on.

"That's it," she moaned. "Send me. Beat me, daddy, eight to the bar. . . ."

# Chapter Ten

That evening around nine-thirty after I'd eaten at the restaurant Rill ate a second can of dog food . . . sex made her hungry she said and smiled. And I puffed up like a proud peacock.

We checked on Zeke but he was gone, so Rill wanted to go look for him. I agreed. It was about time I got out of the house and saw more of the town. We walked up the promenade toward the Gas House. Rill went barefoot.

Twilight was in its last stages and the cement beach side benches were mostly empty of the old folks who compose the bulk of Venice West's population. They come from all over the country to die of boredom sitting in the sun all day, day after day, always bundled up in coats and sweaters as if still warding off the cold winters of the east.

As we walked past them they followed us with their sharp old resentful eyes. Rill ignored them. To her they were part of the scenery, curious specimens of the ultra-square world. They didn't exist for her as human beings. And I'm sure they held the same opinion of us.

A police car on patrol crept along the walk and passed us. The cop inside gave us a long look. His eyes flicked over me and fastened on Rill speculatively. But the car didn't stop. He shifted his hard gaze to some high school kids out on the park that cut into the width of the beach.

"Lousy fuzz," Rill muttered.

We turned into the Gas House. Many years ago it had been a bingo palace but a law had killed it and its fellows and Venice had sickened and died. Now the building was a curiously painted art center and gathering place for Beats. Old sofas and chairs were scattered about. The famous flame painted bathtub was squatting near the door with a cushion in it. The walls were hung with spotlight illuminated paintings. Most were abstract. One or two looked as if they had merit.

Zeke wasn't around. Rill took me over to a tall blond giant with a beautifully proportioned body. His hair was long and he had a black patch over his right eye. He was playing chess with a lean and hungry looking guy with a straggly brown beard.

"Al, seen Zeke?" Rill asked.

Black Patch looked up slowly. He grinned and revealed two teeth missing in front. I wondered what he was doing in the Gas House. He could have played pirate roles in the movies all his life.

"Hi, chick." He took me in with his good eye. The other fellow leaned back in his chair and scribbled something on a clipboard on his lap. It looked like poetry. "He was here ten ago but he split to the Pup. He's recruiting for a blast in Beverly."

"Yeah." Almost as an afterthought, Rill said, "This is Jeff."

The two nodded at me. I nodded back. Al jerked his head at his chess partner. "Dick."

Dick asked, "Man, you making it with Rill?"

I glanced at her and nodded.

"How about laying a couple on me? I'm flat. The old turnkey'll toss me tonight unless I cross her palm with green." He saw me reach for my wallet. "Like, five?"

I gave it to him. He whistled at the sight of my money. "Look at all that bread. Think of the wheat germ that would buy." He folded the bill and put it in his shoe.

Rill moved off and I followed her. Once outside we walked toward Windward. I noticed a tram up ahead loading for a trip to Ocean Park.

"What was that bit about wheat germ?" I asked.

"He eats it."

"Is that all? Just wheat germ?"

"Bananas and milk with it."

"What does Al eat?"

"Vitamins."

I raised mental eyebrows. Wheat germ. Vitamins. I was living in kook harbor. Weirdsville, as the kids say.

We walked up Windward to Pacific and turned right. The Pup was a sleazy drive-in. Zeke wasn't around there either. Rill sighed and we started back to the apartment house. It was ten o'clock.

There was a note on our door to come up to his pad.

As we entered apartment seven, Zeke was sitting in the dark with a girl. He lit a candle. I saw it was the teen-ager I'd seen in the convertible, the one in the bathing suit and shirt in front of the Gas House.

Zeke got to his feet. "Hey, Jeff, the breadman. Let's get your wheel and roll. We got to pick up Al and Dick on the way."

I was busy taking a close-up of the girl, Rosemary. She was wearing a skimpy red bikini that her skinny frame had no business trying to fill. The top punched out more than it should. Falsies for sure. The ponytail was long enough to reach halfway down her back. She didn't look more than fourteen.

I frowned. "Is *she* going with us?"

She was quick to take offense. "What's the matter with me, mister?"

Zeke said, "Sure, she's wanted. Don't worry about it."

"She's not going like that, is she?"

Zeke looked at her. "Square thinking all the way. But right this time." He dug into a corner and threw an old shirt and pants at her.

Rosemary looked at me resentfully. "You'd think he was my old man, for Pete's sake!" She put them on.

We trooped down the stairs, out and down Speedway. Zeke chuckled. "The native squares call this queer alley."

We reached the parking lot. The Caddy sparkled under the street lights. Rosemary's eyes got big. She looked at me. "Jeez, is this *yours?*"

I nodded and we got in. Rosemary managed to sit next to me. She breathed admiration at the rich interior and ran her fingers over the spectacular dashboard. "Wowee, man, this is class. Feel that carpet." She was impressed. Obviously her scale of values placed Caddy owners at the top. She was as square as I was.

I backed the car out of the lot and started down Speedway. We stopped and picked up Al and Dick at the Gas House. Then Zeke directed me onto Pacific and we hummed toward Santa Monica.

We stopped and picked up some liquor, Zeke buying with my money, then hummed on to Wilshire boulevard where we turned inland.

Rosemary had gotten a look at my money. Suddenly her manner changed even more. Now I was a friend. A good friend. She snuggled up to me and placed her hand on my leg. I could feel her fingers squeezing and sliding on my inner thigh.

Al grinned wolfishly at her and talked about cars. "Detroit iron, a drag, but I'd like to let this one out just to hear it sing. Good motor but too much weight, too much play in the wheel. Rides like mush."

Zeke directed me into Beverly Hills. We crept along a street of immaculate lawns and deep set rambling houses. "Here," he said, "the stone front. Pull into the drive." There were three expensive cars parked before the door and a Mercedes Benz in the open garage.

We piled out and Zeke pushed a signal pattern on a buzzer by the kitchen door. After a moment the door opened a crack and a slurred female voice said, "Who dat?"

Zeke replied, "Who dat say 'Who dat?'"

The door swung wide and a busty fortyish woman in a leopard skin lounging outfit burst into a raucous drunken laugh. "Zeke, you hype bastard, come on in." She motioned us down narrow stairs to the basement.

As I passed I recognized her as a former female lead in B-pictures. She was currently doing important character bits in pictures that aim for Academy Awards. It startled me. You don't really believe those shadow stars exist until you see them in the flesh.

She ignored me and smiled widely at Rosemary and Rill.

The basement was a plush pad. There were hundred dollar mattresses on the nylon carpeted floor. The candles were thick and red in fancy brass holders. Flickering yellow light half filled the room. The hi-fi was stereo, tape deck, AM-FM radio and twelve feet of polished mahogany. It was playing muted cool jazz. In a nearby corner was a low-boy bar. Two feet high. You sat on cushions.

The other people in the room were pure Hollywood.

## Chapter Eleven

Zeke looked around, spotted a black haired blue jowled man with a pretty young woman, nodded, and appeared immensely relieved. "We brought you an offering," he said to the busty actress as she came down after us. "Great!" She took the two bottles of scotch and set them on the low bar. "You!" She pointed at Al and Dick. "Start pouring. We need liquid reinforcements." She turned to Rosemary, Rill and I. "Sit down, make yourselves at home. It's going to be a long night." She laughed. Her voice had a resonant theatrical quality. She took Rosemary's arm. "Child, where on God's green earth did you get those clothes?"

Rosemary smiled at her. "They made me wear them so the cops wouldn't stop us or something." She unbuttoned the shirt. "Bunch of jerks."

Zeke leaned close to the woman. "She's hip, Sylvia, smart."

She watched Rosemary take off Zeke's old clothes and stand nonchalantly in the brief swim suit. "Oh, lovely," she said. "Lovely, lovely, lovely."

Rill slumped down to a covered mattress and I followed. She was very quiet and I got the impression she was a bit wary. She looked around at the other people in the room.

The room was covered wall and ceiling with black acoustic panels. It was long and narrow, with an L-shape at the far end. The bar was at our end next to the steps. There was a door at the far end. Cute signs indicated it was a bathroom.

Lounging and sitting with drinks on the other mattresses were a tall gaunt young woman in a flaring green dress that rustled loudly when she moved, and a sullen young man of incredible handsomeness. Near the bathroom door sprawled a very fat man in a bright sport shirt that folded over his big round gut like a colorful maternity outfit. His bald head was fringed with grey streaked hair. Across from Rill and I, next to the hi-fi, were jowled well-dressed man and a striking brunette. She wore a white ruffled blouse and pink walking shorts.

Zeke whispered something to Sylvia, the hostess. She nodded. "Child, you look old enough to drink. Tell those two to give you a glass. Zeke and I have something to attend to." Her hand trailed along Rosemary's arm.

The kid grinned knowingly. "Thanks."

I watched the two go up the stairs. Al, grinning like a one-eyed Viking, padded over to us with two drinks. His forearm was as big as Rosemary's thigh. "Enjoy," he said. "They're bombs."

I tasted mine. Whoosh, almost straight scotch. The ice cubes seemed to be the only mixer.

"She's queer," Rill said.

"Who?"

"Sylvia. I can tell. She's up there laying it on Zeke for bringing Rosemary."

A shiver went up my spine. "What do you mean?"

"Daddy-o, Rosey is the new blood, the virgin, the sold slave. The old one likes it y-o-u-n-g."

I looked at Rosemary. She was sitting on a purple cushion at the bar, sipping a big drink. She didn't like the taste but she didn't show it much. Dick was talking to her.

"Does she know it?"

"Sure. This isn't her first blast with Zeke. She gets part of the loot."

I felt a little sick. I took a swallow of my drink and a fire started in my belly. "Some life she's going to have."

Rill shrugged. "A frantic night. The connection is here." She was looking across at the well fed man and his girl.

The guy had an effeminate look despite his close shaven blue jowls and heavy body. His black wavy hair was thick and oiled. A long white hand held his glass with precise grace. He was too well groomed.

"What's his name?"

"Long John."

"Is his last name Silver?"

Rill looked puzzledly at me and shrugged. "Nobody knows his last name."

I watched the girl next to him. She was the diminutive Dresden china type. Very delicate features, small pink hands, enormous brown eyes accented with emerald eye shadow, small apple breasts and a tinkling musical laugh that came from a perfect little mouth as Long John smiled and said something into her ear.

I was about to ask Rill who she was when the gaunt young woman a few feet to our left said loudly, "You make me sick, Robby, sick, sicker, sickest." She got up on her knees and walked on them over to us amid a snap, crackle and pop from her stiff taffeta dress. The young man threw her a black look and slid down to talk to the sport-shirted fat old man.

Her face reminded me of a good natured horse. She sat back on her heels and fluffed the crinkly dress around her knees. "Hi." She smiled like a horse, too. "I'm Maggy. You mind if I talk? I have to talk to *somebody* after listening to *that* malformed mind for the last hour. God, what a creep."

"I've seen you on television, haven't I?"

Her smile widened. "I do guest shots all the time, but mostly I'm night clubs. You ever catch my act?"

"Just on TV. You're very funny."

"*Thank* you." She simpered and looked at me boldly. "I think this is going to be my night for men."

An open invitation. But I was pooped from my many labors with Rill the previous night and this morning. And I felt Rill needed me. I wanted to be faithful to her while we were shacking up together. She was sitting close and quiet with caution still in her eyes. But her drink was sitting empty on the carpet and her hands were under her sweatshirt.

Maggy had noticed and was watching her curiously. I was the one who blushed. "Rill, do you have to do that now?"

She ignored me.

"Rill, for God's sake!"

She sighed and said, "Daddy-o, you got a bill of sale on me?" She didn't stop.

I looked helpless-apologetic at Maggy. She laughed like a horse, too.

Dick walked over with a bottle of my scotch. "Chick, you need filling up?"

Maggy looked up at him and showed all her white teeth. Yards of them. "Oh, *do* I. In more ways than one, hon." She watched him pour a big slug into her glass. She reached up and played with his straggly brown beard. "Isn't that *cute*? That's the cutest thing I ever saw."

Dick looked down into her low cut bodice. "You need fattening up."

Her mobile face instantly became sad. "I know. I live too fast. On the go, cigarettes, coffee, this stuff," she took a gulp of the liquor, shuddered, "and sex. I dearly love sex."

"You'n me should talk," Dick said and squatted down. "I can put you onto something real fine."

She grinned. "Any position is fine with me."

"You ever eaten wheat germ?"

"Hon, I've eaten everything *but* wheat germ." She pulled him around beside her on the mattress. "Tell me all about it."

Zeke and the hostess came back down the stairs. Her pouched eyes found Rosemary at the bar. "Child, come to mama! I see they fixed you up good." As the girl started to get up Sylvia motioned her down and sat on a red cushion beside her. "Hey, Atlas," she said to Al, who was setting up another drink for himself, "pour a big one for me. God, will you get a load of those muscles." She shook her head in mock wonder at his build.

He grinned evilly and poured her drink.

She yelled at the men at the end of the room. "Hey! You two need refills?"

The fat man held up his glass and said, "Yeah."

The handsome boy nodded.

"Take a bottle down to them, will you, sweetie?"

"Crazy," Al said and walked over to them. That walk was beautiful to watch. It was perfect grace in motion. He was like a tawny lion padding along a jungle path.

Zeke sat beside Long John and murmured a few words to him. The man nodded and smiled. He turned and whispered to the girl. Her gaze lifted from her glass to me. Zeke and Long John got up and walked to the bathroom. The girl smiled radiantly at me.

I smiled back. She was something!

There was a terrified screech from the left. Al had picked up the impossibly good looking young man and was shaking him in the air like a rag doll. The fat old man was bellowing with laughter.

Sylvia bounced up from her cushion. "Goddamn that little faggot! I warned him!" She rushed over to them. "Put him down, Atlas."

Al looked at her and let loose. The boy fell to the floor, bumped his head and began crying.

Sylvia touched Al's arm. "I'm sorry, sweetie, I should have warned you. Ordinarily I wouldn't mind if you smeared him, but I'm sort of responsible for him tonight and that pretty face is worth a couple million dollars at the box office."

The fat man's laughter trailed off into chuckles. "To theenk I haf to direct that in war peecture." He chuckled more. "Life . . . life is tragedy."

Sylvia bent over the sobbing boy. "Robby, for Christ's sake, knock it off! Maybe you'd better leave."

"No. I . . ." His voice was broken by sobs. "I want to stay."

"Then behave yourself!" She took Al by the hand and led him back to the bar.

Zeke and Long John came out of the bathroom. There was a blissful look on Zeke's face. I stared at him, fascinated.

They joined the girl and then arranged to change places with Maggy and Dick. Zeke sat on my left and Long John next to him. The girl smiled lazily and stretched out behind me on the mattress. There was a tiny star-shaped beauty mark on her cheek. I felt surrounded. Rill was still on my right side, still feeling herself.

John offered me his hand. I shook it, but it was like shaking hands with a snake.

Zeke said dreamily, "Ackerman, this is John and Lee."

Lee offered her delicate little hand, too. My big paw covered it completely. Her skin was hot.

"Hello," she said. Her voice was flute-like. "What's your first name?"

"Jeff," Zeke supplied, and I was angry with him for not letting me tell her myself.

"Jeff . . ." She made it sound like a priceless jewel. "I like it."

"I like Lee, too." I held her hand. She didn't seem to mind.

"Good." She smiled and wrinkled her nose at me.

I noticed Rill watching us with her Mona Lisa smile. It irritated me.

"Zeke tells me you're an advertising man," John said.

I looked at Zeke but he was smiling at something invisible.

John took a gold case from his inside coat pocket and extracted a long thin cigar. "Would you care to try a little pot? It's harmless. I might say it's easier on you than that drink."

"Is that solid marijuana?"

Rill came alive at my side. "Man, a blockbuster."

Lee sat up and put a tiny hand on my shoulder. "Light it, John, let's get high."

He flamed it with a gold lighter and passed it to her. She inhaled deeply several times then held it out to me. She smiled invitingly. "Want to try it, Jeff?"

I took it and inhaled a small puff. It made me dizzy. I passed it to Rill. "What is this stuff supposed to do to you?"

John answered. "It accentuates everything you see and feel. Concentrate on a mood and it'll put you into it big." He excused himself and went over to Sylvia. He gave her a similar cigar from his case and lit it for her.

Rosemary was getting tipsy from the drink. Sylvia took a deep drag with closed eyes, then bent over the girl. She offered the cigar. One of her hands toyed with the elastic waistband of Rosemary's bikini.

John came back to us. He took the blockbuster from Rill, sucked on it and handed it to Lee. She inhaled deeply and handed it to me. It went around like that for several minutes.

The stuff was getting to me. The shapes around me seemed curiously warped, as if the room were filled with water. I was giddy. John and Lee were speaking to me but I couldn't make sense of their words. She was smiling and trying to pull me down next to her.

Rill was flat on her back, smiling, the sweatshirt suddenly in a pile at her feet. When had that happened? I felt one of her large nipples between my fingers and realized I was toying with her with one hand. Everybody was smiling. Zeke sat like a happy Buddha in a trance.

Lee's voice got through to me as I passed up the cigar for a minute. "I don't think you like me, Jeffy."

I turned my head dreamily. "I do."

"Why don't I get the same attention she gets?" Lee's tiny fingers were unbuttoning her blouse. "I'm in the mood." She was breathing shallowly, her cupid's mouth partly open.

I took my hand from Rill and slid it into Lee's blouse. She was wearing a thin lace bra. Her breast fitted my hand like a tennis ball. "Good," she said as I gently squeezed.

Rill's brow had furrowed when I took my hand away. Automatically her own hand took its place.

John said, "Lee is beautiful, isn't she? She likes you, too. Why don't you come with us for a while? We're going over to her apartment for a few minutes."

"What for? Why leave?"

Lee sighed with pleasure and her smile became more inviting. "I'd like you to come, Jeffy. There's lots of things we could do."

"She knows a lot of tricks," John said. "And there are things I can do for you, too. This pot isn't anything."

My mind had cleared even more. They were pushing too hard. Lee was the bait and John had the hook all ready.

"I want to stay."

His eyes narrowed but he said nothing. Lee pouted with disappointment but still enjoyed my hand. She took the cigar from Rill and urged it on me. I puffed on it but didn't inhale. Her hand crept around my hip.

Sylvia and Rosemary had slid off their cushions and were laying tight against each other on the floor. Rosemary was giggling and trying to keep her half-filled glass from spilling. Sylvia's hand was inside the bikini as she kissed the youthful lips.

Al sat behind the bar with the pot cigar clenched tightly in his teeth. He watched them with detached interest.

Dick and Maggy were sprawled side by side, talking, drinking from a bottle.

The fat old man was smiling and talking low into the ear of Robby. The young man was nodding, licking his lips, and had both hands deep in his pockets. I watched the furtive movement a long minute to be sure. My sight was still wavering.

A doorbell rang above us. Activity stopped for a second. "Good God," Sylvia groaned. The bell rang again.

She separated from Rosemary, adjusted the opened top of her lounge suit and looked hard at Zeke.

He smiled airily at her and waved a hand. "The entertainment, the cool cool entertainment."

A wide smile broke over her face. "Oh, yeah, the act. I forgot." She went up the stairs.

There was an exchange of women's voices, then a nice pair of legs in a bright red dinner gown came clicking down the steps on wobbly high heeled red pumps.

This girl is dressed for the grand ball, I thought, as the rest of her came into view. The dress was cut breathtakingly low in a familiar way. Then I recognized Dawn! She had on too much make-up. Her arms jingled with too many bracelets. Big eye-catching earrings swayed by her beautiful throat.

"Surprise," Zeke said.

"Did you invite her to this party? Did you know Dawn and I are married?"

"I'm playing God tonight, man. I'm high in the sky. They picked up the act for me."

Behind Dawn came Tex in grey flannel slacks, tartan vest and a wine colored sport coat. I was beginning to realize that Zeke was a "power" in Beatland. It paid him to know things about people.

Then down the steps came a small Negro and Negress. They wore native African robes of rough purple cloth fastened at the shoulder. Incongruously, he carried a narrow leather attaché case. All four stood peering uncertainly into the candle-lit gloom as Sylvia came down behind them.

## Chapter Twelve

I drew my hand away from Lee's breast and twisted away from her seeking hand. "Jeffy . . ." she complained.

Dawn's eyes were wide with curiosity and excitement as she looked around. She stared at Rill's naked breasts and busy hands, then recognized me. Her lips closed firmly and she looked away. Tex saw me and scowled.

Sylvia put a hand on Tex's shoulder. "Kiddo, you and this ravishing doll get yourselves a drink and sit down somewhere." She addressed us all with a sweep of the hand and a raised voice. "Zeke arranged to have these two people from Africa put on a special dance for us. Something very few white people get to see." She said to the Negro, "Do you speak English?"

He nodded. "Yes, but imperfectly." He had a French accent.

"Are there any preparations you have to make?"

I looked closely at the two as he conversed with Sylvia. The Negress was even smaller than he, with a child's round face similar to his. Their hair was kinky black. Standing side by side, only her smaller size was indicative of her sex. She couldn't have been over four feet. The robes showed only their arms, heads and feet. Their skin was blue-black.

I looked over at Dawn. She held a drink self-consciously in her right hand. I felt ashamed of her. She was overdressed, done up like a cheap whore. She had no dress sense, no taste.

Her mother was responsible for that. The old bag always rouged two dollar-sized spots on her cheeks, made her mouth into a red rimmed wound and powdered the rest of her face white. The poor creature always looked like something relatives peer down at with sad smiles before they bury it.

I saw that Dawn had worn an up-and-out bra with the dress, making her wonderful figure into a ridiculous caricature of an impossibly endowed body. She had plenty. Why did she have to do this? Then I knew. Zeke had told her a director and some stars were going to be here, too. This was her way of getting attention. It was pathetic.

The Negro was objecting to something. His voice was silky. "For best effect the lights should be turned off at just the right instant. We were not told about candles."

"Does it make that much difference? I think candles set a perfect mood. Nice effect for the dance. Besides, I'm paying for it."

A pained expression passed over his young-old face. "That is it, the effect! Without the quick darkness there is... how you say... anti-climax. There should be only a controlled spotlight."

"Well, I'm sorry . . . what's your name again?"

"I am Andre. She is Ynez."

"Andre, we haven't got a spot. How about my adding another fifty to the tab. Will that soothe your artistic temperament?"

He bowed his head for a few seconds, glanced at his partner, the room, and nodded. "It will not be very good, but . . . we will try." He produced a record album from the small case. "Will you put this on the machine?"

Sylvia took it, looked at it curiously, and sailed it over to Dick where he sat next to the hi-fi. "Groove it, will you?"

Andre and Ynez went to the center of the room, directly in front of Zeke, Rill and I. They stood silent as Dick set up the record and started the player in motion.

Sylvia gestured to Rosemary and they walked behind us along the wall to an empty mattress on the other side of John.

There was a scratching sound from the speakers then a full fidelity roll of jungle drums. Andre and Ynez reached to their shoulder fastenings and with a loud beat from the drum, let their garments fall. Both were stark naked.

There were gasps. Their bodies were black statues in the candle light; not an ounce of fat, beautiful rippling muscles . . . and something else. The Negress was young, with high conical breasts and tight narrow hips. Her eyes gleamed.

But it was Andre who drew the stares. Somebody on nature's assembly line must have made a mistake. Behind me Lee said, "Oh, my God!"

I was well hung, and proud of it, but this man, this little black Negro smiled with white teeth and stamped his heels to the drum beat and turned slowly, showing himself to all.

Rill was sitting, rigid, forming words without sound as she looked.

Zeke laughed low. "That spade's the most. The most."

"What do they do?" I whispered.

"Watch the chicks, that's the show. Watch the audience. When that mule comes up they flip or faint."

I glanced at Dawn. Her eyes were saucers. Tex looked dazed. At the other end of the room Rosemary was swallowing repeatedly, her chest rising and falling quickly. Reside her Sylvia was smiling. Robby was visibly shivering. The fat director looked amused. Across the way Maggy laughed too loudly and said, "He can have me any old time."

"Does he connect with that thing?" I asked Zeke.

"For five hundred. Sylvia wouldn't spring for it. Just the dance."

"That little Negress can take him?"

"I picked up on them downtown three months ago. He looked a long time before he found her."

I imagined so. But it figured if a small man was equipped like that, somewhere there was a woman as small who had equivalent organs.

The drum beat steadied and they began an elaborate pantomime. Ynez was bathing modestly in a pool of water, splashing herself with childish glee. Andre circled slowly around her, legs wide, moving sideways with his feet making little hops, peering through imaginary bushes at her.

She climbed out of the pool and began rubbing herself sensuously in the sun, her hands rubbing up and down her body, over the young breasts, down to her flat belly, over the taut thighs. Andre circled more slowly, watched more intently, then hesitated an instant.

The room was hushed.

Ynez cocked her head to listen. Her hands stopped in mid-air, her eyes were frightened. Behind her Andre leaped forward with a silent cry. She whirled and stared. Terror was on her face. They were barely a foot apart.

Then began an immensely graceful enactment of feet remained in the same place. He held her, yet never actually touched her. She pushed at him but her hands pushed an invisible shield an inch from his skin, They fought and swayed in slow motion, their muscles coordinated to a wonderful illusion of reality. Their bodies filmed with perspiration. The dance must have taken hundreds of hours to perfect.

Andre finally pinned her arms to her side. He kissed just away from her purple nipples and they responded as if he actually had kissed them. Her head lowered in shame.

Then, for the first time since the beginning of the struggle, she noticed the size of him and the slow effect of the phantom kiss. She watched in horrified fascination as he stirred.

She didn't want to believe it. Her hand waggled from side to side . . . no, no, no . . . but her eyes never left it and a barely perceptible look of greed came into her eyes.

I was spellbound. The acting was incredible, the tremendous discipline and muscular control they were displaying was hard to believe.

One of the viewers was moaning. I could hear hard breathing all around me. I kept my eyes glued to the act. The tempo of the drums changed to a deeper, more urgent beat. They adopted a throbbing primitive rhythm.

Ynez' hips jerked slightly. Again. She appeared at first surprised, then eager. Andre's hips moved with hers in hesitant shallow thrusts. He smiled at her and she smiled back. The drums became more insistent. Their hips swung in wild sensual abandon.

Lee pressed herself against my back. She was panting as her hand groped for me, slipped under my belt and squeezed and moved in time with the drums.

I was hot. Just watching would've aroused anyone. I reached back and felt for her. I heard a zipper and she guided my hand between her thighs. Her skin was warm and humid.

I felt impelled to glance at Dawn. She was watching Andre and Ynez while trying to stop Tex from wrinkling her dress. She had no eyes for me.

Ynez sank slowly to her knees, not missing a beat with her swinging hips. She arched back onto her elbows, her knees wide, her head touching the floor almost at my feet. There was a crazy uncontrolled grin on her upside down face.

Andre hovered before her, coming closer, his face stiff with desire. He was on his knees, in position, still matching the beat. He drew back as the drums neared a frenzied climax.

The record ended and that was all. Panting, he sat back on his heels and wiped sweat from his brow. Ynez collapsed from her strained position.

Lee's hand stopped but still held me. I could feel her cheek on my arm. She was peeking at the two from between Zeke and me.

Andre looked around at the staring people. "The lights should be out."

Rill stirred at my right. She slid off the mattress and began wriggling dreamily toward him, her breasts rasping on the carpet. He watched her approach, a wide smile on his face. He shifted position so she could crawl between his knees.

"No! It's mine! I want it!" Robby dashed over to him.

Andre pushed him away. "No, monsieur, it is for the ladies only. I am sorry."

"No, me . . . *me!*" Robby hit ineffectively at Rill and tried to recover his position.

Sylvia got up from beside Rosemary. The top of her outfit was off and her great white breasts jiggled to and fro as she came forward. In her hand she held Rosemary's bikini top. "Damn it to hell, Robby, I *told* you this was out of bounds for you! Behave yourself or leave! You've got a big hunk waiting for you at home, why don't you go to it?" She pulled him away.

"He's cheating on me," Robby sniveled. "I hate the sight of him."

"I can't help that! Get back to your corner and stay there or I'll throw you out myself!"

Rill had continued crawling and was up over Andre, sliding her hard nipples over his sweat slippery chest. They spoke no words. None were needed. They crawled off to the alcove at the far end of the L-shaped room.

I was shocked and angry. I'd thought Rill and I had an understanding. "What goes?" I asked Zeke.

"You bugged?"

"She must be crazy to do a thing like that."

"Lots of chicks go for color."

"But the way she acted."

"That's why her folks busted her into Camarillo."

"The State insane asylum? When? She didn't tell me about that."

"You have to know everything? She flew the coop six months ago."

Sylvia watched Robby crawl back to his place and then she realized what she held in her hand. She held it up like a trophy and dropped it in Zeke's lap. "Here, you bastard. You brought me a fake." The bikini top was self-formed, with built-in falsies.

I looked over at Rosemary. She was giggling constantly and trying to drain the last of her drink. Her real breasts were the faintly rounded swellings of a barely pubescent girl.

Zeke shrugged eloquently.

"And she giggles too Goddamned much!" Sylvia stood for a minute undecided. "But I guess I'm stuck with her. She knows the score all right."

Al moved out from behind the bar with a towel. He knelt beside Ynez as she lay recovering her breath and began wiping her down. He stared fixedly into her eyes. She examined his build and ran a small child-like hand over his lithe muscles. She nodded gravely. He draped the towel over her middle and picked her up easily, cradling her in his arms like a baby, and moved back behind the bar.

Robby crawled over where Andre and Rill lay hidden from view. "Let me watch," he begged. "Please let me watch. I'll give you money."

Sylvia was back with Rosemary. She threw the girl's bikini pants at him. Rosemary was a naked white shape beside her. "Get back there, I told you!"

"He said I could watch, didn't you hear? He doesn't care if I just look."

"Look, then. I don't care if he kills you."

Dick and Maggy were far gone in their discussion. His hand was far under the rustling green dress. She whispered to him and began blowing out candles nearby.

Lee began moving her hand on me again. "Come along with us, Jeffy. I want you."

I shook my head no. I was worried about Rill. I looked at Dawn. She wasn't used to drinking as much as the empty tumbler beside her indicated. Not straight whiskey. She was trying to get to her feet at Tex tried to hold her back. They were arguing fiercely in low pitched voices.

Long John hadn't said a word all through the performance. Now he glanced at me like I was something he'd like to step on and whispered into Lee's ear. She made a face but obeyed. She took her hand away and zipped up the side of her shorts. She got up and walked into the bathroom.

Dawn finally broke away from Tex and staggered to the center of the room. "I can sing and dance, everybody. I can entertain." Her face was flushed. She wobbled unsteadily on the spike heels.

"Sit down," I said. "You're making a fool of yourself."

She looked down at me with a foolish drunken smile. "Oh, no, no no nonono. I'm going to show you." She struck a pose and began singing. "Don't know why, there's no sun up in the sky, stormy weather . . . since my man and I ain't together. It's raining all the time . . ."

She couldn't carry a tune in a bucket. Her voice was sweet and resonant but she had no style and sang without sincerity.

". . . all the time . . . keeps raining all the time . . ." She stopped, furrowed her brow and looked desperately at the director and Sylvia who were watching. "When . . . when he goes away the blues come get me. . . ." She stopped again.

It was painful to watch. She couldn't remember the lyric. Only the director was watching her now, curiously, as if she were a strange bird in a zoo.

"I can dance, too . . . look at me dance." On the first step a heel turned inward and broke. She sat down abruptly . . . hard! She began to weep. She pulled off the shoes.

I wanted to stop her and hold her close. I wanted to end this humiliating scene for her, but I knew she'd struggle. Besides, I wanted to see her finally convinced about her chances in Hollywood.

Tex seemed to feel the same way. She sat against the wall and gazed stonily into her glass.

Lee came out of the bathroom and settled down beside the director. She smiled and appeared to be asking for a cigarette. He hastily produced a pack and lit one for her. She stayed at his side.

Dawn struggled to her feet and kicked the red shoes away. Her dance was conventional and too ambitious for the small space between the mattresses. Twice she nearly fell. After a minute the director was pouring himself a drink, no longer paying attention. Sylvia was murmuring to Rosemary as the girl suckled on her breasts.

Dawn's dance died like a run-down mechanical toy. She was breathing hard, her eyes searching for an audience, yet avoiding my gaze. "I know what you want to see tonight. I'll show you something!"

She reached under her arm and unzipped the side of her dress. In a second it was a pile of red wool at her stockinged feet. "Look at me!" she commanded, and everyone looked. She was clad only in frilly black lace panties and a more substantial wired bra. She reached up behind her to unfasten it as her hips jumped in a raw amateurish bump and grind routine.

In another second the bra came loose and fell to the floor. Her breasts sprang free of its warping contours and bounced on her chest, round and full.

She cupped them in her hands and worked her hips harder. She was exhilarated by the attention she was getting. Every face was turned to her, like white moons in a flickering night sky.

Tex reached for her and Dawn slapped her and pulled away. There was a ripping and her panties came off.

I tried to get up. "Dawn, for God's sake, stop it!"

She pushed me off balance and I fell back to the mattress.

She was beautiful, a wanton blonde goddess throwing naked sex at all who looked. She slapped Tex again and ran to the director. She threw herself down beside him. "Did you like me?"

His face wrinkled into a gargoyle grin. "You are very beautiful. You have many possibilities." He spoke further to her in a low voice and she nodded eagerly.

Lee was staring daggers at her from the director's other side. Tex was mad as a kicked box of scorpions. She stalked down the room and dragged Dawn away by one arm and her hair. She was cursing her. She threw the dress at her and told her in no uncertain terms to put it on.

I was grateful to Tex then. She was my ally in this at least.

Dawn wept but complied. The second she was presentable Tex dragged her up the stairs without a word of goodbye. I felt relieved.

John asked Zeke, "Where does that girl live?"

I learned toward him. "You keep away from her buster, or I'll break her neck!"

Zeke smiled between us and said nothing.

"I can help her in a career," John said smoothly.

"Like hell you can! You want to hook her on dope and add her to your string! Like Lee!"

"Watch what you're saying, Mr. Ackerman."

"I'm just warning you to keep away from her. Do we understand each other?"

He glared at me and looked away. I waited for a minute, ready to clobber him, but he ignored me.

## Chapter Thirteen

Zeke said, "You're not just square, Ackerman, you're cubey. You still want to go back to your buggy job with your buggy wife. Why should you care if John hooks her?"

"She's just a spoiled kid. I feel responsible for her."

"She bugs you, she flies with your bread, she shacks with a butch and you still want her back. Crazy. You're really married to the social lie."

"I don't understand you."

"Money man. Bread. It's screwed up your marriage. Dawn wants it, you work like a whore for it, and it's killing you both. Is your Caddy that important?"

"Nuts! Marriages are broken by emotional and personality problems. It isn't just wanting money that's at fault. There are divorces in Russia too. And the Beats don't stay hitched with one partner for life, either."

"The Beats are free, not chained by a social shuck like the marriage vows. They stick as long as they enjoy life together. Why louse up a relationship with "Till death do us part' a twenty thousand dollar house, a fifteen thousand dollar mortgage and a lifetime of slavery to bigger cars, bigger refrigerators, and a carload of mechanical junk you're constantly yakked at to buy buy buy? Who benefits from those sacred marriage vows? The guy who marries you, the state and city, and the shysters who make it when you break up. They've got you by the balls with their laws."

"I love Dawn. I can't expect her, or any other woman, to bring children into poverty. Women need security."

"You're like a sick parrot. You throw up all you've been told by the schools, the movies, the papers, TV, all the mass media. It's all lies! It's all there to make you and schmucks like you stand still for slavery. Instead of living free you slave away to keep the crap from piling up in the warehouses. You work to make and use useless gimmicks. Do you *really* need an electric can opener for Pete's sake?"

"Women still need security for their kids."

"You're confusing emotional security with physical security. And even so your square women don't have either. A Beat mother can have as much emotional security as a woman with a million bucks. More, probably. But what about the wondrous physical security you and your masters have created for today's mothers? It's a lie. When they're not worrying about the Bomb they're worrying about junior's Social Adjustment scores and about moving into a bigger house because their man finally got the promotion she's schemed him into. Then she has to worry and fret about another jump up the ladder of 'Success' and another, bigger house. Houses aren't lifetime homes any more, they're just another lie, another keeping-up-with-the-Joneses status symbol."

"Zeke, you sneer at my Caddy, but it's an envious sneer. You'd like to have it. You're just not willing to work for it. Why do you rave like that against the system if you're really alienated and disaffiliated as you Beats claim you are? Why do you *care* so much?"

"Man, we're idealists. We hate to see people *used* like they are."

"Like hell! If you're so right, how come your movement isn't sweeping the country?"

"It is, man, it is. People are getting the word."

"Nuts! You Beats make necessity a virtue. You're a bunch of perverts, addicts, neurotics and weirdos. You're down and out so you make out that's a good way to live. I like my life and the good things it buys and I'm going to stick with it if I can."

"A word whore."

"Now you're calling names. I'm in advertising. I still say it's an honorable profession. Nobody forces people to buy what I help bring to their attention. I can't help it if people are suckers. I can't change the *fact* that most people are stupid and only a few smart.

"So they run out and buy aspirin for 89¢ a bottle when they can get it for 19¢ without the highly advertised brand name, is this my fault? Should I run around wiping their noses for them the rest of my life? This is the way things *are*. They haven't changed since the dawn of recorded history. You people should face a few facts once in a while! You want to protect man from every little danger or possible psychological hurt. Nuts to it! In spite of your ideals man will continue to be exploited, lied to and sacrificed. The smart man avoids these and is wise to them."

"You surprise me, Ackerman."

"You don't surprise me. I don't respect a junky."

"Once a square, always a square."

"Nuts!" I went over to the bar to get out of the argument. That sort of discussion is useless. Okay once in a while to help a person give and take points of view and solidify his opinions, but with Zeke and I it was like trying to knock down the Great Wall of China with feathers. Neither would budge an inch.

I reached for a bottle and looked over the edge of the bar at what was happening behind. Ynez was making small squealing noises and riding

Al's naked body for all she was worth. Her small hips pistoned up and down. She was like a frantic black monkey on a bare white stallion.

I watched for a few seconds, blew out two candles and then moved away to an empty mattress nearby. Zeke and John were in a low voiced conversation. I took a swig from the bottle and choked on the raw burning liquor. A deep depression was settling over me to match the deepening darkness. I felt lonely and betrayed.

Another candle was snuffed out. I saw Sylvia stretching to extinguish another near her, the feeble light showing the bottom of her outfit gone. Then the tiny yellow died and near total darkness filled the room.

"No, no," came the complaining voice of Robby from the alcove. "I can't see." There was a click and a fluttering glow lit that corner of the room. He was using his lighter.

There was a constant murmur of sounds: rustlings, sighs, whispers, cries of delight, groans, panting exertions, and rising through it, louder, the wild babbling of Rill.

I set my jaw, swallowed, and tried to ignore it. I took another swig of whiskey. How could Rill keep it up? She'd nearly exhausted me the night before and yet now she was taking that huge. . . . And enjoying it. God, was she enjoying it!

Minutes, maybe hours passed. I kept at the bottle, belting it down, feeling the bitter tide of alcoholic oblivion slowly rising in me.

The yellow light in the corner diminished and died and Robby wept. I could hear the repeated scrape of flint as he tried to rekindle the exhausted lighter.

More time went by. The darkness was complete. I looked drunkenly at the luminous dial of my watch. Two a.m. My bottle still had an inch or two left.

Light flared and the director carefully lit a candle at his side. Lee was curled at his side eyes closed, her hand in his pants. Her blouse was wide open, the white bra loose, one firm apple breast pushed into sight.

The old man sat benignly in his puddle of light and patted the exposed breast. Then he took the candle in his other hand and put the flame to her erected nipple.

John cursed and lurched toward them as her shriek rang out. Her doll-like face was contorted, grotesque, and she jerked away from him, whimpering, pressing her breast with both hands.

The director held the candle steady. "Ach, I couldn't help it. I'm sorry, so sorry, mien liddle beauty. Such a shame."

John kicked him once and leaned close to speak angry guttural words. Sylvia, barely visible, rolled over toward them and yelled, "Otto . . . oh, God, I give up!" She rolled back into the gloom and pressed Rosemary to her again.

Otto reached into his coat and pulled out a fat wallet. He took out some bills and pressed them on John, apologizing profusely. John accepted the money and demanded more. The director sighed and pulled out two more bills. John took them, helped Lee to her feet and they left.

I was more and more glad Dawn was away from this accumulation of twisted people.

The director put out his candle and plunged the room into darkness again. The love sounds began again. More time went by. My bottle emptied and I considered crawling to the bar for another. It seemed a long long trip. I lay flat on my back and wondered if I could do it. My muscles didn't seem connected to my brain any more. The little man at the switchboard was falling-down drunk. Shame on him. No sense of responsibility.

I sank into a semi-conscious state. Thoughts whirled and spun in my mind. Pictures in sharp color, distorted, swam around behind a film of pale aqua.

I became aware of somebody trying to reach my wallet, A hand was working its way under my hip. I rolled over on the hand, trapping it, and found myself half laying on a small naked body.

"Ow . . . get off." It was Rosemary.

Words formed in my mind and slowly worked their way out. "Naughty . . . naughty . . ."

"Get off, you're breaking my arm."

"Shame . . . shame . . ." I didn't move.

"Please, mister. I like you a lot. I was just trying to wake you up," Her other hand moved on my leg. "I figured we could have some fun." She waited a few seconds. "Could you please get off?"

I was too far gone for that kind of fun. Too drunk, still too high on pot. Sexual desire had been drained like old crankcase oil. The little man roused himself and flipped some switches. I raised up enough for her to pull free.

"Thanks." She lay silent beside me for a moment, then said, "I liked you from the first, when you walked past the Gas House yesterday."

"Thass nice."

"Then when I saw the car you've got! What a dreamboat." Her hand explored. "Can't you do it?"

I pushed her hand away. Even if I could . . . no, she was too young. Even if she was a child call girl . . . too young. "Go back to Shylvia . . ."

"Not her! It's all one way with her. She went off like a string of firecrackers and then went to sleep. Can't you hear her snore? She sure expected a lot for ten bucks."

There was somebody snoring but it sounded like a lumberjack. Was that Sylvia?

Rosemary held my hand on her. "C'mon, help me. I don't like to do it alone."

"'s not nice ..."

"C'mon, will you? What do you care? I'm human, too."

I saw myself cursing Dawn in Portland and retiring to the bathroom of our home. I knew what Rosemary meant. She was human, I was human ... I moved my fingers for her.

"Thanks. That's good." She kissed my cheek.

"How'd you get shtarted doing thish?"

"You mean parties? Six months ago."

"Mean ... sexsh."

She laughed. "You live in my neighborhood you learn everything by the time you're five. The big ones teach the little ones."

I struggled with words. "What about your folksh?"

"What about 'em? Mom works all night at the Pup. She doesn't care what I do. I got my own money now so I don't cost her anything. My dad left six years ago."

"Where you live?"

"What do you care? That's none of your business, mister. Just stick to what you're doing."

Nothing more was said. I felt her body stiffen after a few minutes. She held her breath.

She sighed a minute later and said, "Thanks a lot." Her gratitude made me feel good, as if I'd done something meaningful and constructive. It didn't seem shameful or sordid. I'd helped her when she needed help. To my drink fogged brain that was enough. I felt warm and protective toward her. She put her head on my shoulder and slept. She was just a kid.

I gradually lost consciousness. Zeke had started talking to himself in the blackness and his voice lulled me to sleep.

I awoke with a hand shaking me and a bright ceiling light casting a flat white illumination over everything. Zeke shook me again. "Wake up, Ackerman, time to split."

I sat up, blinking, still fuzzy with a pile-driving headache. I looked around and mentally cringed. The place was a mess. Spilled drinks had discolored the carpeting and mattresses. Candles had overturned and caked melted wax in the nylon fibers. There were small burned spots from cigarettes and wicks.

All around me people were coming awake, naked, soiled hungover. They avoided each other's eyes as they donned their clothes. Rosemary was sleepily hunting for her bikini bottom, the falsie-formed top trailing from her hand. My watch said five-fifteen.

Zeke went around gathering our group. Al put on his Beatnik garb without a look at Ynez as she hooked the robe over her shoulder. Dick was still entwined with Maggy. It took Zeke five minutes to pry them apart but it did no good. They cursed him and coupled again, unheeding. He shrugged and sought Rill. She crawled out of the alcove stark naked trailed by an exhausted Andre. He was limp. Rill looked satisfied for the time being. She climbed into her capris and sweatshirt and stood close beside him, taller than he, yet obviously his slave.

Robby and the director were gone. Sylvia lay on the floor still snoring away, her broad white body flabby in the pitiless white glare.

Zeke made Rosemary put on his old clothes again and we all trooped up the stairs and out into the soft indirect radiance of pre-dawn.

I couldn't drive and told Zeke, giving him the keys. He motioned for Al to take the wheel as we climbed into the Caddy. Andre and Ynez were with us. "We got to drop them off," Zeke said.

It was crowded. Rosemary sat on my lap and fell asleep again. Rill and Andre were beside me in the back. Up front Ynez sat between Al and Zeke.

Al seemed to come alive with the motor. He tromped the gas and jerked us out of the driveway in reverse. He braked, turned, tromped again and we accelerated down the winding residential street.

He was a madman at the wheel! We howled around curves on two screaming tires. On the straightaway he floored it and the big new car opened up. Cold morning air whipped in the open windows.

Al crowed and yelled in delight. He was hunched over, his huge wide shoulders tense, his ham-hands tight on the wheel. We shot down into Hollywood at over a hundred miles per hour.

I was petrified. Rosemary woke up and became breathless with fear and excitement. Ynez had scrambled around in the front seat and was facing us over the back, her eyes clenched tight.

At last Al slowed and squealed to a stop before a modern apartment hotel. The sun was just peeping over the eastern horizon. Yenz, Andre and Rill got out. The doors shut.

"Hey," I said. "What goes on? Rill?"

She didn't look at me. Nothing was said. The three walked toward the entrance of the hotel and Al gunned the car away. The last I saw out the window was Andre putting his arm around her waist as Ynez followed. The sun turned Rill's long wine colored hair into a rich violet cascade.

Al seemed to have had enough of speed and cut down to a law breaking sixty or so. Rosemary settled against my shoulder and closed her eyes for sleep again. "Don't worry, mister," she said, "i'll be around whenever you need me."

In fifteen minutes we were in Venice. Al parked in the lot and we all went our separate ways.

# Chapter Fourteen

My eyes were glued shut when I awoke. The headache was still with me; power driven spikes were splitting the two halves of my brain apart. I groaned and forced my eyes open.

My room was ceiling deep in hot yellow sunshine. I closed my eyes against the brightness and rolled over. There was something about today that was special . . . what was it?

I opened one eye and peered at my watch. Three. Three in the afternoon. Tuesday. Tuesday was the deadline for my return to Portland and dear ol' Kingman's, I wanted to laugh but all that came out was a choked sob.

I heard a telephone ring somewhere in the building. Out in the hall? It rang unanswered for a few minutes and finally stopped.

My mouth was dry, like it was coated with cobwebs. I remembered the party and groaned again. I hit the pillow with my fist. Dawn. . . .

A series of minor explosions went off in my brain. "Stop it," I pleaded, "stop it." A voice said, "Jeff?" and the explosions continued.

Somebody was knocking on my door. Mercilessly pounding. I had to stop it. I fell out of the bed, staggered to the door, unlocked it, and staggered back to bed.

I heard the door open and close behind me. "Jeff?"

I turned over. It was Dawn. She was all tricked out in a thin print dress that showed her bra and panties clearly, a cute white hat, purse and gloves. As usual she was coated with too much make-up. She looked like a two-bit whore.

"What do you want?"

"Last night at the party . . ." She bit her lip, looked down and was unable to continue. Then she looked at me. "You must have slept in your clothes."

I peered down at the wrinkles. "So what?"

"Jeff, you look awful. Are you going to stay down here and . . . just go to pieces?"

"If I want to! What is it to you?"

"I don't like to see you like this. Aren't you going back to your job and everything?"

"Not without you."

"Stop it! I don't want you on my conscience. You can't make me believe . . . You're just trying to force me into going back with you. This is all an act, isn't it?"

"Sure."

She swallowed and looked away. "Stop it. Go back to Portland. I've got a chance now. Don't ruin it for me."

"Dawn, why did you come in here?"

She hesitated. "I want to borrow your car."

I laughed bitterly. "Who told you I've got a car?"

"Zeke. I asked him just now if he knew where I could borrow one and he told me you had one."

"What's the matter with your precious Tex? Doesn't she have one?"

"Oh, *her!* She wouldn't let me use it. She needed it for work, she said, but she's like you. She doesn't want me to succeed either. She wants to keep me tied to her in this dirty slum! She never once intended to move to Hollywood. She was lying so I'd stay with her. She was using me. Everybody tries to use me."

*Use. Use.* There was that word again. "Dawn, for God's sake! What have *you* been doing? You used me until I wouldn't do all you wanted, then you came down here and started using Tex. Anything to make a career! You use anything or anyone that comes to hand. Last night you used your body like it was a flag with S-E-X written on it."

"I had to do *something,* didn't I? With all those stars and Mr. Kluge there. It worked, too. He told me to come to his office this afternoon."

"He's not interested in your acting or singing or dancing talent."

"What do you mean?"

"I mean he's going to use *you!* The man is a sadist. He gets his kicks by torturing. He did it last night after you left."

"I don't believe you. Why, you'd say *anything* to get me back. I don't know why I ever thought you might be willing to help me."

"Dawn, cut it out. Why don't you just call a cab? You've got lots of money."

She bit her lip again. "No . . . I don't, Jeff,"

"Oh, no! What happened to it?"

"I gave it to Tex to keep for me and now she won't give me any."

I sighed. "Well, maybe it's worth losing to keep you away from Otto Kluge."

"Stop saying that! Please, Jeff, let me have the keys. I'll be careful. I *can't* miss this chance!"

"No! Ask Zeke if you don't believe me. No, don't ask him, he might—"

On a sudden inspiration Dawn grabbed my coat off the floor, plunged her hand into a pocket and cried out in triumph as she came up with the car keys.

"Give me those!" I lunged out toward her and crashed to the floor. She threw the coat over my head and dashed out. I struggled to my feet and the room whirled. I heard her heels clacking down the hall and on the back stairs. I lost my balance and fell heavily. Blood was pounding through my split skull like coastal artillery.

I lay on the floor and cursed. Slowly I got up. The room spun, then steadied as I braced myself against the table. "Damn you . . ." I couldn't live with her and I couldn't live without her. All right, I thought, you go to hell your way and I'll go mine. Serve you right if Otto tries something. And under it all I hated myself for not stopping her. I could have chased her to the parking lot. How fast could she go with high heels? The dizziness would have gone away if I'd exerted myself enough. But I hadn't. I wanted her to be taught a lesson . . . one she'd never forget. I wanted her to be hurt and I hated myself for it.

I tried to blot out of my mind what Otto might do. I was like a man who has just slashed one wrist and is watching the blood spurt . . . not too late to get to a doctor . . . but he does nothing.

Self-loathing welled up in me. I slammed my fist down on the table. I noticed the two bottles of whiskey, still in the sack, I'd bought the day before. I'd become involved with Rill then and hadn't opened them.

I snorted. Good old Rill. In a way she was as square as I was. I had traded up to a bigger and better car. She'd changed to a bigger and better sex machine.

I uncorked a bottle and sniggered. A piston with a ten inch stroke is a wonderful thing. I took a deep gut-melting drink. Hair of the dog. Great prescription. I sat on the bed and raised the bottle to my lips again.

Sobriety, I decided, was the curse of the square class. Squares, do as I do. Throw off your advertising chains. You have nothing to lose but your frigid ambitious wives.

That telephone began to ring again. Endlessly, persistently, it rang on and on. I began counting. Fifteen . . . sixteen . . . seventeen. . . . Somebody answered it and I was disappointed. I heard a mumbling in the hall.

I took another drink. Somebody knocked on my door. "Go away. I'm fresh out of cars."

A woman's deep voice said, "It is a telephone call for you. Very long distance from Portland, Oregon."

It was Lena's voice. A vivid picture of her lush body flashed into my mind. Who was calling? Bob? "Okay, I'm comin'." I got to my feet and weaved to the door. Nobody was in the hall. I heard Lena's door close. So where was the phone? I walked carefully down the hall to ask her. Then I saw a wall pay phone opposite her door by the stairs. The receiver was hanging down, swinging back and forth.

I took it up. "Hallo?"

"Mr. Jeffrey Ackerman?"

"Yeah."

"Just a moment, please."

There was a click, then old man Kingman's dry voice crackled in my ear. "Jeff? You there?"

"Yeah, I'm here."

"What's going on down there, boy? My secretary's been calling that apartment house for hours Are you going to be back up here tomorrow?"

"As to that, shir, I am not very sanguine. Not at all. Not—"

"What? What? Are you drunk?"

"Feeling no pain, feeling no—"

"Now, listen here, young man. I could sympathize with the troubles you've had with your wife, and I don't begrudge you a day or two to bring her back from that place. But if you're down there boozing in the afternoon—"

I laughed out loud. If he only knew. . . .

"You are drunk. It's always that way with you creative types. Intellectuals. New ideas, new methods, but when it comes to the basics like marriage and drinking . . . Now, you look here, Jeff. I need you up here immediately. Bob has come through with a very creditable idea for the Centennial theme but we need your flair to make it go."

"I'll juss bet he has. Juss tell me what his idea is. Is it a covered wagon with a rocket rising up behind it?"

"He told you about that, did he? Good thing he had it up his sleeve. With you letting us down this way-"

"The bastard stole *my* idea! I gave it to him on the phone two days ago and told him to work on it."

"Yes? Well, Jeff, he claims you were hardly able to talk when you called. All he could understand was the name of your apartment house."

"He's a liar!"

"Those are pretty strong words, Jeff. He's been with me a lot longer than you have. And be that as it may I need a head for my Advertising department! Now, I'm going to lay it on the line. I'm laying down the law! If you're not back and at your desk Thursday morning, I'm giving you another day, if you're not back by then, you can send for your things because you won't be working here any more! That's fair, I think. Fair warning. You understand me?"

"I can't leave here without Dawn. She's playing with fire." *And I've given her the matches.*

"And that's why you're drunk, eh? I don't know what you think you're doing, Jeff, but it's Thursday morning or out! I think I'm being extremely generous as it is."

"Yes, sir, you are the *soul* of generosity."

"What? What was that? Are you—? Never mind. Goodbye!"

Click! And I was left holding a dead line . . . again. I thought about Bob's double-cross. Everybody was chewing on me, taking me apart for the little goodies I should have for myself. Everybody wanted something from me.

My anger and self-hatred mixed with the alcohol in my system and changed to self-pity. I could get drunker . . . is that a word? No, I wanted to talk to somebody. I wanted sympathy. I wanted Shirley.

A part of me sneered. He wants mother-substitute Shirley, poor little weeping boy. He wants her to kiss his ego and make it well. He wants her to kiss his conscience and tell him he did right.

Yes, that's what I wanted! And heaven help Lena if she tried to stop me!

## Chapter Fifteen

She opened the door in response to my irregular pounding. Her grey oriental eyes narrowed. A dishcloth was in her hand. She wore tight blue Levis and an old faded blue T-shirt with small damp water spots near the waistline.

We glared at each other with mutual hatred.

"Well?"

"I want to see Shirley."

She started to close the door in my face but I stuck out a hand and pushed hard. It ripped out of her grasp and cracked against the entranceway wall. I lurched forward and shoved her aside. "Bitch!" I stood in the dining room. "Shirley?"

"She is not here."

I looked at her near bursting shirt. I could see bra straps through the thin cotton. The Levis seemed sprayed on so closely did they follow every contour of her hips and thighs.

"Like hell!" I went into the front room and then into the bedroom. I stood, baffled, and then looked in the closet.

Lena had followed me. "Satisfied? Go now!"

"Don't tell me what to do, you queer bitch!"

"Who are you? A bum! You are drunken. You cannot walk straight. You stink of whiskey. You are not a man, you are a bottle that drinks itself."

"Shut up! I wouldn't be this way if it wasn't for perverts like you!"

Her full lips curled in contempt. "Shirley does not want you. Go back to your room and drink more."

I didn't move. I looked at her body again, seeing through the shirt and Levis, seeing her glorious abundance again as she had taunted me Saturday night. "You're afraid of me, aren't you?"

She laughed with that damned sexy voice. "I have a pity for you now. You are not much man any more." She cupped her breasts and made a motion to hand them to me. "Would you not like to have them in *your* hands?"

I began to sweat. She was goading me, torturing me. "I'm warning you . . ."

Her laugh became throaty, superior. Her hips jerked in a derisive bump and grind. "I hate you, man. I hate you! I see the want in your eyes! Come, touch, touch!" She thrust her breasts at me and when I reached she stepped back and laughed again.

I lost control. I lunged for her and grabbed at her arm. She twisted away, her gloating face wiped clean by sudden fear.

"Now you're scared, aren't you?" I lunged again and ripped a sleeve and half the back off the T-shirt. The bra straps showed white against the tan of her skin.

"You leave! You go away!"

I stood panting, slowly backing her into a corner. "Oh, no, not this time. This time the man is going to get it. This time he's going to touch plenty!"

"Drunken beast!"

"Not that drunk. Not as drunk as you thought. Now you're going to pay for what that lesbian bitch in Portland did to my wife. You're going to pay for what Tex did to *me!*"

"No, please." She was getting desperate. "No, I beg of you. I am sorry for what I said."

I pushed her against the wall and deliberately tore away the rest of the shirt. She recoiled into a crouch and began weeping.

I grunted in disgust. "Tears won't work. I thought you were a butch. I thought you liked to take the place of a man."

She looked up and the hate was back. Suddenly she sprang and threw a punch. I was surprised and it caught me on the neck. I staggered back, pain filling my throat, and she made a dash for the kitchen.

I caught her as she was opening a drawer and spun her back into the dining room. Off balance, she back-peddled and fell into an armchair. The drawer contained silverware . . . knives.

I went after her and threw her to the floor. I raged at her between gasps. "You . . . wanted to . . . stick me . . . bitch . . . I'm . . . going to . . . stick you . . . in the right . . . place!"

I straddled her waist, holding her arms wide on the floor. She writhed and twisted under me, her face a mask of panic. Her white clad breasts rose and fell with her deep frantic breathing, filling the bra to overflowing with every expansion of her lungs.

We had reached a stalemate. She couldn't get away and I couldn't spare a hand to undress her further. We glared at each other.

I tried to kiss her and she nearly bit my lip through. I tasted sharp pain and salty warm blood in my mouth.

I was shaking with fury. I'd never in my life been in a rage like this. I spat crimson blood on her face and cursed her. She spat back. I slapped her hard and she used the free hand to rake my face with long pointed fingernails. They were like claws and I felt the ripping skin and running blood on my cheek.

I became a brute, primitive and savage. We rolled on the floor, all stops out. She tried to gouge my eyes and I slugged her mercilessly on the face and jaw. Then her knee came up and sent waves of agony burning through me. I screamed like a wounded jungle animal and she tried to knee me again. I deflected the blow with my leg and held onto her until the first terrible pains washed away.

She tried to pull away and I was dragged across the floor toward the bedroom. She kicked me in the face. I got a better grip on her legs and waist as she made a supreme effort to free herself. It didn't succeed. She collapsed and lay inert, her body wracked with great sobs, her muscles trembling with exhaustion.

I was nearly done in myself. I rolled her over, unsnapped the bra and rolled her back face up. She couldn't resist when I dragged the thing from her body. Her eyes were swollen with tears, her face lax, mouth open for great gulps of air.

I paused for a minute and touched. I filled my large hands with her softness. She went rigid and screamed, tearing the air with the sound. I clapped a hand over her mouth. She tried to bite my palm and I had to hit her again. She relapsed into semi-consciousness.

I unsnapped and unbuttoned the fly of her Levis, peeling them down, taking along a pair of white panties. She was as perfect below as above.

I watched her warily for a last escape attempt as I sat on the floor beside her and stripped. She was dazed. Ugly black and blue marks were blooming on her face, jawline and arms. She was like a feeble newborn baby as she made ineffectual crawling movements. She was moaning.

I flopped her over onto her back and forced her thighs wide with my knees. I kissed her again but she was unresponsive, her lips flaccid. I kissed her breasts, her flat nipples. In a minute they rose under my tongue.

It wasn't good enough. I wanted her awake, aware of what was happening. I slapped her and got her eyes open, unfocused. Then they gradually filled with understanding and horror.

I gritted my teeth and lunged onto her.

Her eyes snapped shut, her neck corded with taut muscles and a horrible sucking gurgling sound came from her throat.

I moved again and again. Her fingers dug into my back and she tried to throw me off. It was no use. She went limp and tried again. I clung to her as she bucked, her belly muscles contracting under me as each succeeding effort became weaker.

She wept again and screamed alien words at me, Chinese or Japanese. Her face twisted like a rubber mask, her eyes bulged. Her face enacted a story for me, the words explained themselves, and her body joined in the terrible pantomime.

She was a child in the islands. A man, a big man, was doing it to her and it hurt. He forced her, hit her and forced her again. It was a traumatic nightmare of pain and humiliation for the little Christian half-breed girl.

The deep reservoir of Lena's subconscious fear and hate was gushing to the surface and playing itself out before my eyes.

But I didn't stop. My frustrations, my revenge, my anger, and above all my guilt were channeled into my attacking loins. I had been temporarily beyond intellect, beyond reason, beyond morals. I was an animal in the grip of a powerful urge toward self-destruction. This rape was not the end of my degradation.

Lena's emotional charge spent itself. She lay passively beneath me, a dead piece of meat, and I continued doggedly, wearily, wondering how long I could keep it up, wondering why I bothered. There had been an atavistic delight in conquering her. That was past. Shame was enveloping me.

Then her expression changed subtly. Deep within her I felt a slight muscular contraction. Her thighs twitched. She was coming alive as a woman.

I forced my aching body to move faster. I looked into her eyes and she evaded my gaze. Her hips began a barely perceptible response. She closed her eyes and moaned, "No . . . no . . . no . . ." And a blush reddened her face and neck.

But she couldn't deny her body as the floodgates of passion opened. She was carried away on an irresistible tide of pleasure. Her teeth found my shoulder and brought blood. It hurt like hell and I responded like a spurred stallion. My last reserves of strength were expended in her. Her thighs became wild greedy tigers, wanting more and more, urging me on and on and *on*.

At last it ended. She went limp. Her breathing slowly subsided. I rolled off and lay on my back, gasping in exhaustion, too tired to think.

I fought a sweet desire to sleep and struggled into my clothes. Every little movement was charged with pain and weakness. I looked at Lena. She was touching her bruised face and crying. There was nothing I could say to her.

I tottered to my feet and staggered out of the apartment.

## Chapter Sixteen

Back in my room I flopped on the bed and reached for the bottle. I missed and it crashed to the floor. Amber liquid splashed in a wide puddle on the linoleum. I was too tired to care. I carefully opened the other bottle and swallowed. The stuff burned my throat and pooled in my gut like molten lead. I shuddered, took a deep breath and tipped the bottle again.

God, how I ached and hurt. I was a mass of large and small pains. My shirt was spotted red in places where Lena's nails had raked and tore the skin. It was hard to open my mouth because of my lacerated lip. My clawed cheek was stiffening with dried blood. My groin ached still from the knee she'd brought up.

I was back where I'd started an hour ago. Getting stinko. It was like nothing had happened. But it *had* happened.

My mind skidded around the yawning pit of memory. I wanted to blot out Lena, erase her screams and tortured face. Yet there was a disgusting satisfaction in me, a pride in having taken her, forced her, and made her like it! In the end she'd liked it!

And maybe the beast had done her some good. Maybe the violence of her released emotions had drained the childhood trauma of its power over her life. Maybe now she'd be a man's woman. She could never forget that she'd made it with me, with a man. She could never forget the feel of me and the ecstasy it brought.

And I could never forget I had raped. The guilt and shame pierced the alcoholic wall I'd built. The room became hot and small. It closed in on me. I drank feverishly, desperately. Soon the second bottle was empty.

I lay on the bed and passed out. I awoke weeping. I took a piece of the broken bottle and tried to slash my wrist. I couldn't. I held the sliver of glass tight, tighter, and couldn't make the convulsive movement that would do it. My hand trembled with effort and the glass broke in my grip and cut my thumb.

"Dawn . . . oh, God, Dawn . . ." I sprang to my feet with a cry of anguish. The room whirled and I fell. I had to get out! I had to get more liquor, more forgetfulness.

I got to my feet again. I made it to the door. Then the back stairs. I was careful. One small objective at a time. In the alley I used my hands like a blind man feeling his way along the sides of unfamiliar buildings. I reached the Speedway and lurched toward the promenade and the mama-papa store.

I staggered into the small store and nearly overturned a used magazine rack. "Shteady . . ." I leaned heavily on the counter.

The old man's round droopy-jowled face showed irritation. "Get out, get out. I don't want you in mine store." He made shooing motions with his hands.

He wouldn't stay in focus. "Want shome whishkey."

"No, no, I can't sell. Go away." His fat little wife came up behind him, staring fearfully at my bruised, bloody, unshaven face and rumpled dirty clothes. "Go go, go," she added. "We can't sell you."

I frowned and puzzled over their words. Why couldn't they sell me whiskey? I had plenty of money. I swayed before them and dug my wallet out of my back pocket. I fumbled out a large bill and slapped it down.

"Big bottle."

The money seemed to frighten them even more. They eyed it, then me, and backed away from their side of the counter. "Mama," the papa said, "call the police. Call them." She nodded and edged away behind the refrigerated milk display case.

"Whass the matter? Good money."

I waited for an answer but the old man only looked at me like I was a walking time bomb. I could hear his wife dialing the pay phone. The idea of being picked up by the police appealed to me. They would put me away where I belonged. But if they did I'd get sober and start thinking and remembering again.

The old woman was speaking into the phone. I reached for my money, missed, grabbed it on the second try and stuffed it in my pocket. "Shtupid. Thought you liked money . . ." I aimed myself for the door. On the way I hit the rack again and it clattered to the floor, spilling second hand copies of lurid men's magazines.

I turned right, stopped, and stared into the distance at Pacific Ocean Park. "Windward," I muttered to myself. "Whish-key at Windward." I did a clumsy military about face and nearly fell on my ass. I staggered around in a weird circle trying to regain my balance.

The cement beach-side benches were filled as usual with old people. They watched me as I got my bearings again, muttered instructions to my feet, and weaved past them. Young couples . . . college, high school kids . . . walked around me and laughed.

"Boy, is *he* loaded." "Look, he's all bloody." "He's probably fallen on his face a dozen times." "Trip him, Harry." "Did you *ever* see a walk like that? Just like a drunk in the movies."

Little kids paused in their play and stared at me open-mouthed solemnity. Alarmed mothers called them from my vicinity.

"Hey, mister."

I was trying to walk a very straight line past a parking lot but it veered one way, then the other.

"Hey, aren't you ever sober?"

I felt a hand on my arm. I looked sideways and there was Rosemary. I tried to smile but my cheek was too stiff. Her face wouldn't focus either. "Hi."

"You better get off the Walk. The cops'll pick you up for sure."

"Want shome whish . . . key . . ."

"Boy, are you pickled!"

Close behind her, next to a five year old green Chevy convertible with the top up were her two companions I'd seen before, the short babyfat girl and the hulking overweight boy. All three were in decent school clothes.

"Hey, mister, how about letting us take a ride in your Caddy? Man, what a car."

"Shorry . . . wife hash it." That struck me funny and I laughed. The caked blood on my face cracked and new blood seeped out.

Rosemary looked at me appraisingly and said, "C'mon, you'd better climb into Nicky's car. There's a cop car cruising up the Walk."

"Where?" I peered blearily toward Windward.

"Come *on!*" She tugged at me and I followed her into the nearby Chevy. I collapsed into the back seat.

The shorter girl climbed into the front with Nicky. "My God, Rosey, what do you want with *him?*"

"Babs, will you shut up and let me do the thinking around here? Is it five-thirty yet?"

Nicky raised a hairy wrist and looked at a shiny thin watch. "Five-forty five." His voice was surprisingly high and squeaky. "Your ma's at work by now."

Rosemary turned to me. "I was just thinking, mister, maybe you'd like to get cleaned up and come with us to the drive-in movie. It's one we want to see real bad and we don't have enough dough."

I shook my head. "Want to shtay drunk. Whish . . ."

"Nobody'll sell you liquor the way you look. Come over to my place and I'll give you some gin ma has in the ice-box."

"Alri . . ."

She smiled. "Get with it, Nicky. Let's bug out of here."

Babs' face was a picture of puzzlement. "I don't get it."

Rosemary leaned forward and whispered in her ear. The girl's eyes widened and she looked at me. She whispered back loudly enough for me to hear: "Has he got it on him now?"

"Be quiet!"

Nicky hunched his thick shoulders over the wheel. The engine sputtered, coughed, and WHOOOMED into life with a shattering roar. It shocked me into a short-lived normal awareness. What did he have under that hood? He geared in and we shot out of the lot onto Speedway. The blur of movement past the window made my stomach turn queasy.

"Lemme out. Feel shick . . ."

"Take it easy, mister. I only live up on 26th Place."

The ride was short and fast. I watched the back of Nicky's fat black haired neck as he squirreled into a vacant lot just off Speedway and braked the car to a sliding, dust raising stop. He WHOOMED the engine once and let it die.

Nicky came around and half pulled me out of the back. He was big all right, and strong, but his muscles were soft and spongy, like a woman's. His face was pudgy and empty. Rosemary told him exactly what to do.

We went into a falling-down wooden house next to the lot. Inside it was dirty, bare and dark. The windows were filthy. Nicky dropped me on a 1930 vintage sofa, once blue velvet, now worn and discolored by thirty years of dirt, grease and spilled liquids.

"What now?" Babs asked.

Rosemary grinned. "Now we give him a bath, Nicky, go turn on the hot water in the tub."

"Want gin."

"Later, mister." She leaned over me and began unbuttoning my shirt. Babs stood by and giggled. Rosemary snapped, "Do something! Take off his shoes and socks."

"Don't want bath." I tried feebly to stop them, to push them away, but I was still weary from my ordeal with Lena and the only energy in my body was from alcohol. I couldn't remember when I'd eaten last.

"It'll do you good. You stink like hell. I'll put some mercurochrome on those scratches, too."

"Hell with it. Lemme 'lone."

She was undoing my pants. Nicky came into the room. "What ya doin'?"

"We can't give him a bath without taking off his clothes, can we?"

"Yeah, but . . ."

"C'mere and lift him up."

Nicky blinked and obeyed. Rosemary slid my pants off, coaxed me out of my opened shirt, and directed Nicky to help me into the bathroom. Only my shorts were left on. Babs had dissolved into a storm of giggles.

The tub was old and the enamel had cracked and flaked in many places. Rust showed in the bottom. The water was gushing out of the spout in a noisy torrent. It reminded me of the bath Shirley had given me. Things were working in cycles. Who would I rape next? "No, *no* . . ." I said aloud.

"It's not too hot. Stick your foot in." Rosemary dropped my shirt and pants in a corner, stooped and pulled my shorts down.

Nicky was supporting me from behind. Babs had crowded in last, her eyes eager and curious. I jerked when I felt the shorts go and nearly pitched head first into the tub. Nicky grunted and held me up. Rosemary was on her knees, tugging at my ankles. "Step in, step in!"

Babs loosed a hail of giggles. "Oh, wow," she said. "Look at that!"

I was embarrassed. The alcoholic mist was being torn to shreds by shame and anxiety. The nearest haven in my weakened condition was the tub. There at least I could use my hands to cover myself from their curious eyes.

I sank down into luke-warm water. "At last," Rosemary said. She took up a washcloth and gently sponged off my face. Babs and Nicky just stood there, watching.

"Nicky, go check the paper and see when the show starts."

I brushed off her hand. "I c'n do it. Go 'way."

She went right back to her task. She flinched sympathetically as she concentrated on cleaning my wounds. "Don't act stupid." Her voice took on the tone of an admonishing mother. "After last night. And don't worry about Babs. You haven't got anything she hasn't seen before."

Babs was washing my feet and legs. Her fingers boldly reached to my loins and washed there, too. She giggled again. "But he's sure got a lot more of it."

I pushed her hands away. That damned giggle. She'd been deliberately trying to get me worked up.

Rosemary banished her from the bathroom, too. A few minutes later the bathing was finished. I was relatively sober. I refused her help and dressed myself.

"Why did you pick me up and bring me here?"

"I just thought you needed help. You were nice to me at the party."

"But you wouldn't tell me where you lived then. Now you've got me in your house. How come?"

"I figured you were safe. No vice squad goonie is going to get busted up and drunk like that."

"I wish you'd've let me be. Where's that gin?"

"What's the matter with you, mister?"

"That's none of *your* Goddamned business. Now bring me a drink."

Nicky poked his blank pasty face into the bathroom. "The first show starts in twenty minutes, Rosemary."

"Okay, thanks." She looked at me critically. "You still look like hell, but if you sit in back it'll be okay."

"Okay for what?"

"For getting into the drive-in as my date. Nicky and Babs will be in front, and you and me in back."

"What do you want me for?"

"Well . . . I don't want to go without a guy. And besides, I kind of like you."

"The hell with it. I want a drink." What she said didn't ring true. She was attracted to me by more than my kindness . . . what a laugh . . . and my current good looks.

"If I bring along a bottle will you come?"

I didn't hesitate long. A bottle, a couple of distracting movies and a 14 year old hustler were what I needed. Anything to keep Dawn and Lena out of my mind.

We left the house and got into the deceptive Chevy. Nicky was proud of his car and his skill at driving it. It wasn't long before we were creeping in the waiting line of cars at the Drive-In. The bill for that night was Jerry Lewis in "A Visit To A Small Planet" and an English picture with James Mason.

As we drew near the pay booths Rosemary said, "Could you treat us tonight?" The bottle of gin was up front in the glove compartment and I was thirsty for it. My whole body cried for it.

I agreed and forked over a ten dollar bill. I caught Rosemary glancing sideways at my wallet as I pulled out the money. So sneaked a look at it too as she twisted on the front seat and pretended to admire a sports car behind us.

So that was it. I was the sugar daddy for tonight. A flash of the intense anger I'd known with Lena surged through me. It shook me. I wanted to forget that terrible rage. I called for the bottle as soon as we cleared the booths. Babs handed it to me.

I didn't get any change back from the ten. I hadn't really expected it. As we pulled into a center stall and parked I had the cap off the bottle and was working my throat, sending the colorless fluid into my gut, searing it into churning activity.

## Chapter Seventeen

Before the first feature came on I was tapped for another five . . . for candy and pop. All three of the kids went off to the refreshment shack and left me with my thoughts. I sucked on the bottle all the harder.

The drive-in lights dimmed, the kids came back loaded with junk for their bellies, and the Jerry Lewis comedy came on first.

Rosemary climbed carefully into the seat beside me with a big paper cup of coke and a big pizza pie. Candy bars stuck out of the pockets of her school blouse like twin rows of high caliber cartridges.

She extended the pizza toward me. "Want a piece?" In the front seat Babs laughed. "Can't you wait, Rosey?"

"Huh!" She still held it toward me. "Go on, take some."

I pulled off a section, stuffed it in my mouth and washed it down with gin.

We watched Lewis's slapstick butchery of Vidal's satire. The kids liked it. They laughed a lot at the Beatnik sequence.

"Jeez," Rosemary said, "Wait'll I tell Zeke about this. They use words I never heard of!"

"Yeah," said Babs. "You ever see a *real* Beatnik dress like *that?*"

"Bunch of squares," said Rosemary.

Nicky responded to all the jokes and pratfalls with a high cackling laugh.

"God, Nicky," Rosemary complained, "lay it or get it over with."

Babs giggled. "You mean me?"

Rosemary sighed. "I guess so. You won't be happy till Nicky gives you some. I know how the picture will end anyway. C'mon, roll up the windows."

The windows squeaked up out of the doors. They were dirty. So dirty you couldn't see through them. Smart, I thought, very smart.

Up front, Babs' blonde ringlets settled close to Nicky's black crew-cut hair. Rosemary leaned against my shoulder, took the bottle from me and capped it. "Don't get too drunk."

I played with her pony-tail. Dawn used to have a pony-tail. Where was Dawn now? What had happened at Otto's office? Or... what was *happening?* I cursed and drove the thought away. I had to *do* something! I couldn't just sit and *think!*

I seized Rosemary and kissed her. She gave a little grunt of surprise and then cooperated. Our tongues met and I forgot for a moment that she was so damned young. I was getting heated up when I put a hand on her breasts and remembered they were mostly fake. I broke away and found the bottle.

"What's the matter?"

"You're just a kid."

"So what? I'm human." She opened her blouse and pushed down her bra. "I got enough, don't worry." She took my hand and pressed it against a warm budding of firm flesh. I caressed a nipple experimentally and felt it come out, hard and erect.

So I played with her and kissed her and watched the picture. And she played with me. I soon became aware of her hand opening my pants, searching, grasping and lifting.

In the front seat Babs giggled and slumped lower. Nicky was breathing heavily. I could hear clothes being rearranged.

I drank from the bottle again. It was halfway empty.

She moved her lips to my ear and breathed, "You remember what you did for me last night?"

I nodded.

She tickled my ear with her tongue. "Do it again." She slumped down as Babs had done and I heard the whisper of rayon against flesh as she pulled her panties down and off. She spread her knees.

I felt disgusted with myself. Then I snorted. This was nothing, minor league, compared with my earlier day's work. I had to shake that thought away with a quick forgetting kiss of Rosemary's eager young lips. I shifted my hand for her.

Rosemary came quickly and relaxed. She pulled my head down and whispered, "Thanks. I can go again in a few minutes."

I shrugged. Why not? It was something to do. I took a swallow of firewater, threw my head back on the top of the seat and closed my eyes. Her hands became active on me again. It was nice, balancing the heat in my belly against the slowly rising heat of my loins.

Then it changed. I felt something hot, wet and moving. I stared down incredulously. The pony-tail bobbed up and down.

"No!" I croaked and pushed her away.

She looked puzzled and hurt. "Don't you like it?"

My God, I thought, is that all they do in this sex mad city? Fourteen years old and she does that . . . matter-of-factly . . . a whore . . . nothing but a little whore. And Babs too, judging from the regular slapping sounds coming from the front seat.

Then I thought, why not? Why not sink this low? What difference did it make? In a back corner of my mind under the gin fog and repression was a steadily growing certainty that it did not matter in the least. Nothing I did now would matter because my guilt was already too great to be borne. It was going to pile up and cave in on me soon and then in one desperate act of atonement I would wipe it all off the books . . . the only way I could.

"What's the matter?" she whispered. "You look funny."

"I like it. Go ahead."

She hesitated doubtfully, then shrugged and began again.

I watched, fascinated, and finally gritted my teeth and gasped as sweet agonizing sensation darkened the world and shut out all sound.

She moved away as I recovered and then silently placed my hand under her skirt.

That once had been my limit for the night, but Rosemary used my hand often. I lost track. I concentrated on the James Mason movie that had been filmed in England, a truly humorous story about a clever plan to get rich off the British Admiralty . . . that worked.

The gin wasn't doing me any good any more. I might as well have been guzzling water.

We buzzed out after the first complete show. The windows came down and the night air flowed in. It was eleven-thirty. Rosemary cuddled up to me and urged me to take a drink. I refused.

"You're a kook. First you want to get drunk, now you don't."

"You wanted me sober, now you want me drunk."

"Well, I showed you a good time, didn't I? You enjoyed yourself."

"Sure. Good gin."

"What is it with you? You liked what I did and you know it."

"All right, so I liked it!"

We gunned down a street near the ocean and turned onto Speedway. Nicky and Babs seemed unusually quiet and nervous. At last we stopped at Seaside Avenue. Nicky left the motor idling and turned in the seat to face me. So did Babs. Rosemary made a quick grab and pulled my wallet free.

"Hey!" I tried to grab it back.

"Nicky!" she commanded.

"Leave her alone!" His black eyes were mean. I suddenly saw six inches of switchblade weaving in front of my face. Rosemary passed my wallet to Babs who whistled and pulled out my sheaf of money. "You were right."

"What's the big idea?"

Rosemary was contemptuous. "Go on, get out. What do you think I picked you up for? Because I liked you? A kook like you who carries that much deserves to have it lifted."

"You little bitch."

"I don't go down for anything but money, mister. Lots of it."

"What if I go to the cops?"

"Why do you think we dragged you along to the show? You've been contributing to the delinquency of minors all night. You try turning us in and we'll send you up for five years! The guys at the drive-in booths will remember you going in with us. With that face. A big tall guy like you. So just get out!"

I was defeated and knew it. Besides, it didn't matter. Not any more. I climbed out and said, "Don't spend it all in one place."

"Don't worry about us."

Babs giggled and yelled, "Here!" and threw my emptied wallet out onto the road. Nicky turned back to the wheel and the car blasted off.

I picked up my wallet and slipped it into my pocket without thinking. If I'd thought about it I would have left it there.

I stood by the side of the street and considered what I wanted to do first. Yeah . . . I should leave a note. It was in the best tradition.

I walked past the posts that guarded the narrow walk-way and on into the front entrance of the Seaside Apartments.

## Chapter Eighteen

As I wearily climbed the stairs to the second floor I heard a door open and quick slippered feet on the hall carpeting above. Shirley's voice called, "Lena?" Then her worried face peered down over the railing and she saw me. "Oh, it's you." Her voice dripped venom. "I want to talk to *you!*"

She waited till I'd reached the top of the stairs then she walked angrily to the open door of her apartment. She was wearing the terrycloth robe again and apparently nothing under it. . . again. The robe swirled open as she turned quickly and showed a thick meaty thigh.

I followed her in like a cow to the slaughter. I knew what was coming. I owed her the pleasure of chewing me out. It was part of my penance. A very small part.

She faced me in the middle of the living room. "You bastard. You *filthy rotten bastard!*"

She waited for me to say something and when I didn't she continued. "What did you do to her? You raped her, didn't you?" She waited two heartbeats. "DIDN'T YOU?"

I pushed the word out of my mouth like it was a piece of decayed food that was making me sick. "Yes."

"What kind of a man are you? I came in and found her on the floor where you left her. Just lying there, crying like . . ." Shirley began to cry herself. "She wouldn't tell me what happened. She just repeated your filthy name. I cleaned her up and put her to bed. Then I went to the store to get some linament and when I came back she was gone."

Shirley sat on the couch and clasped her hands together like they were two wet clothes she was trying to wring out. "I don't know where she went. I've been worried sick."

"I'm sorry . . ."

Her eyes raked over me. "Did Lena do that to your face?"

I nodded miserably.

"Good! I wish she'd killed you!"

I stood in the center of the room and felt like a blood-bloated spider.

"She was hysterical and . . . different . . . some way. She wore one of my dresses when she left. She doesn't have any of her own." Shirley looked up and screamed, *"Why did, you have to hit her like that? Was that the only way you could make her do it? WAS IT?"*

I couldn't answer. She didn't wait for an answer.

"Eight hours. She's been gone eight hours . . . my poor baby . . . after what happened to her when she was a kid . . . now you doing this . . . *If somethings happened to her I'll kill you!*"

"You won't have to."

Shirley's face twisted. "Why not? You figure somebody else you've raped will beat me to it?"

"No."

"No? Oh, I get it. You're going to commit suicide. Isn't that just dandy. You come down here to Venice, get knocked around, lose your wife, rape somebody, and think you can make it all square by opening a vein. I bet you thought of it all by yourself. Your type always does."

"What do you mean?"

"You make me sick. What did Dawn need but a little understanding? You let her get away then came down here blaming it all on her. You cried on my shoulder for an hour about her. She's immature, she's selfish, she's unfaithful. What a laugh. You're *both* guilty! There you were moaning about how she was betraying you with Tex and all the time you were hot to trot with *me!* Suicide! What a perfect romantic solution to a screwed up life."

Shirley moved angrily on the sofa and the robe opened wide. She didn't seem to notice. I didn't care. It seemed a million years ago that I had massaged those full pendulous breasts and enjoyed her scalding muscles.

She pressed her fists between her knees and glared at me. "You thought you were so damned sophisticated! What a laugh! You come down here from a hick town like Portland that closes up at midnight and you think you're hip. You know it all. Your kind always does. A big frog from a small puddle.

"I'll bet I can tell you exactly what your parents are like. They're prissy middle class. Your mother thinks she can hide unpleasant things by pretending they don't exist . . . like the girl next door getting knocked up by the boy across the street. She preaches sermons, doesn't she? And she'll never admit you're grown up and don't need her. And your dad is a sucked dry fly, isn't he? But you still love your mother, don't you? The silver cord is still there. You can cuss out your mother but you never deep down mean it. She's your *Mother!* That's why you liked me so much, wasn't it, baby? I'm older and motherly and I called you baby, baby, baby."

"Shut up!"

"The truth hurts, huh? Don't you want a little before you kill yourself? I know your type. Square. Cubic. Wiseacre Babbits in modern dress. I make my living off your kind, baby. I studied psychology and figured I'd last longer with a motherly routine. It works real well."

Her bitter acid words ate at my mind. "Damn you. Do you want me to cut my throat for you right here? You want to see me die at your feet?"

She sneered. "You haven't got the guts to do it anywhere. All you're good for is fooling yourself. I'm surprised you haven't figured out a way to blame Lena for the rape."

I winced.

"Rape. That word bothers you, doesn't it?" *Rape!* She looked down and saw her robe hanging open. "Here I am, baby, why don't you try raping me? I'll fight you if you want a little resistance to add flavor." She threw the robe open further and made a lewd movement with her hips. "Come on, don't you want it?"

"Please, stop it." I sank to my knees. I was so tired, so hag-ridden with guilt.

"You didn't stop with Lena! No, sex comes first with you. You're actually proud of yourself, aren't you? She was a beautiful piece who wouldn't have anything to do with men and that was a challenge to you. You couldn't let her get away with *that,* could you? It was a terrible blow to your ego. You had to prove no woman could resist your charm!"

"It wasn't like that."

"The hell it wasn't. Don't lie to me. I can see it in your eyes! You just had to have her, didn't you? I know what went on in your mind: 'Once I'm in she won't be able to resist me.' I know all about you studs."

Shirley was mostly right. The rest didn't make much difference. There was no excuse for me. I stood up and felt weaker. My body had been going for too long on nothing but alcohol for food. I moved toward the door.

"That's right, leave. I hope to hell you do have the nerve to do it!"

Everybody yelled at me to get out! Tex had, Dawn, Lena, Rosemary. All right, I would get out. Out of the world . . . out of life.

I went out into the hall to the stairs. All I had to do was walk into the ocean. I had strength enough for that. Then swim out till I couldn't swim anymore.

I glanced at my door and saw light under the bottom edge. Had I left the light on? I'd gone out for more liquor in the afternoon. Maybe I'd left the door open. Anyway I had to write that note.

## Chapter Nineteen

The door was locked. The key was still in my pocket along with the fifty dollar bill I'd used to try to bribe mama and papa. I'd leave it to Dawn, too. She just might need it.

I went in . . . and stared.

Dawn was face down on the bed, sleeping, her print dress rumpled and torn at the hem. Her hat and gloves were missing. The purse was on the floor next to the bed. Her closed eyes were red and swollen from crying.

My throat tightened. She was beautiful. The light glowed in her yellow hair and filtered through the thin print dress wherever it folded away from her small body, making the white skin underneath come alive in barely seen shadow.

Like a sleepwalker I went to the side of the bed. I wanted to fill my mind with her beauty before leaving.

But the view wasn't nice. I'd let her go to Otto and look what had happened. Start with her face: the childlike innocence was no longer there, even in sleep. It was changed. Something had happened to the mouth and eyes. The muscular set was different. She looked older . . . wiser.

She twitched in her sleep, her hands made small incomplete motions, one leg abruptly straightened and showed the smooth creamy lines of knee and half a thigh. She moaned.

Continue the inspection: small black and blue marks on her upper arms. Her hair mussed. The thin dress was drawn tight across her back and twisted under her. The white skin showed through from her shoulders too . . .

I stared down at her. She was naked under the dress. No bra, no panties. The dress outlined her bare hips and small round buttocks with obscene truthfulness. I could see part of one full unhindered breast push against the blanket. The dress hid nothing. She looked like a cheap whore sleeping off a ten man sex binge.

I buried my face in my hands. My God, what had she done? I swayed on my feet as terrible images swam out of the rotten depths of my brain. I saw her with Otto . . . obeying his depraved instructions, sacrificing her self-respect, everything, for a chance in the movies . . . everything for a promise.

Shirley had been right: I could have prevented it. A little understanding. Instead I'd been petty and egotistical.

I went to my suitcase and quietly got out the report Grimes had prepared for me. I could use the back of it to write on. There was irony for you. I got a pen from the pocket of the coat Tex had ripped. I sat on the lone chair in that dirty room and wrote against a tattered copy of the *Post* some previous tenant had thrown in a drawer.

"Dear Dawn," I wrote. I scratched it out. "Darling; I'm leaving. I've caused so much suffering and pain in such a short time that I think it best to get out of everybody's life for good. The car and house are yours. I hope you'll go back to Portland and live with your folks. Don't blame me too much."

It sounded corny. Something you'd find in a tear-jerker movie. I was a top flight advertising man and I couldn't do better than that. The one time in my life I wanted to be sincere and I came out ridiculous.

I signed it and was about to put it beside her head on the pillow when she frowned in her sleep, said, "You're filthy . . ." and rolled over on her back, mumbling.

I waited till she'd lapsed deeper into slumber and put the note beside her head. I took a last look at her.

The neckline of her dress was twisted to one side and creased deep into the ice-cream softness of her left breast. I wanted to reach down and adjust it to ease the pressure. Both nipples had been excited by brushing against the silky material as she had tossed and turned. They were like two camouflaged pink cannons guarding a fortress no longer repulsing the enemy, but still alert, still blindly responding.

I sighed and went out. As I closed the door the lock snapped loudly in the silence. I heard Dawn stir on the bed. "Jeff?"

I forced myself hurriedly down the stairs and out into the starlit night. I walked quickly toward the beach. It was past twelve. Few lights were on in the houses. I crossed the promenade and crunched into the dirty sand. The electric mercury lights that lit the empty Walk stretched for over a mile along the beach to Ocean Park like a string of forgotten pearls. The only sounds were the hissing rumble of the breakers and a whisp of juke box from the High Water. I smiled grimly. Full circle.

My shoes quickly packed with sand again. I thought about taking them off and decided against it. It would be easier to drown with them on.

I was close to the water's edge when I heard a faint cry behind me. I turned and saw Dawn running across the Walk and into the sand after me. She called my name, a weak plea to wait.

I pointed my sand filled shoes at the ocean and willed them to move. My whole body tensed, my jaw was so tight I thought my teeth would crack, but I could not take those few steps into the surf. I sank to my knees. Shirley had been right about this, too. I was botching everything.

"Jeff . . . Jeff . . ." Dawn's voice was nearer and I despised myself as I waited for her to arrive.

She threw herself down beside me, panting, gasping her words. "Don't, Jeff, please don't! I love you."

I howled and hid my face in my hands. "No! You can't!"

She pressed against my side, a breast flattened and curved around my bare arm, sending tiny electric currents radiating from my skin. Her arms were around me, protectively. "I *do*. Oh, darling, I do."

I leaped up and ran along the beach away from her.

"Jeff! Please . . ." I could hear her following.

I couldn't go far. My strength gave out and I fell. I lay there cursing my weakness. She knelt beside me and touched my shoulder. I jerked away. "What do you want with me? I'm no good for you. I never was."

"Jeff, *listen* to me. We both should walk into the ocean for what we've done to each other. I'm as guilty as you are. But I found out I loved you today. I found it out the hard way."

I turned on her, spitting words savagely. "Love! What do you want now? I've given you the car, the house, every damned thing I own. There isn't anything left! Go back to your career. Go back to Otto and let him burn your tits in exchange for a bit part in his next movie!"

"Stop it!" She began to cry. "I love you . . . I love you . . ."

The night wind was cool and I noticed she was shivering. All she had on was that silly print dress. She was barefoot. I wanted to take her in my arms and warm her.

But I didn't. Something in me pressed a button and a new flow of hurting words cut at her. "Don't tell me Otto turned you down? In that case you'd better go looking for Tex. Tex will take care of you. She'll give you what you like!" Then I thought of Lena and a wave of black disgust washed over me. My voice was bitter with self-contempt. "You don't want me. I'm worse than any of them."

She said nothing. She bowed her head and continued to weep.

I crawled away and got to my feet. I could do it now. I walked down the slope of sand to the advancing hiss of a wave as it swept toward me. It broke over my feet and felt icy cold. I followed its retreat and the next wave wet my pants to the knee. I nearly fell from the undertow.

Then Dawn was at me again. She clutched my arm and tried to drag me back. "NO!" she screamed. *"I won't let you!"*

I pushed her away and took another few steps forward. She recovered and grabbed me again. She was screaming, hysterical, sobbing. I yelled at her and thrust her away. She went over backwards as a wave hit and threw me off balance. I toppled with her, end over end, bitter sea water getting in my mouth, throat and nose. Salt burned into the scratches on my face.

She was on her knees a few feet away, coughing, swallowing, crying her heart out. Her hair was a dripping mess that she had to push away from her face. She was like a half drowned kitten mewing piteously for help.

I went to her and helped her up. She clung to me, shaking, and her arms locked around my waist. "Take me with you," she sobbed. "We'll both do it. I don't want to live without you."

I became enraged. I roared at her above the roar of the surf. "What movie did that line come out of? Stop acting!"

"I'm not! I'm not!"

"All right! We'll see if you are or not!" I dragged her out of the water and across the beach to the nearby hummocks and tall sand grass that mark the edge of the picnic grounds. She pressed against me as we walked and her body heat penetrated my wet shirt and pants. The dress was glued to her like a second skin. Light from Windward and the Walk sifted through the trees and picked out glistening highlights: her small pert nose, the full round thrust of her breasts, her flat belly and the long thighs.

How could I resist her? Yet I had to.

We were deep in the shadows there. I threw her to the sand and went down on my hands and knees over her. Her hair was spread on either side of her head, a wet tangle, dry sand caking to it. I felt the sand sticking to my sopping pants legs and on my hands. The glimmering starlight showed her face as an indistinct blob under me.

Her voice betrayed fright. "What are you going to do?"

"I'm not going to do anything. I'm too damned weak. I can't drive you away, can I? You won't let a guy kill himself in peace, will you? You've got to make the big play, the big scene. You love me, only me. I suppose you're not interested in a career anymore."

"No, I'm not."

"And you want to go back to Portland with me and be a good wife and bear children."

Her voice took on a low vibrant sureness. "Yes."

My body tensed again. I crouched like a big wet hound over her. "Damn you, *prove it!*"

"How? What do you want me to say?"

"Don't say a word, miss frozen lips. Don't say, 'Aren't you finished yet?' or 'You're hurting me' because I'm not going to do a thing. If you want to be a loving wife and mother . . . prove it. Otherwise stop being a movie heroine and leave me alone!"

I lowered my head and kissed her. Her lips were salty, but warm and yielding. Her lips parted and her tongue flicked up in tentative initiative. I put a hand on a breast. Sand clinging to my palm grated on the wet dress. "Yes," she whispered, "oh, yes . . ." and her own hand pressed it tighter.

We kissed again and again, deep kisses, kisses that turn your guts to jelly and make you gasp for more and more air. Dawn threw her arms around my neck and tried to pull me down. But I stayed crouched as I was and said, "Prove it."

"How can we? The sand . . ."

The sand was everywhere. Her back was caked with it and it clung tenaciously to her legs. I could feel it even inside my shirt. I rolled over onto my back, almost in a sitting position against a small steep dune. "Come on. This way is recommended in all the better sex manuals."

She hesitated. "Jeff, do I have to do it out *here?*"

"Suit yourself. I don't give a damn about it one way or the other. I just want this settled."

"Jeff, I *do* love you. Can't you see that?"

I said nothing and waited. I was splitting down the middle with conflicting emotions. YES, I loved her, but I didn't want her as she had been in Portland and as she'd been when she'd taken the car keys only hours ago. Could she have changed that much? I had to find out. Maybe she had changed some. I had to push her along.

And even if we did save our marriage, what about Lena? Could I ever forgive myself that? No civilized man can live with the raw knowledge of his inner beast always fresh in his memory, always rising to haunt him at odd moments.

Dawn sat on her heels and shivered in the cool night breeze. I felt goose bumps on my own skin. At last she said, "I'll have to take off my dress."

I waited as she unzipped the back and slipped it off. She stood for an instant in the pale radiance of stars and sea, a Woman, eternal, a magnificent awe-inspiring vision. And then she left the universe and came to me with her hands and lips.

There was a clink and tinkle and my belt was undone. Seconds later she pulled my pants down to my knees. I watched her come forward and rise up. Her lips were trembling and she kissed me with sudden passion. Her hands guided and her hips sank.

She was not afraid of bruising her body or of pain this time. She gripped my shoulders and squirmed lower, taking it all for the first time. She made a funny sound deep in her throat. She moved with a violent aggressive rhythm. *"I love you!"* she whispered fiercely and repeated it again and again as her hips came down.

To the left of us a big wave hit the rocky Venice breakwater and sent white spray thirty feet into the dark night sky. I closed my eyes and kissed Dawn's breasts as they bobbed before my face.

Another wave hit and I could feel the beach shiver under the impact. Still another struck, then another. They came faster and faster, shaking us, and the white spray was continuously before me. Only it wasn't spray any longer, it was Dawn's white moving body.

I groaned her name and clutched at her like she had clutched at me in the surf. I couldn't let her go now. A big wave, the biggest there is, was building off in the distance. She knew it. She was with it, riding it, pushing it toward the breakwater, panting, gasping working hard to stay on the crest until it broke and spewed up into the heavens.

It rose high, higher, closer and closer. It would drown us, sweep us away. Then it broke over us with the power of a thousand locomotives. It engulfed us. We held ourselves together desperately. We were lost, beyond help, tumbled, cartwheeled, flung around the world. And still Dawn worked unconscious, dazed at the immense thing she had unleashed. Still she rode it to the end, until the sea calmed and subsided and was still. Not till then did she collapse into my arms.

Gently, tenderly, I kissed a soft cheek pressed close to mine. Her mouth was open and her breathing was deep and ragged as her lungs caught up to her body's recent exertion.

I petted her head and neck and shoulders. "Darling," I whispered. "Darling, darling, darling . . ."

She raised up, her face transformed, her eyes wise and awed with new-found knowledge. "I didn't know . . . I never dreamed it could be like that . . ."

"I didn't either, darling."

We smiled and separated slowly, peeling ourselves apart reluctantly, unwilling to break the immediate closeness and memory of what had happened.

Dawn chuckled and put on her still wet, still sandy dress. "I hate to think what I look like."

"You look lovely to me. And that's all that matters."

"I feel so different . . . so happy. I think I like proving myself to you."

I took her hand in mine and we walked down the beach toward our street. "I have the feeling I may not stay convinced. You'll probably have to do it all over again tomorrow."

She put her arm around my waist and pressed close. She took my hand and kissed it. "I'd like that."

Yeah, I would, too. Everything looked lovely . . . except for what I'd done to Lena.

Dawn looked at me, smiled, then looked again more closely. "Jeff, what happened to your face? I never noticed before . . . things happened so fast."

Involuntarily I touched the deep scratches. Could I say: *Darling, I raped a woman today. I'm sure you'll understand.* I had Dawn back now, a Dawn I'd always dreamed of but never seriously believed could be real. I couldn't risk losing her by telling about Lena.

I didn't want to think of what Lena might have done to herself. Even if she were safe I would have to live with that sickening half-hour the rest of my life. If it turned out worse . . . I would have another date with suicide.

"You know how it is," I answered. "I got drunk and a fairy tried to pick me up. We got into a fight. They fight like a woman."

She seemed to accept the explanation. "Poor Jeff. I'll bet you'll be glad to get away from this town." She kissed her fingertips and placed them on my cheek.

"As long as I have you." Then my heart sank. I had no money. That damned Rosemary. Just when everything looked good. It was way past midnight and the new day was Wednesday. Old man Kingman had given me till Thursday morning to get back on the job. We had to take a plane.

"Dawn, do you have any money?"

"No." Her eyes were twin pools of misery. "I told you, I gave it all to Tex. I don't know how we'll ever get it back. She told me this morning if I went ahead and saw Mr. Kluge I could forget about the money and her, too. She said we'd be through. But I didn't really believe her. Now I don't know what to believe."

I brought out my soaked wallet. The credit cards were a mess. I was glad then I carried them even if I hadn't been in the habit of using them. They were what Zeke would call a shuck, a part of the social lie; the exorbitant interest charges more than offset their usefulness. I had carried around the whole set as a sort of mark of distinction . . . like a general wears ribbons I carried credit cards. They were status symbols.

I thought we could dry them out in my room. But did I have a key to my room? I couldn't remember keeping it after letting myself in and seeing Dawn. I felt in my pants pocket and breathed a sigh of relief. I'd automatically slipped it back after opening the door. The fifty dollar bill was there, too, but soggy now.

We cut diagonally across the wide beach toward the deserted promenade. I was exhausted, beat, frazzled, all those rolled into one. My feet dragged. It took a great conscious effort to keep putting one foot in front of the other. Sleep was coiling slowly around my mind.

Too late I noticed the creeping police patrol car on the Walk. We were only fifty feet away from the Walk and there was no place to hide. We stood out in that empty well-lit fringe of beach like two scarecrows.

There was nothing to do but continue on. The car stopped and waited.

Dawn became conscious of her thin wet sand encrusted dress. It clung to her as closely as before, showing clearly her nakedness underneath. Her breasts especially were displayed. Every lovely contour, every line was there to be seen. Her nipples appeared to stick out a full inch. She flushed and crossed her arms in front of her.

We tried to cross the Walk behind the car but the cop got out and stopped us. He was about six feet, near forty years old, dark, stocky, lantern jaw, spick and span uniform. He had trouble keeping his eyes off Dawn.

"What were you two doing out on the beach? Who are you?"

I told him our names. "We're down on a short vacation." I handed him my dripping wallet and wished I could wring it out for him. "We climbed out on the breakwater and my wife fell in. I had to go in after her."

"Yeah?" He looked us over again. He looked at the cards in my wallet and looked at Dawn again. "But, are you sure she's your wife?"

"She *is my* wife!"

Dawn started to shiver again. She had been staring at the ground all during my explanation. She looked up at him defiantly. "I *am* his wife!" Her gaze faltered. "Do you have to look at me that way?"

"What way?" His eyes stripped the flimsy dress from her body. "Let me see your hands!"

She uncrossed her arms and showed him her hands palm upward. He glanced at them then fastened is eyes greedily on her thrusting breasts. She flushed and instantly crossed her arms again.

I got mad. "Goddamnit, you—"

"Shut up! This is quite a piece you picked up, bud."

*"She's my wife!"*

"Yeah? Why isn't she wearing a wedding ring?"

Dawn reacted beautifully. I realized Tex had made her take it off when they'd gotten together, and at the time Dawn probably didn't give a damn. But at that moment she gasped and looked stricken. "Oh, Jeff, I've *lost it!*"

I took her in my arms. "That's okay, honey. We're lucky you didn't drown out there. We'll get you a bigger one."

The cop looked suspicious. "I don't know . . . There's something fishy." He looked again at her obvious lack of underclothes. "I think I'd better run you two in. Maybe in a couple days you'll tell a different story." He handed back my wallet.

I started to sweat. "Look, officer, I've got to get back to Portland for work tomorrow. We have to fly out of here in the morning."

He opened the door of the patrol car and motioned us into the back. "We'll see."

"Wait." I reached into my pocket and handed him the fifty dollar bill. It was raw, but the only chance I had. "This paper got ruined when I dived in after my wife. Maybe you can dry it out and use it for something."

He looked down at it for long seconds. He cocked his head and looked at me. "Where are you two staying?"

"Just up this street at the Seaside Apartments."

He sucked a tooth and slowly pocketed the money. "Okay, get going."

We didn't wait for another word. In one minute we were climbing the front stairs to my room, leaving a fine trail of sand as it fell from our clothes. The danger the cop had represented had passed and a deep reactive exhaustion was setting in. Each upward step was a mountain to be climbed. Dawn helped me as best she could and at last we reached the second floor. The door to my room was ajar, the light still on as Dawn had left it in her hurry to follow me.

There was a small noise to the left and I saw Phil Carling, the writer, peaking at us from his door. He appeared astonished. He saw me looking at him and drew back.

We entered my room and locked the door behind us.

## Chapter Twenty

I stumbled to the bed, stripped off my clothes in a daze of weariness and crawled under the covers. I heard Dawn go into the bathroom, lock the outer door and start the shower. Through the wall came a series of staccato bursts from Carling's typewriter. With those sounds in my ears I sank down and out into sleep.

I was dreaming of a storm at sea. I was being buffeted, something was . . . It was Dawn beside me on the bed, shaking me. My God, I'd just barely fallen asleep!

I blinked at the sunlight in the room. "What time is it?" I groaned.

"Seven-thirty."

I groaned again. My body itched from dried salt water. I was aching and still tired. I was ravenously hungry. "Why did you wake me up this early?"

"Darling, I thought you wanted to get away as soon as we could. Tex should be leaving for work in a few minutes." Dawn threw the covers away from her lush compact body and rose to her knees to peer out of the window at the alley. The pink tips of her breasts pressed lightly against the old wallpaper. I felt a warm stirring in my thighs.

"So what has Tex to do with us now?" Her body, leaning so close before me, was distracting. I couldn't think. I was just beginning to realize what had happened the previous night and to appreciate it. It had been like a wild nightmare, a wet-dream and three magic wishes rolled into one.

"Well, silly, I can't wear that dress I had on yesterday. Can't you just see me getting on a plane in that? And with nothing on underneath? My clothes are all in the penthouse."

I laughed with her as she continued to keep watch on the alley. Then I stopped laughing. She'd come back from Otto Kluge's office without her underclothes, hat and gloves.

"Dawn, I can't really believe you've changed so much in so short a time."

She glanced at me and smiled lovingly. "I did, though." The smile turned to a mischievous grin. "Want me to prove it to you again?"

My body did. I could feel myself getting excited. "I mean, how did it happen? What caused it?"

"Jeff, I suddenly realized it was you. All the time I wanted you. Not Tex or a career or anything . . . just you."

Still I picked at the scab. I had to know. "But why did you suddenly realize it? What happened with Otto Kluge?"

Her eyes darkened. "I don't want to talk about it."

"I have to know, Dawn. No matter what happened it can't harm us now, but I have to know."

"Well . . . he was very nice to me when I got there. He said I had a lot of talent and ability. He just oozed niceness. Then he said it would be a good idea to talk over my future career with Sylvia . . . the hostess at the party. So we went out there in your car, I really thought I was on the way."

Dawn kept looking out of the window as she spoke. "Sylvia thought I was a great potential star, too. A whole hour went by and we had a lot of happy drinks. I guess I got a little woozy. I never could hold my liquor. You always told me that and I never wanted to believe you.

"It got warmer and warmer and somehow or other we all began taking off our clothes. Everybody was laughing. We went down in the party room and they wanted me to do my dance again. I did and . . ." Dawn bit her lip and glanced at me. "Must I tell everything?"

I nodded.

"While . . . while I was dancing they both took off the rest of their clothes. I honestly didn't know what to think. All the time they kept saying how beautifully I'd photograph and wouldn't such and such a part be perfect for me. I didn't dare say anything wrong.

"Then Sylvia set up a camera and started showing some dirty films. They were awful. Men and women doing everything. Sylvia was even in one of them. And they acted like there was nothing wrong with such movies. They laughed and made all kinds of horrid comments. Then they started to feel me.

"It was like an initiation, they said. Every young star had to go through it. They said maybe it would be a good idea if I acted in one of those films as a sort of screen test.

"I didn't want to. But all the time they kept at me with their hands. Then they said I'd have to do it or forget about acting in a regular movie. I didn't know what to do. I wanted to be a star so bad. And they said some of the biggest stars got started that way and they named some of them. I couldn't believe it.

"And all this time the films were going on and I was seeing what they wanted me to do . . . all kinds of horrible things. There was one scene with a woman and a specially trained snake—"

Dawn shuddered. "I got sick. I couldn't help it. All at once I realized I wanted you and that they were too much for me. I thought for a minute I had grey hair I felt so old all of a sudden. I knew I'd made a terrible mistake and all I could think of was getting back to you and trying to make it right.

"I made an excuse and went upstairs. My dress was up there and my purse. I left my bra and panties downstairs. I don't think I could've got away if I'd tried to take them with me. I just threw on my dress, grabbed my purse and ran out. Then I came here looking for you."

There was nothing for me to say. I pulled her away from the window and kissed her. She had changed but I wondered if I had. I wondered now if I deserved her. "Dawn, you've proved yourself to me, now I've got to prove myself to you."

"What do you mean?"

"Lay down on the bed."

"I've got to watch and see if Tex leaves for work. I need some clothes!"

"Let's forget Tex for a while."

She sighed and obeyed. Her body had a clean fresh female smell. She frowned up at me as I leaned over her on my elbow. She raised a hand and touched my scabby cheek. "Your poor face. You've really taken a beating, haven't you?"

I shrugged. "You remember up in the penthouse when we were alone and I didn't want to prove I loved you the way you wanted?"

Her eyes became very grave. "Yes."

"I want to prove it now."

She looked at me for long seconds. "You don't have to."

I kissed her. "You went all out for me on the beach last night, Dawn. You came running out there in that thin dress in the cold and you did everything I asked to convince me. Now it's my turn."

"But I'm already convinced, Jeff. I know you love me."

"You broke all your old rules for me. You were willing to do anything in spite of the way I treated you. I wasn't willing to do the same for you in the penthouse. I am now."

"But—"

"I want to do it. I want to break some rules of my own for you . . . because I love you."

She smiled a wistful loving tremulous smile and kissed me on the nose. "Dear Jeff. Everything has to balance, doesn't it? Love is like a game and you have to catch up."

"I can't help the way I feel."

Her smile widened. "I'm glad you feel that way because . . . I want you to do it."

We kissed and our tongues played sensuously, sending delicious chills through us. I was gentle with my hands as I slowly kissed my way down her body. She ran her fingers through my hair again and again.

"Tell me if I do anything wrong."

Her belly rose and fell quickly under my lips. "I'll make you do it over and over again till you get it right."

It was over very quickly. As I moved up beside her she whispered, "You did everything right, darling." Then she said what I wanted her to say. "You were better than Tex, better than anybody."

"It's good to be on the varsity. When do I get my letter?"

She laughed and touched me. "Dear, will you look at that. You're all swollen up. What can we do about it?"

"I don't know. You're the doctor."

She became serious. "Jeff, after last night I have a feeling I'm surely pregnant."

I squeezed her free hand. "I hope so."

"I do, too." She laughed gaily, some of the little girl sound coming back. "Wouldn't it be funny if it did happen last night? Wouldn't it be romantic and exciting?"

"It would be wonderful."

## Chapter Twenty-One

It was eight-thirty, I had taken a quick shower and dressed in my crusty pants and a clean white shirt with an expensive grey tie. From the waist up after I'd shaved as best I could and combed my hair, I looked pretty good. Below the waist I was a disreputable bum. My shoes were warped, sandy and still damp.

During the night while I was sleeping, exhausted, Dawn had had the same ideas about the credit cards. She'd spread them out on the table to dry. They didn't look bad, some were warped and water marked, but in a pinch that could be explained.

While I was cleaning up Dawn had packed my suitcase and dressed herself as best she could. She put on a pair of my spare white jockey shorts under the ruined dress, and over it she wore one of my shirts. I couldn't help laughing when I came into the room from the bathroom.

"Stop that!" she said in mock anger. "I can't go around the halls showing everything I've got."

"You've got plenty to show, too."

She blushed just a little bit. "From now on, darling, you're the only one who's going to see it."

"After last night and this morning I'm going to want to see it a lot."

She rolled her lips in a playful bump and grind. "You won't have to force me."

My face must have drained of color when she said that. I remembered Lena.

"Darling, what's wrong?"

I came very close to telling her then, but I was still afraid to test her forgiveness, Lena, Lena, Lena . . . why had I done it? What had happened to her?

"Jeff, something is wrong. What is it?"

"I . . . I was just thinking about my job." I told her about the call from old man Kingman and the next morning deadline.

"You can always get another job."

"Not as good. And he could blackball me."

"Don't worry about it, darling. We'll make it in time."

"Sure we will." I forced a smile. "You wait here, I'm going down the hall and call about reservations on a plane north." I went out then had to come back and get some change from her purse. I was penniless.

As I called the airlines the door of apartment four haunted me. The third airline I called had two seats open. I made the reservation. We would have to move fast. The flight left at ten-forty two . . . in less than two hours. We had a lot to do.

I stared at the door. I had to find out.

It opened as I was about to knock. I faced Lena. She had changed. Her hair was done differently, more feminine, and she wore a skirt and blouse. I winced at the sight of her battered face.

She stared at me without expression. I couldn't stand the silence. "How are you, Lena?"

Tears welled in her eyes and coursed down her cheeks. "I am—"

Dawn came out of my room and joined me by the door. "Did you have any luck, darling?" She saw Lena. "Oh . . ."

I waited helplessly for the blade to fall and chop off my future. Anything that happened I deserved. I felt a hundred pounds of lead break loose in my stomach and start sinking.

Lena brushed away some tears and smiled at Dawn. "You are lucky. He is a good man. I thought all night on the busses on it and he is a good man. I am a woman now."

I stood thunderstruck. Dawn reached for Lena's hand and squeezed. "I know. I'm glad for you, Lena. He made a woman of me, too."

Lena turned the smile on me. "Goodbye, Jeff." She stepped forward and awkwardly kissed me lightly on the cheek. "I am sorry about . . ." and she touched the scratches.

I found myself beginning to cry too. "God, Lena, I'm sorry for what happened. There's no excuse—"

"No. It was a good thing. I am glad." She stepped back and slowly closed the door. "Go now . . . be good to her." And the door clicked shut.

I felt drained and lightheaded. Dawn took my hand and pulled me away. "Come on, darling. Let's get my clothes. You won't have to worry about her any more."

"Did you know?"

"Yes. That man in five told me. He sees everyone who comes in and goes out. He peeks at them like an old woman. He went to the bathroom last night when I was waiting for you and he talked right through the door at me. Shirley told him what you had done to Lena and he told me. He sounded like he was gloating.

"I was worried sick over you. I must have fallen asleep because the next thing I knew I heard the door close and saw your note on the pillow."

"And you still loved me?"

"Yes. You still loved me after I took your money and left you. Darling, I guess we're stuck with each other."

We headed for the rear of the building and the penthouse stairs. Dawn stopped halfway between the second and third floor. "Jeff! What if she's up there? What if she's got that gun?"

I remembered the look on Tex's face and the ugly wavering black hole of the muzzle. "We'll just have to take the chance."

"No! I can borrow some clothes from Shirley."

"To hell with that! I'm not going to crawl away from her like a scared dog. We go up!"

We were just starting up the last flight when we met Zeke coming down. He was carrying two fat suitcases.

"Those are mine!" Dawn said.

Zeke nodded and handed them to me. "Tex just kicked you out, chick. She came around early this morning mad as hell and told me to get your stuff out. She packed it all up for you."

"Is she at work?"

He nodded. "But you better not go up there now. She moved in another chick to take your place." He frowned at us. "You two high on something?"

Dawn and I were laughing hysterically, the tension and anxiety of the last few days flowing out in helpless mirth.

"Squares," Zeke muttered as he went past us down the stairs. "I'll never understand them . . ."

## THE END

# THE FAR-OUT ONES
## by Dell Holland

# ONE

"Let me have another pull at that jug," Sam Mackey said, reaching out a long arm to where Charley Bluejacket sat near the wall, his legs crossed beneath him, looking as if he was posing for a painting with his dark, stolid Indian face and ramrod straight back.

"Sure, Sam. Prime stuff," Charley said, placing the jug of hard cider in Sam's large hand.

"Shame this is about the last of it," Sam said, raising his head up from the cot where he was lying just far enough away so he could drink with comfort. "Jake still running that still up on Hawkin's Mountain like last year? Maybe I could mosey up tomorrow and pick up a few jars. He puts out a good product."

"Naw, Old Jake, he's laying low. Scared of the Feds. Supposed to be a few of them around."

"Shame about that. Sometimes I don't know what the country's coming to, they won't even let a man make a living."

"Well, you're rich now, Sam, ever since you inherited the Inn here. You can afford store-bought stuff."

"That just ain't got the bite like Jake's liquor. Ain't got that much folding money, anyways. When Brother Zach died, about all he left was the Inn."

Carefully placing the jug on the ground, Sam let his head down, stretched out his legs and relaxed so completely, he seemed to sink into the cot and become part of it. A big, lanky man in his early forties, sprinklings of grey lightened his glossy black hair at the temples. Though distantly related to Charley Bluejacket, his features didn't look particularly Indian with its thick growth of beard and slate-grey eyes.

Though generally considered to be rather shiftless and lazy by many of his neighbors, Sam didn't think of himself that way. There wasn't a man in the hills that he couldn't out-walk coon hunting or out-lift on a bet. He'd never gotten the knack of exerting himself for money although he'd watered the forty acres of rocks he called a farm for some twenty years with sweat.

Small farming in this day and age, of course, is a losing proposition, as Sam knew full well. But the idea of working for someone other than himself was something he just couldn't take, so he stuck it out until his brother Zach got killed in an automobile accident, then sold the farm and moved into the Inn with his daughter Emmy.

Zach's Inn was a ramshackle affair on Route fifteen, a seldom used road that snaked through the desolate mountains in this section of New York State. Zach had always had great hopes for the place but it was too far off the regular tourist track for him to do much except break even at the end of the season.

Zach had offered to let Sam come in with him several times but Sam had known that they wouldn't be able to work together. Zach was just too nervous and jumpy, always worrying and scheming, for Sam. Now the Inn would be run the way Sam wanted.

This would be somewhat different than the way Zach had operated. While he never expected to make any big money out of the place, Sam expected to have a lot more fun with it than Zach.

Unlike his brother, Sam enjoyed boozing, fighting and tomcatting around. When he got his liquor license, he expected to have all of these pleasures close at hand. Instead of having to go over a few miles of hills to raise a little hell, everything, including those wild women from New York with their eye-popping swim and sun suits, would be right within his long reach.

The fresh green leaves of the trees that covered the surrounding mountains gleamed in the bright June sunshine. Occasionally, a cooling breeze would sway the tree-tops, making the underside of the leaves ripple as though a giant, invisible hand had stroked the mountains. A flock of crows were loudly cawing someplace on the slope behind the Inn. The road leading past was empty of cars.

"Nice day," Charley said, reaching over to take the jug. A full-blooded Mohawk, twenty-five years old, he had a lithe, runner's build in spite of the fact that the most athletic thing he had done in the years since his discharge from the Marines was to shoot an occasional game of pool in Boys' Corner, the nearest town.

"Sure is. Damned glad to see this miserable winter over. Thought it'd never get over. June's here now, though, and pretty soon all them tourists will be coming around. I tell you, Charley, I'm damned fidgety, after being holed up here all winter!"

"Same here. It's rotten, having to stay around here where there's only two or three women around who put out!"

"More than that, Charley. You just have to hunt them out hard, that's all. Not that they're really worth too much bother when you finally root them out."

"OK for you to say that but it ain't easy trying to make these damn ridge-runners when you're a Mohawk."

"Well, why don't you run up to the reservation? Ought to be able to pick up something there."

"You kidding? Listen, I'm strictly on the outs with the tribe ever since that time I tried working with my old man on that high-tower five years ago and fainted dead away from being up so high. All the kids stand around and laugh whenever I come around."

"Sure is funny, you being a Mohawk and being so afraid of height when your tribe makes a living putting up those skyscrapers and things. And, for an Indian, you're just about the clumsiest guy I know in the woods! How in hell you managed to get lost that time I took you hunting for three days is something I've never been able to figure out! All you had to do was walk in any direction and in less than half a mile, you'd of hit a road."

"It gets damned difficult, alone in all those trees. I kept trying to remember all those things, like which side of a tree the moss grows on and everything but I kept on going around in circles. That's something else the tribe won't let me forget."

"You're sure one hell of a Mohawk," Sam laughed.

"I don't know, I can't help thinking that way back in my family, there must've been a white man hiding behind the wigwam. That's an expression we use."

"You sure look like a full-blooded Indian, though. Say, there's another gimmick you might try. You know what I'd do if I looked like you, Charley? I'd go off to Hollywood, try and get into the movies or television. Seems that they're always making these westerns and things. All you'd have to do would be to *look* like an Indian and that seems to be something you could do without half trying."

"Don't talk to me about movie acting! When I got out of the gyrenes, I gave that a try."

"Yeah? What happened?"

"Well, they took me to this guy who was casting director and when he seen me, he nearly flipped! Says I'm just what he's looking for and gives me this real crazy outfit to wear. You know, feathers and all that jazz. So I put them on and he gets real excited. Tells me he'll fix it up with the Apaches so's I can join their union and he'll get me all the work I can handle."

"Sounds like a good deal."

"I thought so, too. I figured I'd have it knocked, making good bread and chasing all those starlets around in my free time. But do you know what that crazy clown wanted me to do to get the job? I nearly decked him when he told me!"

"Nothing immoral, I hope?"

"Naw, worse! The crazy bastard wanted me to ride a *horse!* A big, ugly, mean-looking *horse!* I sure told that silly sap what he could do with his job!"

"I don't know, Charley. You can't seem to be able to make it as an Indian, why don't you try making it as a white man? You're still young enough to learn a trade, maybe even get some education."

"Live like a white man? Listen, I've got *some* pride left! Besides, there's plenty of gimmicks I got left."

"You mean like that camp for kids you were running last year? You never did tell me the inside story about that. Heard a lot about it. There was even talk about lynching you."

"Camp Cowattimie? Listen, that was a damn good deal for everybody! The kids liked it, the parents liked it because they got rid of their brats for the summer, and *I* sure loved it!"

"How'd you work that deal anyway, Charley? You sure ain't the guy I'd let my kids go off into the woods with."

"I tied in with this Italian girl from Syracuse I used to go with. She had black hair and eyes and was dark enough to pass for an Indian. What we did, we got these buckskin outfits and put an ad in the New York papers with our pictures saying Chief Running Bear and wife are opening a co-ed summer camp for kids aged twelve to seventeen, nature lore, camping and all that."

"You? Nature lore?"

"Don't laugh, it worked. We got a whole herd of kids. I rented the old Barkley farm and fixed it up good. Now, naturally, I didn't take them hiking or any of that business."

"Glad you had that much sense."

"I mean, like what good's that stuff in this day and age? I taught them things they ought to know. I brought up a pool table and tried teaching them how to shoot a good game. Now, you know that the only way you can learn pool is by playing somebody better than you are for money and some of those kids got up to ten bucks a week spending money. I taught them a little about how to bet the right odds on dice and how to bet in poker, too."

"Makes a bit of sense but how about the girls?"

"Well, I let the broad take care of the little ones but the older girls, I took care of myself. Some of them were fifteen, sixteen, even seventeen years old, you know."

"Pretty young but, the way things are now. . . ."

"Sure, that's the way I figure it. Besides, sooner or later, they are going to say yes, those of them that didn't already, and it's better some guy who's been around breaks them in than one of these wild young kids that're running around."

"So you gave them some sex education besides all the rest of it, eh, Charley?"

"I'll say I did! One of the kids was a Boy Scout and I had him put up one of those things with the branches making like a roof, what do you call them?"

"Lean-to?"

"Yeah, that's it, a lean-to. Anyway, the older girls, I'd take them up there for what you might call overnight camping trips. Oh, man! Talk about your wild times! They weren't a bit shy about it at all once they caught on, either. I tell you, Sam, you ain't lived until you're wrapped up in blankets with maybe half a dozen sexy teen-aged broads. Man, they really kept me hopping all night from one to the other. In the beginning, we used to take sleeping bags up with us but carrying all that stuff knocked them for a loop."

"How come the whole shebash blew up on you like that? You get a little careless?"

"Naw, I got a little tired. It was that dago broad what blew the whistle. She started getting mad at me because she wasn't getting enough. Well, I had six paying customers to take care of first but she just couldn't understand. And you know how bitchy a female can get when she sees other broads getting more than she is."

"I sure do!"

"So she goes off and writes letters to the parents and everybody else and the trouble started. Took all the profits I made just to keep out of the can. It was worth it, though."

"Guess this country just ain't progressed enough to handle an idea like Camp Cowattimie. Give it a few more years and maybe you'll be able to get back into that field."

"I figure on giving it another try one of these years when I get a stake built up. This time it's going to be for adults only. No women unless they're over eighteen. I figure I can call it a health camp or something. You know, a place where wives can go to get away from their old men for the summer. I figure there won't be any complaints from anybody then."

"How about the husbands?"

"What the hell, I'm taking the wives off their hands, ain't I? Giving them the whole summer to play around on their own. I'll have to wait until the stink about Cowattimie dies down before I try it, though. This time, I won't try to handle it all by myself. You could ruin your health that way! I already got a bunch of guys lined up who want to go in with me."

"Maybe I'll sign up myself if this place doesn't make a go. Or are you only taking Indians?"

"Naw, no racial business in my place. You ought to do pretty well in the business, Sam. You've got the right inclinations. Maybe you could try the same bit here, call the place Mackey's Health Farm, run the guests around the place a few times every morning and charge them double rates for the privilege."

"Hell, they want exercise, I'll take them up to my old place and let 'em try to sweat a crop out of that miserable ground! A season of that'd sweat an elephant down to the size of a dog. I don't see getting into that sort of thing, though. I didn't come into this business to run around any more than I have to."

"You ought to give them something of that sort. They expect it nowadays. Maybe you could take a bunch of them out coon hunting with you some night?"

"Naw, I go hunting for pleasure and I don't call it no pleasure trying to keep a bunch of greenhorns from breaking their fool necks out in the woods. I ain't going to exert myself no more than to stick out my hand when the tourists come to take their money. Unless, maybe, I try that art business that you talk about."

"Now, Sam, you promised me I could have that concession all for myself. Besides, I'm a natural for it. You wait and see, it'll be just like it was up at Bond Lake a few years back. One of those broads with nothing to do'll come around with one of them easels and ask me if I'd mind posing for her. Sure, I'll say, for five bucks an hour. Say, maybe I could put up a little sign over at the desk, kind of advertising my services?"

"Sure, it's OK with me."

"The first day, I'll wear the full regalia, you know, buckskin pants and all that. The next day, the broad'll ask if I mind stripping down to one of those loin cloths and, after awhile, she'll give a little giggle and ask if I'd mind taking that off, too. After awhile, she'll stop even trying to draw and it'll be clear sailing from then on in. Those tourist women are really something and some of them ain't too bad to look at, either. You ever score with any of them, Sam?"

"Oh, sure. Not as much as I'd of liked to because of the farm but on a Saturday night, me and my guitar'd both get a good work out. All them pretty little secretaries really went for that old guitar of mine, I tell you!"

"Yeah, those broads really liven up these hills, all right. Only a few more weeks and they'll be coming here. It's going to seem like a long time, though," Charlie said, stretching out his arms.

"One little thing I meant to ask you about, Charlie," Sam said, a little embarrassed. Just as he never liked taking orders from somebody else, he disliked giving them.

"Yeah, what's that?"

"Well, you're supposed to be the handyman around here and there seems to be a few things that still need to be fixed."

"What do you mean?" Charlie asked, aroused at the prospect of having to do any work. "I painted all those cabins out back last week, didn't I? And didn't I fix the door yesterday?"

"Yeah, but I was thinking of the roof. That old roof really needs shingling and it's a nice day for it."

"You trying to be funny or something? You ain't going to get me way the hell up there on some ladder!"

"But damn it, Charley, it ain't no more than two stories high at the most!"

"Uh-uh. I'm not going up there. You know how I am about heights. Go get Emmy to do it."

"But I've been working her pretty hard for the past few weeks, moving furniture and everything."

"So what? She's a healthy girl, ain't she? Besides, she's a lot better than me at carpentering, anyway."

The conversation lapsed into silence. Sam was in a dilemma. The place was just starting and he was running into labor difficulties already. He could threaten to cut Charley's salary except for the fact that he wasn't paying him anything since Charley was willing to work for what he could milk the guests for. Of course, he could cut down on the booze he was giving Charley but that was just a little too low-down and mean a way to treat anybody.

Sighing, he finally gave up and did what he knew he'd end up doing. Besides, as Charley said, Emmy was a lot better at general work than he had ever been.

"Hey, Emmy!"

"Emmy!" he yelled.

"Hold on, Pa," Emmy's voice called.

A few minutes later, she came striding in, her tall, robust body encased in a pair of skin tight leotards. Both Sam and Charley picked their heads up to look at her. There was plenty to look at. Eighteen years old and extravagantly curved both fore and aft, she made the black leotards strain to contain her.

Sam shook his head as he always did when Emmy came around. His daughter, what a hell of a joke that was. Fortunately, all she'd inherited from him was her height and coloring for her features were delicate and pretty. Charley let out his breath in a soundless whistle.

"Emmy! Do you have to run around dressed up in those things? It gets a mite disturbing, I don't mind telling you."

"Oh, Pa! Don't be silly."

"And do you have to wriggle so damned much when you walk? I swear, you look like you're doing a coochi dance every time you so much as walk across the room."

"I can't help that, it's because I'm a natural born dancer. That's what the book says, that a girl should have a natural sinuous kind of walk if she wants to be a dancer."

"Well, you got that, anyway."

"I'll say!" Charley said.

"No comments from you, Charley!"

"What is it you want, Pa? I *see* you got your whiskey handy. You want me to pour it down your throat for you?"

"Don't give me any back talk, young lady. Maybe a swift kick in the rump'd learn you some manners."

"Oh, get off it, Pa. What do you want?"

"Well, Emmy," Sam said, changing his tone, "I was thinking that today'd be a good time to fix up the roof. Why don't you grab a hammer and some of those shingles and fix it up?"

"For Pete's sake! Why can't you or Charley do that instead of just lying around, drinking?"

"Why, Emmy, I'm not just lying here, I'm thinking and making plans about the season. Charley here is afraid of high places so he can't do it. That leaves you. Come on, be a good girl, it won't take but an hour or two. You want us to make a lot of money this summer so's you can go to that dancing school in New York the way you want, don't you?"

"Oh, all right," Emmy said, leaving.

"Charley, it sure is a rough thing, having a daughter at her age when you're my kind of man. If she was a boy, it wouldn't matter none. I'd encourage him to go out and raise hell whenever he got the urge but what do you tell a daughter? I mean, it's kind of different somehow where a woman's concerned."

"Well, what the hell, a woman's human, too."

"That there's a dangerous way to start thinking, Charley. By the way, about Emmy, you ain't been . . . ?"

"Naw, I seen you fighting mad once when you cleaned out Colin's Bar a few years back. I ain't touched her but I can't help looking. You'd better get some other women around here or I may weaken."

"Oh, I don't mind telling you, raising a girl's rough," Sam said, taking another swallow of the applejack. "I guess the only thing to do is marry her off."

"If you want a husband for her, you're sure going at it in the wrong way, beating hell out of any guy that comes calling on her the way you been doing."

"Well, Charley, I wouldn't want her to marry any weakling, would I? If one of them'd stand up to me like a man or come back for a second try after I whopped him, why I'd take to him right kindly. But if they don't think enough of my daughter to lose a few teeth over, they can't be worth much."

"That's an interesting theory but I think you'd better cool it a little."

"Maybe you're right at that, I don't know. It's just that I see them sneaking around and I sure know what *I'd* do if I was in their place."

"At least you won't have to worry about her after this summer, what with her going to New York and all."

"That's when I guess I'll really have to start worrying. That poor defenseless young girl alone in the big city. Say, we're starting to run a little short, Charley. Why don't you run into town and pick us up another bottle?"

"OK, but I'll wait until it gets later. It's too damn hot out now to be going any place. We got enough 'jack to last till then, don't we, Sam?"

"Just about."

Above them, they could hear Emmy as she started hammering away at the shingles.

It was hot work, fixing up the roof. Emmy worked swiftly and surely, spitting out nails whenever she needed one. Sweat started staining her leotards. They really weren't the best kind of outfit to wear for this kind of work. Standing up, Emmy looked down the road. There wasn't any traffic on the road and, if necessary, she should be able to duck down behind the porch if anybody came along.

She took off the leotards, put them by the sign and, naked, went back to work.

She made just about the most attractive carpenter that could be imagined. Swinging with gusto, she nailed down shingles at a high rate of speed, black hair flying and sturdy breasts swaying with her motions. Gentle winds caressed her damp bare skin, cooling her.

Emmy liked going around naked this way. She used to do it all the time but Sam had stopped her in the past few years. Her body was a fine one and she welcomed any chance she got to free it from clothing. Glancing down the road, she giggled at the thought of somebody coming by and seeing her.

When she was a dancer, she thought, everybody would delight in seeing her body. Of course, she'd have to wear some kind of outfit but that wouldn't matter much. She'd be in New York then and she gave a little shiver at the thought.

New York, oh how wonderful that would be! Not that she really had any great dislikes about her current life. Sam was pretty easy to get along with but it would be so *nice* to meet some half-way decent men for a change without having Sam clobber them! It had gotten so bad that, in spite of her looks, none of the local boys wanted to have anything to do with her.

Not that she was a virgin.

It had happened the previous fall. Phil McCabe had been the boy's name. While not particularly handsome, be had been so insistent and anxious to have her that she'd finally gotten excited and agreed to meet him in the woods after school.

Why should Sam have all the fun?

Trees were ablaze with color in the warm October sunshine as they tooled along the highway in Phil's jalopy and turned onto a dirt road that led to a deserted logging camp. Somehow, knowing that in a few minutes, she'd be actually doing it, didn't thrill her the way she'd hoped.

Phil was thrilled, that was for sure. He could hardly keep his pale blue eyes off her and nearly sent them into a ditch several times before he brought the car to a stop. Brushing back his long, yellow hair, he turned to her and grinned, showing most of his teeth.

"Well, we're here," he said.

"That's right."

They commenced necking then. Gradually, she got to enjoying his kisses and the way he fumbled around at her body. She was wearing a light summer dress under her coat that kept getting in his way so she finally broke free.

"Let's get outside," she whispered.

The thick covering of dead leaves on the side of the road crackled under their feet as they stepped out of the car. Phil nearly stumbled to the ground as he followed her to the base of a big sycamore. Her heart was beating a mile a minute as she stripped down. When she finished, she had to laugh at Phil, he looked so funny, standing there looking at her with his mouth hanging open.

"Well, what are you waiting for?" she asked.

"I'm not waiting for anything."

Then he was on her, pressing against her as the leaves noisily crackled beneath them, pounding at her with ever-increasing urgency as he grasped and dug at her body with his fingers.

It was disastrous.

Phil was just about as inexperienced as she and much, much more excited. They struggled clumsily on the ground and she felt pain but she expected that; but she also expected more than the pain and the awkward wrestling. For a few seconds, she thought they would make it and they started working together and she began to feel herself falling into it the way she'd always thought she would but then—

He finished. It was over.

When he pulled himself up off her, she remained lying on her back, looking up through the tree branches at the distant blue sky through half-opened eyes as a great sadness settled over her. Was that it? Was that all there was to the whole business? She could hear him moving about where he'd left his clothes and, raising herself up to her elbows, she watched him dress.

He was grinning!

Grinning as if he'd just done something worthwhile, striding around triumphantly as if he was the greatest lover the world had ever produced and not even bothering to look at her! She realized then that he really didn't give a damn about her or even care about doing *it;* all he wanted was to be able to brag about having her to the gang that hung around the pool hall.

"You better get dressed, Emmy. Somebody might come along. That was pretty good, wasn't it?"

"No, it wasn't."

"Well, what the heck, it was the first time for you. The next time'll be a lot better."

"There's not going to be any next time," she said. Rising to her feet, she turned away from him and pulled the dress over her. "You had your chance and you muffed it."

"Huh? Well, if that's what you want. . . ." he said, hesitantly.

"No, that's not what I want! You know what I wanted and you couldn't give it to me!"

"Hey, now! What are you getting so mad about? Don't start giving me a hard time. You wanted to come up here as bad as I did so don't start crying now."

"I'm not crying about it. I just don't want to have anything else to do with you, that's all."

"That suits me fine! There's plenty of other girls around that are better than you."

"They're welcome to you, Phil McCabe. Just one more thing. You know what my father would do to you if he found out about this somehow, don't you?"

"Hey! Don't you tell him, Emmy!" Phil said, sounding worried.

"Don't worry, *I* won't say anything, I'd just as soon forget it If you start bragging around about how you . . . did it to me, it'll be sure to get to him eventually. You know that, don't you?"

"OK, OK, you don't have to worry about your reputation. I wasn't going to say anything, anyway."

"I'll bet you weren't! Just keep quiet about this, that's all. I don't want your killing to be on my conscience."

They rode silently back to the farm. He let her off about a mile away and she walked home. What a mess! Why couldn't she have been born a boy the way Sam had wanted? Everything would have been so simple then. When she wanted sex, she could just go out and get it. As a girl, though, she had to be careful.

She was just entering the farmhouse when it suddenly struck her how careless she had been about the whole thing. That—that jerk, Phil, had been so stupid, he hadn't bothered taking any precautions. Just because it had been so close to nothing for her didn't matter; it hadn't been completely nothing, she still could get pregnant!

The next month was hell for her.

When she realized she was safe, she resolved never to have to worry about that sort of thing again. Ignoring everything but graduating from high school, she waited out the long winter. Spring would come and she would be free to go to the city where she could live her own kind of life, do *it* with whoever she wanted whenever she wanted.

Now it was spring but she was still staying until the fall. Not a stupid girl, she had enough sense to realize that it would be better to go to New York with some money. Besides, things might be a lot of fun around the Inn when all those people started coming around. Maybe one of them might be the sort of man she'd been waiting for so long.

When she finished the work, she lazily stretched out on the roof, an arm over her eyes, letting the sun bake into her skin, dreaming that she was on some sandy beach in the south of France.

# TWO

Jim Perkins walked slowly along the roadside about seven miles from Zach's Inn. Dust coated his stout walking shoes and khaki pants and the straps of his hiking pack chafed against his shoulders. Jim wasn't what anyone could call a particularly handsome man, being less than medium in height, chunkily built, red-haired and with a face that seemed to have been put together rather haphazardly. But his eyes, continually bright with amusement, saved everything and made him particularly appealing to women.

He had such great success with women, as a matter of fact, that one of the comments frequently heard about him back on the West Coast was that he was a first-rate lover and a second-rate poet.

Yes, Jim Perkins was a poet, of the semi-beat school. He didn't agree with the above comment. Secretly, he considered himself to be a third-rate poet. This belief didn't bother him because he sincerely believed that it was better to be a third-rate poet and a first-rate lover than to be a first rate anything else.

Jim was thirty four and had been on the outskirts of the Beats during that movement's brief life, having wandered into an expresso house the week after he'd gotten discharged. There, he'd developed a taste for Italian coffee and poetry that he never lost.

The Beats! What a thing that whole idea had been. One hundred and eighty million people worked themselves into an uproar, presidents made speeches about national morality, preachers made sermons and everybody made noise because a few thousand people scattered throughout the country admitted that they didn't know what was coming off and decided to stop giving a damn about it all.

Yes, they had a lot of kicks back in the old days. Jim never went completely in with the Beats but he hung around for ten years, picking up odd jobs when he had to, working as a bartender, construction worker, bell-hop, factory hand and what have you. One time, he let a woman support him for half a year but he finally decided that it would be easier to get another factory job.

Gradually, without his realizing it, he stopped being a young man or, at least, a very young man. The kicks started coming slower, the big poem he was going to write never got written and all the people he'd known began changing and dropping away.

Some pushed the drugs too hard, going past pot and shooting heroin and becoming junkie ghosts haunting the places where they'd once been so alive; others fell back into jobs where they put in their forty hours and lived it up after work; others went back to college and graduate school; others died, others got jugged and others simply disappeared.

Jim hung around.

Those that were left or that joined were different. There was a meanness, a viciousness about the crowd now that he didn't like. When the laughs came, they had a cynical edge to them and the underlying self-pity showed too clearly. Jim decided to take off.

He'd originally come from Rhode Island and had spent some time in New York so he began beating his way back across the country, taking his time. He hitch-hiked to Chicago and spent the winter there, working in a meat packinghouse. When the weather warmed up, he quit and continued on his way.

He had enough money to take a bus or train or even to fly but he hadn't seen the Eastern half of the country in some ten years and he liked the idea of wandering through the countryside in the spring, looking around amd maybe knocking off a few poems.

The sun blazed down and he turned around in circles as he walked along the highway, the bright green grass alongside the asphalt soft beneath his feet, the heady smell of the growing leaves and grass rich in his nostrils and the tree-covered hills massed up around the thin band of the highway.

Jim couldn't get enough of looking and savoring every sight and sound and smell. Oh, if only he had some woman to go romping through the woods with him, her nude body running through the sun-dappled shade and her silvery laughter hanging in the air as he madly pursued and finally caught her! Oh, for a smooth-skinned beauty, giggling in the ticklish grass beneath him, the fertile earth touching her shoulder blades and wide hips and a bright, welcoming smile on her lips as he gently lowered himself down!

On a day in Spring, anybody would be expected to have thoughts like this but Jim had special reasons. He'd just done thirty days on a vag charge in a town some thirty miles back up the road.

He'd been hitch-hiking and a woman, in her forties but not too bad, had stopped the Caddy she was driving and motioned him to get in. A little surprised—most women driving Cadillacs don't stop for hitch-hikers—he joined her on the front seat. She was over-weight and overly made up but seemed friendly enough.

"How far are you going?" she asked.

"New York eventually but I'm in no hurry."

"Well," she said, after giving him a long look, "maybe you wouldn't mind spending an extra night on the road then?"

"Sure. Why not?" he said, flashing her a grin as she put the big car into gear.

That's one good thing about this type of woman he thought as he leaned back against the seat, you don't have to waste much time beating around the bush. Not a bad looking woman at all. She was probably very pretty when she was young. He decided to take his time and make her speak first.

"You can call me Elaine Hamble," she said after they'd gone about a mile.

"Hello, Elaine. I'm Jim Perkins."

"Jim Perkins. That's an all-American name."

"I'm an all-American boy."

"You don't seem to be very surprised about this. Does it happen to you often when you're hitch-hiking?"

"No, it's just that I usually take things as they come."

"You know I don't do this sort of thing often, don't you? I mean, I hope you don't think I'm some kind of nymphomaniac or anything really abnormal?"

"Of course not."

"It's just that it's the first decent day we've had and it's been such a long winter and my husband spends so much time at his work; he's a sales manager, you know."

"Sure."

"But what about you? Why are you hitch-hiking this way? I've always wondered about it when I see you men standing by the road. I've never picked one of you up till now, though. Carl, that's my husband, Carl always says that people like you are always looking for a woman to rape if you get half a chance. Do you want to rape me, Jim?"

"Not unless you want me to."

"I don't think that'll be necessary, Jim. Tell me, are you good in bed? I hope you don't think that's an embarrassing question, it's just that I'm taking a chance, doing this, and I'd hate to be doing it unless it was, er, worth my while."

"I'm very good."

"I'll bet you are! Carl is, oh, adequate, I suppose but he's so wrapped up in making money that he's been neglecting me recently and I'm at an age where a woman doesn't like being neglected. But you still haven't told me about yourself. You don't talk the way I'd expect you to if you were a casual laborer."

"I am very casual about laboring, though."

"What do you *do,* when you're not casually laboring or casually letting some woman pick you up?"

"I write poems. Very casually, of course."

"A *poet!* Well, isn't that interesting! I wish I could tell my friends about this, they'd be *green!* Imagine, having an affair with a poet! Jim Perkins, let me see. No, I don't think I've ever heard of that name. I don't know, Jim Perkins just doesn't seem to *sound* like the name of a poet."

"I know. I've frequently thought that if I was a Welshman or a Scot or, best of all, a mick, I'd have it made."

"You mean people like Dylan Thomas and Brendan Behan? But are you as good as they?"

"They're much better artists than I could ever be but I know I can drink and raise hell as good as them. The trouble is that if you're an Irishman and you break up a bar or a theatre, everybody just has a good laugh about it but if some *smuck* named Perkins trys something like that, the fuzz clamp down in nothing flat."

"'Fuzz'? That means police. Are you Beat?"

"Somewhat."

"How interesting, a real Beatnik! But I thought you all wore beards and berets?"

"I always shave mine off when the weather starts getting warm and berets are out this season. I even take a bath once in awhile, as you may have noticed."

"Yes, I have."

"Anyway, I never really was in with the Beats although some of them were my best friends. No, all I've ever been is a bad poet who liked to drink and kid around as if I were a good one."

"But if you're a bad poet, why did you stay with it. I mean, what's the sense of living the way you do if you don't have any confidence in your talent?"

"Why, I think that's a tribute to my character. Anybody could put up with poverty and non-recognition if he thought he had talent but to do it when you *know* you're second-rate at best, why, that takes courage, damn it!"

"What an interesting way of looking at things! You're very entertaining, Jim. I'll bet you *are* very good in bed! I'm so excited, I almost feel like a girl again," she said, giving a high-pitched giggle.

Jim blanched a little, having had some experience with middle-aged women who began feeling girlish. Elaine was starting to display some of the most alarming characteristics of the species. A little brain-numbing alcohol seemed to be in order.

"Any good bars around here?" he asked.

"Oh, yes, the motel we're going to has a fabulous bar. We can have a few drinkies first, then go beddie-bye."

"That sounds good," Jim said, keeping from retching with an effort. "Drinkie" was a word he hated. She would probably have to go to the little girls' room after having a few drinkies, too. He began thinking that it might be better if he told her to forget the whole bit but still, with a few drinks in him and in a dark room, it might be as good a way as any to kill a night.

"Here's the motel," she said, turning the car into the driveway of a flamboyantly gaudy structure. "I've never been in here so there won't be any chance of anyone seeing us. I suppose we'd better register under your name?"

"Why not?"

"Do you have any money or should I give you some now?"

"I don't give a damn. I have enough to buy a few drinks but if this joint is as expensive as it looks, you'll have to pay for the room yourself."

"Aren't you going to argue about me paying?"

"Of course not. You obviously have much more money than I have. Besides, this is your idea."

"Good, I'm glad you're not being silly. Do you want to register first or have a few drinkies?"

"I think I could use the liquor."

They entered the bar, which could be described in one word: Phony. Everything was chrome and vinyl. The bartender wore a red jacket and a supercilious sneer when he saw that Jim wasn't wearing a suit and tie, but he had noticed them coming up in a Cadillac so he didn't make any audible comments when they went to a booth.

"Are you hungry, Jim? I feel like ordering a sandwich or something before we start drinking."

"No, I don't feel like eating," he said looking around. The walls were painted an orange-green color and effectively killed his appetite. The bartender came over to the table, glared disapprovingly as Jim, making Elaine burst out with an explanation of his outfit.

"My husband is one of those hiking nuts even though he is a Republican, ha-ha. That's why he's dressed that way. I hope it's all right for us to be here?"

"Well, as long as it's a week-day, I guess it's all right."

"Could I have one of your club sandwiches, turkey with mayonnaise dressing and a slice of chocolate cream pie?" she asked, surveying the menu. "I'd like to have some kind of a cocktail to go with it, too. What's this House Special?"

"Oh, that's very popular," the bartender enthused. "It's creme de menthe, scotch, pineapple rings, rum and orange bitters all topped with whipped cream."

"That sounds yummy! I'll have one!"

"Very good, Madame," the bartender said. The horrible concoction was a lot of trouble to make but it went for four-fifty and if the broad and her boy-friend wanted to spend the price, it was all right with him. The joint could use any money it could get until the warm weather came. "And what will you have, sir? The same?"

"No. Schenleys and water'll suit me fine."

"Very good, sir," the bartender said, frostily, and left.

"That was quick thinking on my part, wasn't it?" she asked. "I mean telling him you were a hiker and all that."

"Why did you bother? I'd imagine that you had enough bread so you wouldn't have to give a damn."

"It doesn't work out that way, Jim. When you are well-to-do, you have to be even more careful about what people think."

"That's a problem I've never had."

Getting up, he walked over to the juke-box and started looking through the listings. There, amongst the Mantovani Strings, Mitch Miller Sing-a-Longs and Jackie Gleason mood pieces, he found a recording of *Sinfully Yours* by John Dexter's band. Putting in two quarters, he hit the designated button four times and went back to the booth as the mellow music began its pulsating rhythm.

She was wolfing down her sandwich and occasionally sucking some of the amber-colored drink through a straw. Jim gazed in horror at the huge glass filled with its stomach-turning contents, the chunks of fruit and congealed globs of cream floating listlessly on the surface, as she avidly brought the level down.

Stopping at the table just long enough to gulp down his whiskey, he hastened to the bar and had two more shots before returning to where she was sitting.

"Oh, that was good!" she said, daintily wiping a fleck of whipped cream off her lips. "I think I'll have another one. First, I think I'll go over to the little girls' room."

"Hell, yes, by all means. The little girls' room. I think maybe I'll go for another Schenleys."

"This is all so exciting!" she said, skipping off.

"Give me a refill on this, Mac," Jim told the bartender. "The life of a gigolo is a tough one, believe me."

"Yeah. That's Hamble's wife, ain't it?"

"That's right. Know her?"

"See her around. Her old man's in here a lot with *his* dates. You don't have to sweat him, he's on the road now. You figure on making her here?"

"Any objections?"

"Naw. It's nothing to me."

"Right now, I don't know if I can go through with it or not. Maybe another few shots and I won't care."

"Well, you know what they say. Turn them all upside down and you can't tell the difference."

"I doubt turning her upside-down would make much improvement in her but maybe I'll give it a try."

She came back to the booth and he joined her. They drank, played kneesies and, later, hands across the knees. She was, as he expected her to be, a very stupid woman but he always was good natured and tolerant when he drank so he wasn't too annoyed. As a matter of fact, the more booze he put away, the more he liked the idea of sharing a bed with her later in the evening.

It would be, he imagined, something like plumbing the depths of a billowing sea of soft, white flesh. Certainly, she was losing her inhibitions at a rapid rate. The whole affair might turn out to be an interesting experience.

"Say," she giggled, "I hope you're not drinking too much, for *later*. That happens sometimes, you know."

"I never had that problem."

"You never had any problems, have you? None that you couldn't just walk away from, that is."

"Had more than my share."

"Not really, not like me. Married to a stuffed shirt who's got about as much emotion in him as an iceberg. I used to be pretty, Jim, do you know that?"

"I'll bet you were."

"I like that," she laughed. "Anybody else, any of the men I know, would start sayin' how I'm still pretty."

"Oh, you're not hard to look at."

"Tell me, Jim, you're a poet, you probably think about things a lot, deep things, I mean. Why do you do it? Are you looking for anything or are you just running away. Sometimes I think that everybody is just running away."

"They are."

"But what about you," she persisted. "What are you looking for, what do you want? I mean, what's the sense of all this? Come on, tell me, why are you a poet?"

Questions such as these, he well knew, were best left unanswered since they were unanswerable but he was drunk and somehow they seemed to be as important as when he'd first asked them himself more than ten years previous. He decided to try and explain himself to her, even though he knew he shouldn't try. After all, they were drunk together and soon would be in bed together, why not try and know each other better?

"Look," he said, making vague motions with his hands as she rested her chin on her hand and stared earnestly at him through her cigarette smoke, "Look, Elaine, I never tried telling this to anyone, at least not since I was a kid but it's something like this. I figure the only reason the human race is around or any life is in existence is to know things, to be aware of them."

"You mean science and school and things like that?"

"Yeah, anybody or anything that's more aware or at least is trying to know about itself or the world, like a bug's more aware than a plant or a man, supposedly, is more aware than a bug."

"But how is the way you're living doing that?"

"Because I think that a poet is on the right track too. He's the one who's trying to feel his emotions more deeply than anyone else. I think the universe is trying to know itself, I think that poets are the eyes of the universe."

As soon as he said it, he wished he hadn't. It was too late, though, and he could only sit and watch her. Her eyes grew wide and she lifted her head up.

"Why, that's—that's *cute!*"

Picking up her drink, he poured it over her head. He had to do it, there wasn't any choice left for him.

She screamed.

Then she cursed him, using language that would have done a longshoreman credit and he slapped her across the mouth to shut her up. That brought the bartender running and a nice little brawl commenced that broke various articles of furniture, bottles and knuckles.

Jim wasn't very big but he'd picked up a good saloon-fighting style in his day and had palled around with a Zen enthusiast who taught him a few *Judo* and *Akido* tricks so he was able to give a fair account of himself. It wasn't until the manager of the motel along with a handy-man had entered the fray that he was subdued.

So he presently found himself in front of a judge.

Elaine, he knew, wouldn't press charges against him as she wouldn't want her husband to find out about how she spent the days when he was on the road. The motel, he knew from hearing the bailiff mention it, didn't want any publicity so they wouldn't make any trouble either. He still wasn't out of the woods, though.

"What's your occupation, young man?" the judge, strictly something out of *American Gothic,* asked.

Jim knew he was in for it then but he didn't falter. Looking him straight in the eye, he answered:

"I'm a poet."

"What!" the judge cried, face and neck turning red with anger. "You say you're a . . . *poet!*"

"Yes, that's right."

"Have you no shame? I've heard about fellows like you and am only glad that there are no women or children in the court. How much money does he have on him?"

"About thirty-odd bucks, your honor," the sheriff answered.

"James Perkins, you are hereby found guilty of vagabondage as you have no means of support and are fined thirty dollars and sentenced to thirty days in the work-house. *That* should knock all that poet nonsense out of you!"

The next thirty days were, as might be expected, rather miserable ones for Jim. He was the only prisoner at that time and the sheriff and his deputy used to amuse themselves by belting him around from time to time. He got his revenge on them all, however, by writing an obscene poem about the judge, sheriff and deputy and printing it on the courthouse wall when he was free. It was by far the best thing he'd ever done and made them all the laughing-stock of the county. None of them ever won an election after that.

Thus it was that Jim was in a jovial mood that day. A truck driver had given him a lift that morning and staked him to a donut and coffee for breakfast, so he had regained his faith in human nature and it was such a fine day, his customary good spirits returned.

There still remained the problem of food and lodging for the night but something would probably turn up. If it didn't, he could walk until he hit the next town and wash dishes or something.

Spying a flower with delicate blue petals growing alongside the road he stooped and picked it. A pretty little thing, he thought, sticking it into his shirt-pocket so that it hung over. Shame he didn't know the names of plants and trees. Something else he'd have to do now that he was free.

The mountains around here, he thought, were like old, tired beasts sitting on their haunches. Hmmm, not too bad, at that. Maybe he could make something out of it:

"Great tree-pelted cats, dozing in the sun, smooth bodies worn
and wearied by time, dreaming of ancient youth and heights
forgotten, of upward slanting slopes and torrid clime, before the
advent of that presumptuous slime, Life.

What do you think of those two-legged fleas scurrying madly
through your trees?"

Pretty rotten poem, all around, he thought. He just wasn't in the mood to write about nature and that sort of thing. What he really wanted now was a woman, a real woman, not like that soft, over-grown doll, Elaine. What rhymed with breasts again?

Lost in contemplation, he almost let the battered '55 Chevy go past without sticking his thumb out The brakes squealed and it came to a jarring stop some fifty feet away. Automatically, he began trotting over toward it. As he approached, he could see that there were two people sitting in the front seat.

Two women.

Remembering his recent experience with Elaine, he stopped short. Then one of them turned around. She was a young woman and, even from where he stood, obviously quite good-looking. The other one didn't look bad, either, not bad at all.

"What the hell," he said aloud, "here I go again! I hope the jug in this county is better than it was back in Crawford!"

A smile on his face, he commenced trotting again, the hiking pack jostling against his back.

## THREE

"Hey! What are you stopping for?" Joan Barton cried out as her friend, Sue Lindquist, hit the brakes.

"Why, I'm going to pick up that hitch-hiker, naturally," Sue replied.

"Are you crazy or something? That's the way girls get killed and worse, picking up strange men that way."

"Oh, Joan, stop being so suspicious all the time. You'll never have any fun if you keep acting that way."

What's the use, Joan thought, giving up the struggle of trying to make Sue use a little sense. She'd been trying for several years now and hadn't gotten anywhere. Sue simply insisted on treating life as though it were a ball. It was really her own fault for having such a kook for a friend.

They were dissimilar types although both were very good-looking and about the same age and had lived together for the past year. Sue, a big busty blonde Swede, was the one you noticed first. You generally noticed her because she was doing an impromptu can-can on top of some bar, or challenging some truck driver to a beer-drinking contest (and winning) or enjoying herself in some other lusty manner.

Joan Barton was the dark-haired girl with the horn-rimmed glasses trying to restrain her.

Not that Joan was a dried-up, unattractive prudish type, quite the contrary. When you got to know her, she turned out to be a very delightful girl with a sharp, ironic sense of humor. Built on a somewhat smaller scale than Sue, she still had a supple, well-curved body that was nearly as remarkable as Sue's, although Joan dressed much more conservatively.

They had met in college where Joan had consistently held down the highest grades in the school, while Sue made merry with most of the male student and faculty body. She majored in physical education, most appropriately, and twirled the meanest baton in the state. Somehow, they managed to hit it off well together. Each had a deep respect for the other's qualities.

Most men shied away from Joan because of her braininess but she hadn't been completely wrapped up in the scholastic bit, having experimented with sex several times. The first time had been with a brawny football player. While she had enjoyed grappling with him in the back of his car so much she went the whole route, his tedious boasting about his exploits on the field grew so tiresome, she broke off with him.

The other man she'd gone with was an intellectual. Everybody knew he was an intellectual because (a) he told them so and (b) he had long hair and wore thick glasses. He was going to do great things and, single-handed, would raise the American theatre to a higher level with his powerful, earthy plays.

A month after he graduated, he got a haircut and a job in an insurance office run by his father.

After these two losers, Joan decided to cool it for awhile. Sooner or later, she would meet some man with whom she could have a serious, adult relationship. However, girls who are looking for serious, adult relationships usually don't get too much action, as she found out. Often, she wished she could be like Sue and go skipping from bed to bed without any desire for anything besides the immediate gratification of sex but she knew that she was just too reserved to be able to act like that and enjoy herself.

Joan reluctantly opened the door so that the dusty hitchhiker could get into the car.

"Hello, girls," Jim said. "Do you want me to get into the back seat or the front?"

"Sit in the front. How far are you going?"

"I don't know," Jim said, shucking off his hiking pack and throwing it into the back. "Maybe up to the next hotel or restaurant. I figure on trying to get some kind of dishwashing job. I'm stone broke and a little hungry."

"We're going to have to stop and eat soon," Sue said, starting the car moving again. "That should give you a chance to ask if there's anything open."

"That sounds fine."

"Where are you coming from?" Joan asked, moving as far away from him as the seat allowed.

"Crawford Jail."

"Oh, no!"

"That's funny," Sue said with a laugh. "Joan here was just saying that we shouldn't pick you up because you might assault us or something. Why did they put you in jail?"

"For assaulting a woman."

"No kidding? You really don't look like the type. Do you do that sort of thing often?"

"No, as a matter of fact, that was the first time I did it. It was just one of those urges that come over you."

"Yes, I know what you mean. I get urges like that all the time. Joan here never gets any urges like that,"

"Poor Joan."

"Look here," Joan said, "just in case you get any urges about us, I'd better warn you that Sue's a very powerful girl and that I took Judo lessons in college!"

"Really? I was thinking of going for my black belt when I was out on the Coast," Jim said.

"Don't be silly, Joan. Anybody could see that he's harmless. Aren't you harmless?"

"Well, I'm not *completely* harmless."

"What's your name? Or shouldn't I ask you that? I'm Sue Lindquist and she's Joan Barton."

"I'm Jim Perkins, known as Wild Jim occasionally."

"That's only when you get those urges of yours, I bet. How'd you like jail?" Sue said, ignoring Joan's frantic kicks at her instep. Joan was such a worrier! It was obvious to Sue that this Jim Perkins was all right so what difference did it make if he did a little time? The way things were, *anybody* could find himself in jail. Besides, the woman probably deserved getting assaulted.

"I found jail rather confining," Jim said, answering Sue's question. "How far are you girls going?"

"New York."

"That's where I'm heading, eventually. What are you going to do there? Sight-see?"

"We're going to get jobs there. We had good jobs, the both of us, up in Atkins. We worked for an electronic firm but one day, the boss followed Joan into the ladies' room and—"

"Please, I'd just as soon you didn't talk about that!" Joan said, turning a deep shade of red.

"Followed you into the ladies' room, eh?" Jim said. "Strange tastes, that. Still, I used to know a guy up in 'Frisco who—"

"We're *not* interested in any of your friends' perverted adventures in San Francisco or anyplace else," Joan said in icy tones.

"Well, I'm interested!" Sue protested. "Honestly, Joan, how are you going to learn anything acting that way?"

"If Joan doesn't want to talk about it, we may as well let the matter drop," Jim said, magnanimously.

"So, anyway, we both quit our jobs and decided to try our luck in New York. What about you? What do you do?"

"No sense in lying about it, I guess. I'm a poet."

"A poet!" Joan exclaimed. "Wait a second, James Perkins, I think I read something of yours in the *California Quarterly* a year or so ago. Was that you?"

"Guilty."

"It was titled '*Pipes of Pan*' wasn't it? I must confess I read it and thought it was, er, rather . . . oh, a little . . ."

"Is 'bad' the word you're looking for?"

"Well, yes. Aren't you going to argue with me about it?" Joan asked, surprised at his attitude.

"Hell, I just said I was a poet. I didn't say that I was a *good* one."

"But how can you think like that? After all, if you're going to go around saying you're a poet, then—"

"Listen, the last time I tried explaining my life to a woman, I ended up doing thirty hard days and I sure don't want to go through that routine again!"

"You mean that woman you . . . ?"

"Assaulted? That's right, that's why I did it."

"Served her right," Sue said. "If you ask me, there's too many nosy people prying into other people's business."

"You're OK, Sue."

"Thanks, I like you, too, Jim. I knew you were all right when I saw that flower sticking out of your shirt."

"I recently read," Joan remarked, "that when the Russian soldiers entered Berlin in what was to be called the Great Rape, a lot of them were wearing flowers stuck to their uniforms."

"But Jim isn't a Russian. Are you?"

"Not that I know."

"See? It's all right, then. You mustn't mind Joan too much, Jim. She just acts funny like that all the time. If I didn't know better, I'd think she was still a virgin."

"Sue Lindquist, one of these days, I'm going to brain you for coming out with things like that!"

"See what I mean? She gets so excited over things like that. She's a very nice girl, though, and I don't want to hear you say anything against her."

"Oh, I like Joan a lot too," Jim said, giving her a friendly pat. "I think she'll get to like me when she gets to know me a little better than she does now."

"Oh? And what's that supposed to mean?" Joan asked.

"You girls aren't in that much of a hurry to get to New York, are you? Why, the people there would give anything to be up here now in the mountains with the birds and the trees and the clear running streams. It's June, Joan, and believe me, Joan, June isn't any time to be riding subways if you can help it."

"What's your suggestion, as if I didn't see it coming from a mile off?"

"Simple. New York won't run away if you decide to spend a few extra days up here with the fresh air, the trees, the mountains, the birds and—"

"You, I suppose?"

"Exactly. Think of all the fun we'll have, wandering through the woods and getting drunk and making love."

"James Perkins, you take the cake for sheer, one-hundred proof gall! We've just picked you up on the highway where you've been begging rides, we've never seen you before in our lives, you admit you've just gotten out of jail but you still have enough gall to make a proposition like that!" Joan cried.

"I think it's a great idea," Sue said. "Let's do it. After all, we haven't had a vacation this year yet."

"Sue Lindquist!"

"Oh, loosen up a little, Joan! I know I'm in no hurry to sit in front of some typing machine while an old creep trys to put his hand up my dress. What's wrong with having a little fun before we have to go to work again? What's that they say, half the fun is in getting there. He's a nice guy—"

"He's a jail-bird, a lazy, loafing bum, a sex maniac, and a bad poet!"

"I'm not that bad a poet," Jim protested.

"You are too!"

"I don't care how bad a poet he is," Sue put in, "I'm not interested in having him recite to me. Haven't you got any romance in you? What do you have running in your veins, ice-water?"

"No, but I have a brain in my skull, which is more than you've got, it seems!"

"Girls, girls! It was just a simple little suggestion of mine, there isn't any sense in getting so excited about it. I wouldn't want to ruin your friendship. Tell you what I'll do, Joan. If you'll go along with the idea, I'll promise you, on my honor as a bad poet, that I won't even try to touch you the first night. Of course, I'm not saying anything about the second night."

"No! Stop the car, Sue, and let this moth-eaten Casanova go back to where he came from."

"Why, that wouldn't be friendly at all, Joan. I wouldn't do any such thing."

"I don't know why you're getting so mad, Joan. I'm just being honest about asking for what every man wants from you. Would you prefer that I beat around the bush and try conning you about how I'm interested in what you think of my poems?"

"I think as much of your miserable poems as I think of you, you, you rapist!"

"Look, I may as well explain that once and for all. All I did was pour her drink over the stupid broad's head."

"Speaking of drinks," Sue said, "what do you say we stop up at that Zach's Inn ahead of us and have a few?"

"Splendid idea. That'd be the civilized way to continue this discussion. It looks like a—wow! Do you see what I'm seeing or have I gone stir-crazy?"

There, up on the roof, Emmy was going through some ballet exercises. Her nude form stood out finely against the backdrop of the green mantled hills and her black hair flew behind her as she hopped and skipped and leaped about over the dark shingles. Seeing the car, she ceased her interesting performance and slowly stalked back behind the sign, looking back at the car over her shoulder.

"She's naked, all right," Sue said. "It looks like a swinging place, Jim. I hope the food's as good as the free floor show."

"Pull the car in, old Wild Jim's getting another one of his urges!" Jim cried.

In spite of her protests, Joan couldn't talk Sue out of bringing the car over to the parking place in front of the Inn where two rustic types in bibbed overalls were stretched out. When they got up, she noticed that one was an Indian. When Sue and Jim got out of the car, she shrugged her shoulders and followed them. Everybody else seemed to be going mad so she might as well join in the gaiety.

When the car stopped, Sam noticed it first. Getting up, he shook Charley Bluejacket's shoulder until he awakened from his sleep, knocking over the applejack in his excitement.

"Charley! Charley! Customers are coming!"

"What? Where?"

"Over there, you idjit! Jumping catfish, will you look at them two females!"

"Hey, you're right! Hey! I think that's—it is! It's Wild Jim Perkins!"

Jumping on top of the railing, Charley gave an ear-splitting war-whoop and launched himself flat out at Jim. They merged in a mass of wrestling bodies and rolled over and over on the ground, scattering gravel as they pummeled each other briskly.

"Hey, Charley!" Sam Mackey yelled from the porch, "That ain't no way to greet a guest!"

"Naw, it's OK," Charley cried. "This ain't no guest, this is my old pal, Wild Jim Perkins! Hiy'a, Wild Jim!" he said, digging a fist into Jim's stomach.

"The Shmohawk Kid himself, I'll be damned!" Jim said, tripping Charley and laying him out on the ground.

"What're you doing in this part of the country?" Charley inquired, kicking at Jim's shins.

"Just passing through on my way to New York," Jim replied, falling on him and getting a good head-lock.

Gradually, the two old friends grew tired of the boisterous exchange and, gasping for breath, they continued their talk on a less strenuous level.

"Yeah, I just did thirty on a vag charge over in Crawford. They let me out today," Jim said.

"Those bastards! They had me for a drunk and disorderly last year. Three hundred years ago, the tribe massacred that town. Sometimes, I'd like to get them to try again and do a better job!"

"If you need an extra gun, give me the word."

"This is our chance, Sue," Joan whispered. "Let's sneak away while we've got a chance. That Indian is as bad as he is and the old one leering at us from the porch looks like the worst of the lot."

"Sneak away? What for? This looks like a fun-place," Sue said, waving at Sam. The motion attracted Charley's attention and he stopped talking to Jim to gape at Sue's buxom form.

"Wowie!" Charley enthused, coming toward her with his eyes showing a lot of their whites. "What a body! Oh, those big, busty blondes! You ain't nothing but curves, are you, honey?"

"You're an Indian, aren't you?" Sue asked.

"I'll say I am. Hey, Blondie, I bet you ain't never done it with an Indian before."

"No, I haven't."

"Well, you ain't never done it if you ain't done it with an Indian, believe me," Charley said, breaking out into a dance and hopping around Sue's robust form while slavering at the mouth.

"He's kind of cute. I like a man who isn't afraid to show how he feels. What's his name, Jim?"

"Sue Lindquist, meet Charley Bluejacket, a guy I used to know back on the Coast."

"Hello, Charley Bluejacket. Are you a poet, too?"

"No, I ain't nothing but a lover," Charley replied. "And I can't hold it back any longer! You and me, Baby, and me and you, right now!"

Howling, Charley grabbed hold of Sue and tried wrestling her to the ground. During the struggle, Sue's dress ended up wrapped around her waist and Jim and Sam stopped to admire this interesting sight before coming to her rescue. Their help proved to be unneeded, however, since Sue, as mentioned before, was a very strong girl. The brief struggle ended with her straddling Charley, her full-fleshed thighs pressing down on his shoulders.

"Now, Charley Bluejacket, are you going to try and get control of yourself?" she asked.

"Oh, Blondie, I don't care what you do to me now! Like, I'm in another world!" Charley cried, lifting his head up and drumming his heels against the ground.

"You have to excuse this here simple savage, Ma'm," Sam said. "He just don't have no self-control when he sees a fine looking girl like yourself. Of course, in your case, I can't rightly blame him for it very much."

"Say, you're a *big* one, aren't you? I always did like big men. Who are you?"

"Sam Mackey, the owner of this here place. Allow me to welcome you to it."

"Hello, Sam," Jim said, shaking his hand. "I'm Jim Perkins, I used to know Charley back on the Coast. The girl with the glasses screaming over there is Joan Barton."

"Howdy, Jim, Miss Barton. Right nice-looking women you have traveling with you."

"Speaking of good-looking women," Jim said, "who was that nude nymph I noticed dancing on the roof when we pulled in?"

"Oh, that must have been my daughter, Emmy. Emmy, come on down here!" Sam yelled.

Emmy appeared on the edge of the roof. Grasping the rain gutter, she hung suspended over the side for a second and then fell lightly to her feet. To Jim's intense disappointment, she was wearing her black leotards now.

"Yeah, Pa?"

"Damn it, girl, how many times do I have to tell you not to run around without any clothes on?"

"I got hot up there, Pa, fixing that roof. If you'd of been up there, instead of laying around on the porch drinking that liquor, I wouldn't have stripped."

"Emmy, let's not have any squabbles. I don't know what's become of this younger generation. So damn lazy they can't do a little work without complaining about it. This is Jim Perkins, the girl sitting on Charley is Sue Lindquist and the other girl yelling over there and trying to get the car started is named Joan Barton."

"Hello, everybody," Emmy said.

"They're going to be guests here. You are going to stay over-night, ain't you?" Sam asked.

"The girls are but I'm flat busted and can't afford to pay for a hotel room," Jim said.

"Shucks, son, no worry about that. If you're a friend of Charley's, you shouldn't mind bunking out with him in the tool shed. As a matter of fact," Sam said, stroking his unshaven chin as he examined the girls' fine figures, "seeing as how you're all the first customers we've had yet, I'll make a special rate and won't charge you nothing at all and throw in a few meals, too."

"Why, that's very friendly of you," Sue said, pushing Charley's head down with one hand. "Did you hear that, Joan? It's not going to cost us anything. You might as well stop trying to get the car started, I have the key."

"So, now that it's all settled, we can all go into the Inn and have a few drinks and maybe get something to eat. We still have a little of that 'possum left, don't we, Emmy?"

"Yeah, but I'll have to stretch it out with a lot of grits to feed this crowd."

"What about Charley here?" Sue asked. "It's going to be hard for me to eat with him hanging on to me."

"You settled down yet, Charley?" Sam asked. "Come on, now, you have to give these girls a chance to eat at least before you start bothering them that way."

"If you'll promise to behave, I'll let you up," Sue said.

"OK, OK, you blonde bombshell. Anything you say, but there's going to be a full moon out tonight and I ain't responsible for what I do when it's like that," Charley said.

"Neither am I," Sue replied, getting off him and finally pulling her dress all the way down.

They all began ambling inside except for Joan. She had given up trying to start the car and sat there with the dazed expression of someone who's just experienced an earthquake. Sue walked over to the car, grinning happily.

"Come on, Joan. They're heating up the 'possum and grits for us. I've never eaten 'possum before and just think, it isn't going to cost us anything."

"You're not serious about this, are you? Do you actually want us to spend the night under the roof with those lunatics?"

"Why not? They look like a lot of fun."

"Even that wild Indian who attacked you right in front of everybody like that?"

"Sure, any girl likes to know that she attracts men. Besides, I know how to handle him."

"How? With a whip and a chair?"

"No, I'll just give him what he wants. Any man who wants a woman that badly ought to get one. Damn it, I'd like to take on all three of them, at the same time, they're so nice."

"Sue Lindquist, I always knew you were uninhibited but I didn't know you were a raving nymphomaniac!"

"Who's raving? That's your trouble, Joan, you always put a label on something and then worry about whether or not you should do it. I do it first and *then* worry about it. Besides, anything that feels so good can't be wrong."

"You're rationalizing!"

"And you're sounding like a raving prude, that's what you sound like! Come on, Joan. You know you really want to."

"Look, Sue, just give me the ignition key and I'll go someplace else for the night and pick you up tomorrow."

"No. For your own good, I'm going to make you stay. You haven't had a man since you ditched that phony play-writer. You need a good orgy even more than I do."

Whistling merrily, Sue went over to the porch where they were already killing the remnants of the 'jack. Joan didn't know what to do. In spite of everything, she had to admit to a kind of curiosity about what would happen at Zach's Inn that night.

"Oh, what the hell, anyway," she finally said and went to join the rest.

# FOUR

"Emmy'll show you your rooms," Sam said when the two girls entered the Inn.

"No sense in bothering Emmy, I'll take them up," Charley volunteered, trying to get around Sam to Sue.

"No such luck, Charley," Sam said, blocking his way. "These here girls need a chance to rest up a little. Now, if you feel like doing something, why don't you and Jim take a run into town and get us some liquor for the party tonight?"

"What, and leave you alone with these lovely babes?"

"Now, that ain't no way to talk about guests, is it? You don't want these young ladies not to have anything to drink, do you? Where's your hospitality?"

"Well, all right, unless Jim here's brought along some tea? Got any pot, Jim?"

"No, I'm sticking to booze for the past few years. Pot is too risky to bother with."

"That's a wise decision, Jim," Sam said. "Straight, honest liquor made from corn, that's the thing to stick to. Can't beat it for keeping you healthy."

"Seeing as how we're just about out of apple-jack, I guess I'll have to go," Charley said. "About how many bottles do you want me to bring back from the store?"

"Let me see," Sam said, taking out a handful of crumpled bills and silver. "I got about six bucks and change on me. Guess that should be enough for two bottles of that *Old Doc Hensley.* Get me some tobacco with the change."

"OK, I'll get it but don't try beating my time with these chicks while I'm gone."

"Wouldn't think of it, Charley."

"Yeah, I bet. Come on along with me, Jim, and tell me how it's been out on the Coast since I left."

"It's changed a lot, Charley," Jim said, following him out to where Sam's rusty 'forty-seven Pontiac was parked. "You were around just about at the end as far as my bunch's concerned. Everybody sort of dropped away in the last few years."

"Any of them do any of the great things they were always talking about?" Charley asked as they got into the car.

"No, most of them are doing the nine-to-five bit, those of them that aren't hung-up on something, in the jug or dead, that is. I felt something like a ghost, hanging around the old places. That's why I decided to come East again."

"Got anything lined up in the City?"

"No. I'll just have to hustle up something. I'm hoping that the change'll do me good. Funny that I stayed out West so long. It feels good, knowing I'll be back in New York in a few days, even if I don't have anything going for me. What about you, Charley? How are you making it?"

"Oh, I had a few deals working for me. I'm supposed to be handyman over at the Inn with Sam now. You never can tell, I might be able to pick up some bread from the tourists. Sam ain't paying me anything but he's easy to get along with."

"How about that daughter of his, that Emmy? Are you getting any of that?"'

"Hell, no! Don't you go trying anything with her either. For a guy who likes chasing women as much as Sam does, he's sure a square when it comes to Emmy."

"Happens that way sometimes."

"How about those two you brought in? You been making out any with them?"

"No, I just met them today. They gave me a lift on the road a few miles from here. Seem like a nice couple of kids."

"That Sue, what a live one she is! Listen, Jim, I hope you ain't got any plans about her because I'm moving in on that! I just have to. That big blonde sends me."

"Go ahead, it's all right with me. The one I like is that Joan. I sort of get a kick out of her."

"The little brunette? She's nice looking, all right, but she seems to be pretty stiff, yelling that way when I grabbed the blonde and everything."

"I have a hunch she'll come around when she gets to know me better, that type of female's like that."

"Maybe, but I prefer them when they're like the blonde and are nothing but ready to go."

Back at the Inn, Emmy had brought Sue and Joan up to their room. It wasn't very luxurious, consisting as it did of a huge, sagging brass bed, several chairs and one small tattered rug over the scarred wooden floor. Being city girls, they had to ask Emmy what the use was for the white crockery placed under the bed.

"So that's what one of those things look like," Sue said when Emmy had explained it's function to them. "I can't wait to use it. See what we'd have missed if we hadn't stopped here, Joan?"

"Yes, it's an experience I wouldn't have missed for the world," Joan replied, testing the mattress. "Say, aren't there any soft spots in this thing?"

"That there's the best bed in the house," Emmy said. "Tell me, are you really going to New York?"

"I thought we were but I'm not so sure now," Joan answered.

"That's where I'm going, soon's the season's over. I'm going to be a dancer, see?" Emmy said, proceeding to leap lithely around the narrow confines of the room.

"I must be dreaming or something," Joan murmured, closing her eyes.

"That's very nice, Emmy," Sue said. "Tell me, is that Charley really an Indian?"

"Oh, sure. He's Pa's second or third cousin, that's why he's working here although I ain't seen him do any work yet. He sure has a yen for you, hasn't he?"

"Well, he was pretty impulsive, trying to rip my clothes off even before I knew his name."

"Yeah, but you don't have to worry about him much."

"*That's* about the best news I've heard since we've come to this squirrel factory," Joan said.

"Now, Pa, *he's* the one that you're really going to have to watch. I got to go now. I got about four cords of kindling I have to chop up by supper," she said, dancing out of the room and down the stairs.

"Sue, I don't know how I let you get me into these things! This whole idea is completely mad."

"You said you were getting bored with Atkins and the clydes there, didn't you? This is certainly different than there, isn't it? Where else could you find people like this?"

"Nowheres outside a production of '*Tobacco Road'* I guess. That sex-mad beatnik poet and the crazy Indian and that big, hulking, lecher of a hillbilly—"

"Aw, I think they're all cute. I think that Jim really likes you, too, Joan."

"Sue, I like a good time as well as the next person but these people are dangerous! There's no telling what any of them are going to do from one minute to the next!"

"That's what we left Atkins for, wasn't it? Because it was so damn stodgy and dull there, we were ready to start climbing the walls! And just think, if it's so wild here in the sticks, think how it's going to be when we get to New York!"

"I give up. I just give up!"

"That's what I'm going to do the first chance I get," Sue said, smiling with relish, "give up. I'm going downstairs now, are you coming too? You don't want the 'possum to get cold, do you?"

"Possum and grits and that—that *thing* under the bed and to think that I wanted to leave Atkins because it was so backward!"

In spite of her complaints, Joan followed Sue down the steps. She hadn't eaten anything since that morning and was quite hungry. Whether or not she was hungry enough to eat roast rodent was a matter she preferred not to think about.

The meal wasn't quite as bad as she expected. The chunks of dark, greasy meat weren't really to her taste but, to her surprise and, it must be stated, chagrin, not much effort was made by the men to try making her. Charley and Sam flanked Sue on each side and, from the way she giggled at unexpected moments, were engaged in undercover activities.

Jim proved to be a witty and intelligent conversationalist and between his talk and the fiery whiskey that he and Charley had brought back, Joan began enjoying herself in spite of her previous doubts about the worth of the group of people.

Charley and Sam were getting in each other's way in their pursuit of Sue and were in danger of knocking each other out of the running. They were beginning to get annoyed with each other but Sue kept them in good humor. When the meal was over, they started drinking in earnest. Sam brought out his guitar and led them all in singing obscene folk songs. He had a mournful, deep voice and played a first-rate guitar, displaying nimble finger-work which didn't surprise Sue any.

"By golly, I'm sure enjoying this," Sam said somewhere during the second bottle. "You girls don't know how dull and miserable it gets up in these hills in the winter."

"It seems pretty now," Sue answered.

"Oh, it's pretty enough, all right. It's just that it ain't no fun having all this scenery around without no gal to show it to. Say, how'd you like to take a little walk up the top of the mountain, Sue? Ought to be pretty tonight with this full moon and all."

"That sounds like fun."

"Hey, you ain't taking her up there alone, Sam," Charley protested. "She goes, I go!"

"Why, sure, Charley. I wouldn't think of going without you. I figure we can take what's left of the bottle and my guitar and your mouth organ and have a fine time. Charley play's a fine mouth organ, you know."

"Let's do it," Sue said. "How about you two? Feel like joining us? It should be crazy! Later, we can strip and chase each other through the woods."

"No, thanks!" Joan answered quickly. "No orgies for me! I'm staying here."

"Same here," Jim said. "I'll stick around and keep Joan company until you come back."

"Don't do me any favors."

"All right," Charley said, getting up. "You wait for me and I'll go get my mouth organ although I don't know why you want to leave a house to go out in the woods at night for."

"Why, haven't you ever done it in the moonlight outside by the trees and everything?" Sue asked.

"Yeah, and I liked it better in bed. I'll be back in a jiffy, Sue. Watch this Mackey character while I'm gone."

"Ah, those Indians!" Sam laughed. "For some reason, they never do trust a white man. Come on, Sue, we might as well start walking up there now."

"But shouldn't we wait for Charley?"

"Why, hell, he won't have any trouble catching up with us on the trail. He's like a bloodhound that way."

"Oh, yeah, I forgot: How about it, you two? Are you going to change your minds and come along, too?"

"No, I plan to just sit on the porch and admire the mountain venery— oops, pardon my Freudian slip," Jim said.

"All right, I'll see you two sometime tomorrow morning. Have fun, kiddies."

Leaning against Sam's lanky frame and holding the almost empty bottle of whiskey while he carried his guitar, she went with him out the door and into the thick trees that grew just outside the back door. Joan and Jim could hear her laughter ringing out as they began ascending the slope.

Jim didn't say anything and the loud ticking of the grandfather clock in the kitchen made the only sound. Taking some of Sam's tobacco, Jim filled his pipe with it, fired up and puffed contentedly away. Joan studiously ignored him, leafing through a two-year-old copy of the *Farmer's Almanac*. Charley came dashing down the steps and came running into the room.

"Well, I found it! Hey, where'd they go?"

"They left without you," Jim answered. "Sam said you'd have no trouble catching up to them on the way."

"Oh, that dirty bastard! That dirty bastard!" Charley cried, leaving the kitchen and disappearing into the trees.

"Charley sure doesn't trust Sam too much, does he?" Jim asked.

"Apparently he hasn't any reason to trust him. Anymore than I have for trusting you."

"You shouldn't say that, Joan. Remember, I promised, on my oath as a bad poet, that I wouldn't touch you the first night if you stayed in some place like this. Come on, let's go out on the porch and look at the stars and talk a little."

At that moment Emmy began practicing her dance steps upstairs. The thuds of her rather large feet made the whole building reverberate and shake.

"All right but just because I'm afraid she'll bring the building down on us. Don't go getting any ideas!"

"Take it easy, Joan. I was just kidding with you out on the road. If you don't want to, that's your business. Hey, what's this?" he asked, taking a light-weight spinning rod out from the corner. "A fishing rod. Maybe I'll ask Sam if there's any good streams around the area. Haven't done any fresh-water fishing in a long time."

"That's surprising, you wanting to do that. You don't strike me as an outdoorsman or anything."

"Oh, I get my best kicks out of nature, it's all those damned people that I can't stand. I used to work on a sport-fishing boat out on the coast at one time, I liked it so much. How about going out with me tomorrow? Some fresh trout should be a change from that 'possum and grits that seem to be the specialty of the house here."

"Maybe I'll take you up on that. I don't know if I care to try that meat again two days in a row," she said as they went outside on the porch. "It's insane for us to even be here! All we're doing is wasting time. The sooner we get to New York and get jobs and settled down, the better off we'll be."

Outside on the porch, they sat on rockers and looked out over the valley. The bright moonlight made the trees cast dark shadows. All she could see of his face was the part illuminated by the burning red flare of a match when he relit his pipe. Out in the back, Sam's Redbone coon hound howled disconsolately a few times and then was still. Propping his feet up on the railing, he leaned back against the chair with his hands clasped behind his head. They could hear leaves rustling in the deep silence.

His silence bothered Joan for some reason. She had been brought up to believe that a stoppage in conversation was something to be avoided at all costs but he obviously was content to simply relax and keep quiet, enjoying the scenery.

"Of course, as far as you're concerned, I suppose it doesn't make any difference when or if you get to New York," she said.

"I could never see anything particularly attractive in this idea of settling down. It seems to me that the only time you ever really can say you're settled down for good is when they bury you. Until that happens, I plan on playing it loose."

"But what are you *doing* with your life, that's the important question, Jim. You seem to be fairly intelligent and I have to confess that I like you more than I thought I would—"

"See? I said you would."

"But what have you accomplished with yourself? You have to admit, very little."

"I don't agree, Joan."

"You admit you're not a good poet, you're broke and wandering around like a hobo; you haven't anyplace to go to or anything to do so how can you disagree? If you were a kid, laying around like this might be all right but you're not."

"Sure, but I've knocked around a little, I've seen various things, I've felt various emotions. All this must be worth something. Certainly as much as if I'd have stuck to one of the jobs I've had in my life. I remember talking to this guy on the first job I had when I was a kid. He was about fifty and all he wanted to talk about was how he'd gone on these two-weeks hikes during his vacations when he was younger. I realized that the only time he'd ever done anything he really wanted to do, the only time he ever really lived, was during those two weeks. I quit the job the next day."

"But what if everybody acted that way?"

"There'd be a lot of miserable jobs open. The thing is, everybody *doesn't* act that way."

"But they—oh, what's the use? I don't know why I'm talking to you this way, I don't have any right to tell you how to live."

"That's OK, Joan. I don't mind."

"I think I'll go to bed now."

"So early? I'll see you tomorrow morning. We can take a walk down to the river and see if I can get any fish."

A serious expression was on Joan's face as she climbed the stairs. It was crazy and ridiculous but she had a very strong hunch that she was about to get involved with Jim Perkins.

Out in the woods, Charley Bluejacket had succeeded in getting lost. Every once in awhile, he'd let out a yell but it was no use, Sam had taken the big blonde off someplace for himself. Oh, that dirty white-eye of a rat! What Charley'd give to have him tied to a stake like in the old days!

Brushes and branches scratched at his face and he kept running into trees and tripping over roots in spite of the moonlight. There was, he knew, supposed to be ways of telling direction from the stars but when he looked up, he couldn't remember anything of what they'd tried to teach him in the Marines about night maneuvers.

The Inn, Charley knew, should be directly down-slope from the direction he'd come, but *what* direction had he come from? He'd been wandering around the mountain for an hour or so and might have blundered onto the other side where there weren't any roads for miles. Slipping, sliding and cursing, he half fell and half walked down from the mountainside, hoping he'd find a road on the bottom.

He didn't.

Succumbing to despair, Charley sat down on a log. There wasn't any getting away from it, he wasn't going to nail the big blonde that night. Taking out his harmonica, he began wailing out the *"Gone Woman Blues"* and waiting for dawn.

Up on top of the mountain, Sue and Sam were sitting side by side in a little clearing. The strong moonlight made the guitar strings glimmer as Sam strummed them and changed the still leaves of the trees to a dark silvery color. Stars blazed haphazardly up in the black sky. When Sam stopped singing, aside from an occasional rustling in the tops of the trees, there wasn't any sound. Far below, they saw a lone car's headlights turn and twist as it followed the road.

"Damned pretty up here when you got a good-looking woman like you along, Sue," Sam said, taking a pull at the whiskey and putting his arm around her waist.

"Glad I came," Sue said, snuggling a bit closer and nestling her head against his shoulder.

"Ain't nothing can be better than holding a well-built woman like you on a night like this. So soft and scrunchy-like," he said, laying the guitar down on the ground and devoting both hands to Sue.

"I like it too but what about Charley?"

"Charley? Forget him, honey. You know how these Mohawks are, always flitting from one thing to another. He probably changed his mind and went off to some bar."

They were in each other's arms then and Charley and the rest of the world outside them was forgotten. His big hands roamed and wandered unhindered up, down and across her supple body. Pushing herself against him, she rubbed her breasts against his chest while her hands did some reconnoitering of their own.

"Say, honey, this here'd be a lot more fun if we didn't have all these clothes on," he said after a few minutes.

"Funny, I was just thinking the same thing," she said, starting to unzip her dress.

"Let me do that, Sue."

"Be my guest."

Gently, he removed the dress and placed it out of harm's way. She could see his eyes gleaming in the weird light as he surveyed her mouth-watering figure. Running his fingers down her back as if he was playing an arrangement on her spine, he found the catch to her bra and loosened it.

"Oh, that black lacy underwear! What it does to a man! I feel like a seventeen-year-old younker again!"

Taking the bra away, he placed it on top of her dress. Sue's breasts were round and full and soft to his touch as he kneaded skillfully, tweaking the pointed nipples and making her giggle.

"Say, you must have had a lot of practice at this sort of thing," she said.

"Well, gal, all those cold winter mornings when I had to milk the cows when I was a boy weren't a complete waste, you know."

"I don't particularly care for the comparison but I sure do go for the results, Lover."

When she began breathing faster and he felt the nipples harden into firm little nubs in his hands, he lowered his reach down to her well-filled panties, kneeling before her as he did so, his bristly cheek pressing against her pliant skin. Lovingly pulling the panties over her wide hips down to her ankles, he reached up again and began rolling her stockings down, taking his time and squeezing her thighs and the area above them.

"What are you doing now?" she asked.

"Taking off your stockings."

"But my stockings don't go that far up."

"You complaining?"

"No Sir! If there's one thing I hate, it's somebody telling somebody who's doing a good job how to go about his business. And you sure know your business."

"I aim to please."

"*Ooooh!* You're doing that all right."

"You ain't seen nothing yet," he said, standing up and holding her close, his fingers grasping her bare buttocks as he kissed first her breasts and then her lips.

"Sam, Sam, I'm nearly going crazy. Let's go ahead and do it before I burn up! I'm ready!"

"So'm I. Just give me a chance to shuck off these duds of mine and we'll really go to it," he said, stripping.

"You're a big man. Big and strong."

"Eager! Eager as a bull busting through a fence after a cow. Eager as a big old buck pawing the ground in the rutting season," he said. He took her by the shoulders and started to lower her to the rock-strewn ground.

"Wait a second, Lover. There's too many rocks around here. Let's look around a bit."

"Why, honey, as far as I'm concerned, we could do it on a bed of nails and I wouldn't mind."

"*You* wouldn't mind but I'm the one who's going to be feeling them, remember?"

"All right, let's go over there in that fresh spring grass. It'll be soft as any mattress you've ever been on."

The thick, springy grass tingled the soles of their feet as they moved further out into the center of the clearing. Embracing each other, they sank down and lay facing each other, hands exploring each other eagerly. They kissed again, their tongues meeting and bodies touching. She could feel her heart beating a mile a minute and she dug her fingernails into his hard muscled back.

"Now, Sam. Now!"

"Yeah, honey. I think so, too."

In her eagerness, she lifted her hips up off the ground to him, her legs spread wide. Bracing himself on his hands placed on either side of her body, he slowly lowered himself and—

"Oh, honey! That's just—about—it!"

"Yes, yes! That's what I want! You, *there!*"

"Where I wanted to be ever since the first time I saw you. Hang on, here we go!"

They fell to with a will, their bodies meshed and working together with increasing speed. He drove forward into her again and again, awakening her to frenzied activity, holding her down as she squirmed and twisted beneath him, pressing down the grass and flattening it all around them.

"Oh! Oh! Oh!" she cried with each of his thrusts.

Above, past his neck and shoulder, she could see the stars, seemingly closer than she had ever seen them before. They seemed to sway and rock in the air just above them, dancing and shaking in place. Their frantic motion increased and, just as they strained against each other's bodies one last time, she thought she saw a shooting star flare up in a flaming path across the horizon, burning up its short-lived life as she trembled and then was still.

Again he began and again she responded to him, feeling the hard ground and soft grass beneath her dissolve as he lunged forward, again and again. Arching her back, she threw back her head as the stars and the moon and the trees all whirled about like lights on a merry-go-round gone berserk with a mad-man at its controls.

Still and warm, they lay, not moving, breathing deep and fast. The air grew cold on their damp skin and they finally separated. He stroked her well-used body and she could see his teeth gleam in the moonlight. Smiling to herself, she shook her hair and stretched out her limbs while he fondled her tenderly.

"Nice way to spend a night, isn't it, Sue?" he asked.

"Beats television."

## FIVE

Joan was still awake when Sue came into their room late that night. The bed was too uncomfortable with its sloping sides and sharp springs and she hadn't been able to stop thinking about Jim.

"Hello, Joan," Sue said, throwing her wadded up lingerie onto one of the chairs. "Still up?"

"Yes, I couldn't sleep. I guess there's no need of my asking how it went with Sam?"

"Fabulous, Joan, fabulous! This mountain air really does something to you. That Sam is all man. You know what he did? It's hard to believe but—"

"Spare me the details, I don't want to know."

"All right, if that's the way you want it," she said, taking off her dress and letting it fall to the floor. She turned herself around in front of Joan, asking, "Are there any marks on me? He's one of those guys who doesn't know his own strength and he got plenty excited out there on the mountain."

"And I guess you were calm, cool and collected? No, your skin is as lily-white as ever."

"Don't worry, Kathy Winters, I was plenty hot and bothered too. But he cooled me off and he did it the right way, the best way. How'd you do with the poet?" she asked, getting into the bed.

"He's not really such a bad guy at all, he was a perfect gentleman all night."

"Gee, that's too bad. I thought he was a live one, too."

"Well, he did promise before that he wouldn't lay a finger on me the first night, remember?"

"Oh, yes. Well, maybe you'll have better luck with him tomorrow."

"He said something about going fishing. Say, do you have to lay all over me that way or haven't you had enough loving with that hillbilly up on the mountain?"

"I can't help it, it's the way this bed sags. I bet this old bed could tell some stories, eh, kid?"

"Well, can't you at least put something on? It's kind of disturbing, having you plastered all over me naked this way."

"Disturbing? Don't tell me you're getting a little gay on me. Don't worry, I won't say anything to anyone."

"Sue Lindquist!"

"It's all right with me if you go that way but nothing tonight, Joan. I've had my sex-quota already."

"Will you stop talking foolish? You know I'm not—oh, what's the use? Listen Sue, I let you railroad me into this situation but I think it's time we decided what we're going to do. We've had our fling and we'd better start making plans for leaving here. I think we should go the day after tomorrow."

"The day after tomorrow? If you're in such a big rush to get away from here, why don't you want to leave tomorrow morning?"

"Well, Jim asked me to go out with him tomorrow and I sort of hate to disappoint him."

"Aha! So that's the scheme! I guess you were doing more than just roasting pop-corn and listening to the crickets while I was gone with Sam. Go on, you can tell me."

"Nothing happened and if it did, I certainly wouldn't tell *you* about it. It's just that I found he's really not such a bad person after all. It's just that he doesn't have any common sense and he's lazy and he's irresponsible and a little crazy but aside from that, Jim's really very nice."

"Well, suppose you tell me about all those good qualities of his tomorrow morning? I've had a pretty good work-out and have to get some sleep," Sue said, curling up against Joan so that their backs touched one another.

"All right. Good night, Sue."

A little after dawn, Jim came into the room, carrying the spinning rod he'd found the previous night. Walking over to the bed, he looked at the sleeping girls and grinned. The concave curve of the mattress had thrown them into each other's arms and the blanket had fallen to reveal Sue's bareness to her navel. He admired her for several seconds before swatting Joan on the fanny.

"Oh!" she yipped, coming awake almost instantly. "Goodness, what are you doing here?" she asked, trying to burrow underneath the blanket and also waking Sue.

"Humm? Oh, hi there, Jim. Welcome to our bed. Want to join us for awhile?" Sue asked.

"That's the best offer I've had today. Hope I'm not breaking anything up between you girls but we're supposed to go fishing, remember, Joan? Come on downstairs, Sam's got breakfast cooking for us."

"Will you get out of here?" Joan cried, pulling the blanket up.

"OK, if that's the way you want it. Speed it up a little, will you? I don't want to waste any more time. See you later, Sue."

"Come again soon," Sue said as he left.

"How did he get in here? Did you leave the door unlocked?"

"Lock that door? What a laugh that is. All the keys in the hotel are the same. Sam told me last night."

"That's reassuring," Joan said, getting out of bed and taking off her pajamas. Hunting thru the bag she'd brought into the Inn, she finally selected a pair of shorts and a red striped blouse.

"That's a real sexy figure you have there, Joan," Sue said, watching from the bed as she dressed.

"Stop kidding. We all know you're the reigning sex-pot in this room."

"Don't sell yourself short, Joan. Well, have fun out there with the fish and Jim. I have to get some rest if I'm going to go another round with Sam tonight."

When Joan came down the stairs and into the kitchen some ten minutes later, she found that Jim was the only one there. He was standing at the coal stove, cooking something in a frying pan that smelled good. A few dishes were set up on the table.

"That smells good, what is it, 'possum again?" she asked.

"No, it's something better than possum. It's smoked hog jowl and scrambled eggs. Sleep good?"

"Don't go bringing that up again. I'm still mad about you sneaking in the room like that."

"I didn't sneak in, I walked right in like a man. You looked very chummy in bed."

"Don't go starting that business again."

They ate breakfast which turned out to be very good. The coffee was black and strong and the sliced strips of hog jowl were much tastier than any bacon Joan had ever eaten.

"Where are we going, Jim? I haven't seen any streams or lakes nearby where you could use that rod."

"Sam told me about a little creek way up behind the mountain. He says there's some nice pools in it where he's picked up some good trout. It'll be a few miles hike but he makes it sound good. Besides, I won't have to worry about any game wardens back there."

"Oh, yes, I forgot about licenses. When were you talking to Sam? I don't see him around anywhere."

"He took his hound out to track Charley. He's lost, you know. Sam says he gets lost every time he so much as steps foot into the woods. I don't imagine Charley'll give him much of a friendly welcome after that trick Sam played on him last night."

They left shortly after eating breakfast in the cool of the morning. Joan had some skepticism about being alone with him but he acted the gentleman still. Carrying a few sandwiches and some beer, they walked easily, taking their time and carrying on a lively conversation that covered many diverse topics.

After a couple of miles, they came to the narrow creek that Sam had mentioned. As soon as Jim saw it, he knew that there would be some good trout in it. It just looked fishy. Leaving Joan in a small meadow bordering the stream, he took off his shoes and socks, rolled up his pants and proceeded to wade slowly downstream, drifting a worm he picked out of a clump of grass roots before him.

The bait was snatched off the hook before he'd gone ten feet. Stopping to fill one of the pockets in his jacket with a handful of worms, he continued downstream. Several hits later, he picked up the first trout, a strongly colored native brown about eleven inches long.

He came to a surprisingly large pool where the current from the stream had under-cut a sycamore, causing it to fall into the water. The submerged tree looked like a natural place for the boss trout of the stream to hang out. Putting on a small wobbling spoon, Jim cast over the sunken branches. The golden spoon winked in the sunlight as he retrieved. It was just past the tree when a shadow, the size and shape of the wide end of a canoe paddle, rose up from the deepest part of the pool and snagged the spoon.

The slender rod bent double as he screwed the drag down tight to keep the fish from fouling the line in the tree. Splashing into the water, he waded in over his waist, trying to scare it away from the tree. The trout didn't jump but stayed deep, making long, stubborn runs.

Coming to the top, it ran parallel to the stream bank and he saw that it was a big, hook-jawed brown, the spoon's treble hook hanging barely by one barb from its mouth. Loosening the drag, he let the fish run out into the center of the pool again, slowing it just before it reached the tree.

Finally, the fish tired enough so that he could work it within his reach. He was just sliding it into the shallow water when it suddenly made one last run. Shaking its head, it broke off the hook and the lure was yanked into the air, landing in the branches of a bush behind Jim. The trout was in sight for a few seconds and then disappeared into the gloom of the deep water.

"Damn! I bet it would have gone over five pounds, too," he said aloud.

Sitting down on the bank, he lit his pipe. There wouldn't be any sense in trying to fish the pool for the rest of the day. He'd put the big one down good. The thing to do would be to come back early in the morning, before sunrise, and float a live minnow down into the hole. That might work.

He decided to work his way back to where he'd left Joan. Maybe he'd have better luck with her.

When Jim had left her, Joan had felt a little puzzled and more than a little insulted. Here she had let him lure her into the woods and he was ignoring her for some fish! How was she going to rebuff his advances if he didn't make any?

The day grew warmer and she stretched out on her back, closing her eyes, feeling the warm sun on her face. Birds sang and the wind skimmed through the trees. Reaching out, she grabbed a handful of grass and smelled the sharp, heady odor of the fresh spring juices. It seemed to go to her head, charging her body and making her tremble with sudden, rushing desire.

Nothing like this had ever happened to her before. An aching longing engulfed her, a lust for Jim and his maleness, an awareness of her youth and her woman's need. Her hips moved against the ground of their own accord, her thighs pressing together as she grasped her breasts and squeezed them.

Realizing what she was doing and what she would look like if he should happen to return, she stopped but the fires of spring ran riot through her, leaving her panting and tense. She got up, her feet strange and weak beneath her, and looked down the stream to where he was slowly approaching.

What was happening to her?

It was as if all of the restraints and checks of a life-time were dissolving and falling away. Giving herself wholly to the mood of the moment, she began taking off her clothes in a torrent of ever-mounting lust. Her clear skin glowed ruddily in the downward slanting rays of the sun and she lifted out her arms to his far-off form.

"Jim! Jim!" she cried.

Seeing her nude figure beckoning him forward, Jim reacted as one might expect him to act. He dropped his fishing rod. Hurrying toward her, he stripped on the way, leaving a trail of his discarded clothes behind him on the bank. By the time he reached her, he also was naked and in the mood.

"Hey, Joan," he said, scrambling up to where she was standing, "What set you off?"

"Don't talk, just—"

Not a complete fool, he didn't bother saying anything else but just snatched her off her feet onto her back. She was rising to meet him just as he moved over her. Not bothering with any preliminaries, each wildly excited, their bodies met and strained toward each other, meeting and joining.

The ripe smell of spring in their nostrils along with the odor of their thoroughly aroused bodies, every muscle taut and tense, sliding and jerking against each other, they rode a wild race with each other's lust.

Faster and faster, they gave themselves completely to the frantic coupling. Limbs entwined, slippery with sweat in the hot day's sun, they both reached their goal at the same time. She gave a soundless cry as he drove into her, her arms raised straight up in the air and then fell limply in the sharp-bladed grass.

Ceasing, they lay in the same position for possibly a full minute and then, releasing his breath, he took himself off her. Her eyes opened and she looked at him. He put his arm across her, stroking her smooth skin and smiling.

"And I thought Sue was the sexy one! When you make up your mind to do something, you go right ahead with it, don't you?" he said.

"I don't know why I did it that way. I've never let myself go like that with anyone before in my life."

"Should do that more often."

"But why did I do that? It was like something had taken hold of me, as if I couldn't help myself."

"Well, *I* was around. Isn't that enough of a reason for you to get a little, er, excited?"

"Be serious, Jim."

"You don't believe in flattering people, do you, Joan? Here I was, thinking that you finally realized what a virile and handsome kind of guy I am."

"Well, you *are* very virile, not that I've had too much experience along that line."

"Thank you."

"I just remember crushing some grass and then—wow! I couldn't control myself any longer."

"I'll have to remember about that grass business. Might be a fortune in it if I could bottle it."

"Jim, you don't think I'm turning into a nymphomaniac or something, do you?"

"Nope. I just think you had a slight case of delayed spring fever. I recommend you stop worrying about it and just enjoy it."

And that's what they did the rest of the day.

After swimming in the cold, clear water of the stream, they wandered naked through the forest, feeling as if they were the only humans on the planet. Coming to a copse of towering hemlocks, they spent most of the remainder of the day laying in the thick carpet of pine-needles, exploring with ever-growing wonder the glory of each other's bodies. When the tree shadows lengthened, they regretfully put their clothes on and went back to the Inn.

Sam didn't find Charley until late in the day. Charley didn't express joy at Sam's approach. As a matter of fact, he narrowly missed bouncing a rock off Sam's head as he approached.

"Now, cool off a little, Charley!" Sam called out, ducking behind a tree.

"Oh, you dirty rat! What a mean, miserable trick to play on somebody who's worked hard for you like I have! Sending me out in these damn woods with who knows what kind of wild animals and snakes around, not to mention all those bugs!"

"I'm right sorry about all this, Charley."

"Sorry!" Charley cried, shelling another rock towards him. "I'll bet you're sorry. What a rotten, white-man's trick you pulled. And to think you claim to be my kin!"

"Ease up, Charley. I brought a bottle of liquor up here for you. I figured you could use a snort."

"I need a drink all right but that's all I want from you. Don't talk to me."

"I did it all for your own good," Sam said, coming out of his shelter.

"What do you mean, *my* good? It was *you*. That's all you were thinking about. That's all you ever think about. You never think about other folks, even a good friend like me what's kin to you and working for you," Charley said, taking the bottle and drinking. "As far as that goes, I ain't working for you no more. I quit!"

"Listen, I know it wasn't a nice thing to do," Sam said, sitting on a stump. "I just didn't want you to feel hurt, that's all."

"Didn't want me to feel hurt! How do you think I felt wandering around running into trees and falling all over myself all night? I nearly got myself killed, walking off a bluff."

"I just wanted to save you from that cruel, cold woman, that's all. After you'd gone, she kept on saying how little she thought of you, saying how ugly and ornery and scroungy you looked. I didn't want you to get your feelings hurt by having her turn you down when you tried getting her."

"Don't give me that baloney, Sam. I know that girl goes for me, I knew that when we were wrestling around out in front of the Inn yesterday. I love that girl!"

"Love her! Who are you trying to kid? You know damn well that there ain't a woman in this world can keep you for more than a week or so at most."

"I didn't say that I loved her for all time or anything like that. I just mean that I want her more than anything in this world, at least until I get her."

"I didn't know you felt like that."

"Hell, you know I always feel like that every time I see a good looking gal."

"I'll tell you what I'll do, Charley. I'll give you a fair crack at her tonight, no competition."

"Huh? Hey, that must mean that you—? That you and she must have spent the night?"

"Well, yes, we did, now's you mention it."

"Oh, you big bastard, if you were forty pounds lighter, I'd take you apart, here and now! Don't spare me, tell me how she was. No, don't, I couldn't stand it!"

"It was right interesting, I have to say."

"Oh, hell! Listen, Sam, let's get this straight—you promise to keep out of it tonight, right? None of your white-man's tricks or anything?"

"Sure, I promise you. I won't even stay around the place. I hear that Chuck Rebly's organizing a coon hunt tonight I'll take old Blue down and join them."

"OK, Sam, I'll give you one more chance. If you do as you say, I'll even come back to work for you."

"Now that's a relieving thought."

"But if you double-cross me again, I'm coming for you! I know I can't handle you in a fair fight, Sam, so I won't even try that. I know how to handle a gun fairly well, though!"

"I don't think you know what you're saying. Don't go threatening me, Charley. I don't like it."

"And I don't like spending a night out in the woods, either!"

"OK, don't go getting yourself het-up," Sam laughed. "I guess I was wrong in doing that to you last night. I'll give you this one free night with Sue and you better make the best of it because I have a hunch I'll be getting that old urge again pretty soon."

"Listen, one night with me and you might as well forget her."

"We'll see, we'll see."

\* \* \*

When Joan and Jim came out of the woods, arms around each other, Sue saw them and came out of the Inn.

"Have a good time?" Sue asked. "No, don't bother answering that question, it's very easy to see that you have. Glad to see that you took my advice, Joan."

"Pretty country back there on the other side of the mountain. Where is everybody?" Jim asked.

"You've got me. The only ones left in the place have been me and Emmy. She says that Sam's out hunting for Charley. Claims he got lost looking for us last night."

"There anything to eat in the kitchen? I picked up one trout but then I got distracted from fishing."

"Emmy cooked up some corn-pone if you're hungry enough for that. How'd it go with Jim, Joan?"

"Why don't you two go up to your room and talk about it? I think I'll take a nap on the porch for half an hour or so," Jim said.

"Must have had a hard time this afternoon. Still, it's nice work if you can get it, as the song goes," Sue said.

Jim had just started dozing off when Charley and Sam came out of the woods and sat down on the steps, the bottle of whiskey resting in between them.

"Hello, Jim," Sam asked. "Any new guest arrive yet?"

"Not that I've heard."

"Good. I'm pretty satisfied with those we have now."

"You're certainly not going to make much money out of us, Sam."

"Maybe so. I don't know, Jim, I'm beginning to think that I'm just not cut out for the hotel business. Sure don't want to have to go back to farming again, though."

"It's a miserable thing, this having to earn a living. Never could quite get the hang of it myself," Jim said.

"I don't know, you seem to be a fairly smart fellow. Poet and all that. Any money in that kind of work?"

"None at all. The only way you can make a buck out of that racket is if you're a heavyweight fighter or an Irishman, particularly a drinking Irishman."

"Well, you ain't big enough to be a heavyweight fighter but maybe you could tell people you're Irish and work it that way."

"You know, that's an idea. I might just try that when I hit New York. Yup, I think I will! It'll be great kicks to see how long I can pull it off. Not a poet, though, a playwright, that's the thing that they go for in the City!"

"Playwright? You ever done anything like that before?"

"No, but I bet I can work it so I can get something produced. I only know a few people in New York and they'll keep quiet about it if I give them the word. What I'll do is write something for the Theatre of the Absurd."

"How do you go about that?" Sam asked.

"I think the accepted method is to get stoned on pot while you're writing the play, but I won't bother with that. The important thing is to insult your audience and keep everything moving so fast that they can't follow the action. I think I can do that. It'll be boss kicks. What do you think of the idea, Charley?"

"Charley's sleeping. He's plumb tuckered out from walking around all night."

"I'm going upstairs and tell Joan. She's just been yapping about how I don't have any goals. I'll have to brush up on the accent before I hit New York, too."

"Say, I have some old Barry Fitzgerald records down in the cellar. What you can do is play them a few days and imitate the way he talks. He's Irish, I think."

"Good move. I'll see you later, Sam."

When Jim opened the door to the girls' room, he found Joan lying on the bed wearing a towel around her head while Sue, equally unclothed, sat on a chair, applying polish to her toe-nails.

"Hi, Jim. What's new?" Sue asked.

"Hello, girls. I have great news, I've—"

"Are you crazy!" Joan cried, pulling the blanket over her. "What's the idea, breaking into the room like that?"

"I still don't understand you, Joan," he said. "Here we've spent the whole afternoon naked together and you go getting excited just because I come into your room without knocking."

"It's different now. Besides, what about Sue?"

"Hmmm, yes. What about Sue? You don't mind me coming in here now, do you?"

"It's all right with me. I guess I'd better go downstairs. It looks as if Joan here's getting another one of her attacks of shyness. Throw me that pair of slacks over there, will you, Jim."

"Sure. Here you are. You know, Sue," he said as he watched her wriggle into the slacks, "maybe you'd like to come along with me and Joan the next time we go over the hill?"

"That's what I like in a man, confidence in himself. Think you could last the route, though?" Sue asked, pulling a blouse over her head with difficulty.

"I wouldn't mind trying."

"I'm game but I don't think Joan here's quite ready for orgies yet. She's still a little bit of a square."

"I don't think either of you are being a bit funny," Joan said.

"See what I mean? She still needs a little loosening up," Sue said, departing.

Kicking off his shoes and pants, Jim got on the bed next to Joan and stretched out luxuriously.

"Ah, that feels good. This is the first real bed I've slept in for over a month now."

"Couldn't you have waited until I asked you?"

"Well, I assumed I'd be welcome," he said, drawing her to him and kissing her while his hand slid down her back. "How about it, Joan? Am I welcome?"

"Oh, all right. Say, before you go any further, what was it you wanted to tell me when you came in?"

"Oh, that. Nothing important. I've just decided what I'm going to do when I get to New York. I'm going to be a playwright."

"A playwright?"

"An Irish playwright, which is the best kind there is."

# SIX

Charley possessed a tremendous talent for sleeping and was still out, dead to the world on the porch steps, when evening came. Putting his Ruger twenty-two into his hip pocket and whistling for his hound, Sam started to leave.

"Where are you going, Sam?" Sue asked. "There's still a full moon out, you know."

"Yeah, ought to be prime coon hunting. Kinda promised the boys me and Blue here'd show tonight."

"I guess I must be losing my allure or something."

"I'm getting a mite elderly, you know. Don't have quite as much recuperative power as I used to."

"You couldn't prove that by me."

"Howsoever, I expect old Charley Bluejacket'll be glad to keep you company."

"Charley? Well, I always was a great one for variety. Funny that they call them the vanishing race when they've got such a go-getter as Charley with them."

"Oh, I don't know. I don't think he's got more'n four or five kids scattered around."

"That's pleasant news."

When Sam stepped over Charley's reclining form, he gave him a kick in the ribs to wake him up. Thinking he was back in jail for a few seconds, Charley woke up fighting. A short scuffle followed that ended with Charley being flung down the steps.

"Damn it, Charley," Sam said, "If you're just going to spend the night sleeping, I might as well not go out. I thought you wanted that woman?"

"Don't you worry none," Charley replied, swatting dust off his clothes. "I was just recharging my batteries. I'm all set now and that girl's going to have the time of her life."

"She's all your'n now."

Sam and his hound got into the front seat of his Pontiac. Charley watched to make certain that he really was going then slowly entered the Inn. Tonight would be the night, all right. He wanted the big blonde as bad as he had ever wanted a woman. It was important that he didn't foul things up. He'd have to play it real cool. Subtle, that was the way he'd make his play.

"Hi, Charley. Get a good rest out there on the porch?" Sue asked from where she was sitting by the table. Charley noticed she was wearing a very tight blouse and an even tighter pair of passionate purple slacks.

"Would you like to go to bed with me?" he asked.

"I guess so, seeing how the television set you've got isn't working very well."

"Ain't nothing good on anyway."

They grappled a bit in the kitchen but she held him off, but not without some difficulty.

"You sure are a fast starter, aren't you?" she asked, her face a little flushed from her efforts.

"Can't help it, you're the most woman I've seen around these parts all winter long," he said, reaching a hand out for one of her two most prominent features.

"Cool it, will you? I thought you wanted to use a bed, not a kitchen table!"

"OK, let's get up to your room then."

"Can't. Joan and Jim are using it. They're listening to old Barry Fitzgerald records."

"Old Barry Fitzgerald records?"

"Yeah. It takes all kinds to make a world, you know."

"No matter, there's all kinds of rooms up there and they all have beds in them."

"Let's go, then."

Charley was something of a romantic and had been a great fan of Clark Gable. When they got to the staircase, an impulse came to him to try and emulate Gable in the famous scene in *Gone With The Wind* where he carried Vivian Leigh up the stairs. However, he forgot that Sue was a considerably hefty girl and that the lifting of heavy weights had never been one of his strong points.

As it was, he managed to carry the giggling girl halfway up to his goal before he began staggering from the wall to the banister, gasping for breath and almost falling.

"Charley!" Sue yelled, "I think we'd better scrap this bit! If you ruin yourself, you're not going to be much good for me when we get upstairs."

"I think you're right. Give me a hand the rest of the way, will you?"

By the time they got to an empty room, Charley was recovered enough to give her a hand, stimulating her into letting out a delighted squeal of pleasure. Wrapping his arms around her, he nuzzled at her neck. Then he reached under her blouse with both hands at the same time and fondled the soft half globes of flesh he found there.

"Hmm, that's nice," Sue purred. "You're pretty good at this, aren't you? I didn't know you Indians were so romantic."

"Baby," he whispered, taking his lips off her fair skin for a second, "What do you think we do in those wigwams all winter?"

"Hooray for wigwams then!"

Pushing the blouse up until both fine breasts were freed to his glittering gaze, he kissed them thoroughly from their wide base to the pointed pink-tinted tips, straining his body against hers and maneuvering them both to the beckoning bed.

"Oh, Charley my boy, you merry Mohawk, give me a little room to get the rest of these things off," she said when she felt herself touching the end of the bed.

"Mmm-mmh!" Charley replied, being somewhat occupied.

Unwilling to remove his mouth from its succulent position, he held his face to her bosom while feverishly divesting himself of his clothes while she, giggling all the while, stripped also. When she was bare in the glaring light of the unshaded lightbulb, he stepped back several feet in order to get a good look at her.

"Oh, boy, what a set of boobs!"

"Like me?" she asked, turning slowly so that he could admire every smooth, clear, curve she had.

"I've always yelled about how the white men have fouled this country up but it's almost worth it, if they bring such wild-looking broads like you with them."

"From looking at you, I have a strong hunch I'm going to be glad I came here."

"You said it, you big Scandinavian squarehead, I'm going to make you so damn happy, you're going to zoom up to the moon!"

"Squarehead? I never did like that name. You see anything, anyplace on me that looks square?"

"No, baby, you ain't nothing but round," he said, grabbing her at some of her roundest parts.

Smiling happily, she let herself fall backward onto the bed and he came onto her like a dark tide roaring into a white sandy beach, his fingers making deft forays around and over different parts of her body while his lips kissed her in places where she had never expected to be kissed.

Up and down, fore and aft, topside and down below he went his ticklish way, making her twist and roll as if she was trying to work her way through the mattress with anticipation. Squeezing her breasts so that nipples stood up, she held them while he alternated kissing first one and then the other.

Her light blonde hair hanging loose on the pillow like a golden cloud, she moved her head from side to side. Her lips pushed out and only a sliver of white showed between her eyelids as she moved her thighs against him.

"Oh, Charley, Charley," she murmured.

"All right, baby. All right."

"Now, honey, now."

"Yeah," he said, raising himself over her.

Things were progressing nicely in the other room with Jim and Joan, also.

Jim had just played *"They Sailed Away From Galway Bay"* for the sixteenth time. Joan lay on the bed, the sheet wrapped around her and a pillow pressed against her ears. When the record came to its rousing finish, she took the pillow away.

"Jim Perkins, has anybody ever told you that you were more than a little crazy?" she asked.

"Faith and many's the man that's told me I was a wee bit daft, my buxom Coleen."

"And stop with that phony Irish accent! I think I must be crazy, myself, to be in the same room with you!"

"Sure, and name me a gossoon that wouldn't be driven stark, staring mad by the sight of your loveliness? What there is of it I'm seeing, that is," he said, sitting next to her and stroking the smooth sheet where it covered her hips.

"No, Jim! Stop that!"

"Ah, Joan, my black-eyed lass, I'm not understanding you a bit, at all, at all. We've spent the day tripping through the trees with nary a stitch on and you not minding it at all but here, in this great, lovely room, you wrap that beauteous form of yours like you were a mummy in a museum."

"This afternoon was this afternoon, but now is now!"

"Sure, and a pretty bit of logic *that* is!"

*"Will"* you stop that? It's time we started thinking about things, making plans so we can decide what you're going to do."

"Aha, but I know what I'm going to do," he said, bending over her and kissing her forehead.

"Be serious, will you?"

"That I am, that I am," he said, lowering his face to hers again and getting clouted with the pillow.

"I warned you!"

"You're a darling girl, Joan, but I wish at times you weren't so everlasting serious."

"Somebody's got to be serious around here! Look, Jim, I still don't understand what you're trying to do. You claim that you're going to be a playwright, which is crazy enough, but you're not even trying to write! All you're doing is listening to those records of Sam's and talking like a character out of a Sean O'Casey play."

"But, Joan, me lovely, don't you be seeing the method behind my madness?"

"Will you be stopping the Irish accent? Goodness, now you've got *me* doing it!"

"Nowadays, my naive girl, the writing of the play is the last thing you worry about. It's establishing the fact that you're a character that really counts."

"You shouldn't have any trouble with that part of it!"

"And the best kind of a character to be is an Irish character. Look at Dylan Thomas—"

"He was a Welshman."

"Same difference. Now tell me this. Do you think if Robert Frost had carried on like Thomas did the authorities'd let him? Do you think he'd of attended inaugurations and everything if he'd gone around pinching college girls on their bottoms? Do you think an American playwright could get away with raising hell the way Behan does? Why, they'd have him before a psychiatric board in nothing flat for daring to enjoy himself!"

"But, you big lug, these men can write! They succeed in spite of the way they act, not because of it!"

"Sure, my wise little filly, but do you think the men who put up the money for plays'll see it that way? All they'll know is that a few wild micks have also been wildly talented and when they see Shamus O'Shaugnessy—"

"Oh, no! Shamus O'Shaugnessy! You!"

"With his little frizzy mustache I'm going to grow, wearing a cloth cap and a scarf though its mid-summer, why they won't dare *not* back my play. All I have to do is throw a few good drunks, something I have a natural talent for, and I'll be set."

"How about the play?"

"Oh, I'll knock that off soon's I'm able to borrow a typewriter from somebody. Something wild with a typical American family. You know, domineering mother, useless father, hideous kids, a little incest, some homosexuality. All of the current clichés, in other words."

"But why? If you do get enough rich lunatics to produce your play, you still know it won't last past its opening night, if that far. What's the purpose of it all?"

"Why, think of the laughs we'll have when it's over."

"Laughs! That's all you think about, isn't it?"

"No, there's other things I'm thinking about this very instant," he said, sliding his hand beneath the sheet and touching her cool, sleek skin along her belly.

"Jim, I'm trying to be serious!"

"Call me Shamus," he said, caressing her in slow circles around her navel.

"Now listen to me, you—oh! Oh! *Oh!*"

"Yes, my wild rose of the Catskills, let me be getting this shroud of a sheet off that fine figure of yours and my own clothes off and I'll be joining you on that bed and if you want to keep talking, why that's all right with me. But I don't think I'll be doing much listening, I'm afraid, Joan, my love."

"Damn you, Jim or Shamus or whoever you are! I don't know what you do to me to make me act like this, but get out of those clothes and over here! Fast, fast!"

At the very moment Jim started to join Joan on the bed, Charley was likewise engaged with Sue. Alas, though. As the poet might have said, the best planned lays oft go astray.

It all happened down in the kitchen where Emmy had put a flame beneath the coffee pot. She was wearing, naturally, her leotards and was practicing bounding energetically from one end of the kitchen to the other, thinking of the wonderful time she would have when she reached New York. A strange man would meet her there; a very handsome man, tall and dark and young, and they would travel all over the city and he would make love to her, really make love to her; not just use her like Phil did that time in the woods.

And it would be fine and wonderful from then on.

Lost in her imaginings, she didn't notice the gust of wind that blew the curtain toward the stove or the way it somehow burst into fire when it flapped near the coffee pot. When she did notice it, the window sill, old and dried out, was already burning.

"Fire!" she yelled, picking up the dishwater and throwing it at the blaze. The water didn't seem to stop it at all, it was going too strong for that. The wind gave another gust, sending the flames in toward her and singeing her eyebrows. She started to run outside but, remembering the others upstairs, ran up the steps instead, as billows of smoke began filling the corridor.

"Fire. Hey, Charley, the place's burning down," she cried, dashing into their room.

They were at a time and position where one finds it almost impossible to think of anything but the business at hand. With the strength born of desperation, Emmy rolled them off the bed and broke them apart. The shock of landing on the hard floor brought them back to this world, but they still didn't seem to notice the smoke pouring into the room from the door.

"Emmy!" Charley cried, outraged. "What the hell are you trying to pull, in here?"

"Run you crazy idiot! The Inn's burning down!"

"What do I care? Get out of the room if you're going to carry on like this, pushing people out of bed and everything."

"Hey, wait a second, Charley! I think she's right. The joint does seem to be on fire," Sue remarked.

"Oh, hell! I think you're right. Just my miserable luck! I guess we'd best shag out of here, eh?"

"That sounds like a good move. Joan! I just remembered her! Are they still in their room, Emmy?"

"I guess so."

"Come on, we've got to get them out of there!"

The three of them ran into the room where Jim and Joan were, crashing through the door with a cloud of smoke. Joan had insisted that Jim turn the light off and they had to waste time searching for the switch. When they put the light on, they discovered Jim and Joan in roughly the same position that Sue and Charley had been in. Jim and Joan did not welcome the interruption.

"For the love of Mike," Jim said, looking up, "I know there isn't much to do up in these parts but can't you find something else to gawk at?"

"The place is burning! The place is burning!" Sue, Emmy and Charley all cried out.

"Well, what do you want me to do about it? Say, now that you mention it, it does seem a bit warm and smoky in here. What do you think, Joan? Should we shag or try to make it first?"

"I'd think it best we leave."

"I guess you're right. I wouldn't be able to keep my mind fully on it anyway. Wrap the blanket around you, Joan, in case of cinders. What's the best way to get out of here, Emmy?"

"The stairwell seems to be gone. I guess we'd best get on the roof over the porch and drop off from there."

"OK, let's go!"

The floor in the corridor was hot beneath their feet and wisps of smoke were rising from between the boards as they made their way to the window that led to the porch roof. Hurrying to the edge, Charley and Jim jumped down first. On the ground, they held the blanket out and caught Sue and Joan in it. Emmy came down in her usual manner.

The flames lit up their bare bodies luridly as they spread quickly throughout the building, roaring out the windows. Black smoke blotted out the stars and the terrific heat forced them back toward the highway where they stood, watching.

"Sure makes a good fire, don't it?" Emmy remarked.

"Yes, it does at that," Jim said. "Well, Joan, there doesn't seem to be much we can do about it so shall we go back to what we were doing before it broke out?"

"Are you out of your mind?"

"You know, Joan, it gets a little tiresome, you asking if I'm nuts like that all the time."

"Then stop making those crazy suggestions all the time!"

"What do you think we should do then?"

"Well, we could . . . why, we could call the fire department, that's what we could do!"

"Yes, I guess we could do that. Seems to be too far gone to be able to stop it now, though."

"Hey," Sue said. "Speak of the devil, look, isn't that a fire engine coming? Yoo-hoo, firemen!" she cried, waving and standing in the middle of the road.

The Boys' Corner Volunteer Fire Truck, with its full complement of incompetents aboard, came roaring down the road, stopping with a great screeching of brakes just in front of Sue's stalwartly standing body. Zeb Hawkins, the leader of the group, was at the wheel and he bit the end of his cigar off when he saw Sue.

"Hello, there, firemen," she said, smiling politely at them.

"H-h-how do, Ma'am. What seems to be your problem?" Zeb asked.

"Well, we have a fire. Right over there, see?"

"Huh? Oh, yeah, so you have."

"We were wondering if you'd care to put it out for us?"

"Well, mebbe so. Kind of caught you a little by surprise, didn't it, ha-ha."

"Come on back under the blanket, Sue," Charley said, taking her by the arm and leading her to where the others were huddled. "Old Zeb'll never even get started with you around looking like this."

All under the blanket, they watched as the fire burned fiercely away through-out the whole structure. Emmy began crying.

"There, there, Emmy," Joan said. "It's not that bad. At least no one's hurt."

"But now I'll never be able to get to New York!" she wailed.

"Don't worry, maybe Sue and I'll take you with us when we go there. Do you think you'd like that?"

"Oh, boy, would I! Go ahead an' burn down, you big, ugly building! Burn till you're nothing but black ashes!"

"Too bad we don't have some frankfurters or marshmallows," Jim said. "We could at least get some good out of this."

"Youch!" Joan yawped. "James Perkins, can't you think of anything except sex?"

"It wasn't me," Jim protested. "Hey, Charley, what gives with you? Ain't one woman at a time enough for you?"

"Sorry, my mistake," Charley apologized. "There, is that you I have now, Sue?"

"Yep. It's me all right."

"I think it's starting to get a little crowded, all of us under the same blanket," Jim said. "Why don't you and Sue slip away into the brush, Charley?"

"Yeah, I think that's our best move. How about it, Sue? You can watch a fire any old time."

"All right. Maybe we'll set a blaze of our own that'll make this one look like nothing."

Sue and Charley moved back in the brush and no more was seen of them, except for an occasional rustling of leaves, for the rest of the night. The blanket draped over their shoulders, Jim and Joan stood next to Emmy, their arms around each other. The fire brigade stood around, seemingly more concerned with looking at Emmy and Joan than with the blazing building.

"Say, Joan, what say we sneak off and emulate Sue and Charley for awhile?" Jim asked, giving her a hug.

"I'd like to, but they'd all *know* what we were doing."

"Who, those so-called firemen standing around out there? Hell, Joan, they've probably got the right idea about us anyway. After all, standing around naked underneath a blanket together . . ."

"I know, we can go over to where the car's parked and I'll be able to get some clothes out of my other suitcase."

"How about me? I don't feel like wearing one of your outfits. Think I'd just as soon stay the way I am now."

"Don't you have anything except what you left in the room?"

"I've got some extra duds in the toolshed but the way these yo-yos are acting, that'll catch fire from the main building any second now."

Adopting as casual an air as possible under the circumstances, Jim and Joan walked past the leering faces of the firemen to the car where Joan slipped on a light summer dress.

Out in the hills, the coon hunting party had just gone to work on the second jug as the hounds struck up a trail. There were seven of them, standing and squatting around in a clearing on top of a mountain, passing the liquor around, smoking and chawing while they listened to the dogs bay. Chuck Rembly noticed the glare of the fire first and he pointed it out to Sam.

"Looks like a bit of a blaze over there, Sam. That's around where your place is, ain't it?"

"Hell, yes. Ain't nothing around there but my place. Must be burning down."

"Too bad. Guess you'll be heading down that way, eh?"

"Guess I'd better see if anyone's hurt."

"Too bad it had to happen tonight and spoil the hunt for you."

"Can't be helped. Old Blue comes back, bring him around to my place, or what'll be left of my place, tomorrow, will you, Chuck?"

"Sure."

It was a two mile down-hill walk back to where Sam had his car parked but he made good time. Hell of a thing, the way things turn out. Here he was, figuring on taking it easy for the rest of the summer, maybe even the rest of his life and this here silly fire had to come along and ruin everything. He'd have to go back to that miserable farm, damn it. Wasn't anything else he knew how to do. He groaned out loud, thinking about it.

When he got back to the Inn, he found the firemen standing around, passing a bottle from hand to hand and watching the blaze. The whole structure was covered with streaming flames and the noise it made was audible for over a mile around.

"Hello, Sam," Zeb said as he came up to join them. "Mighty nice fire you got here."

"Glad you're enjoying it, Zeb, but don't you think you should be doing more than just watching it?"

"Well, hell, Sam! It's too far gone to be able to do much."

"Where's Emmy? Hey, Emmy, you all right?" he called. "How about the others?"

"I'm OK and so are Charley and the rest of them, Pa."

"That's good. Now listen here, Zeb, I know the Inn's gone but I think we can still save the shed. I think we'd better save that shed or else I'm liable to get a little mad about all you just standing around like this, understand?"

"Well, don't just stand there!" Zeb cried, running up to the others. "Let's see if we can save the shed at least."

They all began moving then, including Jim who had the blanket wrapped around his shoulders like a cloak. Several times it looked like they would lose everything but, after several long, scorching hours, the house collapsed on itself and burned itself out. Charley came out of the woods with Sue and went into the shed where he and Jim put on some clothing. Sue also, to the disappointment of the fire brigade, got herself dressed.

Nothing was left of the Inn except the shed and a great mound of smoking cinders when dawn came. The fire brigade left after standing around for awhile. Sam, Charley, Jim, Emmy, Sue and Joan were left standing where the porch used to be.

"Well, I guess it's back to the farm for me," Sam said.

"How about insurance?" Joan asked.

# SEVEN

"Insurance? Your uncle Zach have any insurance on the place, Emmy?" Sam asked. "I seem to remember some sort of papers around mentioning insurance."

"Yeah, I think so, Pa. They're in that there metal box with all the deeds and things."

"Fire insurance?" Joan asked. "Do you know when the policy was supposed to lapse?"

"Don't remember. I never did pay any attention to those things. I last saw the box in that little desk just inside where the front door used to be. Soon's these ashes cool down a bit, I'll try to dig it out though I guess they're probably all burned up, too," Sam said.

"That doesn't matter," Joan said. "The insurance company'd have their copy of the policy. All you have to do is check up with them. What company was it?"

"I ain't sure but I imagine Zach had the deal through that Carson fellow over in town. He's about the only one who handles that sort of thing around here."

"Let's go in and check up on it."

The whole crowd got into the girls' car and drove the five miles into town. Jerome D. Carson had his offices over a feed store. They all climbed up the rickety stairs and piled into his cluttered office. Carson was a small man in his fifties with a habitual sour expression on his pinched features. He looked up from his desk when Sam led the others in.

"It certainly didn't take you long to show up here, did it, Mackey?" he asked sarcastically.

"We came about that insurance that Brother Zach had on his Inn. It burned down last night, you know."

"So I've heard."

"I'm wondering if he carried fire insurance on it?"

"You damn well know he did! I've just been going over the policy he took out, Mackey, and I've made a very interesting discovery about an amazing coincidence. I suppose you know what I'm talking about, don't you?"

"No, I don't," Sam said, resting his fists on the table and leaning over.

"The fact that that policy was due to lapse today! And you have your fire last night!"

"Do tell? Sure was lucky, wasn't we?"

"Get off it, Mackey! I'm not buying that and neither is the company. Who are all of these other people? They figure on getting some of that money too?"

"They're friends of mine."

"Well, you can all forget about it. Not only aren't you going to collect but if I have my way, you'll all end up in jail for arson because of your stupid little scheme."

"Disagreeable little bastard, isn't he?" Jim said.

"Who are you? The one who thought up this idea?"

"Knock it off, Carson," Jim replied. "You're bluffing and we all know it. That was a legitimate fire. Hell, I nearly got burned to death in it."

"Let me handle this, Jim," Sam said. "I'd like to get this straight, Carson. You're claiming that I set that fire a'purpose; that I risked the lives of my own daughter and these other people just because I wanted that there insurance money?"

"You're damn right that's what I'm saying. You—"

Carson was unable to finish his sentence because his voice was choked off by Sam's hands around his throat. Sam lifted him up off his feet while Carson kicked out his feet frantically. Sam still hadn't changed his facial expression.

"You know," he remarked, "I bet I could throw you right through that there window over there."

"I don't know, Sam," Jim said, rubbing his chin thoughtfully. "He doesn't weigh too much, it's true, but that still would be a hell of a good heave."

"Bet you a beer he could do it," Charley said.

"On the fly?"

"Sure. Sam's strong as hell. Go ahead, Sam. Heave the little bastard."

"Wait a second Pa," Emmy said, "I think he's trying to tell us something. See how purple his face is getting?"

"Oh, yeah, so he is," Sam said, lowering Carson to his feet but still retaining his grip. "I don't suppose your throat feels so good you want to talk too much for awhile, but are you trying to say that you're apologizing to me and my friends here about what you said?" Carson nodded his head vigorously in the affirmative. "And that you're not going to give us any trouble about the insurance? That's good. Now you just get over there and keep out of the way unless I want you. Joan, you seem to be a right smart girl. Why don't you take a look at that there policy for me?"

"All right, Sam," Joan replied, examining the document "Hmmm, that brother of yours, Zach, he wasn't very loose with his money, was he?"

"Zach? He was cheap as hell. Why?"

"Well, he only insured the Inn for one quarter of its value which comes to four thousand."

"Four thousand! Hot damn!" Charley exclaimed.

"Why, that's a right nice pile of cash," Sam said, breaking out into a grin.

"That's wonderful!" Emmy cried, leaping around the room. "Now I can go to New York!"

"This calls for a celebration, everybody!" Sam yelled. "We'll all head for the White Oak Bar. And you, Carson. You get right to work on getting that money for us, understand? Don't answer me 'cepting to nod your head. I feel so happy, I might just twist your neck off out of good spirits if I heard you open your mouth again."

The noisy procession went its way across the street and into the large, dimly-lit bar. The bartender looked a little worried at seeing Sam and Charley come into the place but he made himself look friendly when they lined themselves up in front of him.

"Hi, Sam. Ain't seen you for quite a spell. Hear you had a little trouble out at your place last night."

"A mite, just a mite. Burned down, you know. Old Zach, he had some insurance on it, though, and we ain't as bad off as we might've been. Set 'em up all around," he said, throwing his last twenty dollar bill on the table.

Beer, booze and coke (for Emmy) flowed freely as they toasted Sam's good fortune in not having to work any more, at least not for the rest of the year. There was a recording of *The Stripper* in the juke-box and Sue gave an impromptu performance that nearly sent the several farmers who wandered in climbing up the walls. When one of the farmers tried grabbing her, a lively argument followed that ended with Sam throwing the farmer out the back door, without opening it.

"Sure is nice, being rich this way," Sam beamed, coming back to the bar, rubbing his skinned knuckles.

"What are you going to do with all that bread?" Charley asked.

"Hardly been able to think about that, everything's been happening so fast. Just think, a few hours ago I was sweating having to go back to some farm or a factory or something and now I don't have to. Kind of makes a man think, it does."

"What are you going to buy?"

"Oh, I figure a new guitar first off. Maybe even one of those electrical kind."

"Don't forget New York," Emmy said.

"Sure, sure. Maybe a new car, too."

"Sam, don't be silly and spend it all at once," Joan said. "It really isn't that much money when you think about it. What you should do is invest it in something safe and secure, possibly go into another business."

"Joan's right," Charley put in, "you don't want to just let all that cash blow away. What you want to do is put it into something that's sure fire. Now, with that four grand, I could open up another summer camp that'd probably double your investment in less than a season! All we'd need to do is buy—"

"That's not the sort of investment I mean!" Joan protested. "What you should do is put it into the bank and forget all about it. Get a job someplace until you can make up your mind about it."

"That don't seem like much fun!"

"What about me, Pa? What about that trip to New York you said I could go on?" Emmy complained.

"I think you should just take the money and have one big party with it until it's gone," Sue said.

"No! That'd be silly. Save it!" said Joan.

"Damn it, I didn't know it was such a bother to have money! What do you think I should do with it, Jim? Everybody else's had their say about it."

"I always thought travel was a good thing for a man. There any place you ever really wanted to go to, Sam?"

"Hell, yes, there is, now that you mention it. Always had a hankering to go back to New York myself when I had a little cash. Only was there once when they shipped me overseas during the war. I didn't have too much fun there 'cause I was broke and that ain't no place for a poor man but now, with all this cash, I could set myself up proud!"

"That's a pretty good idea in a lot of ways," Charley said. "There's plenty of ways to make a buck in the City if you've got some cash in back of you. The trouble is, Sam, you're really nothing but a country boy at heart. Those sharp city-hipsters'll be on you like a chicken chasing a bug for your dough."

"Yeah, I'm afraid you might be right, Charley. What I'd need would be some younger, smarter man to kind of look after me. I don't suppose you'd be willing, would you, Charley?"

"Sure I will! What sort of friend, what kind of kin do you take me for, Sam? I wouldn't think of deserting you now that you've got the burden of all that cash bothering you."

"That's mighty white of you, Charley!"

"I don't like the way that was put exactly but I'll let it go for now," Charley said.

"How about you, Jim? Care to stick around with me when we get to New York? Maybe I could back you in that play you were talking about. I think I'd like that, grabbing at all those chorus girls and everything. I could be an important man then."

"Not with the play I'm thinking about. I tell you what, Sam. If you'll stake me to a place to sleep and chow-money, I'll split anything I make out of that deal with you. It's best that you be calling me Shamus from now on, though."

"Fair enough. How about you girls? You're all not going to desert me now, are you?"

"I don't know, Sam. What is it you have in mind?" Sue asked.

"Why, I figured you could live with me for a spell, Sue."

"That's a straightforward answer. Sure, why not? I'm certainly in no rush to get back to a desk in some office. You're going to have to rent an awfully big place for all of us, though. Still, me and Joan will be glad to—"

"Hold it!" Joan cried. "I've been involved in this madness long enough! Sam, don't you see what they're all doing?"

"What are they all doing, girl?"

"Why, they're—they're *using* you! All of them just want to stick around you while you have the money so they won't have to go to work. I don't like to say it but it's true."

"Hell, I know that. Doesn't matter, though. I'd do the same if it was them who had the money."

"Sure. What's wrong with wanting not to work?" Jim asked.

"It's wrong, Jim," Joan said. "There is, after all, such a thing as morality and decency and—"

"Listen, Joan," Jim said, "If you start making a speech about morals, I'll pour my drink over your head. It's a tendency of mine to do that when I've had a few."

"Hear, hear!" Sue said. "I'll join you in that."

"All right, all right, do it your way," Joan said. "But, when it's all over, don't say I didn't tell you the right thing to do, Sam."

"I wouldn't want to deprive you of that pleasure, girl. Now's the time to drink, though."

"On to New York!" Sue cried.

"We'll take Manhattan," Jim said.

Part of Joan, her practical, sensible part, told her to leave them all but somehow she couldn't bring herself to do it. In the several days since she and Sue had picked up Jim, she had to admit to herself that she had the most fun in her entire life. Like a gang of happy lunatics, the whole bunch seemed to go along carrying a cloud of madness along with them, sweeping you in with them whether you wanted to join them or not.

A very serious person, Joan knew that it was every citizen's duty in the current crises to spend at least a few hours a day worrying about the national and world-wide state of affairs but, since she'd met Jim and the others, she hadn't even been curious about them.

A shocking state of affairs.

Jim was the worst one of the lot. Not half as stupid as he acted, he was more blameworthy than any of the others. Where did he get the nerve, someone as intelligent as he was, to go around being happy? Worse still, she found herself reacting to him more strongly than ever. He had only to enter a room where she was and she could feel herself responding joyfully to his presence.

The whole group spent the next week in an alcoholic daze. They all lived in the tool shed. Sam sold his Pontiac and used the money to buy food and whiskey. Joan could not help but join the rest in the long orgy. It had about everything a successful orgy should have; a lot of sex (naturally) much drinking and eating and a great deal of plain and fancy loafing.

Jim spent a few days trying to catch the big trout he'd hooked earlier but had no luck since he brought Joan along with him and they usually ended up in the meadow where they first made love. For awhile, time ceased having any meaning.

As the weather grew warmer, more and more car-loads of tourists started appearing. As they passed the ruins of the Inn with Sam and the others laying around in the sun passing a bottle around, they would shake their heads in a superior manner, thinking, the way some people let themselves live! Then they would speed past, not wanting to waste any of their precious two weeks.

The money finally came through and everybody sobered up to go to town and pick it up. Sam insisted on taking it all in cash. They went into the White Oak Bar and looked in stunned silence as Sam stacked the big pile on the bar.

"Man oh man! Ain't that pretty!"

"What a sight," Charley said. "What do you figure on doing now that you finally got it, Sam?"

"Hell, I figure on doing what I said I'd do, take it to New York and see what happens!"

"Hot damn, New York! When do you figure on leaving?"

"Right now! That's one good thing about that fire, we won't have to worry none about packing. We'll have one drink, pile into the girl's car and be on our way!"

"New York, here we come!"

"Say, Sam, before you go, don't you think there's something you should do first?" Joan asked.

"Huh? Can't think of anything we can do here we can't do better in the big City."

"I'm talking about your daughter. She hasn't had anything to wear except those leotards for over a week now!"

"Oh, yeah. They do look a little ragged at that. There you go, Emmy. Take some of this money and buy yourself another pair of those things if you want."

"Gee, thanks, Pa! I think I'll get some that's flesh-colored this time!"

"I'll go over to the store with you, Emmy," Joan said, taking a handful of money. "Maybe I'll let you buy some leotards but no flesh-tones! With your figure, that'd drive every man around you insane. Of course, the crew you have around you now has given you some experience so you could probably handle them."

"There you go with that crazy talk again," Jim complained. "Hell, you can't say you were acting so almighty sane and sensible last week up on the mountain when you—"

"Never mind that! Come on, Emmy, we're going to get you properly clothed again."

"What a kill-joy!"

"Say, you boys think I ought to spruce up a bit, seeing as how I'm going to live in New York now?" Sam asked.

"Sure but don't buy anything here. Get it in the city where the prices are cheaper," Jim said.

"This is all so exciting," Sue said, getting onto Sam's lap and downing a stein of beer. "I'm so glad we stopped and picked you up that time, Jim. Look at all the fun we would have missed."

"That's, going to be nothing to the fun we're going to have when we hit New York. It's been a long time since I've been in that town. I wonder if it's changed much."

"Where do you think we should look for a place to stay when we get there? There's quite a crowd of us, you know."

"If it's anything like it used to be, there'll be only one section where this bunch'll be able to live without any questions being asked. Greenwich Village."

"Greenwich Village?" Sam asked. "That sounds kind of small townish, don't it? I was figuring on raising hell in the big town."

"Don't worry, Sam. The Village is where the rest of the town comes to raise hell. Besides, it's not that far to go uptown."

A half-hour later Emmy and Joan came back to the bar, carrying an arm-load of boxes. Emmy had on a lemon-colored dress that made her figure even more voluptuous than when she wore the leotards.

"Emmy, you amaze me," Jim said, "you look even sexier with a dress on than without one."

"I tried to get something conservative to sort of tone her down a little," Joan said, "but it wasn't any use. She'd have to wear a space suit or something if she didn't want to look sexy."

"Well, folks," Sam said, gently pushing Sue off his lap, "I guess the time's come to get on the road if we want to get to New York before it gets dark."

"Let's go then."

Stuffing his pockets with the bundles of bills, Sam waved farewell to the bartender and led the way outside to the car. The six people had a tough time cramming themselves into the close quarters of the car but they had been living so intimately in the preceding weeks that none of them minded too much.

They took their time, stopping frequently to stretch their legs and refresh themselves at the many bars that lined the highway. Emmy and Jim were the most excited; Emmy because she was going someplace that she had wanted to go for many years now and Jim, because old memories came back to him with every mile of the trip as they approached the great city.

Strange, the way things worked out, he thought. When he'd gotten out of the service, he'd really intended going back to New York but somehow, it just hadn't worked out that way. While he didn't consider the years he spent on the Coast wasted, he couldn't help thinking of how different things might have worked out had he come back East the way he'd planned.

"What are you thinking about, Jim?" Joan asked. "You're the most serious-looking I've ever seen you."

"Just ruminating about my wasted life, Joan," he said, putting his arm around her waist, she being seated on his lap. "Sort of wondering if things'd be any different if I'd have come back East the way I planned instead of staying on the Coast."

"Don't tell me you're finally coming to your senses after all these years? What were you thinking of doing back here if you'd have returned then?"

"Oh, I had the G.I. Bill then. I had some vague idea about going to school around New York and killing four years that way. I wonder what I'd have done if things'd worked out that way? Maybe I'd have some kind of good racket going for me by now. More likely, I'd have spent all this time hanging around the Village and wishing I'd have stayed out on the Coast."

"It was stupid of you to just let that chance fall through your fingers, Jim. You should have tried to go to school out in California someplace."

"Hell, I used the Bill, I went to school on it."

"You didn't tell me that. What college did you go to?"

"I didn't go to a college, I went to bartender's school for a year. I did pretty good at it, too. I'm a pretty good bartender, Joan, except for the fact that I can't stand having people around me all the time, particularly when they want those damn-fool concoctions you have to mix like a chemist."

In the late afternoon, they entered New Jersey. The sun cast long shadows when they got onto the George Washington Bridge and saw the far-off towers gleaming in the reddish light.

"Well, look at that, will you?" Sam said. "New York itself. Makes quite a sight."

"Oh, ain't it lovely!" Emmy said. "I don't think there's anything I've ever seen I thought was prettier. Where's Times Square at, Jim? Can you see it from here?"

"No, Emmy, not good. Cut off onto the right when you get off the bridge, Sam. If I remember right, that's the best way to get down to where we're going."

As they tooled down the Westside Highway, fighting the rush-hour traffic, every occupant in the car began to feel the faster beat of the city infuse their bodies. Jim felt as if he was returning home again after a long absence. Pulling Joan closer to him, he kissed her on the back of the neck and sent his hand exploring beneath the folds of her dress.

"Feel it, Joan? Feel the pulse of the city taking hold of you?" he whispered.

"I feel something, all right, and it isn't the pulse of the city!" she said, trying to fend his hand away.

"You like it. Admit you do. There! I felt you that time. You sure have nice legs."

"Are you crazy? The others!" she whispered hoarsely.

"Don't mind us, Joan," Sue said. "We've got our own affairs to keep us busy."

"See, Joan, me fine beauty, there's nobody else to worry about so just be relaxing and enjoying it."

"There you go with that accent again! Are you serious? And stop tickling me with that mustache!"

"Sure and you'll know how serious I am when you see the name of Shamus O'Shaugnessy up in lights on Broadway."

"How far do you reckon we have to go before we turn off, Jim—I mean, Shamus?"

"Not too far, Sam, me bucko. What we'll do, lassies and lads, is stop at some bar, pick up a paper and see if there's any places around where we can get a big, cheap apartment. Will you look at all the new buildings they went and put up since I've been here last? And it's hardly been ten years."

"Jim, don't these buildings and everything kind of make you feel a little, well, scared?" Joan asked.

"The name is Shamus, remember? Shamus O'Shaugnessy scorns the word fear, he does! And what's so frightening about all these big piles of masonry and concrete anyway?"

"Oh, be serious! This is a big city, Jim. It's one thing to have all of those wild schemes and dreams up in the mountains where it doesn't really matter but the time's come to stop playing around. This is a big place, Jim, the biggest in the world! You can't go around acting so impossibly irresponsible around here. Look at those buildings. They look ready to grind you to nothing at any second!"

"Hey now, my girl! I thought I was the one with the imagination here! Sure and the buildings are nothing but bigger versions of Sam's building and you saw what happened to it! And the people are nothing but . . . people. 'Tis just that there's more of them."

"Stop talking that way, Jim! I mean it!"

"You are serious, aren't you? What is it, Joan? What's bugging you? Beside me, of course."

"This whole wild jaunt we've been on for the past week or so, that's what's bothering me! Are you actually planning to try and work that wild scheme of yours?"

"Sure, why not?"

"And the rest of you, you're just going to go your merry way the way you said you would back in the mountains, I suppose? All live in the same apartment and just spend your time drinking up Sam's money while Sue just goes from one to another like a bouncing ball?"

"That's the idea, Joan," Sue said. "What's wrong with it?"

"It won't work, that's what's wrong with it. You must know that. Why don't you wake up now and save yourself all that grief?"

"You're trying to say something, Joan. What is it?" Jim asked.

"Just this. I've had it. It was great fun up in the mountains, I have to admit that. Now the time has come to be practical. Sue, I think we'd better live the way we planned to before we met Jim. Get a little apartment for the two of us, scout up some work and then go out looking for fun."

"Hey, what about me?" Jim asked.

"It's been great fun, Jim. I've never met a man I liked as much as I like you but I think we'd better not see each other for awhile after this."

"Awhile? What does that mean?"

"It means until you straighten out and start living in the real world! I'm sorry but that's how it has to be. How about you, Sue?"

"Damn it, Joan, I'm going to miss having you around," Sue answered.

"All right if that's the way you want it. Just let me off at the YWCA."

"Oh, no! The *YWCA!*"

## EIGHT

They dropped Joan off after going up-town and then came down to the Village again. Losing one of their members was a big let-down for all concerned. Sue was crying and Jim looked as if he wanted to. It was too late to look for an apartment so they took rooms in a grimy roominghouse over on the East side.

After leaving their gear there, they went to a Village bar and started drinking dark beer. Everything seemed to be turning into a drag although Emmy was still excited about being in New York and asked Jim if he'd show her Times Square.

"Sure and why not? 'Tis like a morgue in here. How about it, everybody? A bit of the bright lights might brighten us up ourselves. I wouldn't mind it myself."

"Fine with me," Sam said. "The last time I was there, I was stone broke but I don't have that trouble now!"

"Say, Sam, I'm thinking it'd be best if you were to put all that money in a safer place than your hip-pocket. Why don't you put it in traveler's checks or something 'till you can bank it?"

"Hell, if somebody's able to take this away from me, they're welcome to it! Besides, it ain't as if I wasn't heeled, I still have this," he said, yanking out the Ruger twenty-two. " 'Course it's only a little bitty gun but still—"

"Sam! Put that away before somebody sees you! You'll get jugged!"

"Why, it's all right I got a permit for it from the sheriff back home."

"That doesn't mean anything here. Believe me, Sam, they take that Sullivan Law strict in this town. You'd best take it back to the room and leave it there."

"Well, I guess you know best about the ways of the City. Seems like a lot of fuss to make over such a little gun. Just used it when I went coon hunting. Sorry I couldn't bring my dog with me to the City here but I always heard New York wasn't fit for a dog to live in. That's why I let Chuck have him. Hope he's all right."

"Now don't start getting homesick on us on your first night, Sam! You just got here."

"Ain't that so much. Just that the only two things I had that were any good was the dog and my guitar what got burned up. Hey! That's something I can get tonight, a new guitar! Hey, Bartender! Any places around here where a man can get himself a good guitar?"

"Sure is," the bartender called back. "There's a place where all the folk-singing bit is sold about five blocks down the street."

"Hot Damn! That's for me. You children go off by yourself and have a good time. I think I'll pick me up one of those electrical guitars like I've wanted so long."

"Then we'll be seeing you later. Take care now. I wouldn't be drinking the hard stuff if I was you, not with that wad you're carrying. We have some of the finest pick-pockets in the world working in this city."

"No, fear, Jim—I mean, Shamus. You'd better brush up on that there accent of yours, boy. You keep falling out of character."

"Sure, and I've been noticing that, myself."

All of them except Sam got in a cab and went up to Times Square. It was flashy, cheap, vulgar, silly and more than a little sad. Emmy got a great kick out of it all and so did Sue and Charley. Jim couldn't revive his spirits, though. He kept thinking about Joan.

They did the tourist bit all the way and, close to midnight, they found themselves in front of the *Club Piyaki,* a belly-dancing joint. They were all pretty well lubricated by this time and they stood in a swaying mass in front of the place.

"Hey, what's this here?" Charley asked, hanging on Sue with an arm around her neck.

"Greek place. Haven't been in one of these for quite awhile. Feel like going in?"

"Sure do!" Charley said, looking through the window and catching sight of one of the girls swirling around in a trail of veils.

"Looks like a fun place at that," Sue said.

"Let's go in," Emmy said. "I ain't never seen a real dancer before and that's why I wanted to come to New York."

"I don't know if that's the kind of dancing you've been thinking of, but Sam gave me the money to show you something of New York so let's go in," Jim said.

Since it was a week-night, the *Club Piyaki* wasn't crowded. Most of the customers seemed to be Greeks and the *bozooki* players had turned the sound system off so that it was possible for them to hear themselves talk. They took a table up front and Jim ordered *ouzo* and *raki* all around.

"Oh, will you look at those crazy guitars!" Emmy said, leaning forward. "Too bad Pa ain't here, he'd be interested in them."

"There's some other things around here he'd be more interested in, I think," Sue said.

Charley looked as if he was being hypnotized by the glittering jewel set in the G-string beneath the dancing girl's navel. A dark, exotic-looking wench with high cheekbones and straight black hair and an amazingly supple body, the dancer revealed terrific muscle-control and rhythm as she kept the veils fluttering like pennants flying from a ship in a hurricane.

The wild music picked up the beat and she leaped and shook with abandon from one side of the stage to the other, giving herself fully to the nautch dance. The audience roared its approval at every twitch of her taut torso.

"Ain't she wonderful!" Emmy cried. "And that music! I can hardly keep from dancing to it myself!"

"Maybe you'll get the chance, Emmy," Jim said. "Some of these joints let the audience in on the act. Oh, oh! There they go!"

The number came to its close and the male customers all left their seats in a rush to participate in the old custom where, when a dancer has been especially good, they push dollar bills into her scanty costume. Smiling widely, the girl snake-hipped her way around the stage while the men clustered about her sweat-gleaming body.

"Jim! Give me some money!" Charley cried.

"OK, go to it!"

Grabbing a handful of dollar-bills, Charley bulled his way to the front and began pushing the bills into her outfit while she rolled her hips and belly in a tight circle. A sly grin on her lips, she pressed her moist skin against him, hands joined over her head and hips pulsating rapidly.

The music ceased without warning and she turned and ran off to the dressing room. Charley tried to follow her but was stopped by a husky young Greek stationed at the door who wrestled him back to the table where the others were sitting.

"Take it easy, Sport. She's got another number to do later, just cool it till then."

"Pardon our friend here," Sue said. "He gets a little carried away with himself at times."

"Why don't you girls give it a try yourselves?" the Greek asked, his white teeth gleaming in a friendly leer. "This is Amateur Night, when we let the girls from the audience take a crack at it."

"I'm game. How about you, Emmy? Here's your chance to be a dancer in New York the way you wanted."

"Tell them there guitar players to rev up, Mister and then stand out of our way."

"OK, Boys!" the Greek cried to the band. "We've got a couple of live ones here!"

Emmy and Sue jumped up oh the stage as the band picked up the beat once more. Sue, nearly stoned out of her mind, didn't do much except stand in one place on the stage, laughing and jiggling. At any other time, this would have guaranteed that every man in the surrounding area would have kept his attention on her but it didn't work out quite that way this time.

Emmy was coming into her own.

Somewhere, way back in her family tree, which certainly was varied enough, Emmy must have had some Eastern blood in her for she picked up the rhythm and style of the dance right off. Kicking off her shoes, she stepped back and forth over the stage, head thrown back and hair streaming behind her, stepping high and shaking every part of her body that could be shook.

Everybody came up front, some standing on top of the tables, all clapping their hands and stamping their feet to keep time as they yelled their applause. Though Emmy didn't have anything on except her regular street clothes, with her wild figure and wilder movements, she put on a performance that nearly set the stage afire.

Twisting, turning and stamping her feet, she laughed over the noise of the crowd. Catching the idea from her, Sue began varying her motions, drinking down a bottle of beer as she did so. Unable to restrain himself anymore, Charley jumped up on the stage also and did a stiff-legged grunting dance of his own in front of Sue.

The young Greek also got into the act, kicking at the wooden planks of the stage, yelling and grabbing at Emmy's swiftly moving body. She kept just out of his reach, her eyes glittering with excitement as he maneuvered his way around her.

The club turned into a bedlam then. People were shouting, jumping up and down on tables, pouring liquor down their throats and over their bodies, fighting and falling and generally having a very good time. The musicians played so fast and strong that they began breaking the strings of their instruments.

They didn't stop though and the leaping and yelling went on. After some ten minutes, people began dropping out and staggering to their seats where they sat, gasping for breath and cooling their throats with beer. After awhile, the only ones left on the stage were Emmy and the Greek who were still going at it hot and heavy, the sweat running in rivulets down their faces and necks.

The crowd grew hoarse from yelling and just clapped their hands and stamped feet to keep time now. The two figures on the stage, the tall girl and the muscular young man, whirled about at a faster and faster rate as the bozooki's went mad trying to keep up with the frantic beat they set up.

Finally, as the music rose to a crescendo, he grabbed her, picked her off the floor and carried her back to the table while everyone in the room cheered.

"Oh, baby, you're good," the Greek said, placing her on a chair and falling back on one himself, wiping his face with a handkerchief. He raised his arm and one of the waiters came running. "Bring out some of that champagne for this table, Al. I just worked up one hell of a thirst."

"Quite a performance you two put on," Jim said. "I guess maybe you are a dancer after all, Emmy."

"You're damn right she is! Where've you worked before, Emmy? I'm Nick Mazides, I own the joint."

"Why, I ain't never tried nothing like that except when there wasn't nobody around back home, Mr. Maz—Mazer—"

"Call me Nick. You're a natural, kid, a real natural. Why, if you were to do that bit with one of the girl's outfits on, you'd drive everybody out of their minds!"

"Do you think so?"

"I know so! Ah, there's the champagne! Drink up, everybody, it's on me. You folks from the city?"

"No, we just got in, Nick," Jim said. "I'm Jim—I mean, Shamus O'Shaugnessy, just in from the ould sod, this here is Charley Bluejacket, one of the noble savages of this fair land. The big blonde is Sue Lindquist and the young lady is Emmy Mackey."

"Any of you related to the young lady here?"

"Nope."

"I'd like to make her an offer. Are you interested in working in my joint, Emmy?"

"Sure am!"

"What do you say to an even hundred a week, just to start with, of course. You'd just have to work six nights a week. The other girls will show you the ropes and maybe we'll see about a raise if you come along like you should."

"That sounds—"

"No, I don't think so, Nick," Jim said. "Emmy's father brought her to New York to get an education, not work as a stripper. He probably wouldn't go for it."

"What? Why, Pa wouldn't mind. I don't think," Emmy said.

"Wait a second," Nick said. "What's with this stripper business? All I want her for is a belly-dancer. It's like an art-form, you ask any of the girls."

"I doubt he'd go for it. Certainly not for a measly hundred bucks a week."

"Hell, what's wrong with that? Where else could she make that kind of bread? Besides, she ain't nothing but an amateur. You admitted that yourself."

"So what? You saw what she did to the crowd here tonight and she didn't even have the outfit on."

"Look, I'm out of my mind to do this but one of the girls is going back home next week and I've got an opening. Tell you what, I'll go for one twenty-five a week."

The bargaining went on until the club closed. Waiters were going around stacking chairs on tables and sweeping the littered floor by the time Jim got the price up to one seventy-five.

Nick said, "For a mick, you bargain like a Greek! I tell you what I'll do. I'll take her for one week at that price and we'll see how it works out. Sometimes a girl'll come out of the audience and set the place on fire like that but freeze when it's for real."

"I still have to check with her old man."

"You go talk to him, if you don't have any luck, I'll give it a try. Say, me and Shamus here've been talking so much we haven't heard from you, Emmy. What do you think of the bit?"

"I think it's wonderful! This has been the kind of thing I've always wanted to do."

"Say, you wouldn't need a blonde belly-dancer, would you?" Sue asked. "I know I'm not as good as Emmy here but I need some kind of a job and I think I've got most of the equipment."

"Hmmm, I don't know," Nick replied, examining her closely. "You have the looks, that's for sure. You'd probably go over great just standing there but I don't know how the other girls would take it. Hell of a lot of trouble, having a bunch of women working for you. They'd probably get jealous if you wasn't working as hard as they were and start bitching."

"It was just a thought on my part."

"Why don't you go in for stripping someplace?" Charley asked. "I'd act as your manager."

"It's pretty hard finding work as a stripper in the city nowadays," Nick said. "The only way you can work it is by billing yourself as an exotic dancer and, I hate to say this, you really don't have very much sense of rhythm."

"Maybe so," Charley said, resting his hand on Sue's knee and leering at her, "but I sure do go for what she *does* have!"

"My fan!"

"Look, Nick," Jim said, "what we'll do is get out of here, talk it over with her old man and come back tomorrow."

"OK. I'll be around the joint all day tomorrow so come around if you decide to try it, Emmy. Come around even if you decide not to try it."

"Don't worry, I will," Emmy said, blushing.

It was almost four-thirty when they left the *Club Piyaki*. Except for Emmy, they were all pretty drunk and she was so excited she might have been in another world someplace. While she'd been dancing with Nick, something had happened between them and she knew that he was the one she wanted, the real reason she'd come to New York.

"What do you think, Emmy? Want to try working in that place with the Greek?" Jim asked.

"Sure, I do! Why were you giving him all that about Pa? You ain't really fixing to tell him, are you?"

"I was just trying to use Sam as an excuse to push the price up that way. Aren't you going to say anything about the deal to him?"

"No! I'm old enough to live my own life and this is going to be one time that Pa ain't going to ruin things for me."

"Suit yourself, you're old enough to know what you want. Just make sure that Greek doesn't ruin *you*. From the way he was looking at you in there you could tell he was nearly burning up from the strain of keeping his hands off you."

"Do you really think so?"

When they entered the place where they'd gotten their rooms, they could hear Sam making the building quiver with the sounds of the new electric guitar he'd bought. When they entered his room, they found him seated on the floor, several other guitars lying around him and as happy as a kid underneath a Christmas tree.

"Hey, ain't these something!" he cried out when he noticed them. "Did you ever hear such tones? I'm thinking of getting me a banjo tomorrow. Have a good time?"

"Sure did," Jim answered. "We're figuring on getting some shut-eye now. We really need it."

"Well, go ahead. I think I'll just stay up myself and whang away at these some more. What'd you think of New York, Emmy? Enjoy seeing all the sights?"

"Sure did, Pa. Found me a place to learn dancing the way I wanted, too."

"That's nice. Cost much?"

"Naw, hardly nothing at all."

Emmy was the first one up the next day. She was thinking of asking Sue to come along with her but decided not to, having a good, strong hunch that she and Nick would be needing some privacy before the day was over. Wanting to be sure of making a good impression on Nick, she even went so far as to take a bath before leaving.

Outside, she was a little confused about how to get to the club. Not wanting to get lost on the subways, she took a cab uptown. The place looked different in the daylight; indeed, the whole neighborhood looked different from the way she remembered it. It was sort of dingy and lackluster without the bright lights and crowds of people to liven it up.

The club was closed and shades were drawn over the front window. Peering past the edge of the glass door, she saw Nick seated at the bar, working over some papers. She rapped at the glass with a quarter until she attracted his attention. Looking up, he saw her and came to the door and opened it.

"Hey, how's it going, Emmy! I was scared you wouldn't show. I thought you might've only been kidding last night."

"You should have known better than that. I mean, after the way we were up on the stage and everything."

"Yeah, but I thought maybe my luck wouldn't hold," he said, locking the door again. "So you think you can be a belly-dancer, Emmy?"

"I think so."

"Tell your father about it yet?"

"He doesn't matter, I'm eighteen. Besides, he doesn't care what I do. He knows I wanted to work as a dancer."

"OK, Emmy, what do you say we have sort of a dress rehearsal, or what the girls call an *undress* rehearsal. It won't bother you going around nearly naked, will it?"

"Oh, no. It won't bother me at all."

"It's liable to bother me, though," he said, flashing a grin at her. "Still, that's the main idea of this business, bothering any men there are around."

"I like bothering men that way."

"Yeah, I noticed that. Why don't you go into the dressing room and see if you can find an outfit that'll fit you good? I'll put a few records on the juke and we'll see what happens," he said, patting her on the thigh.

"All right, but I wouldn't mind doing it without any costume at all on."

"Business before pleasure, doll. What we want to find out now is how you come over from the stage."

She smiled at him and went to the dressing-room, her hips swaying nicely. He poured himself a shot of bourbon and once more gave thanks that his father had left him a belly-dancing joint when he died. The kid went for him in a big way, he knew. That had been pretty apparent from the way she'd acted the previous night. He went for her strong, too. If she looked anywhere as sexy as she should stripped down, she'd really be something, too.

Still, he had to remember that he was a businessman and not get carried away just because it seemed likely that he was going to make her before the afternoon was over. Sometimes a woman could have a wild looking figure but just not come across to the audience. It was a funny thing but it happened sometimes.

This girl, he felt pretty sure, would come across like heat from a blast furnace. Going to the juke-box, he put a handful of change in it, hit a few *bozooki* records and took a seat at a ring-side table where he waited for her.

There was a full length mirror in the small, cluttered dressing room. Emmy had never had a full-length mirror before and she had a hard time taking herself away from it. Taking off her clothes, she grinned happily at her nude reflection, running her fingertips over her clear skin and making it tingle.

*He* was out there and he would be seeing all this, she knew. It would be wonderful, she was certain of that just from the way they had danced the previous night. It wouldn't be, couldn't be, anything like that time with Phil McCabe back in the hills. All of that, her life on the farm and the Inn, seemed to have happened to her a hundred years in the past.

She was about to start a new life now!

Grinning, she let her upper body pull back and pushed out her pelvic region toward the mirror, rotating it to the music that she could hear from the juke-box. She let her hands roam about on her soft skin, thinking of how soon, so very soon, it would be *his* hands that were touching her and *his* lips brushing against hers and then . . . and then *him* lunging into her body.

Her hands were trembling a little with desire as she took down one of the outfits that were hanging on hooks around the room. She put the bottom part on first, wriggling into its binding, flexible cloth with an effort.

It was made of a gold-colored fabric and the front of it came well beneath the slope of her belly, ran up in a narrow band between her legs and buttocks to where it was fastened at her back. A few wispy lengths of gauze were fastened to the waist-band with glittering specks of mica sewn into them.

She had a little trouble finding a halter big enough to contain her two beauties but finally was able to get one that covered her enough to keep the cops away. Most belly-dancers are built big in the hips and not so big in the breasts.

When she examined herself in the mirror, she was surprised to find out that she looked even sexier and nuder than when she didn't have anything on at all. Putting on some bracelets she found on the table, she winked at her reflection and went out.

"How do I look?" she asked Nick.

He choked on his drink when he saw her, sputtering good bourbon all over his table. The girl was sensational!

"Wow! If you come out in that outfit, we're going to have to chain the customers to the floor!"

"That's good, isn't it?" she asked, swaying to the music. "This here is some outfit."

"It ain't the outfit, it's what's in it that counts."

"I'm glad you like it."

"Honey, I'm going to show you just how much I like that great body of yours," he said, rising.

"Don't you want to see me dance?"

"You got the job, don't worry. I know you can dance, I can see you got the figure and now we'll go into my office where I have a bed where I sign all the girls up."

"Wait, let me finish here first. I've always dreamed of being in a place like this."

"OK, Emmy, suit yourself," Nick said, loosening his tie.

Letting herself laugh out loud, Emmy moved in front of Nick, gyrating and turning as she stamped her feet on the floor. Faster and faster she jerked her belly, her hands grasping at her breasts and stroking her heaving flesh.

The spangled gauze flew around her as she snapped back and forth, one way and the other, her bracelets jangling and glittering in the bright foot-lights. Nick was pretty used to the business and all but this girl was affecting him as much as if he was some rube just in from the sticks raising hell on his first night in town.

"OK, OK, you've got the job," he muttered, licking his lips. "Now to close the deal."

"Let's close it here," she said, panting.

"Here? All right, you crazy broad, right here!" he said, taking off his coat.

Still keeping time to the music, Emmy got the halter off and threw it off the stage, shaking her breasts and making them jump on her chest as if they had separate lives of their own. Wriggling out of the bottoms, she let them fall to her feet and now was clothed in nothing except her bracelets.

"Nick! Oh, Nick, you're so wonderful," she cried as his strong body came nearer to her.

"Emmy! Emmy!" he cried, moving and taking her in his arms as she let herself fall back on the floor.

And then the hard floor was beneath her and he was pressing against her, holding her and he was *there* and they were joined together under his driving force as the wild music played faster and faster, making the blood boil in their veins.

And it was good.

# NINE

The next day they all moved into a five-room apartment over on the East side. Sam was talking about getting a better place but Jim talked him out of it. It was a roach trap of a place on the top story of a five-story building but the rent was cheap and there was enough room for them all.

Charlie had relations in Brooklyn and he spent a lot of time down there, telling lies about the big deals he had working for him. Emmy didn't bother telling Sam about her job but, as he was so busy learning to master the guitar he'd bought, he never took any mind of her absences.

Sue and Jim were working on lowering the level of a bottle of whisky one evening and listening to Sam playing *"The Hog-Cutter's Stomp"* when the door-bell rang.

"Hey, Everybody," Sue called out, opening the door, "look who's finally come calling! Joan."

"Hello, Sue, Sam. Hello, Jim," she said, entering.

There was a sleek, well-groomed look about her that set her off from the others. She wore a severely-cut gray business dress and coat that made her look like a store-window dummy, Jim thought, looking up at her from the floor where he was lying.

"Hey, howdy, Gal," Sam said. "Decided to come back and live with us again?"

"No, thanks," she said, looking around the place.

"How're you doing, Joan?" Sue asked. "Still looking for a job or have you found something yet?"

"I have, I'm working in a publishing office. Krebs and Norwell over on Fifth Avenue."

"I thought you looked even more smug than usual," Jim said.

"Why, that ain't no way to talk to Joan," Sam said. "The girl wants to work, that's her privilege."

"Anybody follow you into the ladies room yet?" Jim asked.

"I figured that would be your attitude, Jim. It happens that I'm working with gentlemen now but of course, you wouldn't know anything about that."

"Oh oh, I'd watch that, Joan. Those gentlemen types are the worst kind. Never trust a man who isn't honest about his lust, that's the advice your old buddy Jim has for you."

"Jim? I thought you were Shamus O'Shaugnessy now. Or have you some other hare-brained scheme now?"

"No, I'm going to work that bit yet. Just biding my time. It's no good rushing into something like that. Any day now I figure on starting in getting drunk in places and letting the city know that there's a new Irish genius in town."

"Oh, what's the use of talking to you? Sue, you're the one I want to see. I've been talking to my boss and he says he needs a new private secretary. He seems to be a very nice man and the pay's good. What do you say?"

"Gee, I don't know. It'd be nice working with you again, Joan, and I would like to be able to pay my own way again."

"Now, that's right silly, Sue, if that's the only reason you have for working. I still got plenty of money left," Sam said.

"But it just doesn't seem right and I have to work sometime. All right, Joan, I'll drop over at your place tomorrow. What kind of a guy is he? Fanny pincher? Nudger? Hand-on-the-knee-type?"

"I told you he was a gentleman! Of course, the men you've been hanging around with have probably made you forget what a gentleman is like."

"Better watch it, Sue. Pretty soon she's going to be trying to get you to move into the YWCA with her," Jim said.

"It wouldn't be a bad idea! I mean, just look at you all! It simply isn't natural for you to live here with all these men!"

"Are you saying that it'd be more natural for her to live in a building full of other women?" Jim asked.

"Can't you all see that this just doesn't work, living like this in New York? It was one thing up in the mountains but not here where you've got to be practical."

"You're a strange one," Jim laughed, "talking that way. Most people who come from small towns to the city can't wait to start breaking loose from the small-town morality bit but with you, it's just the other way around."

"As for you, Jim, I've asked to see if there's any chance of there being any work you might be qualified for."

"Shouldn't have bothered, Joan."

"I think I found something you might be able to handle. They say they could use a delivery boy in the shipping department. Of course, you're a bit old but you never can tell, they might take a chance and hire you."

"If I was to get some kind of a job like that, I think I'd rather be a night porter."

"That figures."

"It'd be interesting, swabbing down the floors in one of those huge hives of an office building in the middle of the night when it's all deserted, listening to some out-of-town station playing dance music and smoking my pipe."

"Say, you're serious. Why don't you do that? At least it would be doing something."

"Why, Joan, do you think I give up on an idea of mine that easily? I haven't even tried getting the play produced yet."

"There you go with that pipe dream again!"

"Joan, why don't you quit that job of yours and come back here with us?"

"No. And furthermore, I don't ever want to see you again unless you get to work and stop wasting time."

"What? You mean you're not going to stick around tonight for old time's sake?"

"Here, Sue," Joan said, scribbling something on a piece of paper and handing it to her. "There's the address. Show up around ten tomorrow morning. And remember that this is a business office you're going to, so dress up."

"You mean I should wear a bra?"

"Certainly. A girdle too."

"A what? Me? Sounds like a stiff place but all right, I'll give it a try."

"Good, I'll see you tomorrow. So long, Sam. I'm sorry I flew off the handle but this clown's so irritating! If you'll take my advice, you'll kick him out and go back to the mountains while you still have some of that money left."

"Why, I think I'll stick around the city for a spell, Joan," Sam said. "Drop by again when you get the chance."

"So long, Joan. Watch those characters you work with when they try and back you around the water-cooler," Jim said as she left.

"Sure is a cute little filly when she's mad like that, ain't she?" Sam remarked, tightening one of his guitar strings.

"Yeah. I'll give her a few more weeks in that Y and she'll start loosening up again," Jim said. "Some of the things she was yapping about were right, though. I think I'd better start working in another day or so."

"Hell, things ain't *that* bad."

The very next day, however, Jim did proceed to work. He worked his way from one posh East Side drinking spot to another, loudly proclaiming that he was Shamus O'Shaugnessy, genius and playwright, who'd just finished a five-year tour of the United States and was now proceeding to write a play based on his studies.

Most of the places wouldn't let him in and those that did soon threw him out, but he did begin to be noticed in the newspapers. He did this by the simple expedient of bribing several of the gossip columnists. Items about Shamus O'Shaugnessy began appearing at the tail-end of daily columns when the news was dull or the writer had too big a hang-over to write his own stuff.

He took care not to appear any place where a real Irishman might show up although he had several close calls. When someone started talking about Ireland, he usually feigned extreme drunkenness, a feat not too difficult.

In spite of his efforts, he was unable to find anybody who was willing to put money into his play, as yet unwritten. The previous season had been quite disastrous on and off Broadway and the pigeons, also known as angels, were playing it very close to the vest.

He didn't despair for he was made of stern stuff and just went on boozing and brawling from one night-spot to another. He had faith that his efforts wouldn't be in vain. Sooner or later he would have to connect.

His luck finally changed in late July.

He was seated at the bar in a place on East Fifty-Second Street, singing what he claimed was a Gaelic drinking song. It was late afternoon and there weren't many people in the place but, stout fellow that he was, Jim, as we will continue to refer to him, kept up the routine.

A comely woman, about thirty-eight with a sleek, well-cared for body and glaring platinum blonde hair, entered with a handsome youth who had gigolo written all over him. Apparently they had had a spat for she was pouting and his mouth was grim. Jim noticed that she had some very expensive jewelry hanging off her body and he stopped his singing so that he could get a line on her. They sat in a booth just opposite him.

"Really, Marla, you're acting quite impossible," the young man said, lighting her cigarette with a jeweled lighter that she must have given him.

"Impossible? How else do you expect me to act, Randy, when you pull a vile stunt like that on me?"

"Vile stunt? Come now, Marla! Simply because I happened to be out when you called me, there's no reason for you to act like that. After all, I can't stay by the phone *all* the time!"

"For the money I'm giving you, you damn well ought to!"

"Please, Marla!" Randy said, looking around and running his hand through his long, wavy blonde hair. "Someone might hear you."

"What's the difference if they do? Everybody knows that I'm supporting you while you're supposed to be writing the Great American Novel. Ha! What a laugh that is!"

Aha, Jim thought to himself, she goes for that artistic routine. That meant that she'd go for it again if it was presented right. Like a good fly fisherman, he knew that he'd have to make his move at just the right instant. It looked like he might be able to connect with her that very day. Apparently old Randy'd done something to irritate her and she was angry about it. In a way, Jim was sorry for Randy. Having been a kept man himself once, he knew that it really was very hard work.

"Marla, I'm very sorry that you're taking this attitude. You know that writing is something that takes a lot of time and effort when you're trying to do something that's very good."

"Bunk! You haven't done more than two chapters on that thing in the past year."

"That's because I have my principles. I refuse to be a hack! I will not prostitute my talent!"

"Damn it, your only talent is that you *are* a prostitute! Don't go striking any poses with me, I'm getting sick of them!"

"Now, darling, let's not quarrel."

"Listen, Randy, I don't mind you playing around and calling yourself a writer if it makes you feel better but when my husband was alive, he taught me to get full value for any money I spent."

"Well, really dear, you can't say I've been remiss in that department, since you insist on bringing everything up this way."

"Like hell! I'm paying you for your exclusive services, not on a part-time basis."

"But darling—"

"Don't but darling me! Do you think I don't know where you were yesterday when I called you? I happen to know you spent the time in the apartment of that little tart of a chorus girl!"

"So that's who that strange-looking man was that I noticed looking at me. Really, Marla, private detectives! How gauche can you get? I was merely asking her for some background material for that nightclub scene in my book."

"Oh! Your book! Stop trying to play games with me, Randy. For once, be honest!"

"Be honest? Are you sure you want that, Marla, my sweet? Very well, since you insist. I *was* having a ball with Dora. Of course I was and a very good bed-partner she is."

"You bastard!"

"And, of course, I am being kept by you. How else could you even hope to keep a man as attractive as me around except by paying me? What are you again? Forty-something, isn't it?"

"Thirty-nine, you conceited swine!"

"Not conceited, my dear. Just being, as you say, honest. If you had been honest—with yourself, that is—we could have kept this arrangement going. As it is, you're approaching a rather difficult stage when women of your type become quite tedious. In short, Marla, you sloppy, middle-aged bag, I'm dumping you."

Bad form, that, Jim thought. He should have let her have the fun of dropping *him* first. It would have been the gentlemanly thing to do. It's guys like that who give the Profession a bad name. Sliding off his stool, Jim walked over to the table and glared at Randy.

"'Tis sorry I am to be breaking into a private conversation like this," Jim said, "but I couldn't be helping but hearing the way you've been talking to the lady."

"What the hell are you, a refugee from Third Avenue? Beat it and go back to your beer!" Randy said, starting to get up.

"Ah, and it's a very impolite young man you are indeed," Jim said, hitting him in the face with a left that knocked him back against the cushions. Blood immediately began streaming from his nose.

"Hit him again, Irishman, hit him again!" Marla cried, jumping up and down on her seat like a little girl.

"Why, Shamus O'Shaugnessy's always ready to oblige a lady," Jim said, belting Randy again.

"I think you've gone and broken my nose, you clumsy oaf!" Randy cried.

"Why, I don't think you should be calling me clumsy, it was meaning to break your nose that I hit you."

"You damned fool, don't you realize what this could mean to me in my business?" Randy cried, sliding around the table away from Jim and holding his hand to his face. "I've got to get to a doctor!"

"I hope it heals crooked!" Marla yelled, tripping him when he tried to get past her. Staggering to his feet, Randy hurried to the door as the bartender hurried to a phone so he could call up the gossip columnist who's pay-roll he was on to give the word about the latest exploit of Shamus O'Shaugnessy.

"Oh, I'm sorry I went and done that, fair lady, but I just couldn't help myself. I hope you won't think too badly of me?"

"Sit down and let me order you a drink. Did you say you were Shamus O'Shaugnessy? *The* Shamus O'Shaugnessy who writes plays."

"Aye, that I am. Did you just mention something about a drink?"

"Yes. Sit down."

"Why, thank you kindly. Then you're not being angry with me for larruping that young scalawag?"

"Certainly not. I just wish you could have hit that phony writer a few more times."

"Aye, that was one of the reasons I wanted to belt the spaleen. I simply cannot stand someone who's using the arts for his own vile and mercenary ends."

"Naturally, a serious artist like yourself would think that way. By the way, I'm Marla Peters, Mr. O'Shaugnessy."

"It's honored I am to meet you but I wish you'd call me Shamus the way me friends do."

"And you call me Marla. Bartender! Bring us some drinks!"

The whisky and conversation flowed merrily along for the rest of the evening. Jim discovered that Marla had once been Miss Schlager Lager Beer of nineteen forty-five. It was while she was Miss Schlager Lager Beer that she met Roger Peters, the elderly tobacco king, and married him. Roger had lasted some five years before he died, leaving her with more money than she knew what to do with. Since that time, she'd gone through a succession of Randys and had spent a lot of time being associated with various artsy endeavors.

"You've certainly led an eventful life," Jim said.

"Oh, but I bet you've really lived, Shamus."

"No, it's been a rather prosaic life I've led. Fishing off the Orkneys when I was a wee lad, whaling with the Norwegians down in the South Atlantic, prospecting for gold in the Andes, smuggling guns in the Med, fighting the heathen communists with the French Foreign Legion in Indo-China, running a night-club in Paris. Still and all, I've managed to see a few things in my time by keeping my eyes open and my mouth closed."

"My Goodness! The stories you could probably tell! Not to mention the plays. Have you produced any yet?"

"No, devil take the luck. Sure, and I thought here in New York they'd be interested in putting on a *real* play, a play with guts in it and life and thought but all they seem to be interested in is the cheap, sleazy kind of thing that makes money. But why are we talking about my silly problems? I must be daft, talking so, when there's such a fine woman sitting so close to me," Jim said, putting his hand up beneath her dress.

"Oh!" she yelled.

"Ah, forgive me, fair lady but I cannot seem to help myself. 'Twas always that way with me when beauty's about, I cannot help but try and grasp it!"

"Not here, Shamus, not here!"

"You've started a wild fire burning in my veins as if there was gasoline running in them and you, my blue-eyed beauty, you're the one who's touched a match to it!"

"Control yourself, you wild, passionate Irishman! We'll go to my place."

"Yes, yes! I'll follow you on winged feet of happiness, oh Glorious Creature! 'Tis afire I am and only your cool, fair skin can quench the blaze!"

Weaving their way outside where the doorman called a cab for them, they clung to each other while the earth rocked beneath their feet. In the cab, Jim, by now full of enthusiasm for the role he was playing, had her panties down to her knees before they'd gone past two stop lights.

The cab pulled up to a building on Fifth Avenue facing the park. There was a slight delay while Marla pulled her panties up again and then they got out. On the self-service elevator, Jim mauled and kissed her all the way up to the penthouse where she lived.

Rearranging her dress, she led him into the spacious apartment. A Negro maid was making half-hearted attempts to dust the furniture in the livingroom when they entered.

"Jocasta, do we have enough liquor in the house?"

"Yes, Ma'am. A new case just came in yesterday."

"Good, take tonight and tomorrow off."

"Thank you, Mrs. Peters."

"Want to take a look around, Shamus?"

"I can see that it's a fine and lovely place but it's your own sweet beauty that I'm interested in now."

"Le's—let's go out on the terrace, Shamus. Got a terrific view of the park if you go for trees."

They wandered out onto the terrace. South, they could see the lights of mid-town Manhattan gleaming in the darkness. Overhead, a myriad of stars hung. The city noises didn't penetrate this far up. Jim leaned over the railing and saw the headlights of cars streaming along the streets.

"Ah, what a wonderful sight is the work of mankind and the Glory of Creation! The sky, these buildings, all are beautiful but you, my love, my Marla, you are the noblest creation of them all."

"You sure can talk. Come on over here and say all that stuff," she said, laying on a sofa.

"Yes, my blooming flower of the night," Jim said, kneeling beside her and slowly stroking her bare arm. "Oh, what a marvel a fine built woman such as yourself is!"

"Like my legs? Pretty good, ain't—aren't they?" she said, raising her feet towards the distant stars, her skirt falling around her hips in a swirl of cloth.

"Name me a man who can call himself a man who wouldn't like them," he said, running his hand down their sleek surface.

"Hey, that tickles. What do you say we take our clothes off and throw them off the terrace."

"How could I not obey any of your commands," Jim said.

Giggling drunkenly, she lurched to her feet and, with Jim's help, managed to get her clothes off. She really wasn't in bad shape at all. She'd kept her weight down and there seemed to be plenty of bounce in her boobs.

They went over to the edge of the roof. She gave a whoop and sent the dress and the rest of her gear flying down toward the street. Jim was a little more prudent, simply dropping his clothes just on the other side of the railing where he could pick them up later.

"What do we do now, Shamus?"

"Why, I take you up in my arms like this and carry you back to the sofa, Marla."

"Yeah? Gonna tell me more of that pretty talk, Shamus? That fink Randy hardly ever said anything about how good looking I am or anything, the lousy rat-fink."

"You hurt me, mentioning that conniving, thieving rogue at a moment like this. There, lay yourself—"

"What?"

"I say, lay yourself down and let me just stand here a moment or so, looking down and taking in that magnificent beauty of yours."

"Like me, Shamus?" she asked, wriggling herself comfortably.

"Like you? Why, Marla, your eyes are as fine a sight as the moon, full and bright, shining in the Sligo bogs. They're almost that same marvelous color as the River Liffey where it goes sliding past the big brewery, your lips are as soft and sweet as a wet rose and I must kiss them," he said, doing so.

"Don't stop there."

"And your breasts! They seem to be like two soft doves in my hands, I can almost feel them fluttering against my fingers. Here! I'll quiet them with a kiss."

"That'a boy, Shamus! Don't stop there."

"Ah, and what have we here beneath them? That fine, supple waist that would be a credit to a schoolgirl, all white and gleaming in the starlight, the lovely little belly-button staring up at me like an empty glass. Sure, and I'll fill it with a kiss."

"Yes, that's it, oh, yeah! Don't stop there, Shamus! Don't stop there!"

"How could I stop? Can a man falling off a cliff stop? Can a drunkard stop after one glass? Och! And what have we here, beneath all the rest?"

"Yes, Shamus, Yes!"

"Bedad, what a lovely pair of kneecaps! I'll have to be giving them a kiss, too."

He bent his head down over one of her knees and kissed it. Deciding that it was time to get started in the serious business, he brought himself over her excited body, squeezing her breasts with Gaelic gusto, rousing her completely till she lifted her body up to him.

"All right, you crazy Celt, your fiery language and heated passion has been too much for me to withstand. Take me, I'm yours!"

Then he was over and into her in one swift, practiced motion and the legs of the sofa were rattling madly where they rested on the tile floor.

Later, they went into her bedroom where they got into the huge bed and fell into a deep sleep. Jim awoke first. He had a raging hangover. Going into the bathroom, he found some aspirins and gulped down a few along with a quart of water. The bright sun hurt his eyes and he crept back into bed with Marla.

He couldn't get back to sleep, his head hurt him so. The whole bit seemed to be falling right into place. He'd stepped into Randy's place without any trouble at all. The important thing was not to be the one to bring up her backing his play.

"Ollgnn," Marla said, stirring awake.

"And good morning to you, Marla, my pretty."

"Huh? Oh, it's you. I feel awful."

"Want me to get you some aspirin or something? I'm feeling pretty rocky myself."

"Yeah. Hey, there's some stuff my doctor gave me in the dresser drawer's supposed to be good for hangovers."

They tried the remedy and found out that, like all hangover remedies, it wasn't much help. By about noon, though, they were recovered enough to fix up some breakfast for themselves and they started to come out of it about then. Jim went over to the terrace, thinking to get the clothes he'd carefully dropped on the ledge but found that they'd fallen some five stories further down during the night. He called up Charley back at the apartment then.

"Charley? Jim. I think I found our pigeon. Come on over to this address and bring a new outfit for me. I'm up in a penthouse at 2295 Fifth Avenue. Listen, when you come over, don't speak English, talk Mohawk. I'll tell the broad that it's Gaelic and maybe I'll be able to fix you up in the deal somehow."

Jim was still nude around the time they were eating supper when the door-bell finally rang at the elevator. He went to it and let Charley in.

"What the hell kept you so long?" Jim asked.

"Ah, I got off on the wrong side of town and tried to cut across Central Park, see. It's sort of confusing there, you know, all those trees and no street signs and—"

"Charley, you went and succeeded in getting lost in Central Park, didn't you?"

"Don't spread it around, will you, Jim? I'm catching enough hell from the tribe now."

"Got my clothes?"

"Yeah, here you are. Say, this is quite a lay-out. You must've struck pay-dirt."

"Maybe, I don't know for sure yet. Wait a second, I think she's coming now. Remember, don't speak any English."

"If you say so."

"Oh, hello," Marla said, joining them. "Is this your friend that you asked to bring over the clothes? Silly of us, wasn't it? Still, you must know how wild Shamus here gets Mr. . . ?"

"Sean O'Toole, just over from the old country, Marla."

"From Ireland? *Him?*"

"Sure, and you've been hearing of the black Irish, haven't you, me darling?"

"Begorrah," said Charley Bluejacket.

"You'll have to be pardoning Sean here, Marla. He's made a solemn vow, he has, that he won't speak a word of Sassenach till they get out of the northern counties."

"He's the damnest mick I've ever seen but if he's a friend of yours, Shamus, he's welcome here."

"Ah, 'tis a fine, generous creature you are."

"Let's go into the dining room, Shamus. You too, Mr. O'Toole. Does Mr. O'Toole write plays also?"

"To be sure he does. You must know that a true Irishman writes plays easy as a bird sings."

"Shamus, I was wondering if you'd let me invest some money in one of your plays?"

# TEN

Jim and Charley came back to the apartment late that night carrying a typewriter and a stack of paper. Both were pretty well looped and Jim's face was flushed with triumph. With a flourish, he placed the typewriter on the kitchen table with a bottle of Irish whiskey next to it.

"Congratulate me, Sam and Sue, I've found my pigeon!" he said.

"Well, I'll be damned," Sam said. "Just goes to show you never can tell. I kinda had the notion that you were just going through all that as an excuse to get drunk."

"I'm surprised at your lack of faith."

"What happened? Who's backing you?" Sue asked.

"This Peters broad from uptown," Charley said. "She's loaded! Jim here told her I was a mick too and that the two of us have a play written already. We're all of us going to be in it!"

"Me, stand out on a stage and emote?" Sam asked. "I don't think I'd be able to."

"Nothing to it, Sam," Jim said. "If you don't want to act, you can provide the background music."

"Gee, me, an actress! What sort of a play is it going to be, Jim? You haven't mentioned that," Sue said.

"Hell, how would I know? I haven't written the damned thing yet. I'll have to do that tonight, I told Marla I'd have it ready for her by tomorrow afternoon."

"Then don't just sit there jawing, boy!" Sam said. "Get going and start hitting those keys!"

"Then give me some room here! Sue, you start making coffee, Charley, you go get some ice for my drinks, Sam, get that guitar of yours going and make it a fast beat! I got a lot of work to do before I leave this apartment again."

Rolling some paper into the machine, Jim proceeded to write at a break-neck speed. Faster and faster, he pulled words out of the air and his mind and threw them on the clean, white surface of the paper. The coffee he drank boiled in his stomach, the booze mounted up to his brain, and his throat and tongue burned bitterly from the tobacco he smoked but he didn't slacken his fast pace.

The strung-out words took more and more sheets of paper and the stack of sheets next to the typewriter mounted. He wrote quickly, not pausing an instant to check what he was doing or what he was trying to do. He was like a rocket, ascending skyward at an ever-accelerating pace, piercing the black emptiness of space with its flaming trail.

Gradually, the others drooped and dropped off to sleep, lying around the floor like a newspaper picture showing the aftermath of a massacre but Jim kept hammering away at his typewriter, his fingers flying over the keys and hitting them like well-oiled pistons.

As the grey light of dawn began showing at the edges of the window shades, he began to tire, pausing occasionally to run his hand over his face and to rub his bleary eyes for a second. The coffee-pot was emptied but he couldn't take the time out to make a fresh batch and now he wrote on straight whiskey.

Now the dim light grew brighter and the chirping of sparrows sounded outside the window. But now the end was in sight and he forced himself to pound away at the typewriter though his eyes were closing and his head was nodding onto his chest. Indeed, he wrote some ten pages while he was asleep, waking with a start and putting still more words, words, words on the paper, defiling the virgin whiteness.

Then the moment, the wonderful moment, came when he could type the final words, THE END.

He hunched forward in his chair and let his forehead rest on the letter-keys, raising them in a jumble against the paper. After some ten minutes, he got up from the chair and kicked Charley till he sputtered himself awake.

"I did it, Charley. I did it!"

"Hey, nice going there, Jim! What kind of a play did you and me write?"

"I don't know, I haven't read it yet. Get Sue to re-type the whole thing and then wake me up in two hours so we can take it to Marla. I have to get some sleep."

Making his weary way to his bed, he fell face forward into its yielding softness and was asleep almost instantly.

It seemed like no time at all before Charley was shaking him awake. Stripping, he went into the shower waving at Sue who was just finishing up the manuscript as he passed through to the bathroom, still half asleep.

"Hey, Jim," Sue called, "I've been typing this thing for a couple of hours now and I haven't got the slightest idea of what it's all about. It's like trying to read a book lying down in the bottom of a well with twenty feet of water over it."

"Good, that shows it's a deep, profound play."

"What do you want me to title it?"

"Hell, I knew there was something I'd forgotten. Let me see. I got it. Call it 'Oh Pappy, Poor Pappy, Mammy's Run Off to Alabamy and I'm Feeling Real Crappy.'"

"That's snappy."

"Should look real good up in lights if we can get a theatre with a big marquee."

The frigid water cascading over him brought him back to life more or less. He got out of the shower, dried himself, dressed and the whole motley crew went off in a body to Paul's Place, a nearby bar where they were to meet Marla.

There, Jim made a breakfast of healthful, delicious, nutritious dark beer and read his creation. He decided that the play might have some possibilities after all.

When Marla came in, she looked a little surprised at the group clustered about Jim but, as she thought, these imaginative Irishmen did tend to congregate with some weird types.

"Hello, Shamus. Have you got the play with you?" she asked.

"That I have. Not only have I brought the play but I've brought some of the actors, too. This is Sue Lindquist, who's going to act one of the roles, Sam Mackey, who's our musician and, of course, Sean here, who's condescended to play one of the roles."

"But if Sean's made a vow not to speak English . . .?"

"'Tis a non-speaking role. Here's how we'll work it. It'll be sort of an introductory scene to put the audience in the proper mood. Sue here'll be seated in the audience and Sean will come running out onto the stage costumed as one of your wild, savage, heathen Indians. He'll let out a whoop, dash down off stage and start pulling the clothes off of Sue."

"So far, it seems interesting."

"Then, he'll haul her, screaming and yelling, up to the stage where there'll be a four poster bed in the back with the curtains pulled down. They'll be staying there for the whole performance and you won't be hearing anything from them save the squeaking of the bed-springs."

"I like it, I like it," said Sue.

"Now, here's where the revolutionary part comes in. All the audience will be thinking that they're just jumping up and down on the bed and pretending that they're making love, but they'll be doing it for real instead!"

"They'll *really* be doing it?" Marla said, slightly surprised at the idea.

"But sure and they will. Do you not see the terrific breakthrough of it all? The audience'll think that it's just an illusion but it won't be an illusion at all! Illusion and reality will be combined in a new dimension!"

"But Shamus," Marla objected, "if we have a performance six nights a week and twice on Saturday, won't it be, well, quite a bit of a strain on Mr. O'Toole?"

"Oh, and Sean is knowing that it's a very demanding role that he'll have to put a lot into but, for Art's sake, he's willing to give all he's got. Right, Sean, my Bucko?"

"Begorrah," answered Charley Bluejacket, nodding vigorously.

"What's this opus of yours to be called, Shamus?"

"Oh Pappy, Poor Pappy, Mammy's Run Off to Alabamy and I'm Feeling Real Crappy. *'Tis a title that sings.'*

"Tell me more about it."

"Well, all the performers saving the three main characters, the Old Man, the Young Shoe Salesman and the Nude Woman (it's for the sex interest that I'm throwing her in) will be seated behind screens with just their feet showing. This is to symbolize that no human being can ever really communicate with another. Also, this way it won't matter what the actors look like and we can hire ugly ones at a much cheaper price."

"Glad to see that you're interested in saving me money, Shamus."

"The three main characters'll be hanging by their knees from swinging trapezes to symbolize the topsy-turvy condition of the mad world we're living in. They'll hang there for the whole play so we'll have to get actors in good shape for these roles."

"But what will they talk about, what's the play about?"

"Life, my fair lady, Life! And not the customary kind of blathering that passes for dialogue nowadays, either! For it's improvising that they'll be doing, another great breakthrough! You see, we won't have them learn their lines together or even let them know what the other characters lines'll be. They'll each receive all their speeches in one great flood of words without even punctuation marks to tell them when the sentences are over. It'll be bringing the stage to a new level, like Jazz, where each one improvises and takes off in his own wild way!"

"But if I know anything at all about actors, it'll be a madhouse up there with each one stepping all over the other's lines and trying to up-stage each other."

"Sure, and isn't that just the way it is in real life with everybody pushing and trying to pull the other fellow down?"

"To tell you the truth, Shamus, I think I'd have to be out of my mind to invest money into this play of yours."

"That's simply because you're too used to the hide-bound conventional theatre, Marla. Here, have some of this fine brew or perhaps a spot of whiskey and we'll talk about it awhile."

After several hours of convivial drinking, Marla finally came around to agreeing to back the play. After all, as she said, she would be able to deduct the losses from her income tax.

"Bravo for you, Marla!" Jim cried when she came through. "You're now a patroness of the Arts!"

"I'm now the biggest patsy in New York but what the hell, I might as well have some fun with my money."

"A charming attitude, that. Now let's see, we'll have to have a theatre. Do you think the Bryant would be too small?"

"Bryant my foot! It'll be off Broadway in some converted candy store on Second Avenue. I'm not shelling out that kind of money for a certain turkey."

"Ah, me. Well, perhaps a more intimate theatre would be best suited for the play at that. Something small that would make the audience feel as if they were part of the goings on."

"Listen, if the audience starts feeling that way, the cops'll shut us down for sure. When do you think this thing should open, if we get a place and actors willing to appear in it?"

"You show a distressing lack of confidence in my talent, Marla."

"You're talented, all right, but not, I have a hunch, in playwriting."

"Very well, mock me now but when 'Oh, Pappy' etc. opens and you see it in all its glory, you'll change your tune. I see no reason why we can't open a few weeks from now, thanks to the clever way in which I eliminated the need for the actors to study their lines."

"All right, here's what I'll do. You find me a place, a cheap place, where you can produce this thing and a bunch of actors who are willing to work for little else but the experience and I'll foot the bill. Fair enough?"

"Oh, more than fair, far as it goes, Marla. Still there's the matter of my livelihood. Seeing as how you're such a fine person and all, I'll sell you the play outright for the ridiculous sum of—"

"Ixnay, Shamus. What I'll do is split the gate with you, fifty-fifty, if there is a gate, that is."

"But Marla, my Love, that doesn't seem right to me."

"Now who's expressing doubts about your talent?"

"Very well but it was you I was thinking of."

*And so* "Oh Pappy, Poor Pappy, Mammy's Run Off to Alabamy and I'm Feeling Real Crappy" *was launched.*

After searching around the East Side for several days, Jim found a supermarket in a building that was waiting to be torn down and rented it for a month. Emmy went to work during the day doing carpentry work and fixing up the stage. Sam was curious to know why she didn't try to get into the act also but she told him she didn't feel herself ready yet.

Getting actors was fairly simple. All Jim had to was stop by at several of the bars where the would-be actors hung out and sign a batch up. There were some fairly good-looking girls among the applicants and he let Charley and Sam do the picking there.

There was also the matter of ballyhoo. Jim attacked this problem with relish, drinking and raising hell until the name "Shamus O'Shaugnessy" was a household word in the city. He appeared on television drunk, slugged the reporter who was interviewing him, and told the viewers to buy the sponsor's competitor's stock.

The weeks flew past and he gradually almost forgot that the whole thing was just a joke he was playing and came near to thinking he really was Shamus O'Shaugnessy, playwright of the western world.

Still living at the Y, Joan couldn't help but read about Jim in the papers and once had seen him on his lone television appearance. It was all she could do to keep from throwing an ashtray at the screen when he mentioned that he was now living as a house guest of his patroness, Mrs. Peters.

Joan frequently thanked her lucky stars that she was out of the crazy set-up Sue had led her into. Everything was going along fine with her. Already, she'd gotten her first raise at her job and was making more money than she'd ever made in her life. In a little while, she expected to move into a small apartment of her own although she didn't particularly mind staying where she was.

There were some single men working in the office with her and she went on dates with them several times. They were all sensible, sane types who treated her with the utmost respect, never trying to paw her when they returned from the play or movie or nightclub they had attended.

Everything was going along swimmingly with Joan. At last she was living the kind of life she'd always wanted. Everything was in its proper place, there were no jarring notes, no disturbing fractures of routine.

She was ready to go out of her mind with boredom.

During the day, when she had her job to keep her occupied, it wasn't too hard to keep on going but when night came and she lay in her bed, looking at the ceiling and remembering green fields and Jim's arms around her, the miseries hit her.

Deciding that it was lack of sex that was bothering her, she resolved to indulge in a little. After all, *he* was, wasn't he? Picking out one of the more likely candidates in her office, she accepted his invitation to go up to his apartment.

It didn't turn out too good.

He played the whole bit as if he was following directions given in some magazine. There were soft lights, a hi-fi with acceptable jazz playing softly in the background, a wide and comfortable couch,—the works.

When, after making the suitable overtures, he took her to bed he still seemed to be following a set pattern as if he'd memorized some make-out manual put out by a mechanic's magazine. First the lip kissing, the discreet nudging of the knees, the subtle hand stroking various sections of the body then, at last, the Great Moment.

All through it, Joan was wondering whether or not she could get her hair set the next day.

When they finished, she thanked him politely, took a shower in his bathroom and left, leaving him going over a crossword puzzle in the Sunday Times.

As the opening date for Jim's play approached, she felt herself being strongly tempted to catch the opening. It would be good, seeing the whole thing blow up on him that way, she thought. The trouble was that that was what he wanted; a big explosion so he could have the amusement of knowing that he caused it.

She didn't go to the show although she stayed up until the late papers came out so that she could catch some of the reviews. They were all bad, the most favorable one being by Chesley Argyle in the tabloid, the *New York Clarion:*

"Though the miserable collection of *non sequiturs* masquerading as a play on Second Avenue is thoroughly absurd, tedious in the extreme, atrociously acted, hideously staged and an insult to the mind of the audience, one has to admit that O'Shaugnessy does have a certain lyric quality at stray times. It is indeed unfortunate that some of our own writers are unable to achieve that Celtic style. In any event, *'Oh Pappy* etc.' shouldn't be infecting our fair city for too long. I expect it will close by the time this appears in print."

The next day's papers brought word, though, that Marla Peters was going to keep the show open indefinitely. Joan had moved into a one and-a-half room apartment by this time. Although she was only in it a few days, she was bored and lonely with its grey-colored walls. She wished Sue had taken that job with her, then they could have afforded a bigger and better place.

It all blew up a week after the play opened. An article appeared in the *Clarion* under the screaming headline, SHAMUS BOGUS!!!

"It was revealed today (it ran) by Randolph (Randy) Crullers, young man-about-town that Shamus O'Shaugnessy, erstwhile playwright and author of the colossal flop *'Oh Pappy, Poor Pappy, Mammy's Run Off to Alabamy and I'm Feeling Real Crappy'* is, in reality, one James Perkins, beatnik poet from California. Crullers, who was involved in a brawl with Perkins-Shaugnessy several months ago, said he felt that it was his duty as a citizen to reveal this information. Reports of bands of irate Irishmen roaming the city armed with shillelaghs and hunting the playwright have been received."

Joan had just finished reading the article when there was a knock at the door. She opened it and Jim, wearing a dark pair of glasses, came in.

"Hello, Joan. Nice little place you've got here. Been getting any recently?" he asked politely, sitting down.

"Hello, Jim. Make yourself at home, have a seat. I see the great awakening has come."

"I'll say it has. I've got every mick in the city out hunting for my blood. Well, at least I can stop talking with that brogue now. Got a drink for me? Anything'll do so long's it's not any of that Irish whiskey. I've kind of lost my taste for the stuff."

"I guess I can find you something. How's your patroness taking this or didn't you stop to find out?"

"I stayed long enough to get the drift of her thinking on the subject. You know, Joan, people just don't seem to have any sense of humor nowadays."

"I guess she didn't see the humor in losing all of that money, did she?"

"Marla can spare it."

"You know, Jim, you have quite a bit of gall to show up here. I suppose you expect to move right into my bed tonight and we'll take up right where we left off?"

"I don't know what to expect now, Joan. You're right when you say I shouldn't have come here. Silly and stupid of me to be annoying you this way. Let me just sit here a few minutes and then I'll leave. I feel a little tired."

"What? Say, is that you talking? You do look a little drawn and crummy at that."

"It's the way thing's have turned out that've brought me down. I don't know, I must be getting old. I thought that this would be the biggest kick in my life, poking fun at the whole city of New York but it just didn't turn out that way somehow. I guess I finally have to admit you're right, Joan."

"Hey, wait a second!"

"All I've been doing all along is kidding myself. There isn't a single dammed thing in this world that I can do good. Do you know if that delivery-boy job is still open in your place, Joan? I'm about ready to take it now."

"That's a hell of a way to talk to me!"

"You're right, it is. I'll be going now. So long, Joan. We had a few good times, didn't we?"

"Sit down, will you? Haven't you got any manners at all, Jim? You come up to a girl's apartment and start to go without even asking her to sleep with you!"

"Huh? I sort of assumed you wouldn't be interested."

"Don't go assuming anything about me. There's still one thing that you're good at."

"No kidding, you really feel in the mood for it?" he asked, his face regaining some of its usual spirit.

"Damn it, if you won't seduce me, I guess I'll have to start things moving! Come here," she said, twisting her hips out of her slacks.

"Joan! What're you doing?"

"I'm getting ready to make some passionate love, that's what I'm doing! What do you think I'm doing?" Now her blouse was off and she was unhooking her bra.

"But this isn't like you."

"I'm tired of being like myself, I'm tired of being like that idiot girl in the commercials who's always bragging because her armpits don't smell and she's always calm, cool and collected. I want to have some fun with my life!"

"Are you going crazy?"

"Crazy with passion for you, my love."

Stripped naked, Joan threw herself into Jim's lap and kissed him heartily everytime he tried to say a word. After awhile, he stopped trying to say anything and just held her bare body tenderly in his arms while she writhed against him.

Then he picked her up and carried her to the bed. It was a single but they didn't take up too much room for the rest of the night.

Later, when she was cooking something to eat, he walked up behind her and kissed her on the back of the neck.

"Thanks," he whispered.

"Thanks? What for?"

"For acting the way you did yesterday. I was really feeling low when I came in here."

"I was feeling pretty low before you came in! I've been feeling that way since I left you and the rest of the bunch. Living with you all that way has ruined me for the sensible life, I'm afraid. I can hardly stand those people I work with now."

"We've missed you, too. I'm the one who's missed you the most, Joan."

"Oh now, wait just a second! Don't go telling me you haven't been having a ball, running around town the way you were doing and living it up with Marla!"

"Marla was mainly business."

"Some business!"

"The funny part about the whole bit with the play and everything was that I kept thinking how I wished you were in it with me. I even missed having you argue with me all the time whenever I tried to do something a little off-beat."

"I sort of missed those arguments myself," she said.

"You know, every good comedian has to have a good straight man to back him up. You're something like that to me. We kind of balance each other off. We ought to make ourselves a team."

"Like Abbot and Costello?"

"Sure, why not? Without you, I seem to tend to go flying to the sky and when I'm not around you, you get a little stiff. Look at you, living all that time at the Y!"

"Are you talking about a kind of a permanent attachment?"

"Sure."

"A legal one?"

"If you want it that way."

"Without any more Marla-type business?"

"Marla never was anywhere near as good as you."

"Jim, this whole idea is one of the craziest I've ever heard."

"It's a crazy world we live in so we might as well have some crazy ideas and act on them."

"We are talking about marriage, aren't we?"

"I guess so, aren't we?"

"All right but we didn't leave much for the honeymoon, did we?"

"The hell we didn't. I've got a few ideas I've been holding back from you."

"Now I'll have to say yes just out of curiosity."

"I'll try to make it interesting for you."

"What'll you do after we get married, Jim?"

"You mean, how will I make our bread?" he laughed. "There you go, falling back into character again. Good old practical, sensible and sane Joan."

"Well, that's the way I'm supposed to act, remember? I'm the straight man in this team."

"I haven't figured out what I'll do next. I'm a schemer without a scheme at the present time."

"I've got the job so there's no rush."

"Oh, yes. Your job. Quit it."

"Quit it! What for?"

"Hell, I don't want my wife working. Besides, I think better when I'm a little hungry."

"But . . . All right, I'll quit it. I suppose I'll have to show I've got confidence in that sneaky brain of yours."

"Don't sweat it, something'll turn up. Maybe Charley or Sue'll have an idea. Come on, Joan. We'll get dressed and take a run down to the apartment."

When they went outside, Joan called up the place where she worked and quit. She liked doing that. Already, the drop into the old, free and sloppy life was taking hold of her. They took a subway down to the Village and walked over to where the apartment was located. Sue and Charley were the only ones in when they got there.

"Hey, you've brought back Joan," Sue said.

"Yes, and I'm staying this time."

"Anybody come around looking for me?" Jim asked.

"A couple of reporters showed up. I told them you were beating your way back to the Coast so they'd stop bugging me. Your pigeon Marla came around, too, with some punk who has a broken nose. She said she's got no bitch about the play and all since she had some laughs out of it. Maybe you ought to stick with that broad, Jim. She's got much bread."

"I don't think Joan here'd like it if I did," Jim replied.

"Why should she care?"

"We're getting married."

"Married! What do you want to go and do that for?"

"Just a wild idea of ours. Kicks, you know. Where's Sam and Emmy at?"

"I think Emmy went down to the club. Sam took off just after she left."

"Too bad I missed him. I was hoping I could tout that show up so I could give him some of the cash but they went and blew the whistle on me before we could make anything. Say, I haven't told you, Joan. Emmy's been working steady since we hit the city."

"Really? Where?"

"The *Club Piyaki* as a belly dancer. Maybe we ought to go uptown and catch her, the kid's got plenty of talent."

"A belly-dancer! What does Sam think of the idea?"

"He doesn't know and don't you go telling him. According to Charley here, he goes raving mad whenever anybody tries getting anywhere with Emmy and apparently she's been going at it hot and heavy with the Greek who owns the joint."

"Is he really like that?" Joan asked. "I mean, the way he chases after women himself, you'd think he'd be more liberal in his thinking when it came to sex."

"I've seen him a few times back home," Charley said. "He doesn't kid around when he gets going. Hell, he scared me so much that I hardly ever even tried laying a hand on Emmy."

"It works out that way sometimes. Is she still drawing them into the place like she was doing?"

"Sure is. That Greek must be making a fortune out of her."

"Hey, maybe there's an angle in that somewhere," Jim said. "I have a hunch we can make some money, somehow."

"Now wait a second," Joan said. "If you're thinking that I'm going to become a belly-dancer—"

"That wasn't what I had in mind but it's something to think about. Let's run up and see Nick. I'd like to talk some business with him."

# ELEVEN

At that very moment, Sam was looking through the windows of the *Club Piyaki*. He'd begun noticing that Emmy had been acting mighty peculiar around him and it didn't take him long to decide what it must be that was affecting her.

There was some diddling going on.

In a way, Sam welcomed the discovery. He'd been feeling a little left out of things since he'd come to the city. While he got a kick out of working in the play with Jim and Charley and while Sue was still as friendly as ever with him, dropping into his bed frequently, he felt odd and out of place in New York.

Back in the hills, he was somebody, he had things to do. He was Sam Mackey, who could out-walk, out-fight, outdrink and out-shoot any man for miles around his place. Here, none of that counted, here he was nothing but a big rube.

Not that he had any burning desire to go back to the hills, not just yet, anyway. Once he'd seen and smelled the sleek, perfumed city women parading around, he knew he'd be sticking around for quite awhile until he'd gotten his quota of females.

The trouble was, he wasn't getting anywhere near what he considered his rightful share of the female population of New York.

Somehow, he'd lost his self-confidence and when that's lost, it's damned rough to get any women. It all tied in, he knew, to the fact that he didn't have any accomplishments that were of any value in the city.

The money he'd brought was dwindling away and soon, he'd have to look around for some kind of a job if he wanted to stay. Finding work at his age and with his qualifications would be hard enough but with his temper, it would be impossible.

Thus, when Emmy gave him a chance to do something he was quite good at, fighting, Sam felt a little bit like his old self. He didn't admire himself for sneaking after her when she left the apartment and following to see where the man was but it was certain that she'd never tell him of her own will.

When she went into the club, he stopped on the sidewalk and stared at the place with his mouth open.

A hoochie-dancer!

There wasn't any doubt about it. A more-than-life-sized photo of Emmy was standing in the window. Aside from a few wisps of gauze and a meager bit of cloth here and there, she was naked as a jay-bird. The picture had a big sign underneath it.

"Direct from Istanbul, here for a limited engagement at the *Club Ptyaki,* the Princess Marja. Belly Dancer to the crowned heads of the Near East."

She was sitting at the bar with a young man, who had a foreign look. From the way he was holding her hand and looking into her eyes, there was no mistaking that he'd been having her. Sam was glad to notice that he was a husky young fellow. He hadn't had a good fight for a long time now. Maybe it'd perk him up a bit.

When he pushed open the door and came in, Emmy gave a little choked scream.

"Nick! It's my father!"

"Hello, Emmy," Sam said.

The young fellow, Nick, Emmy called him, got off his stool and faced Sam. While Sam was taller, Nick was built heavy and held himself as though he knew a little about fighting. He grinned suddenly at Sam as he approached.

"Hello, Mr. Mackey, I've been after Emmy to bring you over to the club for some time now."

"You're going to wish I'd never come by the time I get through with you," Sam said, taking off his coat. He half expected this Nick fellow to try rushing him when he had the coat half off, in which case he'd have kicked him in the belly but he just watched Sam, grinning all the while.

"Pa! Don't do it! You mustn't, he's—"

"No, Emmy," Nick said. "Don't go telling your father what to do, it's not nice."

The bartender and several of the waiters had begun edging up to the front of the club where Sam was. One of them was keeping his hand in his right hip pocket, Sam saw. Blackjack man, most likely.

"You want we should put the blast on the big farmer, Nick?" the bartender asked.

"No, Tony. Just have the boys clear everybody out of our way. You sure you want it this way, Mr. Mackey?"

"Yep."

Then Sam leaped forward, swinging from the floor. Nick closed in to get underneath Sam's reach and they started grappling, falling to the floor and knocking over tables and chairs as they wrestled, kicked, punched and butted each other all over the floor.

Nick had been the only Greek kid in an Italian neighborhood and had to pick up fighting ability or perish. Always extraordinarily strong, he'd done a little wrestling in the army where he'd learned to use his power more effectively.

The yelling crowd surged around them, shouting encouragement to Nick. Emmy kept moving from one foot to another, not knowing what to do. The two struggling men regained their feet and rushed at each other like two bulls, one old, one young, struggling for mastery of a herd in a field.

The young fellow was too savvy for him at the grappling part, Sam saw, so he tried to keep him up on his feet at a distance where his reach and fists would give him the advantage. Sam had popped him a few good ones in the face that had started him bleeding from the mouth, but Nick didn't let it bother him or stop him from boring in, his hands up high.

Sam felt a little glad that at least Emmy hadn't done it with some punk.

Nick got in close and sent some jolting short punches into Sam's body that staggered him back until he could feel the bar behind him. Sam changed direction, moving back a few steps and then shooting his right with all of his might into Nick's chin, catching him coming into it. It was, Sam knew, as good a punch as he'd ever thrown.

But Nick didn't go down.

He staggered back, shook his head a few times and came right back in towards Sam. When he did that, Sam knew he would lose the fight.

He did.

It took quite awhile, however. Almost half the chairs in the place were broken and the both of them were battered and bloody before Sam caught a punch to the head that sent multi-colored lights racing through his brain.

When he opened his eyes, he was lying on his back on the floor with Emmy kneeling at his head, crying. Nick was sitting at one of the tables while the bartender tried to patch up his face.

"How are you feeling, Mr. Mackey?" he asked when he saw that Sam was coming around.

"I don't rightly know yet. I got licked, didn't I?"

"Yeah. If you want to try again, you'll have to wait until tomorrow and it'll have to be someplace other than here. I got to run a business here, you know."

"I been licked. Damn, but that ain't happened to me since I was a kid. I don't rightly know how I should feel."

"Everybody gets licked sooner or later."

"Yeah, I expect you're right," Sam said, pulling himself to his feet. "That don't make it any easier though."

"Go sit down, Pa," Emmy said. "I'll go get something to wash your face with."

"She's a pretty nice girl, young fellow," Sam said. "I figure she's worth one more go-round."

"You know, you're stubborn. I'm too strong for you, you must know that."

"Yeah, I know that. I just want to make sure you think highly of Emmy, that's all."

"I thought high enough of her to marry her Wednesday, didn't I? What more can I do?"

"Married her! You married her?"

"Yeah. You mean you didn't know?"

"No. You married Emmy, you say? That right, Emmy?"

"Sure is, Pa."

"Well, what do you know. Hey, what's your name, young fellow?"

"Nick, Nick Mahrides," he answered, shaking Sam's hand.

"Mahrides, what kind of a name is that?"

"Greek. I thought that's why you started that brawl, because you didn't want Emmy marrying a Greek."

"Were you born in Greece?"

"Yeah, in a little town way back in the mountains but I left before I was two."

"So you're from mountain people, eh? I guess it's all right with me then. Mountain people are the same all over. Do you work here, Nick?"

"I own the joint. I got half-interest in another outfit over on the other side of town, too."

"Say, that's good, Nick. You got any other hoochie dancers working for you beside Emmy here?"

"A whole slew of them. Emmy ain't going to be dancing any more, not in public anyway."

"You knowing all those wild women, Nick, you might be a pretty good son-in-law at that."

Jim, Joan, Charley and Sue came into the place at that point. They looked around at the broken furniture and the battered faces of Nick and Sam.

"What're you doing here, Sam?" Charley asked.

"I was just welcoming my new son-in-law into the Mackey family, that's all."

"Married? Everybody's going nuts to get married today for some reason. What'd you two do, have a brawl?"

"Yeah, he whopped me, Charley."

"No kidding! I'm sorry I missed that I've been waiting a long time to see you get beat up."

"Hello, Joan," Sam said. "Good to see you again. You going to stick around for a spell this time?"

"For good with Jim, anyway. At least if I can get him to an altar like Emmy did with her boss here. Gee, you look like hell, Sam."

"To tell you the truth, I'm not feeling too sprightly either. What did you think of that there play Jim wrote? Wasn't that something, the way he worked it?"

"Yeah, but now I've got another deal," Jim said. "Nick, you claim to be a businessman. Come on over to one of the tables and hear what I've got to say."

"Sure. You didn't steer me wrong about Emmy so go ahead. Hey, Tony, give this table anything they want on the cuff."

"How do you feel, Nick?" Jim asked as they sat down.

"Like I just put in an hour in a concrete-mixer. That old man of hers can hit! You should have seen that fight, Jim. Say, I heard about that play of yours folding. Too bad."

"I was just doing that for laughs, Nick. Now I'm being serious. For some fool reason or other I'm taking a wife and I've got to get something steady going for me. I was wondering if you'd like to go in with a club down in the Village and let me manage the place."

"The Village?" Nick said, questioningly. "I don't know about that, Jim. Unless you have a good front, you wouldn't do too good down there. Besides, they don't go too much for the belly-dancing south of Twenty-Fifth Street."

"No, I'm talking about a different kind of club, a hootenanny-type thing."

"A what?"

"Folk-singing kind of thing. That's starting to be a big thing, Nick. Sam's damn good at it, too. I've heard him. He whangs away at that guitar a mile a minute."

"It's an idea but I'll have to think about it. I'll tell you what I'll do. You take a look around down in the Village, see what the best deal you can get is and then talk to me. In the meantime, let's get going with the party!"

They closed the doors, pulled down the shades and forgot about cops, laws and everything except their own enjoyment. Emmy gave a farewell belly-dancing exhibition while Sam tried to figure out how to play a bozooki.

Charley didn't stay around long. From what Jim had said to him, it looked as if they were going to open up some kind of hillbilly place downtown. There'd probably be some kind of job for Charley if he hung around but he didn't feel like hanging around that much. The talk about marriage and steady jobs bugged him.

Besides, he had something big in mind for himself.

That Marla Peters broad looked damned interesting to Charley. Not too bad looking and holding heavy, very heavy indeed. Maybe Jim could afford passing up all that bread but he couldn't. In a case like that, Charley could see marriage.

She seemed to go for the exotic stuff so he'd best push the Indian routine. He knew the bar where she hung out and there wasn't anything he could lose in giving it a try. Maybe the gigolo who'd blown the whistle on Jim would be there. That would make it worth his while just to break his nose again. According to Jim, this Randy character was a sucker for any kind of a left.

In the bar to which Charley was heading, Marla and Randy were seated in the same booth where they had been sitting when Jim had made his play. Randy, feeling very certain of himself, was doing most of the talking.

"Yes, Marla, you've acted very stupidly in this whole business. I dare say you're the laughingstock of New York right now, falling for that utter nonsense that Perkins gave you."

"At least I had a little excitement for a change."

"Stick to the kind of excitement that's best for you. The sort that I provide so well in that huge bed of yours. When you go bringing strangers into your bed, there's no telling what might happen. It's like buying a product that hasn't been tested. Stick to the tried and true, Marla."

"When are you going to get your nose fixed?"

"When are *you* going to get it fixed, that's the right question. After all, the whole miserable affair was all your fault although it does give me a certain quality of ruggedness, bent this way."

"You rugged? Don't make me laugh."

"Now, Marla, my pet, be nice to me. Don't you think it was time we started planning our winter trip to Bermuda?"

"Oh, damn Bermuda!" Marla said.

"What? Still stewing over being taken by those penny-ante hoboes? Don't say I didn't warn you about them, I was able to see through them right from the start. What tickles me is that Indian they had acting as an Irish playwright and you taking it right up!"

"Randy, you're becoming annoying again. Do you know something? I got a great kick out of that sleigh-ride that Shamus—I mean, Perkins and the rest gave me."

"You silly fool, they were all just after your money! Don't you have any sense at all?"

"Of course they were out for my money, hell, who isn't out for my money? You are, that's for sure. The difference between you and them was that I got a few laughs out of being with them."

"And the whole town got quite a few laughs out of you and they're still laughing."

"What do I have to look forward to now? A succession of vacations, ever-lasting vacations in various sunny places with shady people and with boring, whining pimps like you? Hell!"

"I'd be careful if I were you, Marla. Very careful. It wouldn't take much for me to dump you again and if it happens again, that's it and I don't care how many T-Birds you buy me, I won't be coming back this time!"

"Big loss! I could pick up another punk like you off any street corner!"

"You're asking for it, Marla!"

"Go on, beat it you bum! Hit the road!"

"I always said you were a vulgar old bitch and this proves that I'm right."

"Go on, scram!"

"All right, all right, I'm going. You couldn't keep me here if you tied me with chains. You'll have to really pay your men from now on! And pay plenty!"

"You stupid sap, haul your butt off before your pretty face gets busted up again."

"By who? Who gives a damn about you nowadays anyway? Whoever cared for you?"

"Me care-um!" Charley Bluejacket cried, entering the bar and coming over to Randy.

"Oh, no!" Randy cried. "Here comes the other wildman from Perkins' Circus!"

"Welcome, Sean, or whatever name you call yourself by now! Slug this over-dressed, loud-mouthed baboon! Kick his teeth out! Scalp the bastard!"

"Now wait a second there," Randy said, backing away from Charley with his arms brought up to protect his nose. "I'm a friend to the Red-Man!"

"You speak with crooked tongue, White-eye," Charley said, belting him in the gut and causing him to lower his guard. Then Charley gave his all in a straight right that sent the cartilage mashing against his cheekbones.

"Hit him, kick him, jump up and down on him!" Marla requested.

As Charley was following her instructions, the bartender came flying over the bar and tried to cave Charley's skull with a sawed-off pool cue-stick. Fending off the club with his arm, Charley punched him in the adam's apple, kicking him in the stomach when he fell down to the floor.

"Come on, Tonto," Marla said, getting to her feet. "We'd better bug out before the fuzz come up and bust everybody in the joint. Follow me!"

"Charley Bluejacket follow white squaw lady to-um ends of the earth."

"Just out to the street where we can get a cab up to my penthouse again. You like-um penthouse, Charley?"

"Like-um heap," Charley said, following her up the steps.

Outside, they hopped into the first cab they could find. Thinking of her wealth, Charley ripped at her clothing like a killer whale attacking a sperm whale.

"Take it easy, you ignoble savage. Wait until we get up to the apartment," Marla said, pushing him off.

"Me no can help um-self. Heart beating like tom-tom ever since first saw you."

"I seem to feel I've been through all this already. You don't have a play you want to get produced or something, do you?"

"Hell no. Have big idea for health camp, though."

"That figures."

"Be good for country. This country. United States of America, I mean-um."

"Yes, thanks, I'm aware of the fact that this is the United States of America."

"Great White Father in Washington say all his people are getting weak and sickly because no exercise enough. Charley Bluejacket fix-um all that with great health camp in mountains. Men and women and girls over statute of limitations only. Run, jump, swim, hike all day. Make-urn love all night."

"I hope Jack hears about this, it'll take a lot of worries off his mind."

They staggered past the doorman who kept a carefully noncommittal look on his face as he held the door open for them. Inside the elevator they went as far as it is possible to go on a very small elevator on a short trip.

Marla's dress was hanging around her shoulders by shreds when they came out of the elevator. Mustering an awesome amount of dignity, when you consider the circumstances, she strode regally into the living room and addressed her colored maid.

"Jocasta, I want you to—"

"Yes, Miz Peters, I'se going."

"Nice looking little spade there," Charley said.

"The hell with *her*! It's me that's come along with the chance to build that camp of yours, remember?"

"Charley Bluejacket remember."

"Come on out to the terrace, Charley. Over here by the railing where we can look down."

"You off your rocker? You no catch-um Charley Bluejacket that close to edge of roof."

"Oh, I love someone with a sense of humor! Come, you sweet-talking Sioux, come over to the couch."

"Charley Bluejacket Mohawk," Charley said, proceeding to take off his clothes.

"Tell me Charley, when you were Sean O'Toole and working on the stage with that big blonde girl, did you *really* do it?"

"Every damn night show last-um."

"How was it?"

"She no complain."

"Sure, but she wasn't thinking of setting you up in a health-camp where you could have all the legal sex you want. For that kind of deal, I have to see if you're qualified to teach the country anything about endurance."

"Charley show-um white squaw he got endurance like eagle flying in wind, strength of bull moose in fighting season, gentleness of rabbit, and—"

"Ixnay on the rabbit bit."

"Grab hold, rich white-squaw. We make-um love now!"

And they did.

Digging into her somewhat faded flesh with furious, driving lunges that quickened the blood-flow through their veins, he raised her like an arrow sent sky-ward, piercing its way through the crystal clear air.

Her heart leaped and strained within her chest like a wild animal trying to escape a cage. Her long thighs enfolded him while his hands grasped and groped at her body.

Faster and faster, his lust lanced into her while she clutched at him, urging him still on. Holding her throbbing body against him, he impelled her to the verge of complete surrender, slackened his pace slightly and then drove forward again, full force, pounding his way into her aroused body.

She uttered a wailing cry. Her face turned up while her whole body yielded itself to him, and they let their muscles slacken slowly.

The late summer sun baked into their bare bodies as they lay, side by side, his skin dark on his lean frame and hers soft and white like a marshmallow next to him.

"How the hell did the Whiteman manage to take the country away from you people is what I'd like to know," she finally said.

"Whites kill off all fighters, only left lovers to make-um babies."

"Charley, do you really want that health camp of yours?"

"Sure, Charley Bluejacket real patriotic American. Just interested in what he can do-um for country, not for what country can do-um for him."

"That's an interesting way of putting it, you know. You ought to write that down someplace. How much do you think this health camp of yours would cost?"

"How much you got?"

"Uh, uh. We don't play it that way with my cash. You name the price first."

"Hard to say. Have to find big mountain with nobody around so we have privacy, maybe have to build a few buildings. Hard to tell how much bread it cost."

"Well, what you could do is stay here for awhile and we can work it out together."

\* \* \*

Meanwhile, the party at the *Club Piyaki* had ascended into the orgy classification. Sue, Emmy and even Joan had donned belly-dancing outfits and were shaking up a storm on the stage while the male members of the party stamped and danced in front of them, grabbing out hands at the ripe female flesh moving just out of their reach.

"This is wild," Sue said. "Hey, Nick, you sure that that door is locked and covered?"

"Yeah, it's closed all right. Why?"

"So I could do this," she answered, taking off her halter and throwing it into his face.

"Hell, two can play at that game," he said, also disrobing and throwing his clothes on the floor.

"Everybody strip," Sue yelled, wriggling out of the remainder of her outfit.

"Is it OK with you, Jim?" Joan called.

"Sure, why not. Just keep close to me, that's all."

In seconds, various articles of clothing were being scattered around the club. The three girls up on the stage danced arm-in-arm while passing bottles of *ouzo* to one another.

A good time was had by all.

A month passed and by this time the folk-singing joint down in the Village that Jim had mentioned was a reality. Unable to think of a title or a name for it, they simply called it *"The Place"* and let it go at that. It was a small, dark and dingy place and when Sam let loose with his electric guitar, people were deafened.

Sam was the featured performer. He wore a gaudy cowboy outfit and acted as master of ceremonies while Jim worked behind the bar with Sue. It seemed like a good set-up for all concerned and they worked very hard at it.

However, the place went out of business within four months and they all ended up working for Charley Bluejacket at his health camp.

THE END

# Beat Girl
## by Bonnie Golightly

# Chapter One

The night before my mother died of cancer of the liver, she got roaring drunk. "One last time," she said (and downing all of those martinis was really heroic in her condition). "Just one last time before I'm catered by the Frank E. Campbell people."

"Oh, *Mother!*" sobbed Joyce, my brother Bart's wife, and went careening out of the room, looking like a drunken circus tent in her mother-to-be clothes.

"I'm sorry she gets so upset," my mother said, really meaning it, "but why does she insist on calling me 'Mother'? She's got a perfectly good one of her own. Or at least adequate," she amended, for she and Ida Bradford had never been friends.

"Oh, Mother," Bart said quietly, repeating Joyce's very admonition, except on him it was something else. Bart understood Mother, probably better than anybody—including me—unless you count Tennie, our maid-cook, who had been with Mother and Mother's family all of her life.

That night Tennie was there too. We were in Mother's bedroom. Mother had insisted she and Jess come in for a drink. And when Joyce swept out on her tidal wave of tears, Jess looked embarrassed, as he always did, and Tennie looked fierce.

"You got no call to carry on this way, Miss You!" Tennie spoke out, her eyes flashing.

"Stop calling me that, you black wretch!" Mother said, and Tennie looked madder than ever.

It wasn't that Mother had race prejudice, or that she didn't love Tennie and appreciate her—maybe even more than she ever loved anybody else—but Tennie had picked up the habit, in the past few very difficult months, of calling Mother what she always called people she didn't consider "quality folks": Miss You, or Mister You, on the pretense that she couldn't remember their names.

"Stop all this," Bart ordered sharply. Then he went out to find Joycie, and nurse her back to peace of mind.

After he had gone, we were all silent and morose. Jess looked miserable. He has very dark skin, but that night it was more gray than black, and he looked as if he were dying, along with Mother. And I guess he and Tennie too both sort of thought it was the end for them. I know I felt it was the end for me.

"Here, Miss Cornelia," Tennie said gently, as she went over to the bed and plumped up Mother's pillows. Then she quietly took her martini glass away from her. "You best get your rest."

"R.S.V.P.," Mother murmured languidly, drunkenly, sleepy, dying. "Or is it something else?" She looked at me.

I wouldn't say it, but Jess did. "It's R.I.P., Miss Cornelia," he told her, his voice husky with dammed-up tears.

I don't know whether she heard him or not, but she made a small gesture with her hand, and, with a little sigh, turned over on her side, facing the wall, her hand still lying where she had dropped it, like a small discarded fan. Such a pretty little hand. It had been a size 4½ (French glove size) when she married my father, so she had said. And now it wasn't much more. It was smaller than my own. I picked it up, placed my palm against hers.

"Darling," she said faintly. But she didn't turn around. And after awhile, after Tennie and Jess had tiptoed from the room, I tiptoed from the room, tears gushing out of my eyes like the hot waters of Old Faithful. That was all. She died in the night.

They wouldn't let me or Joycie go to the funeral because Joycie was so *enceinte* and I was so young. But those weren't the only reasons, for Joyce was still ambulatory and I was seventeen. Actually, both of us were too broken up—I, in my private way, and Joyce in her public one. Had Joyce liked Mother much, that chestful of histrionics she unloaded on everybody would have made healthy sense, but it was so patently a combination of great-acting, guilt, and self-pity on her part that it drove grief right back inside me and bottled it up to ferment, so that I couldn't even cry about anything else, much less Mother, for ages. Further, when I saw the exhibition Joyce put on, I had to force myself to speak. I guess Bart and Tennie and Jess thought I'd been stricken with lockjaw or had gone into Catatonia, that state with the prettiest name. Anyway, their cure for me was to keep me from the funeral and hustle me off on a plane for England the next day, to stay with my Aunt Maude, as had been more or less arranged previously when Mother first found out she was going to die.

Now I wish I had forced them to let me go to the funeral. Had I gone, perhaps I would not have renewed my Holy Grail-type search for the Beautiful People. For when Mother died, I felt that the only one of the Beautiful People I knew had died too. That's why I couldn't talk. Who could I talk to? All the same, I was determined to find someone; you can't live inside a bottle forever. But this, like most searches, led to a lot of trouble along the way.

When I say that the family, or what there was left of it, put me on the plane, I mean it literally. Joycie and Bart were in full command, very much the senior partners that day, and I was a very minor one, will-less, choice-less and next to speechless. But they were quite sanguine about that, and waved me off with heartiness and hope, thinking, no doubt, that if the roar of the plane didn't bring me to, the roar of the British Lion would. I wasn't so hopeful; I knew how much I had lost and how deep I would have to go to retrieve it. More than six feet up or down.

They, of course, were counting on my fondness for my Aunt Maude and her fondness for me. As a child, I had thought of her as a sort of goddess or queen. It was she who had taken me all over Europe, watched over me most of the years between seven and twelve, had been at close call when I was in school in France, and Switzerland. But most important of all, she had been the embodiment of my dead father whom I had never seen, she being his only sister. I can remember how I used to gaze at her sometimes, when she let me sit in her dressing room as she combed her long hair before the vanity mirror, and I thought how heavenly beautiful she was. But once back in England, I soon realized the mirror had the right word for it: vanity. She wasn't beautiful at all, but she was vain.

It must be a terrible thing to be a fallen angel, and I'm afraid it was in my face, the gladness draining out, almost upon seeing her again. In the first place, naturally, she had grown old—quite old—as she was much older than my mother. And she had settled down into thinking of herself as an English Lady, her American girlhood being so far in the past. The lovely waxen features I had once thought of as so beautiful had now coarsened with time, as if the wax had melted and had begun to run. Had I been capable of objectivity at the time, I would still have seen her beauty, but all I saw was a vain old woman who looked at me with cold disappointment. You see, she, too, I now realize, was confronting the vestige of a broken image. Her little chubby baby with the lovely ash-blonde curls and bright eyes had been swallowed by the present me: a dark-haired, neurotic wraith, underweight, funereally dressed, with dark circles under its eyes.

Considering our immediately mutual letdown, I suppose we did reasonably well together for the next long months. But I did not warm to her or my surroundings. More and more England seemed to me rather like a cold forbidding governess—all iron-gray stern and tight-lipped—and I thought my feet would never be warm again.

On the surface, poor Aunt Maudie knocked herself out. She immediately put me in a "best" school full of frightful females with sick-looking teeth way out in front; and when the "season" started the Teeth crew and I moved into town and took our places at the deb "dos" and were admired and talked about. I was also in that last group of debutantes who were presented to the Queen, a fact that floored one and all except me. As I say, I was dead and cold. Even in the summer my feet were cold.

Another thing, Aunt Maude and I found we had simply nothing in common. She had become as thoroughly English as T. S. Eliot, and simply doted on her "town house" and its treasures. (Town house was actually an awful old apartment with ceilings as high as a Norman church and countless drafty, heatless rooms hung with tapestries.) I once remarked to Aunt Maude that it reminded me very much of an ancient castle—a most witless thing to say, for she immediately divined with her astute eyes that I felt trapped, an imprisoned princess held in the tower. But she said nothing, which was her way.

However, what she did not know was that the "castle" gave me the horrors for other reasons. It was more like a boot camp for necrophiliacs than a home for quiet, mending me. Everything about it spoke of the dead, from the priceless hoardings to the private ones of private value; most especially the latter. I was haunted, for instance, by most of Aunt Maude's cherished private heirlooms brought over from Virginia when she was a bride. There were baby shoes circa 1800; there was a ghoulish vomit-making thing under glass which looked exactly like flowers spun from varicolored thin wire. I would have continued in my innocence had I not one day admired it, as it hung in its ornate oval frame, and been told that great aunt so-and-so had artistically woven the hairs of her dead sisters, grandmother, and great-grandmother to form this tender memorial.

But the Longtree relics were not the worst: there was the matter of Aunt Maude's deceased husband, Uncle Philip—Sir Uncle Philip—dead before I was born, but almost as alive. She had preserved everything from crumbled slippers (why all this foot fetish among the Longtrees? Was it inherited?) to hookah, mustache cup and scissors. No fingernail clippings, though, but again locks of hair. And everywhere you looked, his likeness. In the library, of course, it was a painting of him in full military regalia, while elsewhere there were simply old-fashioned photographs, also always showing him in uniform. He was such an army man that I am sure he not only never missed a campaign, war, or skirmish in his time, but I doubt seriously if people were even able to quarrel without him. One picture I had particularly liked when I was ten, and still a great soft-hearted admirer of Aunt Maude's personal tragedies and treasures, was labeled "Sir Philip in the Boxer Rebellion." I had gazed at it with real affection, for at that time Bart had had a fine champion boxer which used to take prizes at dog shows, and I had thought that kindly, pug-nosed Sir Uncle Philip had been the very man who had understood boxers and their puppies and had reasoned them out of their fights. I was under no such illusion now. For me the place was peopled by "he-haunts" and "she-haunts" as Tennie used to call ghosts, and Aunt Maude, with her austere eye and powdery thin skin, rapidly crumbling into dust, was at once their custodian, soon to join them, and my relic. I had enough relics. One primarily I kept in my heart and head and could not forget: Mother.

Constantly I thought of Mother. She was with me in the drawing room, the W. C., the scullery, the ballroom, the schoolroom, and my room in the apartment. And never as she was but always as she had been that last night with her face turned to the wall, like a picture, her pretty hand left behind in discard, behind her once lush and then wasted eighty-five pound body, and her voice hovering over her body like a visible wisp of fog saying, "Darling." My Darling Death. She was my own private ghost. Aunt Maude had hers, and I had mine—only I was even more selfish than Aunt Maude: not only would I not give her up, I wouldn't share her. In all those months, I never spoke of her at all.

Aunt Maude's discretion was as impeccable as her vanity, and, since she had better things to do than pry into the secret grievings of my adolescent heart, she decided to go right on with the pleasures of her life. The chief of these was "The Nobility."

Transplanted to England through marriage at an early age, she had, like a gently lovely but wild rose, taken to the soil. Over the years, and doubtless with Uncle Philip's help, she had espaliered herself over everything British, crawling carefully year by year up the trellis until she had reached the pinnacle, covering all. By all, I really mean all. She embraced and thrived on everything English with a rich full growth. I suppose she expected to start the same process in me—a slip of a girl, as it were. At the age of seven, yes; at forty-seven, perhaps; but at seventeen, no. Especially my sort of seventeen.

She trotted out endless younger sons, Honorable Miss So-Forths, lads who had come into their titles early, and ladies of title no bigger than Goya's "Infanta," but for me they were not the Beautiful People.

It took Aunt Maude a year and a half, thousands of pounds of English money, and a heart-shaped lifetime of shattered daydreams to realize that though I might be her heir I'd never be her idealized heiress. And when I went to her, braced for argument and strong truth, and announced I was going back to America, all she said was, "Oh, dear." It was then I knew she was a really wise woman.

For though I am fairly sure Aunt Maude did not know why I had failed her, I am sure she had accepted the fact that I had, and that was quite enough.

## Chapter Two

The day he called me was the day I began to plan to tell Aunt Maude. His voice over the telephone was enough in itself to creak open the door of Aunt Maude's mausoleum, but then as we spoke that door blew wide open and let in AIR. Air! Fresh, clean American air. And I realized I had been breathing antique, lifeless dust. It was Pritchard Allyn, sort of a member of the old crew in New York, en route home after a summer in Europe. Oddly enough, he was the first of my old friends who had called me, though I knew from home that others had sometimes passed through.

I was cagey as hell at first, putting on my very best British accent, and sounding as aloof as a duchess, even though Pritch was the first man I had "known"—carnally, that is. But then he hadn't been more than a promise of a man. I wondered if he had grown up.

"How about tea?" I asked him after the preliminaries, dropping my accent back into its slightly English cradle where it normally resided these days.

In answer he suggested dinner, saying he had "things to do."

"Very well," I said, hoping I sounded indifferent rather than put out, and we named a time; he would pick me up here.

Aunt Maude asked me if he were anything important, and, quite innocently, I asked her what she meant. Important was one thing to her and another to me. Which was she talking about?

"I mean, is he someone your—brother approves of?"

"I suppose," I said listlessly, for I had never thought of Pritch or any of them in terms like that. What was my brother's approval? In America, it meant he liked the same people I liked; here, to Aunt Maude, it undoubtedly meant that Bart was the head of the house and must *approve* my friends if I were to see them, whether he cared to associate with them or not.

"In that case," said Aunt Maude, "I'm sure the young man will dress for dinner."

It was merely a suggestion, of course. But then, Aunt Maude, being so English, never made anything stronger. I dressed for dinner.

I climbed into the first thing I saw and swished around the drawing room waiting for my "American young man." Aunt Maude had had other plans for her evening, and was, I think, glad that something had turned up to take me off the servants' hands. Even if it was *only an American*. The Italics are hers, even if she wouldn't claim them.

The dress I wore was right for England and the time of year, even if it was wrong for America at any time of year. Aunt Maude's dressmaker had done it, and she is what I can only describe as a dewy-eyed dowdy genius, completely in tune with her time, her town, and her tot of gin. Seldom sober and probably unable to focus her bad eyes on anything smaller than a billboard, she somehow convinced Aunt Maude that she was always "up" on everything; that she worked with Captain Molyneux hand-in-secret-glove and you couldn't go wrong with her at half-the-price. At first, I protested with American-type vigor, but I was soon hushed—by the hush—and gave in. What did it matter, I felt, if I looked like . . .? Name it, you can have it. Anyway, I wore one of her copied original creations that night—my "late summer dinner gown"—as conservative and serviceable as an English walking shoe. Made to last too. As I say, Aunt Maude had resigned herself to me forever.

But that was where Pritch came in. Just as I heard the bell, I methodically checked his arrival on the Ormulu clock (something I would not have done at home except for a Mr. Right, had there been one). And as I heard Cecil, Aunt Maude's butler, admitting him, using that funny intonation on him which as good as said: "*You*, sir, are an *American*," I knew all at once what a hideosity that clock was (if it had been human it would have been strangled at birth), what a fatuous snob Cecil was, how glad it made me that Aunt Maude was out—way out—and how glad I was that Pritch was *in*. My mausoleum door was creaking.

"Baby!" In he walked handsome in his handsome dinner clothes, and held his two arms out to me like an invitation to a seat in a garden swing. I took them. He kissed me soundly on both cheeks.

"You look like a *great lady!*" he exclaimed. "All grown-up, dignified. Like a member of Parliament!"

Cecil, I noticed, heard all this, and, with a smirk hidden behind his decorum, inquired if we would be wanting "cock-tails." The hyphen was his.

I turned to Pritch, who said, "Why not?"

And Cecil went to fetch cock-tails, a concoction, I assured Pritch in his absence, that would be memorable, if not drinkable. But Pritch had suddenly interested himself in Aunt Maude's house.

His back facing me, hands in trouser pockets, he studied one of her cherished Constable landscapes while I studied him. I had seen her Constable often for the last months, but I hadn't seen him.

Yes, I decided; whether or not I had changed, he certainly had. No longer the too-tall, almost wavering silver birchtree-blond-sapling, he was now an adult plant—whatever that meant. And I wondered what it did. I couldn't remember. Pritch was foggy, as foggy as the time we had "made out," as we said in New York, when I was a virgin, and had clung to him with all the fire, passion and hate of a circus animal that night near Montauk. He had taken my virginity. But nothing else. So now he was new to me. And old at the same time. No birchtree stripling. He was a man. How old I didn't know, but a man. I remembered he had been in Harvard in those days. By now he must be out—way out, from the way he looked. For now I saw he was not tall at all. He was going to be one of those men about whom one said: yes, he should have been tall, you can see it in the authority in his glance, the way his eyes are steady and colorless, the expression on his face.

And, as if just for proof, he turned and said, "This is a fabulous house!" It was a statement of discovery, as if I were a Dresden doll which simply belonged in the collection, on some chimney piece or other.

Cecil brought the drinks—Martinis, I think. I drank mine, and Pritch held his. He continued marching around, looking, looking.

How long can one stare at the back of one's dinner escort—especially if one is hungry? I said as much.

He turned, and a knife went through me as the lamplight made familiar all those familiar features I'd forgotten: American, but so Pritch Allyn that he became a nation, a country in himself. I had forgotten his cheek was so golden.

"I guess you still spend a lot of time swimming, and at the beach," I murmured.

He took some of his drink. "Beach? I haven't seen any sun this summer, except through cathedral or plane or train windows."

I took a sip of my drink. "Did you do the Chateaux Country?"

He nodded, then he took my hand, led me to the couch and began to talk about his summer. "I don't know if you want to hear," he said, boyish again, in spite of the serious and direct look of his once blue eyes, now angry sea-gray, "but I've been taking Europe in—in the Grand Tour manner."

Then he told me how he was lost, drifting, didn't know what he wanted to be—poet, architect, pianist, painter—and how he doubted his talent in all. During this, his hand had circled my arm closer and closer, like an ever tightening bracelet. The things I felt because of his touch were like explosions in the distance. But I knew they could come closer. And if they did, I could short-circuit. I had once before.

I stood up. "Aunt Maude would love you for loving her house."

"She must be a great Aunt Maude," he declared, and continued his tour around, admiring this piece of glass, that painting, that chair, and stepping around her Aubusson carpet as if he were afraid he would tread on someone's face. I said this, and added that all these things of hers were in everyday use, that she wanted them "lived with."

"But not lived up," he corrected me suddenly. "I'm glad you live in such a house."

And that's when he discovered the Sheraton table—Aunt Maude's pride and joy, since there were chances it was an original—the first and last.

I thought he'd never stop about it; his eyes were full of love for it—enviably so—as if the thing were human, and female. That's when I suggested dinner, and quick about it. I really was hungry.

In the taxi (and I didn't know where we were going), he still sat like a man surfeited, replete. I had to ask him to give the driver directions before his reverie was broken. "I certainly want to meet your Aunt Maude," was the answer to that, echoed by, "I certainly do, Chloe. I certainly do."

I promised him he'd meet her, wondering what she would make of this particular kind of enthusiast. But it wasn't my business, and how did I know that it wasn't just another creative crush he'd got into? I heard him give the driver the restaurant address. If it wasn't the Ritz, at least it was food, whether I'd been there or not.

But riding along in a taxi with Pritch, an American, I felt awfully sophisticated, well-informed: after all, I did know the places to go for drinks, dinner, dancing, and just to be together—and he hadn't asked me. How grim and square, I thought. And let's have a grim, square evening. Something to take home. And be proud of, Babbitt-proud-of a la the '20s. In a way, we were the '20s, all of us. Only I felt more on the Evelyn Waugh line than the Sinclair Lewis. Maybe I was wrong. Maybe I was rebellious Carol from *Main Street*. But one thing was certain: Pritch was a Babbitt, albeit a young one and slightly less Rotary Club and more couth. But everything about him screamed American. That his sights were rather higher was in a way pathetic, for somehow I felt he would never make it. I wondered what he was doing with his life besides gnawing at culture, and even as I asked him I was just sure he would say he had already been taken into his father's firm.

"Me? I'm taking post-graduate work at Columbia next year," he said.

Which just proved that my insights were scarcely 20-20. "In what?" I asked, and his answer was so detailed and complicated that I still didn't quite know—but he was studying something that had to do with art history and restoration of art treasures; the latter explanation is what hung me up. But no wonder he was such an enthusiastic bore about Aunt Maude's house!

Now that I had him started on the culture theme he didn't seem to want to stop. He went on and on about periods, museums, private collections, galleries in New York and London and God knows what all. How could he have thought I was really interested? Finally he said, jokingly (I hope), "Why, Chloe Longtree, I'd sell your soul to the Devil to own a Tiepolo right now!"

"Why pick on me?" I answered. "Anyway, I'll buy you one instead. It's cheaper."

"I don't know about that," he said. "Tiepolos fetch fancy prices, if and when one comes up for sale. In the world auction record, their price-range history starts at—"

"—A million dollars?" I broke in.

He stared at me. "Are you serious? Of course not." Then he stared again. "You mean you're loaded?"

I nodded, and he gave a low whistle of surprise. "Good J. C.!" he exclaimed. "I always knew you had a few bucks, put you down for a few hundred thou, but—You mean you got real cash? Straight arrow?"

"Straight arrow. I've got bread. By the bankfuls."

"Gee, kid." He was looking at me strangely now. "Gee."

"I don't like those new eyes you're using on me," I told him only half joking, for I'd had about as many lean and hungry looks in the past few months as I could stand.

"Where'd you get it? You mean your old lady left you all that loot?"

That did it. Without so much as a clap of thunder, I had a veritable cloudburst of tears. I sobbed and sobbed and sobbed. I drenched my own handkerchief, his, my petticoat, my evening coat, and even my hair.

When I could speak again, I was hoarse and said all my t's and d's as if I had a cold, and found myself saying them against his lapel, since he had, quite naturally, taken me in his arms for succor. "I haven't talked about Mother since she died," I started to explain, but found myself ending up on a wail.

"Gee, kid, I'm sorry. I didn't know. Look at me, Chloe. I didn't know, I didn't know."

He rocked me in his arms, and after a while it had the desired effect, and I stopped mourning.

Maybe I *really* stopped mourning, or at least shifted into second-gear mourning, for we then discussed quite calmly all my bad blue months in England and what to do about them. The mausoleum door was wide open now, and I was outside.

We talked freely about our parents, aired all our thoughts on the matter. Pritch, it seemed, had plenty of sibling as well as filial problems. All of his brothers and sisters—three boys and a girl—were older by far, and his parents were so old they practically went back to the Stone Age: sixty-five each.

"They're as old as Aunt Maude," I exclaimed, impressed and sympathetic.

"They live in a place rather like hers too," he told me. "Only they don't have any taste. The only good things in the place belonged to their ancestors."

"Oh, a lot of the stuff of Aunt Maude's are hand-me-downs too," I told him to make him feel better, even though it wasn't precisely true; her best things she had bought herself. Then I asked: "They don't live on the upper West Side by any chance?"

He nodded morosely, considering, I guess, that this was another strike against them.

"I'm sure I know where they live. Is it terribly grand, a huge old fortress-type of apartment house built back when apartment houses were a rarity?"

"Yes. You know the place." He named it. "Rather than terribly grand, it's grandly terrible. At least I think."

I didn't at all, and said so. As a matter of fact, it was one of my favorite places in New York, architectural atrocity or not. All of the apartments in it, so I was told, were simply enormous, ceilings so high you could only see the top on clear days, etc. And, since the place had been built for the very rich and the very chic of the period, the first who thought it unstylish to continue living in their tremendous old houses, the architect of the building had included in an effort to pamper these spoiled people a horse-and-carriage-size elevator which could bring milady's equipage up to her very door, so that the only effort she had to expend was that of opening her flat door and being handed in to her carriage by her footman.

"Those heaven days," I sighed.

"You think so. I wouldn't live there again for anything."

"I would," I sighed again. "I've only been there once—" (I didn't tell him it was to visit some people my mother considered déclassé but was sorry for in their straitened circumstances) "—but it was marvelous."

He looked at me rather sharply. "It strikes me as odd, in that case," he said coolly, "that you dislike your aunt's place so much."

I gave him a perceptive and admiring look. "Touché," I said. "Very touché. You've given me something to think about."

## Chapter Three

We hadn't really passed the soup course before I knew that this was no ordinary dinner and that this was no ordinary date. Pritch made me have a new respect for Babbitt-type young men—if that's what he was in the least. He was fun, and yet he was sound at the same time. And he had good intuition, as well as artistic intuition—or sensitivity, as most people are content to define it. I liked him tremendously. So much so that I was thinking of ringing up Aunt Maude and making some excuse to stay out overnight, which, of course, was a little precipitate on my part, because we had only been brotherly and sisterly so far in our embraces, but I had that definite feeling.

Also, one of the things I had learned since I left most of my baby-skin, is when and when not to be the horizontal woman—or whether the choice will come up. I had been, lately, completely upright morally, if these things really are part of morality, but not so at first. I had thought sex was a way out of mental misery and grief, a mistake as universally prevalent as syphilis, and went to bed with so many men I met that I practically forgot the meaning of the word vertical. But that time was long since passed, and therefore, considering that Pritch was my first physical "love," not only was there the initial attraction, but fastly accumulating was a real stockpile of energetic sexual desire, because I found him so desirable in the mind and spirit as well as elsewhere.

I knew something was going on with him too. His eyes had softened and yet brightened at the same time: like a sea, formerly gray, when a streak of sunlight hits it from a crack in the clouds.

Because of this, we began paying elaborate compliments to each other—or entered "the courting stage," as it is known. Our rapport was established, and the time for intimacies would soon be at hand.

Needless to say, I was terribly excited, and I could tell Pritch was too. He said some wonderful things to me—about me—and I listened to them as if the words were as fresh to me as my feelings were, as if no one had ever used them or heard them before. He told me how attracted he was to me, told me how pretty I was, how mature, how intelligent, how et cetera. The language of love.

But, as so often happens in affairs between people who have known each other a long time in too many other lives and relationships, the well-padded brickbat department was as irresistible as the hearts-and-flowers. The fact that we both had clay feet *had* to be pointed out, I suppose, and past private opinions, of a critical nature, had to be aired, in order to clear the air, so to speak. Or at least Pritch obviously thought so.

He started first, and the opening words weren't out of his mouth before I knew I had not steeled myself enough for the probings and insinuations that were to come: the well-tempered clavier was going to make some ill-tempered music when her turn came. What he said was:

"Clo, you know you're a funny girl. The last time I saw you you seemed so mixed up. Not stupid, but goofed up—running wild, like a car without a driver, because you couldn't make it with your mother dying."

I felt my cheeks heat up, and knew I had turned pink. He was after nothing short of my Achilles' heel. How bold and cruel. "Oh?" I said in an aloof voice. "Is that the way you thought of me?"

"Sure. Everybody did." His smile was still warm and intimate, casually disarming. He didn't know he had already gone far too far. "Getting engaged to that guy three times your age," he continued, "and then breaking it up was *crazy* crazy stuff. I guess it didn't bother you too much, but it really threw him. And the rest of us, too."

"That's very interesting," I replied. "Funny nobody mentioned it to me. I suppose all of you thought I should have gone back to Charles and gone through with it?"

"Lord, no, Clo. But the fact that you started it in the first place proved you were like a runaway. But, as I say, you've stopped now. You've really changed. What made you stop?"

"Gravity," I said, my humor still in need of restoration.

"Good sense, I'd say," he further mollified.

But I was feeling very unreconstructible. "Do you mean you and Avery and all the crew really thought I'd permanently flipped?"

"Sort of," he admitted. "But you haven't I guess some of them have flipped instead."

I didn't want to change the subject from me to them. "Do you understand, Pritch, what my mother was really like? What she was as a person, aside from being my mother?"

Pritch thought about it, and looked rather uneasy as he did so. Then he came up with: "I didn't know your mother very well. Anyway, let's not argue."

"Let's not," I returned. "But since we've gone this far, and since you're the first person I've been able to talk with at all about Mother, I . . . I think I should tell you a few things."

And so I told him; tried to explain about the Beautiful People; how I'd felt when I knew she was going to die, then trying to hang onto myself all those months until she did die—like falling, falling deep down in a well; and when I hit bottom all the sense and life and air was jolted out of me, and I just closed up in a vacuum.

"But you're not in a vacuum now, Chloe," he assured me facilely.

"You didn't let me finish," I said. "I was going to say that when the air was knocked out of me grief poured in, and *then* I closed up. So grief was still there, fermenting. And I was simply a bottle. With an airtight stopper in it."

"But you're all right now, aren't you, kid?"

I looked at his beaming face with a very cold one. "No, I'm not really all right. I'm just better." I would not give him the satisfaction of hearing me add: since you came. And anyway, I wasn't sure that he himself had not put the stopper back in the bottle again. I suddenly felt very alone, and wanted to be actually alone.

He continued to grin at me in that self-satisfied and somehow intimate way. Clearly, he did not know how deeply I was offended, else he would not have strolled on toward the quagmire with such a confident spirit: "You ought to come back home," he advised me lightly. "Stay with Joycie and Bart. You should see their kid. That would cheer you up."

"Ugh," I said. "How repellent."

"What? Don't you like kids?"

"It has nothing to do with 'kids'," I said acidly. "I suppose you don't know how Joycie treated my mother, or how she behaved—"

"She was very upset, I know."

"Yeah," I agreed. "Very."

"Don't be that way, Chloe," he said after a time of studying me with now serious, worried-looking eyes. "You should know I'm—well, I knew you before I knew them."

"I suppose you're dear friends with Joyce and Bart now?" I asked. "And they've sent you as an emissary, is that it?"

"Don't get hot about it," he answered evenly. "I am friendly with them, but they didn't even know I was planning to see you. I got your address on my own. Don't you see, Chloe, I wanted to see you. And now I am genuinely concerned because you seem unhappy. I think you should get out of England and go someplace to work things out."

"And you think that place is New York? Certainly not. I wouldn't dream of living with Joycie and Bart and their baby."

"Maybe you and one of your friends from school or something—?"

I shook my head adamantly. "I'm going to stick it out here. I've got to, or nothing will ever work."

"Is it that desperate? You sounded so calm and—"

"It isn't desperate at all, really."

He gazed at me in a way that made me very uncomfortable. "Why is it that you *seem* so close to making it, look so much like you are—?"

I shook my head, feeling as if everything were blurred and melted out of recognition, as if I were going blind. "Let's talk about you," I said tightly.

"We don't have to. You understand me. It's you neither of us understands."

"Words, words, words," I said, really feeling in the dark now, for of course he was right: my motivations were as unknown and curious to me as new germs under a scientist's microscope. But I lacked the scientific curiosity—and courage—to track them down.

I guess Pritch divined this and found my stubbornness both stupid and disgusting. I could almost feel his warmth recede from me, and the light of interest fade from his eyes. Now, he was studying me coldly. "Want to go?" he asked, standing up before I'd even had a chance to nod.

In the taxi there was no doubt about it: he had given the driver my aunt's address; he was taking me home, getting me off his hands. I felt the tingling numbness that always comes when I've made a great and admitted defection; I felt unspeakably sad.

All I could think of was regret, regret that I had fouled this up so entirely that I was being peremptorily dumped. Now we would not go to bed together after all. He would escort me to the door, say goodnight, and that would be that. And in a few days he would be gone. As a matter of fact, he was gone already. All that remained was his duty to deposit me where he had found me. No more phone calls, no more anything. He had had it. The mausoleum door was closing again, with me back inside. . . .

I sat stiffly in my corner, knowing I simply appeared silent and hoping I appeared casually silent, not the frozen and hurt thing I had become. I wondered if he was wondering about the thoughts touring around in my mind. Of course he wasn't. He had lost interest, and I knew it.

Without turning my head, I took stock of him out of the corner of my eye. He was a study in placid indifference. God knows what he was thinking—cathedrals, art, New York. Whatever it was, he had certainly parted company with me, as surely as if we had been riding in separate taxis. It made me furious, but glummer than ever. I felt like something evil, a poisonous snake on the way to the taxidermist's, or disease—gray, horrible cancer—something to get rid of as soon as possible, before I became dangerous.

I'm as bad as you think me, I started to say, but just then I startled myself considerably: tears were simply pouring out of my eyes, scalding hot and uncontrollable. I had pride though, at least; enough to want to keep my tears to myself. If he saw them, all right, but they weren't for him anyway. They were for me. I didn't want his sympathy; I wanted my own. What had I done, what was I doing to myself anyway?

We had stopped in front of Aunt Maude's, and it took me a few minutes to realize he was paying off the driver, that he would not be keeping the cab. He helped me out, took my elbow lightly and we went up the steps.

Cecil let us into the flat, and I averted my face when I returned his good evening. I certainly didn't want to share my tears with him. He told me my aunt had just come in, and I nodded, ducking my head down.

"Great!" I heard Pritch exclaim, and then he wheeled me around eagerly. "Do you think it's too late to disturb her?" He was so excited by the prospect of meeting my aunt that I don't think he even noticed my tears. Dying for a chance to talk about his crush on the 19th century.

I glared at him. What a colossal nerve he had! I started to blurt out at him that these were the first words he had spoken since dinner, then I thought, what's the use? I had already parted with enough of my shabby dignity. "I'm sure she'd like to meet you," I said. "You two have a lot in common."

He missed the irony, of course, and just at that moment Aunt Maude came out of the library saying: "How pleasant, Chloe! Your friend from the States." She had both hands outstretched.

# Chapter Four

They got on like a pair of identical twins, just as I had expected. Her delight was unbounded: such an *appreciative* young man, even if he was an American! I watched the two of them racing about, inspecting everything like a couple of appraisers, and was filled with absolute loathing.

Aunt Maude's British accent was getting thicker and thicker, and Pritch's deference was getting so deferential that I was afraid he'd be on his knees to her in one more minute. So in the midst of this glittering spectacle, this shining performance, I thought I had best extinguish my own small light and creep silently to bed. I tried a preliminary goodnight on them, and they didn't even hear me.

This left me in a peculiar position: should I simply leave? No, that was a childish, pouting way to do things. And after all, if I felt left out, it was my own fault. The best thing to do was ignore them too. With that, I rose and poured myself another glass of sherry; I'd dedicate my attention to that.

They had disappeared into the dining room now; Aunt Maude wanted him to see the Romneys. When they did that room, she would have to do the drawing room—even though he had seen it earlier—and God knows what other cells. Well, if that's what he wanted. No use in having his entire evening spoiled. I decided to be good-natured about it. Did my decision have anything to do with what happened? I don't think so. I think Pritch had had it in his mind all along, all the time I had been having my feather-fight with my own neuroses.

Because what happened was that when he had had enough of his grand household tour, he simply came up to me and said, "Ready to go dancing now?" as if that was what we had planned all along.

Aunt Maude beamed at us as we left. "Have a good time, children," she said, and I knew that I had won her full approval for the first time since my arrival. And through absolutely no fault of my own.

I looked up at Pritch in pure delight when we got outside and said, "Where are we going?"

"Where do you think?" he answered, handing me into the cab that had just stopped for us.

I was just on the point of saying I didn't know, when suddenly I did, for he took me in his arms without a word. Then he gave the driver the address of his hotel.

Going up in the lift I felt as if I could have accomplished the trip under my own power. Joy is as much a physical sensation as a mental one, and I tingled all over with it, feeling as disturbed and excited as an embryo two minutes away from birth.

And it was like that all the way. We walked in his room and he didn't even bother with the light switch, but simply put me back in his arms as if that was the only place I was ever made to be.

I had remembered Pritch as another kind of lover. That night so long ago at Montauk he had been fierce, and we had made love like ravenous wild animals. Now his passion was slow and measured, yet I could feel the strength of it when he kissed me. It was not the ardor of pure desire this time; it was the ardor of love as well.

Gently I felt him unfastening my clothes; he paused every now and then to kiss me. When the undressing ritual was finally completed, he picked me up as carefully as a flower and took me to bed.

Again and again we made love—love that was swiftly and completely satisfying to both of us. And yet before he had moved away I would feel myself desperately wanting him again, and even before I could touch him, to let him know, I would feel his arms around me again, and the sharp deep cry of desire would break from his lips even as it did from mine. And again we would be plunged into that endless silent world of brilliant ecstasy where so few lovers can ever really go.

At last this craving need subsided to some degree and we lay there in warm bliss and love exhaustion—no other fatigue like it. But I knew I couldn't go on lying there in the dark secret heaven I had found in his bed. Insatiety probably would never leave me, but all the same I had to leave it. I made a move to get up, even as I felt his arms tighten around me once more.

"There's always tomorrow," I whispered.

"Stay!" he urged me.

For a moment I gave in, but dimly, a long time back, I remembered having heard Big Ben strike two or three; much too late even then, and now it was even later. Quickly I slipped out of the bed, eluding his arm, and stood beside him, feeling almost irresistibly drawn to return.

In the half-light from the open window I saw his arm reach for me. "Tomorrow," I whispered again, and went to the chair where he had put my things.

My hands trembled as I dressed, then I saw the bedside light go on, and felt his look before I saw it.

I turned. He was sitting up in bed, completely naked, looking at me in the most curious way. It struck me that his expression was somehow alarmingly out of contrast with his nakedness. It was almost the calculating look of an executive giving a job applicant the once-over and should have been accompanied by a fully-clothed body in a business suit.

The smile of happiness which I suppose had been perched on my lips like a silly bird on a branch, simply flew away, and again I turned my back—coolly, I hoped—and continued to dress, taking my time, buttoning each button, getting all the snaps. I hoped he didn't see how much my hands were shaking. Now I fiercely did not want him to know how deeply moved I had been by his love-making.

"You want some help with that zipper in the back?" he asked at last.

"No, thanks," I said with equal lightness. "It doesn't matter whether I get it or not. I have my evening coat."

"Suppose your aunt is waiting up for you."

"She isn't in the habit of so doing, nor," I added with regrettable sharpness, "does she help me undress at night."

"Still no sense in going home half-dressed," he said.

Giving him an angry look, I tugged at the zipper, knowing its tricks full well, knowing it would have defied an acrobat to handle it alone. Then suddenly his hands, cool and efficient, were on me, and the zipper shot easily up making its soft buzzing sound in transit.

"There," he said, but he didn't take his hands away. One slowly caressed my neck, and the other curled softly over my arm as it was something he owned and prized.

"I have to go," I stammered, close to tears, not at all understanding him now, a few minutes before—or, truthfully, at all, ever.

"So do I," he said gently. "In the morning. Somehow I didn't get around to telling you earlier."

I guess I staggered slightly from the impact of this news. No wonder he had behaved as he had. "But darling," I cried. "Must you—must you?"

"Reservation's made. Flying TWA."

I simply couldn't believe it. It had been so short. And for what? Why couldn't he cancel it? Everybody missed planes. I was just about to blurt this obvious suggestion out when he cut me short.

"And there's something else," he said quietly, looking into my eyes, his hand still on my arm. "This isn't just any old flight I'm taking. I'm late as it is. . . ."

Late? My mind jumped ahead like a hurrying crippled animal, desperate for a way out, an explanation. If it was a job, something like that . . . *anything* . . . it couldn't be so important as tonight and. . . . Then suddenly I knew. "Who is she?" I asked, my mouth feeling frozen, as if it could barely open to form the words. "Somebody I know, I guess. . . ."

"Yes, it's Joycie's sister—Les—Lesley."

"Oh," I murmured like Dumb Dora. The whole situation had about it something so familiar, so odiously familiar. . . . And then I remembered: the night before Joyce and Bart's wedding, down at the foot of the stairs at the Bradfords' when I had seen Pritch for the first time since he'd shelved me . . . if you can call it that after only a few dates . . . when he had told me he was there on account of Lesley; that yes, they were very good friends indeed—something of the sort. And I had thought of the color green as it was in one of Mother's paint tubes. Green for jealousy. I could almost smell it now—oily, horrid. "When is it?" I whispered.

"Wedding's the end of October. Lots of parties and things," he gestured, looking almost at ease again, so glad he apparently was to have got it all out in the open. "I thought you knew."

"No," I shook my head, truly dazed now, and feeling the exhaustion from what now proved to be our wasted reunion absolutely overwhelm me. "No," I said again, feeling something more had to be offered. "Joycie never writes since the baby. Occasionally Bart does, and they telephone whenever they both get tight and sentimental. But I guess we've kind of drifted apart—" I said no more. There was no room just that instant for anything more than the huge lump in my throat.

"Chloe. . . ."

I looked at him wretchedly, angrily. If he asked me to forgive him, or asked if I was sorry I'd—

I guess he saw what I was thinking, for the appealing look and voice changed. "I'm not sorry. I love you very much. Also, I'm counting on you. . . ."

"Okay, okay!" I said hotly. "Let's leave it at that, shall we?" Abruptly I stepped back from him.

"You'll never get a taxi at this hour," he said, his voice as calm and smooth as glass. "Let me get dressed, and I'll walk you home."

"It's miles," I told him, knowing my own voice and face were unpleasant and full of contempt. "You've forgotten how spread out London is." Anything to hurt him.

"How will you get home?"

"I'll call Aunt Maude. She can send the car for me."

"At this hour? Won't she be horrified?"

"Heavens no!" I laughed like a wild thing. "She's used to it. I stay out like this all the time."

"Come on," he said firmly. "You and I are walking you home. We have things to talk about."

I wanted to yell: I DOUBT IT! But what was the good? Maybe he did have things to get off his chest. I'd gone this far; listening to him wouldn't change it one way or the other.

It was cold outside; another London winter already promised in something in the early fall air. I hadn't looked at him since we left the hotel, and now I didn't either. I dipped my face down into the collar of my white satin coat, glad I had worn it after all.

"Do you want to go to Lyons' for some coffee or something?"

"No," I said.

"You aren't going to talk to me, I see," he remarked after a time.

"That's right," I told him, still not raising my head.

"You know what I wish?" he said, trying again. When I didn't answer, he said, "I wish you'd come to New York."

"For the wedding?" I asked sarcastically, unable to resist this much at least.

"No. For your own good."

"Suppose you leave my own good to me."

"You know, of course, that I'm going to tell Bart and Joyce that you're not happy here."

"And are you going to tell them why?" I blazed at him.

"No," he said. "But only because I don't know."

I stopped and confronted him in the dimly-lit street. Of all the gall, mitigated or unmitigated! Then my rage fell limp. Of course he was right—he didn't know why. Nor did I, really. I couldn't blame my state of general discontent on him. He accounted for only a few hours of it, as compared with many months. "Don't tell them," I said quietly. "It won't do any good. I'm not going to go back to New York."

He gazed at me in that sad, resigned way wise but weak parents do at incorrigibly wayward children, and we resumed our walk, as silent as before.

We were in the heart of the London night—or rather past it, and in the cold, depressing region of the early morning when all of it seems like a historical ruin, a monument rather than a living city. The breeze didn't help either. As it ruffled my hair it only made me feel more unreal. An unreality moving in the interior of another unreality. Two figures from the past, ancient—timeless—moving in the limitless plains of the past. And so we were. Pritch and I had been here before, walking along the Good-bye Road, which, for us, was indistinguishable from its parallel thoroughfare, Hello. "—'a tale told by an idiot, full of sound and fury—'" I murmured to myself.

"Are you quoting something?" he asked.

"No," I lied, yearning desperately never to have to lie again, yearning desperately for him to say he loved me, as he had back there in his room; wanting to ask if Lesley were prettier, smarter, more fun than I—wanting the world.

## Chapter Five

After that ghastly and ghostly walk, the waters of boredom, complacency, and day-to-day piecemeal peace settled back over everything as if Pritch had never been there for those few terrible and yet wonderful hours. I had my customary feeling of vague but unidentified discontent with my life, except for the always-present dark angel of my mother's death, and a sharper cognizance of my real distaste for my aunt But neither of these two things was strong enough to make me think, as I had that night, of making a change. And, as usually happens, I met Somebody.

Somebody was an awfully nice guy, but he reminded me too much after a while of all the other awfully nice guys, and I knew I just wouldn't be able to stand it. But awfully nice guys don't require dramatic endings to their love affairs, and I was in no hurry to let him down. He would appreciate the slow, easy, painless way, and that was what I was giving him.

He was a sports car enthusiast, and had a terrific custom-built job—a Lagonda. We used to take wild, fast trips all over the English countryside, the only dashing thing about him being his car and his driving. Sometimes, to tell the truth, he scared me out of my American wits. Anyway, I'd never get used to left hand traffic and high speeds on such Lilliputian roads.

One day we had driven up to Windsor for luncheon, and that was the day—perforce—I made up my mind. I got sick as hell and barfed like a dog all over everything, including the car upholstery and my new fall Balenciaga.

He was terribly sympathetic, mopped me up, and talked at interminable length about how everyone got car-sick at one time or another, but I knew I wasn't car-sick: I was afflicted with a slight touch of pregnancy. So that night I told Aunt Maude I was going back to New York, and that's when she said, "Oh, dear."

That was exactly a month after Pritch had gone. And though I knew that I could kid myself another two weeks or so, sooner or later I'd have to face it—and, if I wasn't careful, big as life. I'd made no close girl friends in England, and certainly none who weren't "nice"—*i.e.,* ignorant in the matters where my current interest lay. I had to get back to New York and see Avery. If ever a girl lived who would know about abortions, she was the one.

Aunt Maude thoughtfully cabled Bart my plane schedule, but outside that did not interfere. And before I knew it, I was off.

Whenever I travel—especially when I fly—it seems as if my mind deliberately shuffles through all of its available material and comes up with a selection for contemplation during the trip—this in spite of the fact that I, consciously, always take along a lot of books and magazines. The books and magazines always stay right in my lap, unread, and my mind takes off, almost from the minute the plane leaves the ground, and goes its own way—usually detailed, sometimes devious, and always complicated. I knew this time it had decided on My Problem.

All during the flight as I gazed down almost unseeingly at the tiny white-capped ocean waves, I was thinking: why did you let yourself get pregnant? What good will going back do? He'll be married in two weeks.

Why didn't you just go lose yourself in Paris? They have lots of doctors in Paris. Or why not have his child? It won't ruin your life—only middle-class people let such wonderful acts of nature ruin their lives. How nice to have a child all your own! You'd grow up together, go everywhere, be independent. How do you know you are pregnant? The questionnaire continued. The usual sign plus car-sickness is melodramatically insufficient. And it isn't enough that you've just had that certain feeling all along, ever since it happened. You are a masochist and a fool, just dying to suffer.

By the time we arrived in New York, I felt dead tired from thinking, and had concluded that I was behaving like a fool. Yet why shouldn't I go back to New York, pregnant or not? And looking up Avery to be on the safe side was not an act of further folly.

I suppose the only thing I didn't ask myself was whether or not Pritch was in love with me, and the reason I didn't ask it was because I knew. Pritch was strongly attracted to me, yes, but he didn't love me—he would be slow and cautious about falling in love. And I had even come to the conclusion that the chances were he didn't love anybody, including his fiancée, Lesley. In all likelihood, this marriage was simply the pleasant outcome of "the right thing to do." He had never written me a line after he left London, and actually, I had not expected it—only hoped. Certainly as we came into Idlewild that day, it never crossed my mind to look him up in New York or involve him in my life in any way.

And that's how with all my cold, brilliant thinking and working things out, I got the surprise of my life.

I think I saw them and knew it was them the minute the plane touched the runway, even though they were specks standing with other specks beside a faraway dollhouse-size air terminal.

So when I unfolded myself and gathered up all my unread reading matter, my airplane kit-bag, my purse, my papers, my hat, I did not dare to look outside the plane's door on past the landing strip to where all the meeters stood pressed against the fenced gates beaming rather idiotically in the direction of the meetees, debarking one by one. I did not dare, but somehow it just happened anyway, and there they were lined up in a straight line, cheery as anything, waving and shouting something: Joycie, Bart, Pritch and Lesley.

I think it was my guardian angel who delivered me into their tender, excited and noisy care, for I am sure I could not have simply walked.

Naturally, they were all over me at once, Lesley as enthusiastic as anybody, and we, like most of the other groups around, were a scramble of embracing arms, rather like excited octopuses, everyone talking at once as shrilly and as fast as possible. Or almost everybody. I was like a dead center, the eye of a cyclone, and simply did not protest against the kisses on my cheek (Pritch's were cool and soft as damask—like roses) or who took my arm, and who took the other, and who took them away. I was propelled through brief customs, now borne along by other European travelers rather than my own group who stood aside, beaming again even more radiantly than before, their eagerness in no way abated.

As I waited for my turn with the customs people, I snatched at the thoughts that crowded my mind. But they all raced by like fast-moving clouds on a windy day. Everything was blurred, too fast, too fast. . . .

Then I was with them again, and each was clamoring for something different: Joycie was trying to tell me about her baby, a boy named Cornelius after my mother—an honor my mother would have questioned, as I knew she detested the name. And Bart was trying to find out about Aunt Maude and the mysterious reasons for my sudden return, and both Pritch and Lesley were jabbering about people we all knew and all kinds of frantic parties. Then it occurred to me, quietly, just like that, that they were all really hysterical. Why?

Bart and Joycie had a new car, I saw. They had sold Mother's big one and had bought a perfectly frightful but roomy chrome-covered station wagon. "We bought a house in Connecticut," Bart explained, starting the car.

"Didn't we tell you?" Joycie said. "Oh, Daddy, I know we told her. It's near Mother and Dad," she turned back to me. "Small, but just right for us for the present. We were up there all summer, and we're going every week-end this fall if we can, or until the weather gets too bad."

"Mother loves having them so close," Lesley said, her eyes bright and full of friendship. "And she's simply frantic to see you. My God, Pritch. Look at her!" She exclaimed.

Then they all looked at me and noted my various changes in visage, coiffure, weight, color and attire. I felt very young, and wondered if I made them feel very old. I also felt very lonesome. There wasn't enough togetherness to go around.

"Where are Jess and Tennie?" I asked.

"Oh, they're fine," Joyce assured me, tossing her black long hair slightly to get it out of her way. I had forgotten this gesture. I had forgotten a lot. It seemed incredible to me that Joycie and I had been such close friends all through childhood, and that even understanding, not to mention friendship, had come to such an abrupt stop when she married my brother. Now she was like someone I'd never known, like the daughter of a dear friend long dead who had inherited some heartbreakingly familiar traits and mannerisms of her deceased parent. The truth was that looking at her again after a year and a half, all of my resentment came back. This, plus Lesley and Pritch whom I regarded as gingerly as if I had been seated between two tins of TNT, boded no good for America and me either. Where to go next? I thought. The world, even mine, which by rights should be large at my age, was becoming a very cramped place.

Then I noticed the back of Bart's neck. I knew him so well, and for so long, that even after not having seen him for ages, I knew instinctively he was very uncomfortable, mentally uncomfortable, about something.

He spoke slowly, "Joyce, you haven't answered Chloe's question." That proved it was not pleasant, for he had been calling me "Mole" before—his old nickname for me.

"Haven't I, dear?" Joyce said in serene innocence. And I thought, how vile!

"No," I spoke up. "I asked where Jess and Tennie are."

"Oh, did you? I thought you said 'how.'" She gave a slight cough.

"They aren't with us anymore," Bart said rather flatly. "Joyce felt they would be happier in Baltimore."

"Baltimore!" I exclaimed. "Why they haven't lived in Baltimore for years! They've always been with us. Haven't they, Bart?"

"Oh, come now, Chloe," Joycie said, giving me a smooth smile with just the tiniest bit of jagged edge to her tone. "They've always gone down there to visit. And they really weren't happy here. Things weren't the same after Mother died."

I felt a tight little wad of anger in my throat, threatening to choke me or make me explode. So that was the pitch. Bart had as good as said so: Joycie had fired them.

I still pride myself on the fact that I didn't say a word.

Joycie pitched merrily into the chilly silence like a health swimmer attacking the waves on a December day. She, too, pretended to love it. She splashed and capered, and I didn't listen to one word she said.

Vaguely, I knew she was being joined in her conversational romp by her sister. And morosely, feeling really apart now, except for the knowledge that somehow Bart was still with me in spirit even if he couldn't be in actuality because of his wife, I waited for Pritch to get in on all this small-talk fest. But he was as silent as I. I looked at his profile: neither sad nor glad. It told me no more than a silhouette.

Lesley was sitting on the edge of her seat telling Joyce the latest sick joke, though Joyce begged her to stop, that she didn't get them and she thought they were awful, even when tediously explained. I found myself listening; I did get them and right at the moment sick jokes seemed particularly apt. That's why I didn't hear what Pritch said—anyway, he almost whispered it.

I turned to him. "What?"

"I said I've got to see you by yourself. Have lunch with me tomorrow."

"No," I said quietly, but firmly. "I'm sorry."

"Please!" His tone was as keen as a knife.

"Go ahead," I suddenly heard Lesley say. She had turned around and was staring at me full face. Her expression was impossible to decode. Only something defiant and hurt in her eyes tipped me off. "I know all about it," she told me steadily. "And I wish you would have lunch together."

## Chapter Six

We went to "21" and we made the most minute of talk and were very gay about old times, how we all used to come there together—Avery Stafford, Tim Atkins, he and I. Though actually I think we were all together there only once, and then he and I had not been together: that had been my Tim Atkins period. But the headwaiter I was glad to see still recognized me, as he always had because of Mother. And the food was divine.

Funny how sometimes when you are upset the most, your appetite is heartiest—like the condemned man's last supper. We had that marvelous chicken soup with curry in it, heart of palms, and an entree.

I chattered all through the food without knowing I was chattering. It was like being cold and not knowing it. We made all kinds of inane comparisons about English food and French food, and even compared notes on our stays abroad—I had gotten to France twice and Belgium once while I was there—and we found out we had not only stayed in the same hotel in Belgium, but that we had had rooms on the same floor. At different times, of course. But that's how the conversation ran—scampered. In London we had talked only of ourselves; here, at home, we talked only of selves other than our real ones. And it was all so easy, so pleasant. Right up until the time that I realized what was happening. And again I got that sunk feeling, the same I'd had in London that night after dinner when he was taking me home. This was another—and harder—"never-again." For this time there was good reason. Number one: his marriage; number two: my interesting and top-secret condition.

I was suddenly so full of agony that I thought I was going to be sick. I guess Pritch saw how wan I'd become.

"What's the matter?" he asked starting up in concern. "Don't you feel well?"

I shook my head. No use in being brave if I couldn't hide it. "Too much real food after that English famine," I said.

He helped me up, quickly got the check, and helped me outside. I stood on the sidewalk on Fifty-Second Street and coaxed myself into recovery. He stood by, saying nothing, looking worried, watching me as I fought it out.

"I'm all right now," I finally said.

"You want to go home?"

"No," I said decisively, which wasn't hard. "Home" was a strange place indeed these days. Joycie and Bart had also failed to tell me they had converted the two lower floors into a duplex, retaining the upper two for a duplex for themselves. Of course it was *their* house, according to the will. . . . Mother had left me the equivalent in stocks, and the furniture and things were to be "equally divided" at some future mutually satisfactory date. But I didn't like it at all.

"Feel like walking then? Or a drink? We could go to the Plaza."

"No," I told him. "Why don't we look up somebody?"

"Who did you have in mind?" he said with a slight frown.

I started to suggest Avery, because Avery was so much on my mind just then, but he said instead, "Let's go to my place, Chloe. I really did want to see just you, by yourself."

"So you said," I returned coolly, trying to seem poised and unconcerned. But my heart leaped up all the same, just as if he had whistled to it.

We took a taxi, and I inquired in my controlled mild tone if this were his own apartment he was taking me to.

"Yes," he said. "I can't bear living with Older Generation up there in that massive rockpile."

"Do you have lots of room?" I asked. "I mean, is it going to be big enough, or will you move?" I didn't add, after the wedding, for it seemed to me tactfully implicit in the question.

"Quite big enough," he answered, scowling slightly as if he were mad at the back of the cabdriver's head.

I said no more, but noted we were headed downtown toward the Village. Somehow I had never thought of Pritch as the Village type. He was far too elegant, too fastidious and, admit it, something of a snob. Still, snobs lived in the Village. Probably the biggest ones. I observed and remarked upon the number of new buildings which were going up everywhere, and quite justifiably Pritch had no comment to make on this. He was in another of his silences, apparently a gloomy one. What was he thinking, this guy who waxed hot and then cold? Whatever it was, I loved him so. But I put this thought gently out of my mind, like an extravagant bit of something admired in a shop which common sense told me not to have.

"You really don't care much for Joyce anymore, do you?" he asked in a troubled voice.

Why shouldn't I tell him the truth? "No," I said coldly. "I don't."

"Joyce feels bad about it."

"No, she doesn't," I answered. "She thinks she should, but she doesn't. She wants it this way. She made it this way almost singlehanded. She's what Tennie used to call 'contrary'—she wants to hang on to that cake she's eaten. She won't ever change now."

"You mean she wants to be big grownup sister-in-law, in joint command with big brother, and at the same time play dolls with you on rainy days, or when the juvenile mood suits her?"

"Something like that."

"I thought so, but I promised her I'd speak to you."

"Oh, so *that's* what you wanted," I said. Now I felt fully deflated. But that was nonsense. What else could he have wanted?

"Partially," he said in his noncommittal way.

"Is it about Lesley too?"

"Naturally, it concerns Lesley too."

That, I thought, was the zenith in the enigmatic, or else it was as obvious as a fire engine in a busy street. Probably the latter. Of course it would be to Lesley's advantage too to try to get Pritch to act as go-between for Joyce and me, and in turn, to see how the wind blew as far as she and I were concerned. One big harmonious family. I wondered where they would decide to send me to college, since that was to their minds probably the ideal place for me to go. Or would they, this Board of Directors, make some other plans—all depending on whether I was going to make a happy addition to the family or not? I decided to take up the die—and cast it straight in his face.

"I'm not overly fond of Lesley either," I told him with emphasis, but no particular feeling.

"I didn't ask you that," he said slowly, but interrupting me all the same. "What I really want to know is if you are going to be happy in New York."

"I doubt it!" I cried impatiently. "But I didn't come back here to be happy. I've got other plans."

"Such as?" He looked at me measuringly.

"Skip it," I said. "I won't interfere with your lives—the Bradford-Allyns and the Bradford-Longtrees."

"I understand how you feel," he looked at me with a sort of odious fraternal protectiveness, "but there's no use in jumping to conclusions."

I was so mad I almost jumped out of the cab. "Look here, Pritchard Allyn, if you think I want to gain a brother you're mistaken! Anyway, you're sounding more like Mother Hen. When I tell you I want no part of any of you, I mean it! I intend to live in New York for a short time— maybe with Avery or somebody, move into my own flat—then leave. I hate being around all of you. I think it was simply awful of you and Lesley to turn up at the airport, beaming like a pair of relatives. I want no part of you, her, or your marriage."

"Are you really that jealous of Lesley?"

"What did you expect?" I almost shouted.

"I thought when you saw us at the airport that you would—"

"—Throw my arms around your necks as you did around mine and crow like a baby fed on Pet Milk? The next thing you'll be telling me is that like a good bridegroom you've confessed all, that Lesley wept and forgave, and to prove how courageous and understanding she is, she wants me for her best friend *and* her maid of honor. Stop the taxi, or I will. I'm getting out." I was shaking like a vibrating machine, and the driver had slowed down and was surveying the situation over his shoulder.

Pritch grabbed my arm and firmly drew me back. "Now listen," he said sternly, angrily. "Keep it under wraps. Here, driver. We'll get out here."

"We certainly will!" I said and jerked open the door and tried to slam it in Pritch's face.

He skillfully fixed that, and grabbed me again too, and propelled me across Fifth Avenue into Ninth Street. "Steady," he warned. "Or I'll break off your arm and stuff it down your throat."

What is the answer to this? Certainly, he had me in his grasp, as the saying goes, and I could feel the tips of his fingers boring in. There would be some pretty black and blue marks left, if he ever took his fingers off, that is.

We entered a walk-up, or rather a walk-down, and he pushed me straight ahead toward a white door. No fumbling for the key. He opened it with the swift skill of a housebreaker. He sort of flung me aside, once we were in, and walked over to a closet where obviously he kept the liquor. But I was wrong. He had gone to get a sweater instead, and was shedding his tie, vest and jacket in order to put it on. What a nerve he had, thinking that he felt a little cold at a time like this!

Now I saw that the apartment was one extra-long, and wide room, furnished in beautiful early American antiques, and that the liquor was kept on a dry sink on one side of the room toward which Pritch now strode.

He held up the Scotch bottle in brisk question toward me. I stormily turned my head and he poured two walloping whale-sized drinks, rattled some ice from an ice bucket, and added water from a pitcher. "Now," he said. "Sit down before you really make me mad."

Cool, taking my time, raising my eyebrows in answer to his look, I sat down on the antique settee across the room from him.

"You really are a wild one, aren't you?" he asked.

"When I have ample reasons for making me wild," I replied.

"You nearly made me wild too. I almost never lose my temper."

"Oh, Pritch," I said forlornly. "Look. Don't let's go on with this. You've said enough. I've said enough. I can't help how I feel. Maybe it's wild, or willful—or selfish, or whatever. But I *am* upset."

"And so am I." His voice was quiet, regretful.

"I know you think you've hurt me, well, you have, but—"

"I've hurt Lesley more," he cut in, in the same quiet voice.

"Why? She'll get over it. Just because you told her about our little reunion in London. How could that mean anything to her?"

"It doesn't to her. It does to me. I think. At least that's why we've called the whole thing off. I was going to write you—only I couldn't think how to put it. Then Bart and Joycie told us you were coming back—"

I looked at the half of the drink I had spilled in my lap. Cautiously, my hand still like the last stages of palsy, I eased the glass over to a table. Easy, girl. Easy! was the only idiotic thing I found I had to say to myself. Certainly, the real thinking part of me had just been short circuited. With a loud explosion. I could still feel the reverberation of it in every nerve. "Do Joyce and Bart know that—that you and Lesley—?"

"Have called it off?" He finished for me. "Joyce does. But Lesley and Joyce want you to tell Bart. When you decide . . ." his face was deeply troubled and pale, as if he had just cried a lot. His eyes were pleading.

"When I decide what?" I heard my voice saying from a great distance.

"When you decide whether or not you'd like to marry me."

## Chapter Seven

"Well, aren't you the sly-boots scandal-maker!" Avery greeted me when I went to the phone, and before I could make reply, she continued, "Everybody in town knows that Lesley broke her engagement after you and Pritch had a little night on the town in London."

"What?" I said lamely, but I felt lame. Lame, but serene.

"Am I *persona non* at your address?" she went on. "I'd like to see you. I won't even ask for inside stories, even though I'm sort of ghosting a gossip column these days."

I asked her which one, and when she named it I immediately decided she was lying; that she was just hoping for the job. "When do you start?" I needled her.

"This minute unless you display the proper attitude. What I don't know about you, *Mo-ther!*"

That word still made me a little sensitive, even though things were all set: Pritch and I were flying down to Florida next week. Florida was his mother's idea—don't ask me why. Probably because it was still off-season and "reasonable," as well as remote. Anything to humor the in-laws. Besides, I am sentimental, and what could be nicer than letting the bride pick her own orange blossoms? But this news was not for Avery's ears, columnist or not. The fact that Pritch and I were to be married was very hush-hush. We'd simply turn up in that blissful state a few weeks from now.

I laughed at Avery fondly and invited her to meet me for drinks at the Plaza.

"After five," she said.

Maybe she really was working.

We agreed on the time and hung up.

Joycie asked me who had called. I told her, and in such a way that she would know I considered it none of her business.

She made her usual anti-Avery face. "Pritch agrees with us about her, you know."

"Oh, bug off," I said under my breath and walked upstairs to the nursery—which I forcibly shared with my fretful and very spoiled nephew as a bedroom, since the only other bedroom besides theirs was for the nurse who "slept in." Joyce was being very heroic, thrifty and housewifely these days. She had only a cleaning woman who came in twice a week, in addition to the nurse. The rest of the time she took care of everything herself—including the cooking; and I'll staunchly say she certainly took care of that. Poor Bart. I wondered if even Joyce truly liked tapioca. Anyway, there must have been some better way to make it. The whole thing—this crazy economy drive, the sloppy housekeeping, the bad cooking—made me sick. When I thought of the perfect order the house used to have, the rich, magnificent dinners Tennie served, all those guests, Mother. . . . But it was not my affair.

At any rate, miraculously, somehow, I was getting everything I wanted. Absolutely everything. With Pritch, and the very definite prospect of a little Pritch, the Beautiful People were back in full flower. And I had made up my mind too that as soon as Pritch and I were actually married and settled down in a comfortable house or large apartment, I would ask Tennie and Jess back to work for us. No cramped quarters for the Pritchard Allyn IIIs!

Of course it would mean using my money, since Pritch in his own right had only an allowance, but who could object to good property as an investment? Besides, Joyce and Bart—or at least Joyce—were dying to unload their share of the Glen Cove house, boarded up now since Mother's death, and going to pot—and maybe Pritch and I could buy them out. Or else I could sell too. In any case, there were countless solutions, and I was as busy with ideas as a portable IBM machine.

The afternoon simply took off, and I right after it. Time was comet-fast to me these days; there was so much to do, to see about, think about. And then there was love. Love, a warm, luxurious blanket over everything, shutting out the awful, the cold, the noise. Everyday there was Pritch.

I called him to say I was seeing Avery; despite what Joyce thought, I knew Pritch trusted me to trust my own judgment in such matters. And I was delighted to report to Joyce that not only had Pritch made no objection, but had even suggested that I bring Avery along to Ninth Street to join us for dinner. I told her with such bitchy pleasure, that she reacted with the affronted alarm of a mother insulted by a small child. Just to further enhance the effect I asked her if she really wanted me to stick my tongue out at her.

"You forget this is my house," she said, her nose wings dilated.

"Oh, go back to your comic book!" I advised her, making a home hit. Joyce had simply loved comic books in our childhood.

"I'll be glad when you're gone!" this inspired her to say.

"How gracious of you to tell me," I replied, but I was surprised and hurt by the vehemence of her dislike.

"I don't care! You should see yourself. You're bad, bad—all the way through. Far worse even than your mother!"

"Whose house did you say this was?" I asked icily.

"I don't care! Bart is my husband and it's going to stay that way. I'm no Lesley, uh-uh! You can't snatch away from me what belongs to me!"

"Are you suggesting Bart is next on my list?" I asked in scornful amusement.

"You're not above incest, if that's what you mean!"

I looked at her coldly, levelly. Her still-pretty, but tired face was distorted with anger. And her hair was all awful today. Also she was wearing a perfect bag of a dress and a pair of runover shoes. "You are a terrible mess, Joycie," I said. "Inside and out."

"At least I'm not what you are!"

"You can say that again, fishwife," I told her and went out of the house, slamming the door.

How do you like that? I kept saying over and over to myself. I almost called Bart. But things were bad enough with them—obviously. And my own threshold of pain was still low. Better let the whole thing ride. I'd soon be riding out, and forever, with my Beautiful People.

While I was trying to get a cab, it started to rain, and I made up my mind then and there that the first thing Pritch and I would buy would be a car. Pity I hadn't bought one on the other side.

And while I was riding along, my conscious mind, stuck and pivoted on deep subjects like that: how I needed a car, how hard it was to get taxis in the rain, how Avery would probably not be on time since she never was, etc. But underneath I was as upset as hell. The quarrel with Joycie had really shaken me. In the first place it was bad and rocky to absolutely *know* our rift was permanent, and that Bart, so long as they were married, would have to stay on her side. Which made me feel scary. What if something went wrong with me and Pritch? I'd be even more alone than I had been before. And the baby thing: I still hadn't told him I thought I was pregnant. At first—a few days ago—it had seemed such a warm and lovely idea that I thought I would save it, as a sort of wedding present. Then I realized I was kidding myself about it: the truth was I was scared to tell him. He might not want it; it might change him—and everything. I wanted terribly to talk to someone about it, and semi-consciously knew Avery had been elected. But I would be insane—as well as disloyal to Pritch—to tell her now. Was she trustworthy? Did she have all the good sense I remembered her having? Maybe, I thought, I should just find a good abortionist. But that thought nearly killed me.

Anyway, when I walked into the Plaza she was right there, looking as bright and beautiful as ever, and told me at once that I looked awful.

"I see we're taking up where we left off," I said, feeling miserable but cheered a little—no, comforted is a better word—at the sight of her. "I see you've cut your hair."

"Yes," she said, touching her almost white-blonde curls. "I'm far too sophisticated these days to wear it child-style—long. See yours is still long," she twinkled at me mischievously, giving my own coif a good look.

"Okay. Say it."

"Looks divine," she answered. "Going to cut it for the wedding?"

"Whose?" I inquired with young-cat innocence. "Lesley's and Pritch's?"

"Get you!" She cried in amusement. "Trying to enter diplomatic service? Or are you brainwashing me? Wait 'til you see tomorrow's paper."

"Okay," I gave up. "I'll tell you all about it and you kill the story. Or I'll kill you."

"Why so secretive? Everybody knows it. Far better to be above-board than below."

"Maybe," I said thoughtfully. "But I hate all this mess, believe it or not."

"I believe you, Clo," she told me with quiet sincerity.

It was good, awfully good to have a friend.

We went into the Oak Room and had a couple of martinis. Then I asked her to go down with me to Pritch's and join us for dinner. She was almost touchingly pleased by the invitation and accepted at once.

"I'm sort of on the loose these days, you know," she told me. "You know Madre died."

"No," I said in genuine surprise. "I *am* sorry, Avery."

"Yes," she went on. "And now I know how you felt when—when your mother died. You see, Madre wasn't like just any old grandmother—"

She gave me the details, and went on to say that the Southampton house had been sold for practically nothing. "Of course I have a little money now. But I hate it, really. I so much preferred having Madre."

"I know," I said, because I did. I felt closer to Avery in that moment than I'd ever felt to any friend I'd ever had, including Joyce. Maybe that's what made me suddenly decide to tell her about the baby.

I could tell she was rather horrified. Not at my conduct, but at my predicament. "You've *got* to tell Pritch," she said at once. "Don't wait another minute."

"Why?" I asked.

"Because if you don't," she said, then paused. "Look here, do you know his family well?"

I told her I didn't; in fact not at all. I'd simply met them the evening Pritch and I had made up our minds. "They seemed rather nice—"

"They're cruddy," she said flatly. "About as broadminded as Savonorola. And as vindictive."

I had to admit I didn't remember Savonorola too well.

She sighed, looking distressed. "Well, look here," she explained. "They're heap-big church pillars, number one—where do you think Pritch got all his religious mania from?"

"Aren't they Episcopalians—I mean, sort of high?" I asked.

"Sure, but who says because you're high church you have to be casual about it?"

I pondered this, and at length voiced aloud the theory that I thought they would have objected on the spot, the night they met me, if they were going to object at all.

"I don't mean that," Avery said brushing this notion aside. "You probably think yourself much worse than they do."

"But wouldn't they remember that I was engaged before and broke it up and all?"

"Probably not, even if the word had reached their remote ears. Nobody keeps scrapbooks about us, you know. Besides, they are the kind of conservative squares who have no interest in gossip columns or anything like that."

"Well, that's something, anyway," I said in relief.

"But this baby thing is something else," she said, still sounding disturbed. "They'll think Pritch broke up with Lesley to make an honest woman of you—or that you've tricked him into marrying you and giving your baby his name."

"They wouldn't!" I protested.

"They might," she assured me. "In any case, this is something you *must* discuss with Pritch. After all, it's as much his business as it is yours!"

She was right, of course.

# Chapter Eight

When I told Pritch I was pregnant he turned the color of a glass of milk. "My God, Chloe!" he exclaimed and just stared at me.

I guess I looked pretty miserable, because he came over and put his arms around me and said, "Don't cry, sweetheart. I think it's great about the kid. But you're so damned young, and . . . are you absolutely sure?"

"Pretty sure," I said, looking up at him, not at all certain that he did find it so great.

"Well, God, this *is* something," he murmured, as if he were thinking out loud.

I didn't say anything; it wasn't up to me. I had told him, and that was that.

"What would you have done," he asked, "if this thing with Lesley hadn't—"

"If you and Lesley had gone ahead with your plans? I would have gone on with mine." Then I told him how I had come back here specifically to see Avery and arrange for an abortion, or to have the baby, depending on what seemed best.

"You poor kid," he said sadly, shaking his head over and over. He sat down beside me and took my hand in his and sort of laced our fingers together. "I feel very deeply about these things, Chloe—marriage, babies," he told me quietly, earnestly, his head close to mine. "I would never have forgiven myself."

"You wouldn't have known," I said gently.

This made him shake his head all the more, and his face had the drawn yet relieved look of a man who has narrowly escaped a fatal accident. Finally he more or less came out of it. "Well," he said. "Well." Then he smiled at me, his face brightening like a clearing day. "I guess a celebration is in order. Where the hell is Avery? It doesn't take an hour to buy a package of butts."

"She probably got waylaid," I said, cheering too.

He gave me a sharp look. "You can say that again. I suppose you told her?"

I nodded. "But she's the only one."

Pritch and I were sitting in his apartment, and now that we had had our talk I felt super-giddy and restless. "God, darling, those draperies are *filthy!*" I exclaimed. "Are they washable? Let's take them down and wash them."

He found this perfectly ludicrous. "In the first place, Chloe Longtree, you never washed anything in your life except yourself. And in the second place you can't wash things like that. They have to be cleaned. What kind of wife am I getting anyway? Even Lesley has better sense than that."

I swatted him one, which he more or less eluded, and told him to shut his cotton-picking mouth about old has-beens. "Anyway, let's take them down," I said. "Don't we want everything clean and bridal when we get back from Florida?"

He sort of nodded his head, then looked vaguely preoccupied. I asked him what it was.

"Nothing. Only I more or less promised the elders we'd stay uptown with them after we come back—until we find a place of our own."

"What's wrong with this?" I protested immediately. "I love this place!"

"Oh, Chloe, honey, it's not nearly big enough for two people, and I'd planned all along to give it up. My lease expires at the end of the month." I guess I looked disappointed, because he said, "Baby doll. It'll work out. We'll find something we like. It won't take long."

I was all for looking now, for the thought of staying with the senior Allyns in that huge old apartment of theirs had suddenly become like a combination of going back to Aunt Maude's mausoleum and Juliet's tomb. But I kept this to myself. "It doesn't matter," I shrugged it off. "Anyway, we haven't gone yet, and we can always stay in a hotel when we get back if we haven't found something."

He gave me a strange kind of look, but pursued the subject no further. All the same, I felt as if we had had our first husband-wife tiff. And I wondered if he had the most minute inkling of how little I liked the idea of joining the Allyn parents. Marriage, as a friend of mine once said, certainly makes strange bedfellows.

Avery, who had deliberately found a pretext for going out so I could speak to Pritch in private, was indeed greatly overdue.

Pritch began to pace around the flat, getting more and more like a restless hyena, because he was awfully hungry. And upset, was my addenda to his complaint—the former also unvoiced. I was going to be a tactful wife if it killed me.

"And it probably will," Avery told me while we were in the ladies' room of the restaurant, whence we had repaired so I could tell her how everything went. "Pritch is very difficult. And stubborn." She gave herself a good run-down in the looking-glass, checking to see that all seams were straight, all hairs perfect. Then we went back to join Pritch.

We were having dinner at Henri Soule's "cheap" place which had just opened across from the St. Regis. Only Pritch took on like the bill had given him an ulcer when he saw the amount. I was quite embarrassed, and would have suggested taking care of it myself. Except, as I say, I was going to be a tactful wife.

"From now on," Pritch said outside in the street, "we eat TV dinners."

"Or crow," I heard Avery whisper under her breath, her expression violently disapproving of the scene he was still making.

"You may be rich, Chloe, but I emphatically am not," he addressed me again angrily.

I felt this was no time to discuss finances, and suggested we get a cab back to his place. But I could see from his slightly scowling expression that he really wanted to be alone.

He took a look at his watch. "Aw, Christ!" he said in exasperation, giving both Avery and me rude looks to match his voice.

I said nothing, but Avery spoke up: "Were you going somewhere?" she inquired.

"I was going to study," he said unpleasantly. "If I'd known having dinner would have taken all this time I would have suggested we eat in the Village."

"I'm sorry, darling," I said smoothly, feeling this was the time to step in. I knew his present griping was really left over from his annoyance at the size of the dinner check. It really had upset him, and I wondered why: I happened to know he had at the moment quite a lot of money with him. And this invention about having to study . . . had it been a fact, he would have mentioned it earlier. Was he trying to get rid of us, or what? "I think I'll go home," I said tentatively.

"Oh, sweetie, don't do that!" He said instantly. "I don't really have to study very long, and anyway the book I need I haven't got—this character in my class, who apparently owns no books at all, but borrows everybody else's, still has it."

"Why don't you get it back from him?" I asked, feeling very confused by his off-again on-again behavior. "Where does he live?"

"He lives in the Village."

"Well, why can't we simply stop by there on the way to your house and you go in and pick it up."

"I'd rather not," Pritch said uncomfortably.

Avery gave me a secret look and formed the word "difficult" with her lips. I could see what she meant But everything couldn't be hearts-and-flowers perfect; he had to have some bad traits. Even nasty ones. I wanted a human being, didn't I?

I doubt if Pritch saw Avery make her unspoken comment, but he did notice that I was silent and musing, because he hastily started to offer up his reason for not wanting to pay the call, however circumlocutions the way. "I guess I ought to go by there," he said, "because this fellow has a couple of other books of mine too."

"Well, why don't you then?" Avery wanted to know. "Don't you like the guy? I wouldn't let him con *me* into letting him borrow my books if I didn't like him—"

"Oh, I like him all right. In fact, he's sort of a funny character—one of the true-blue children of the Beat Generation. West Coast displaced poet cum philosopher cum jazz aficionado—primitive jazz, of course—going to Columbia on thin air, as far as I can see, though he must have at least a scholarship."

"What's his name?" Avery said, her eyes oddly bright.

"Seymour—I forget his last name."

"Well how are you going to ring the bell of his apartment if you don't know his last name?"

"His apartment? Good God, I guess you *would* have to call it an apartment. But it certainly doesn't have a bell. It's up about eighty-five flights of the most dangerous stairs you've ever walked on, and when you get there it's a sort of loft—and more or less furnished like one."

"Sounds fright-making," Avery said, and I agreed.

"Anyway," Pritch said rather slyly, "I've forgotten which street its on."

"You devil!" Avery cried. "Tantalizing us like this! How do you know I wouldn't like to meet some beat type and have a nice untidy love affair with him? I've never had a man in blue jeans and a beard—the Bohemian works."

"If you met this one he wouldn't stay in blue jeans long—not from what he tells me, at any rate. He says he likes 'society dolls,' makes him really feel like East meets West—"

"Or West meets East—" Avery giggled. "He sounds divine. I've got to have him for my very own."

"Well, he grows on you," Pritch admitted.

"There," I said, "you have the full definition of a parasite." They both missed it. Avery through absorption, and Pritch for some reason. But I hoped Avery wouldn't get too worked up over the notion of this Seymour. I had already decided he was nothing I needed to meet, no matter how she felt, and I could now understand Pritch's reluctance to visit him. Pritch is very fastidious—to the point of making me look like "Craig's Husband"—and I knew if this book borrower's premises were not clean, it would make Pritch miserable to have to put a foot in the door. I doubted even if Pritch had any intention really of ever trying to get the books back; he probably did not want them after they had been nesting in such repellent-sounding quarters.

All the way to the Village, Avery kept teasing Pritch to have the driver take us over in the direction where Pritch thought this peculiar one lived.

Pritch, however, shook his head firmly; as Avery had said, he was stubborn. "No, we're going to my place and have a nice drink. Wouldn't you like that better?"

"Better than what?" Avery sulked.

"Better than smoking marijuana, for instance," Pritch told her. "Which is the only refreshment he'd offer you."

"How exciting!" Avery exclaimed. "I've never had any. Really, now, Pritch," she pleaded, "can't we go? Just for a few minutes?"

"No," he said staunchly. "Neither of you is dressed for it."

"You make it sound like a hunting trip," Avery pouted, her eyes large and reproachful.

I knew he meant it, and I also knew now that the real reason he didn't want to go was not the distasteful disorder probably to be found, but because he simply did not want to get mixed up too closely with people like that. It was all very well to be hail-fellow-well-met on campus, and even lend books (and possibly money), but no *confrère* business.

By this time we had reached Pritch's apartment, and the cab stopped, and Pritch helped me out. Then Avery. She lagged a little, her heart still set, it was quite evident, on meeting this denizen of the Village. She had no need for disappointment, for there on the stoop, obviously waiting for someone, was a young man who couldn't possibly be anyone but the Seymour in question.

## Chapter Nine

"Hiya, dad," the person signaled Pritch casually, and without being asked, simply followed us inside the door, even while Pritch was still in the "why, hello there" process. I noticed our caller had a couple of books under his arm.

Once inside, and introduced, Seymour nodded to us, and said nothing, as if he hadn't bothered to listen to our names. However, this didn't mean he found us of no interest. When I say he "sized us up" I kid you not. He measured every inch of us, beginning, of course, with breasts, legs, and buttocks. Then we got it in the face. Then our clothes. I started to remark that I was not auditioning for a spot in the chorus line, when he simply turned away and ignored us the rest of the time he was there. He talked exclusively to Pritch, and it was like listening to a dictionary of Beatnik argot. He kept using words like "cool" which was about the only one I recognized, though he made it clear after he switched off campus talk and on to his vivid private life that "going steady with Mary Jane" and "turning on" meant smoking marijuana—or "pot," as he continually called it.

Pritch looked embarrassed and disgusted, and was only too glad when Seymour hauled his obviously sockless sneaker-clad feet to the floor and looked as if he were standing up to go. Instead, he said, "Mind if I have a private *mot* with you, man?"

"Not at all," Pritch said stiffly, and they retreated to the hallway, almost out of my line of vision. But not too far out; after a few seconds of animated but whispered talk on Seymour's part, I saw Pritch nervously shake his head, then reach in his pocket for his wallet. I looked at Avery, but she couldn't see from where she sat, so I decided it was better to just say nothing.

"He thinks we're squares," Avery remarked with feeling.

"He doesn't think we are—I mean, that we exist."

"He doesn't think, period," Avery went further. "If he's a Beat boy, they must have their definition wrong, or else their grammar—he's not beat, he's destroyed."

Then Pritch and Beat Boy came back, both looking somewhat shaken; Pritch for lending money, Seymour for borrowing it. Both knew that the transaction was closed forever, from the looks on their faces. You did not need to study Seymour's visage and attire too hard to know that anything he termed "borrowed" to him meant "gift." His returning the books was an act of barter.

"Now that you've brought back this thing," Pritch indicated one of the books Seymour had given him, "I guess I really will have to study."

"You mean you're throwing us out?" Avery said, looking rather more crestfallen than I had expected. How could she be enjoying this?

"Why don't we all go out and have a coffee first?" asked Seymour quite intelligibly.

"All right," Pritch gave in. "I suppose it can wait."

I shot Avery a thorough look as the four of us started out. I couldn't tell whether she was fascinated or bored, attracted or repelled. She was a strange one sometimes. But judging by the avidity with which she had accepted our dinner invitation tonight, I guessed she was very lonely. And I could guess why too. It had started a long time ago, while we were both going to Chalmers—or maybe even before that, because of her mother. Avery, and her mother before her, had been as thriftless with her friends and reputation as though they were money; the always-plenty-more-where-that-came-from routine. I never did know why, because she was as good-looking as hell and could have had anybody if she'd cared to be selective. But she wasn't, and she had been in the habit of dropping anyone who suggested she improve her ways. I never did, nor, of course, did the Yalies who used to be so crazy about her. But now, I gathered, when the Yale boys called it was more apt to be at dawn's early light, rather than in the gloaming, when proper dates are made with proper people. Now, poor thing, she seemed to reaping all the chaff and none of the grain from that improvident sowing. But I hoped she wouldn't settle for Seymour—that was too far out.

Why didn't I like him? Well, in the first place people in peculiar clothes make me uncomfortable, but the real reason was, and I admit it, that he ignored me. Or rather he looked at me as if I were a commercial product, however a superior one, labeled "doll" with "rich and pretty" in parentheses beside it And I can't stand to be depersonalized. Admittedly, had he exuded charm, been attentive, I would have reacted quite differently, for he was quite good-looking and so was the beard, and his eyes were very expressive, and in a way quite lovely.

And, as it turned out, Avery had the same reaction. It seems he kept calling her—abstractly speaking, of course, and carefully employing the third person—"a rich square dame," insensitive and uncaring for "life." She was really quite furious, and after reporting these results of their chat as they walked along together, she practically turned on Pritch, as if it were all his fault. "Is *that* all you have to offer?" she asked him several times, precisely as if Pritch had deliberately arranged the whole thing, to sell her to the Beat Generation, with Seymour acting as representative.

Pritch kept excusing him, saying it was one of Seymour's off nights, that he was really shy—that was the trouble—and finally adding that he had seemed quite high on pot, and didn't we think so.

"I thought he was high on wine of self," Avery said very heatedly.

Maybe if she hadn't been yakking so much, or if I hadn't become involved to the extent where I was trying to keep her from pulverizing Pritch and Pritch from becoming really quite annoyed, it would never have happened. I was telling them to shut up being angry about one angry young man or whatever it was, and just about that time was when the Corvette skidded up on the curb at Sheridan Square where we were waiting for the eternal taxi, and I got knocked down.

I got right up again, full of Village grime and mud-puddle samples but fine otherwise. Not even any torn nylons or bruises. I assured the driver to this effect who said the accident was due to a mechanical failure of some kind, and that he'd been en route to his garage when he got me instead. We exchanged names and telephone numbers just in case, and he took off while we shakily climbed into a cab.

Nobody said it, but everybody thought it: would this have any unfortunate result on my state of motherhood?

I guess I'll never know for sure, but it certainly was eminently apparent two days after we were married that if I ever had been pregnant, I was no longer. It made me extremely sad, actually, and it made Pritch pensive at least.

"I suppose I never should have told Mother and Dad," he mused.

"You told *them?*" I asked, so horrified that I could not keep from showing it.

"Yes," he said coolly. "Anything wrong in that?"

I shook my head, knowing anything else was folly. I couldn't even quote Dr. Johnson's: "I have furnished you with an explanation; I cannot furnish you with an understanding," for I wasn't even prepared to go along with the explanation bit. All I had was a feeling that their knowing boded the most negative of no good.

# Chapter Ten

Naturally, our honeymoon was something of a frost. We made all the motions and ostensibly had a gay old time. We stayed in a terribly wonderful place in Sarasota and met a lot of people who were fun. But somehow, even the wedding itself was sort of anti-climactic, and I kept getting the awful feeling that Pritch was brooding about Lesley, especially after the baby thing.

Being the wifely diplomat, I didn't come right out and ask to explore his guilt feelings with him, but I did suggest we go back to New York before we'd planned; things were that rocky.

He neither agreed nor protested; we simply took a plane. I had found out these past few weeks that this husband of mine was a silent partner. He hardly said anything all the way to New York, all of which made me as delirious with joy as a throbbing tooth. What can he be thinking? I kept thinking. And it always came back to the same thing: he thinks he's made a mistake, that he should have married Lesley instead. And I reached the point where I halfway agreed with him. But I was determined to make this marriage work—all the way. I did love him very much, even sore and silent as he was. I hadn't forgotten he could laugh and be a warm and lovely Pritch, even if he had.

Consequently, when we left the air terminal and got into a cab, the question of our destination wasn't even discussed: he simply gave his parents' address.

As we rode along that night on those traffic-jammed streets, the city reminded me of my own mental insides—hysterical noise, too much going on at once, no order, and everything panicky with outrage and paranoia. Seemingly insoluble. Yet the streets cleared every night, albeit late at night, and so would I. But wouldn't it be too late? I longed to talk it over with someone. If only my brother Bart were not so all fenced in by his marriage and the family bit. He would help. Maybe he would anyway. Maybe I could meet him for a lunch or a drink tomorrow, away from Joyce. At that moment, it didn't occur to me to appeal to good old Avery.

"Here we are," Pritch stirred me from my thinking, and indeed, there we were—just outside the great, dark old structure where his parents lived, and where I would live too, for a time—or die.

The driver and Pritch unloaded us, while I stood shivering on the sidewalk, bunched up in my Florida-weight coat. Then we went inside.

Even the elevator had that warm mahogany gleam that all handsome old buildings have, and momentarily I felt quiet and reassured. This respite lasted even while Pritch nervously rang the bell, then fiddled for the key. He was just about to use it when an ancient shuffled to the door, opened it, her face an Actor's Studio classic of suspicion, and said, "Oh,"—nothing more as she stood aside to let us pass.

"Hello Olga," he said pleasantly, just as if she had expressed overjoyment at seeing us. "Where is everybody?"

"Out," she said sternly, as if this were an eviction notice instead of an answer to his question.

He made no comment; there was none to make since he had telephoned them the night before, and they knew we were due back. He didn't even turn to me and say, that's strange.

"Maybe, darling," said I, "they thought we weren't coming directly here." Certainly, I hadn't in spite of his earlier suggestion that this was what we would do. Somehow, down in Florida, I had thought he'd come around to my way of thinking, and had more or less decided that we should go to the Pierre or the Plaza or something until we established ourselves. But when people don't talk much, you never know.

In any event, Pritch didn't answer. Instead he said, and not to me but the ancient, "I guess they'll be back soon," and instructed her to "put Mrs. Allyn's things in the guest room."

From the look she gave him, I thought she was going to ask him to put them there himself. Then she gave me a very thorough visual going-over and left without a word.

I hadn't missed the guest-room thing, but at the moment it didn't carry any particular significance for me. I was too puzzled by Olga. "Is she a woodwork product, or just what?" I asked.

"She loves my mother and hates me," Pritch said, strolling about the living room, whence I had followed him, fingering this and that "See?" he said. "Isn't this place awful?"

I wanted to remind him that I had seen it once before, however briefly, and that he had fully prepared me for it that night in London when he had compared it so unfavorably to Aunt Maude's splendor.

"It's not bad, darling," I said, and then with my newfound spouse diplomacy subtly inserted: "we don't *have* to stay here, you know. I'm sure it's an imposition."

"They want it that way," he said, accenting the "they," as if they were foreign agents who had us in their power.

"Well, show me around then," I said brightly. "I want to know where everything is if I'm to live here."

"You'll have your own room," he told me flatly, as if we had been having a long argument about it.

And that's when I simply collapsed on that hideous gray cat-colored overstaffed couch and cried and cried and cried. It was no wifely wile to bring him around; I meant it. But he responded as smoothly as if I'd done it on purpose.

"Chloe, Chloe, Chloe," he murmured over and over, stroking my hair. Then he put his arms around me, and kissed me until I stopped sobbing; then we got up and he led me to his bedroom.

It was wonderful and we were truly together again, only have you ever had your brand new in-laws walk in and find you making love? That's what happened. They ducked right out again, looking after a flash of horrified surprise as if they had merely opened the wrong closet door. Pritch somehow summoned the stamina to give a false chuckle over it. "They'll get used to it," he said.

"Then why am I in the guest room if they approve of legal lovemaking?" I asked as I hurried into my clothes.

"Mother thought it would be best for your health," Pritch replied; meaning, of course, my pregnant health.

I thought a million divine things to say to that, but censored them all myself. "Do you really think," I asked instead, "that it wouldn't be wiser now to wait until morning to go out and say hello? If we don't, maybe they'll just think we're tired from the trip."

But I sensed his negative answer, even before it came, and went on with my dressing. I looked about his room and thought how depressing to have grown up here, and wondered if the guest room were any better. Probably the lumber room, I decided, judging by the rest of the house.

So far, I had seen little of it, but that was too much. The place *was* big, and if the furnishings lacked style, the architecture did not. All of which made the elder Allyn's acquisitions somehow worse. Everything was like the couch—comfortable, but stiff in feeling, humdrum and unfriendly. This house had real Presbyterian austerity, to quote a phrase I read somewhere. I doubted very much then that the Allyns would have even consented to something so frivolous as a listing in the *Social Register*, presuming that they were up to it, society- and family-wise. A large assumption. Well . . . here I was. We made our smiling appearance, hand in hand.

Mr. Allyn, who looked a great deal like Pritch, took my hand in a firm howdy-do type shake, and Mrs. Allyn pecked at my cheek—literally—and said, "Call me 'Mother', dear." I was glad when she took her hands off my shoulders.

Then we all sat down and beamed at each other, and all became uncomfortably aware that Olga was hovering in the velvet hung doorway which separated the living room from the next.

"Come in, Olga," Mrs. Allyn called in false brightness, touching a hand to her cat-colored gray hair which exactly matched her couch.

And in Olga came. "She's almost deaf," my mother-in-law explained to me in a very theatrical aside. Then she said to the servant, "Come in, dear, come in!" And I got my formal introduction to Olga, and was pronounced a member of the family. She took this with her former good grace, gave me a good glare, and switched haltingly to her other foot.

Mother Allyn made some servant-mistress talk about luggage, if there were enough eggs for breakfast, and similar things which sounded so studiedly rehearsed to make me feel at home that I felt positively lost in a forest. And sunk.

Then Father Allyn inquired about our trip, and Pritch told him at such length about our sightseeing, our trip through the Ringling Museum, the circus people, etc., that I could see the poor man's eyes glaze with boredom. All the while, I knew, Mrs. Allyn was boning up on me. She had evaluated my clothes, analyzed my skin, had me down for a nervous type, and was probably planning to tell me what to do with my hair, when Pritch made an elaborate yawn and said we were tired and had better go to bed.

"That's right, Brother," she said to him, utterly serious—that's what she called him; and, looking at me solicitously added, "our new little daughter has to take very good care of herself."

Oh, my God, I thought as Pritch and I exchanged kisses (after the parents turn, of course) and parted for the night; and not so much as a nightcap. Here, I knew already, that term strictly applied to an antiquated, but sensible, form of headdress.

## Chapter Eleven

I won't say that living in the Allyn household was a new life for me, but it was, if deadly, not without its moments, and certainly it was different. And in a way, refreshing.

Pritch and I were summoned from our separate rooms at eight to come to the breakfast table that first morning. And Mother Allyn was as cheery and as active as a robin. She made it quite clear in every way that she liked her life, loved her husband and son, and didn't care a damn (if she had been able to bring herself to utter that word) whether I was Chloe Longtree or Chloe by the song of the same name. I was to her simply her son's wife, and she wanted with all of her wholesome heart to accept me. And I admired her tremendously.

I had known lots of middle-class people before, of the "well-to-do" but modest circumstances group, but I had never been very close to them. Living at the Allyns was therefore a real thing for me. Their rigid sense of morality was completely alien, slightly appalling, but their rigid sense of justice was not. I suppose all might have gone well had the two in our case not been so inextricably mixed together.

It began with my money. Mother Allyn and I were having one of our quiet mother-daughter talks one morning after the "men" had gone to school and office respectively, when I told her we were looking for a house to buy. "House?" said Mother Allyn. "Why, dear, that doesn't seem a bit wise."

"Why?" I asked—innocently, I realized now, so at-home had I become. "Real estate is an awfully good investment. Pritch agrees with me, I know. It's crazy not to in the circumstances—" ("Circumstances," of course was a euphemistic reference to our expected child, which we had decided not to tell the parents was no longer expected.)

"Well," she said, settling back against her chair, looking thoughtful, "it would be *nice* to buy a house, but Father gives Brother all he can afford just now—he plans to retire soon, you know—and until Brother—Pritch—finishes his education . . . well, I don't see how financially—"

That's when I realized that Mother and Father Allyn knew nothing at all about me. "I could swing it," I said quietly.

The look that came over her face would do justice to a Dr. Jekyll-Mr. Hyde performance. At the end she was literally speechless.

"I have lots of money, Mother Allyn," I said, and proceeded to tell her about it.

I can't say for sure, but I think that is when the real hostility started. "Of course," she said, after I'd finished, "that does make a great deal of difference. I didn't realize that Brother—Pritch, as you call him—had married an heiress." She almost added a "huummph." "I recall that he said you had a private income—" She gestured, as if she had just laid it aside and put me on the balance scale instead—"but I hadn't realized that—well, in that case, you certainly don't need *my* financial counsel."

"I do indeed," I told her. "I haven't anybody else's—except my lawyer's and broker's."

"I'm afraid I'm not up to either," she said, standing up. "I just hope you'll use your money judiciously, and not let it spoil—you." I knew her hesitation over that last word was caused by an indecision as to whether she should say "spoil Pritch"—or "Brother," to put it her style—or me.

"Well," she said in an airy tone which told me she was on the verge of making some excuse for closing the audience, "I expect you have lots to do today." (She thought I was going to shop for maternity clothes.) She turned and gave me a great rigid smile that was supposed to be a beam, but her eyes were as hard and cold as rocks.

"Yes, I have lots to do," I murmured. "I'm lunching with my brother, for one thing."

"Where are you going?" she asked, her voice almost shaking with resentment.

"Oh, I don't know," I said casually. "I'll meet him at his office."

The military bearing in her expression changed to something less harsh, though it was by no means an "at ease," and waving her hand vaguely in my direction she went off toward the kitchen. Probably, I decided, to whisper about all this with Olga who would agree, shaking her head ominously, that my money boded no good; that I had rich, ruinous tastes, that I would squander my money, corrupt Pritch, and then being the foolish, sunshiny young butterfly I am, would flit off, leaving them to nurse him back to health and sanity. Oh, yes, I could see it all. And they would also say, perhaps she will calm down after the precious baby comes, she's not a bad sort, just not steady and far too irresponsible.

I described all this to Bart as we had lunch—in the Drake, where we usually went, as it is near his office.

"Also, sweetie," I went on, determined to heave all of it off my chest in one sitting, "when I told her we were having lunch together today—this after my statement of financial worth had been revealed—I thought for a moment she was going up in a cloud of smoke."

This puzzled Bart. "Why, on earth? You mean you can't break bread with your own kinfolk?"

I shook my head. "Don't you see?" I said, really quite upset now that I had a chance to be. "At first she thought *I* would be paying for the lunch, and I'm sure that she thought that I wouldn't settle for anything under the price of Chambord—if she even knows what Chambord is. And I could just hear the cash register going off in her head, and her hand reaching out to snap up everything out of the till before I got a chance to throw it away. What makes people like that, Bart? Why, suddenly, does she consider me so unworthy, so foolish? It's not envy because I have more than she and all her brood could ever possibly hope for in their lives—and it's not simply that standing beside my huge pile of loot I look so small and incompetent in comparison. . . ."

Bart sat back in his chair, speculating about it. "That's a tough one, Mole, but I know what you mean. Sometimes Ida Bradford—and God knows they aren't poor—looks at me as if she hates me. And if there's anything really wrong between me and Joyce it is money. Because I've got so much more, it seems to make her feel inferior, and she sort of humbles herself—no, downright demeans herself—because of it, a sort of Uriah Heep act before the Golden Calf, fawning, pretending to love it, but actually just waiting for a chance to topple it over and kick it apart. You know, Mole," he fixed me with a serious look, "I'll lay you twenty to one that should something happen to me, if I died or something—"

"Bart!" I closed my hand over his in a tight grip. I couldn't bear to hear him even mention it.

"—Or even say we got a divorce and she cleaned up because of it—I'd lay you twenty to one that all this phony money-pinching routine would stop, just like that. And she'd spend it, spend it, spend it, until every dime was gone—like she was whipping it to death."

"What *makes* them that way?" I said feeling all shook up; I knew he was dead center right. "Would they like us better poor? Shall we give it all away?"

He grinned at me. "Give me yours and I'll give you mine."

"Idiot," I laughed. "No, but isn't it true that money, when you have a lot, is as much a part of your personality as your hair, or the way you laugh, or what you say and the way you say it?"

"Yes and no," he said. "You can change all those things, can't you?"

"Superficially. But aren't you a result of your past all the same, just as we are the result of Mother and Father?"

"God, Chloe, don't ask me," Bart sighed. "All I know is that people never get enough—and that people always envy anyone with great holdings, whether they be colossal Einstein brains, or musical abilities like Bach or Mozart had, or even just a dynamic personality. It makes certain people peevish, the kind who always say, 'Humph. *I* could have done that if I'd wanted to.' Or in the case of money, 'What makes her think she's so special? Just because she's so rich?' It's sort of as you said: Everytime they see you, they see a great huge money sack standing right behind you, dwarfing you, because to them money is far more important than people are, I suppose. Only the very rare person—the 'big' man with the open mind—or the very rich can truly accept the very rich as simple, ordinary folk. Money is literally more trouble than it's worth, Mole—something Mother knew. Through and through."

"But what am I going to do about Pritch, Bart?" I said in consternation. "To hell with his stuffy family, but what about him? Do you think he married me for my money?"

"Of course I don't," Bart assured me, whether he meant it or not. "But I would soft-pedal the cash angle, let him pay."

"But his mother will watch every penny he spends now, and if we live beyond his allowance—and oh, Bart, it is so tiny—she'll absolutely think it's my doing, because I'm so spoiled."

"She probably will," he agreed. "But you'll just have to grit your teeth. Wait it out until you and Pritch can get away from there."

"Now you have me really worried," I said deeply troubled. "And I think maybe Pritch did take a fancy to my bank book—it was after he found out I had quite a lot that his real interest began. And then there's Lesley: *she,* even, has much more than the Allyns. How do I know he didn't just drop her and latch on to a better thing?"

"For whatever reason he dropped her, he did latch on to a better thing, Mole. You're a great girl, and you're going to be a great woman. You know I'm awfully proud of my crazy kid sister?"

"Darling," I told him, pressing his hand again.

"You and Pritch will make it," he predicted encouragingly, "just you see. I think a lot of Pritch, and I think he sees you as I do."

"I don't know," I said feeling pretty low. "You know, he really is awfully influenced by his parents, no matter what he says, and if they start hating me now—"

"Hate you? How could they—"

"Well, they might," I told him. "You see, we've sort of cheated them. I don't know what to do." And I explained then about the mock-baby; how I wasn't sure whether I had ever really been pregnant or not.

"Why in the hell didn't you tell them you weren't then?" Bart asked much perturbed. "Now they *will* think—if they want to—that there was something fishy about Pritch breaking up with Lesley and marrying you. Tell me, were they fond of Lesley?"

"I don't know, I don't know," I shook my head, feeling miserable. "Yes, I think they probably were, though they couldn't have known her terribly well. Could they have?"

He shrugged, abashed. "I don't know. Anyway, baby sister, you have got a pot of in-law stew cooking in your kitchen."

"Bart, help me," I pleaded.

"I will in every way I can, Mole, but the trouble is I don't see how I can."

"Talk to Pritch."

"I'll talk to Pritch."

"Without—without Joycie."

He sighed. "I wouldn't dream of doing otherwise these days."

"Things bad with you?"

"Not good. But they'll work. I'm patient, and besides," he grinned, "Ida Bradford, unlike your Mother Allyn, isn't making a dive—quite—for my purse strings. She's got enough money of her own to give her the strength to resist."

"God, God, money!" I sighed. "I was better off when I thought Mother was serious about leaving it to the cats and dogs."

"It works its way down to them eventually," he said, and then looked at his watch and found it was time to go back to the office.

# Chapter Twelve

Pritch wouldn't look at apartments much less houses—and he wouldn't tell his parents there wasn't going to be any "precious little baby." It got more and more embarrassing: Mrs. Allyn watching my girth and diet, and the wives of Pritch's brothers spying on my shopping habits which, to their dissatisfaction, did not include Bonwit's in-waiting department, or all those lovely layette centers in the "better" stores.

We had come to a dead halt in everything, it seemed. Pritch didn't even pay sneak nocturnal visits to the guest room much anymore. And we had only been married four months. I knew he'd had a talk with Bart, but he never mentioned it, and when I asked Bart about it, he told me he had had to do all the talking. And I, feeling disloyal as hell, found I was relying more and more on Avery's friendship and counsel. Which was another thing: Pritch's mother had taken one look at Avery and had found her instantaneously poisonous. She didn't say so, of course, being such a "nice" woman, but I could tell she'd had quite a lot to say about her to Pritch who suddenly knocked her off the "good ole pal" list down to the "to-be-avoided" one. So I never brought her or her name up in that mighty fortress on the Upper West Side.

But what I really couldn't understand—and dared not pry out the explanation to—was Pritch's refusal to try to find a place of our own. He was vague at first, then irritable, bringing up the subject of money, again and again, saying he couldn't afford it, until I pointed out that he had been able to afford his flat in the Village. This brought up further unhappy details: how there were two of us now, how I was used to "certain things"—whatever this meant—how I didn't know how to "do anything." As for a reopening of our original plan to let me buy a house or a cooperative apartment—anything—that subject was as deeply buried as the gold at Fort Knox. Therefore, I knew his mother had lectured him on "self-respect" in the matter of having to cope with an heiress child-bride.

For my part, I developed a keen and well-documented revulsion for the "shabby genteel," and all their rules and ways. I hated the Christmas they made; even hated the way Father Allyn carved the turkey and the fact that they had to have turkey. I certainly loathed the sensible presents they gave me, and the odious dogged devotion to family carol-singing Christmas eve. I longed to go and throw myself on Mother's grave; beg her to let me in. "Nice" people, I learned, are just about the most vulgar in the world.

Pritch's brothers, all of whom were eons older, considered me as a sort of out-of-place and intrusive freak—yet of obvious rarity and monetary value. I was as out of place in their family circle as a piece of Tiffany glass in a hillbilly cabin. But their womenfolk, sensing that I was Tiffany,

handled me with care, as well as suspicion. One and all, I know, made
great sport of me behind my back, mimicked my "upper-Clahss" accent,
almost openly sneered when I forgot myself and mentioned anything
about my international-type upbringing, and thought I was deliberately
trying to humiliate them if I confessed to having seen royalty at close
quarters because my Aunt had married a baronet.

Day by day, I could see Pritch visibly twitching under the strain, and I
wondered: when is he going to turn me in (or out), take me back to
Tiffany's for a refund? Because it was true: I didn't fit with the rest of the
house, the House of Allyn.

Avery, of course, kept saying the Allyns were just peasants, very
common, but I could see that she also had never had any dealings with the
middle middleclass who were a much more complicated bunch than I had
ever imagined: they had all of the bad qualities of the rich and not enough
of the bad qualities of the poor. They were all so Goddamn "nice" and the
snobs of the world! They looked neither up nor down, but straight ahead,
so all they ever saw was more of the same: more middle-class snobs, the
only acceptable things to see.

The day I accidentally found an unfinished letter from Mrs. Allyn to
one of her schoolgirl chums describing me as "an unprincipled child, I'm
afraid, badly brought up—her table manners are simply terrible, for
instance, and she has no sense of refinement, but of course her mother
. . ." was the thing that did it. Clearly, she had bothered to inform herself
completely about my background and Mother's; had checked all of our
loose-lived credentials, probably in newspaper morgues, and found us
uncouth and scandalous. We were just rich. I stormed around the
apartment, longing to hit her. Fortunately, she was out. I cried a little,
then walked the floor a little, then cried, while waiting for her to come
back.

I don't know what I'd planned to tell her, but what I did tell her was
that Pritch and I were moving out, pronto, into a hotel and then into the
first decent house on the market, to be bought with my money—our
money—since what was mine was his. And as a parting shot I told her
there wasn't going to be any little baby, at least not in a few months, and
she could drop her pseudo-concern for my health and let me sleep with my
husband.

"Your language is disgusting," she told me coldly, and proceeded to
remove her tacky hat and with great-lady type presence put it and her
purse and gloves on the hall table before she turned back to deal with me.
I had caught her when she was just inside the door.

"Sit down and let's have a little talk," she invited me with all the
warmth of the dead fire in the fireplace.

I did so, with no particular humility, but without a word to say, as I had said it all when she came in.

She ticked off her complaint items one by one, and in all justice, the first one, at least, was just: I had only myself to blame for reading other people's mail, and, indeed, as she said, it was extremely rude of me to have done so. Then she got on to the business of our moving, pointed out their inequitable finances, when compared to mine, mentioned the danger to Pritch—and to our marriage—of making him dependent on me and turning his head with riches.

Naturally, I challenged this, told her that money never hurt anybody.

"Oh, indeed it has," she corrected me in a tone like a vise. "And I wouldn't want Pritchard to feel weakened, start moving around with a fast, irresponsible crowd, start drinking—"

I made a gesture of impatience and boredom. "Pritch is a grown man, my husband—"

"—And my son. And that's forever, Miss."

"Not if I can help it," I rose up to say. "Either you get him or I do. I'm leaving here. Tonight. Just as soon as he gets home and we can pack!"

"As you please," she inclined her head in what I suppose she thought was a poised, grand manner, befitting her "well-bredness."

"You disapproved of this marriage!" I accused her, just blazing.

"Not at first, no," she said, implacably cool.

"Whether or not," I said hotly, "it's *our* marriage—not yours!" I suddenly knew I was going to cry. "If you'll excuse me now," I said hurriedly, and made it to the guest room just in time.

After I stopped crying, I barricaded the door—a useless precaution, of course, because she couldn't have cared less. Then I sat by it, my ears tuned up like an animal's, waiting for Pritch to come home. I dashed out as soon as I heard his footsteps in the hall, and dragged him, in spite of his bewildered protests, back into the guest room.

"I've had an awful row with your mother, darling," I explained, slightly hysterical. "We've got to leave here. Now. This instant."

"Sure, Chloe," he agreed mildly, and somewhat to my surprise. "But what happened?"

As I began throwing things into suitcases—his and my things, all in a great tangle—I told him what had happened. It wasn't until I got to the baby part that I stopped for a second and thought: she had made no comment whatsoever on this. Why? But then I rushed on with my tale, while Pritch, as bidden, sat down at my extension telephone (installed and paid for by me, much to Mother Allyn's disapproval) and called the Plaza to reserve a room.

We were out of there in half an hour; out without saying good-bye. I don't even know where she was at that point. But I'm sure she knew what was going on. Probably she and Olga, two of a kind, had sneaked out of the kitchen and had had their ears pressed to the door.

Outside on the sidewalk, I took a great deep breath and reached for Pritch's hand to hold as we waited for a cab. Another mausoleum escaped from, and I could breathe again.

"Darling," I said with the utmost love when we were in the cab and on our way. "Darling."

He returned the pressure of my hand in his.

"The first thing we buy with our money is a car," I said, feeling outrageously free and wonderful with release, "and never another taxi as long as we live!"

"Not even on snowy mornings when the car won't start? Or to go and get it when it's been impounded for illegal parking?"

"No!" I laughed like an insane thing, finding it very delirious, hilariously funny, as I would have found anything he said at that moment.

It wasn't until later that I remembered it and knew it for what it was: it had absolutely spurted with sarcasm and worse, his middle-class idea that we would be reduced to street parking and other money-saving devices such as his parents and others like them employed, was hopeless proof, in all reality, of the difference in our orbits, the gulf between our private lives—past and present.

## Chapter Thirteen

The house was sweet, a surprising treasure tucked away in the rear of a drab but neat little tenement on 54th Street, near Third Avenue. We found it late in the day, and it was ours by the next morning. Or mine, I should say, as that is the way it turned out.

We had been living in the Plaza for two weeks, and had rather thought we'd be going on there indefinitely as the situation looked bleak. Then we found this. Our joy was, I thought, unbounded, but that too, I soon realized, was solo. For the night of the day we signed the papers Pritch went home and never came back.

It happened this way: To my knowledge, Pritch had not communicated with his family in any way after we left, simply allowing it to be tacitly understood that he had preferred to leave with his wife. Of course, I realized later he'd probably called his mother every day, but not so then. I was, for those two weeks in the Plaza, really a bride; that was my real honeymoon, and it never occurred to me that Pritch's compliance was the docility and humoring one exhibits for a madman. I thought he was as delirious as I. Every night we did something fabulous—went to some wonderful place that the Allyns could not possibly afford—and afterwards went to bed—together, really together—also something fabulous, and certainly something the Allyns could not, would not afford or condone. So when Pritch casually said, "Now that we have the house, I think I'd better go up and round up all my books and other junk," naturally I didn't realize he was planning to round up his marriage.

I sat in the King Cole Bar waiting for him for two hours—he had agreed to meet me there at seven—and after four answerless phone calls to the Allyn's house, I finally got the pitch. They were deliberately not answering the phone; Pritch had deliberately ditched me. I called Avery, luckily found her at home, and after she came down to join me in my widow-wake we both proceeded to get so roaring drunk that they didn't even want to serve us dinner at the little place we finally ended up.

During dinner, I kept getting up, staggering to the phone to call our hotel room; I did this until the switchboard operator impatiently cut me off because she couldn't understand what I was saying.

"No use, no use, no use," I told Avery, and put my head down on the red-checkered cloth of our table and cried until it was drenched. The next day I woke up in Avery's apartment.

Hungover as a Babylonian garden, I made plans, having persuaded Avery to skip a day at work. I'd move into the house and wait.

She looked at me commiseratingly, but with all the sadness with which one views the hopeless. Finally I asked her to give me her version of it.

"I don't want to," she said rather nervously. "It will—or may—just make you hate me later."

"Do," I pleaded, counting on her, wondering what I would ever do without her.

"To begin with," she said. "I don't think he consciously planned to walk out, but once you had the house—a place for you to lay your head, a place of your own—I think he felt his responsibility considerably lightened—*i.e.,* he could consider other aspects of the thing, and was therefore more receptive to his parents' views."

"Which were?" I interrupted.

"Obvious." She made a gesture. "I'm sure, for instance, that Mrs. Allyn brought up the subject of the non-baby as soon as he hit home."

"Probably," I agreed morosely. "But would he really let her talk him into believing that I'd tricked him into marriage, or that he had married me solely because I needed to be made into an honest woman?"

"You're way out in front, Chloe," she said quietly. "It's nothing we can really know. Anything could have happened. Maybe it wasn't mentioned at all."

"Call the Plaza again for me, will you?"

With a resigned look, she did, but just as both of us knew, there was no answer. "How about calling him at Columbia?" she suggested.

I told her it was too complicated; I didn't even know his class schedule.

"Send him a wire, then. At home."

"I could, I suppose," I said slowly, then I began to consider the whole thing: why should I? He knew where I was, he knew what this would do to me. If he had wanted to be with me, he would have been. "No, Avery," I said at last. "I'll just move into the house and wait."

"You can't live all alone there!" she exclaimed.

"I don't intend to," I answered. "First, I'll send for Tennie and Jess—there's lots of room for them, there's the whole fourth floor—then if he hasn't turned up in a month, you're moving in with me. Absolutely. Don't say a word."

And she didn't say a word, that sweet wise friend, and a month later in she moved.

I must say those first few weeks we lived together in that house, snug, secure, with Tennie and Jess upstairs to watch over us, and we evening after evening downstairs in the living room reading by the fire, or watching TV, or just talking, were serene evenings, but for the fact that I was inside as furrowed as a plowed field, each gaping crevice a mortally bleeding wound of misery. The silent telephone was like a black Frankenstein's monster I could not bring to life. And when I say silent, I mean silent, for no one called either of us, except occasionally Bart, or sometimes a wrong number. And when that happened I jumped like a startled insect.

Avery somehow had managed to keep it out of her paper that Pritch and I were pfftt, as they call it, and since hers was more or less the mouthpiece for such delicacies, no one else had dug up the news. I led in those days such a discreetly quiet life that it was tantamount to a silent life. In the daytime, I watched Tennie cook and clean, or went out furniture shopping, or went to awful grade B movies by myself. Then home for dinner, which was always blessedly Tennie-good, and Avery, then bed. I had bought a car, and Jess drove me around whenever I wanted, which was most of the time, for I was too nervous and unhappy to cope with daytime city traffic myself.

I don't know whose idea it was to shift from low-gear into something higher and slightly faster, but I know it was about the time that I got a legal separation from Pritch, pursuant to an annulment, if possible, and if not, an out-of-state quick divorce.

Anyway, Avery and I decided to go out for drinks and dinner for a change, and she declared herself irresistibly drawn to the Village.

"Memories," I said. "Ghosts."

"Cut them," she said. "Just as you would human beings. It's got to be done, Chloe."

I knew she was right, and I headed us in the car downtown toward the Village.

Still, I would have given a lot to have known what went on sub rosa between Pritch and Mother Allyn those two weeks we lived so happily apart from them at the Plaza; but more, I would have bought my soul back from the Devil to have known what went on *the* night, the last one I saw him. The lawyer, of course, had spoken to Pritch and seemed rather embarrassed by the whole thing. But this much I gathered: Pritch's excuse for breaking up with Lesley and marrying me was that I was pregnant. Somehow going through the legal bit of shearing him was easier after that example of callow cowardliness. From now on he would always be "Brother" Allyn to me, Mrs. New England Allyn's little boy.

Avery tried to rouse me—oh, she did every day. She almost pinched my cheeks, but I would not come back to life. Mostly because I didn't know where life had gone. And I would think: Avery, Dear Muchness: You deserve a rollicking not a sobersides companion. But there we were, curiously stuck together on a small desert island called Manhattan's Upper East Side. We sent up occasional flares; went out on occasional exploratory tours; the trip to the Village was one of them.

We were there—Fifth Avenue and Eight Street—and the question occurred to us simultaneously: now that we're here, what?

We decided to park the car, and we both concentrated intently on this problem, like seamstresses over knots in thread. Then when it was parked, Avery said again, "Now, what?"

"Food," was all I could suggest, and we made for one of the fine Village restaurants where we ate a good and tasty dinner which neither of us tasted. We hardly spoke, but on the other hand, we didn't look around either. All of our hundred-horsepower drive had just faded like fog, and we blinked at each other, each thinking, let's go home, but neither wanting to admit the drizzle of it all.

The check paid, coats put on, we were again outside, in the street. Avery looked up at the streetlights, which shed so much light on so many strangers, interesting-looking strangers, like a child staring at the distant glow of a carnival. "What's wrong with us," she murmured sadly—rhetorically—then asked me where we'd parked the car.

"On Waverly, I think," I said, heading down MacDougall Street.

"Shall we go home? It seems so alive down here somehow. . . ."

I was just ready to say it didn't, when up he strode, Seymour—Seymour whatever his name was, the one we had met with Pritch, months ago.

"Well!" he said heartily. "Hello, there, you two up-towners." He beamed at us some more, sort of 'raring' back on his heels, his hands stuck in the pockets of a worn-out Navy peajacket. I noticed he had terribly bad teeth, even there in the lamplight, and that his beard was worn pointed now, like a Satan's.

We murmured cool hellos, quiet and subterranean as an underground stream; both of us wanted to cut out. Faced with this character again, I remembered he had smelled like stale bedclothes.

"Saw Pritch the other day," he went on, apparently hugely enjoying this confrontation. Or maybe he was just being friendly, and wasn't ribbing us.

"Oh?" I said, non-committedly, and felt Avery nudge me to break it up, move on.

But Seymour barred the way. "Where you dolls headed?"

I made an empty gesture, and he said, "How about a cup of coffee?"

Personally, I didn't want to be rude, nasty as I considered this bearded genius, but I certainly didn't want coffee either. My momentary hesitation seemed to encourage him and with another ingratiating smile, he went to work on Avery. "New espresso place just opened up down the street. The most. Having a show of pix by a friend of mine. Great girl. From the Coast. Great art. Very beat—"

"What do you mean, Very beat'?" Avery put in, bristling strangely, it seemed to me, at this rather innocuous person.

"Beatific! The most!" he went on extolling, and it occurred to me that the reason he was as joyous as hell was that he was high on marijuana, as he had been previously, and probably was most of the time.

I looked at Avery, to see if she shared my slight disgust and strong urge to part company with this type, but she was looking fascinated. He was now talking about Photography, with a capital P, and how his West Coast friend stacked up beside the other greats—Walker, Stieglitz, Cartier-Bresson.

"Come on, let's do go see!" Avery urged me, impulsively. Just one look at her told me she was sold. I hadn't seen her light up that way since immediately after her graduation from Miss Chalmers' when she had embraced me and everybody wildly shrieking, "I'm OUT!" How right she was; she was very far out, which had nothing to do with being free, and now she was OUT even further.

Anyway, the three of us headed for the coffee house-gallery, Avery and this Seymour person walking slightly ahead, talking very fast and enthusiastically—or rather he was, and she was listening at the same rate of speed. She couldn't take her eyes off him. I wondered if they'd even know it, if I simply hung back and disappeared. I was very tempted.

# Chapter Fourteen

Seymour, it appeared, knew even less of our names than we knew of his. Avery's name—Avery Stafford—didn't seem to make any particular impression on him, but mine really threw him. "Chloe Longtree!" he chortled, throwing his head back for another good, rich laugh. "What a name!"

Avery gave him a look as sour as penicillin. Now, I suppose, she was sorry she hadn't introduced me as Chloe Allyn, which, of course, I legally was, but for some devious reason she had decided that Seymour didn't know Pritch and I were married, that he might "tell us something" if we played it quiet and cool, and God knows what other ideas for machinations and intrigue she had in mind. But that was the way Avery was. Open up her tiny little mind, I always said, and inside you'd find a tiny cloak and a tiny dagger—all very harmless, but sometimes tiresomely complicated, as for instance now. Moreover, I hadn't the faintest idea why *she* resented his mirthful reaction to my name; I was the injured party, but was quite used to it, could handle the situation myself. But I didn't get a chance; she was in and at 'em.

"You're something of a humorist, aren't you?" she asked, sarcasm dripping from her tongue, her face as benign as a puff adder's. In fact I was somewhat surprised by it all; it had happened so fast.

Seymour, however, rose to the occasion, recognizing the mating call of competitiveness, and there was much dialogue and much flashing of the eyes between them. He first defended his wit, then his honorable name (which was Marlboro, and sounded very borrowed and made up) and then went into his tortured, sensitive background. I still hadn't had a chance to say a word in defense of the time-honored Longtrees or to smite him across the face with my gauntlet, as I would have gladly done. "—And furthermore, my mother was a poet and a musician—a great musician—with music in her soul," he told Avery, all choked up "—you silly square rich dames don't know anything about people like that—"

"We do now," Avery said drily. "You've just told us."

He ignored her. "—every word she said was a poem, every gesture she made was pure music—"

"Jazz," Avery put in. "Primitive."

But he didn't hear this either; didn't hear me snicker, or see Avery's broad grin. I guess he really was pretty high. His eyes certainly looked it.

Suddenly he groped for, grabbed and held Avery's hand, in a sort of Indian wrestler's deadlock. "—You, you," he told her throatily diving into and drowning in her eyes, "—you could be—you're so beautiful, white, blonde, shining like a goddess—" then he dropped her hand abruptly, as if she had forced a very hot potato on him when he wasn't looking "—but you're dead inside. DEAD! What do you know of the magic of childhood? The sweetness of the mornings, the gold hot noons, The summer-tangled streets of kids at play?"

"With Hoola hoops," Avery again interjected. I couldn't stand it. Both of us were giggling like fools now, and I didn't want to laugh out loud in his poor blind face, so intense now that it was almost incandescent.

"I'm going to look at these famous photographs," I whispered to Avery, getting up to wander off.

My departure, I noticed, received all the fanfare and attention of a pebble cast into a brook, and Avery, for all her wisecracking, was really glued to his side, like a lovely dragon fly next to the house variety on a piece of flypaper. Or so it appeared from here. I scanned the photographs perfunctorily. They were mediocre, as I'd expected, impressive only to those who had a personal concern for the lady who took the pictures, or for those who had never seen any others. The only salient message they had was that the lady had traveled widely, had a good camera, and had used a lot of film up while crouched in some peculiar positions herself.

Through with that exhibition, I turned back to the other: Avery was still in a state of enchantment, despite her amusing asides which she was now delivering to herself or still into his deaf ear. I looked at her, elbows on the table, chin cupped in her short, graceful hands, a bemused expression on her face; yes, she was still being desperately defensive—or offensive—but she was a goner and her rapier of wit was made out of rubber. For he sat, self-satisfied as ever, tuned into himself, the volume way up and blaring, looking incongruously young and pathetic but awful for all his genius-style affectations; the blue-jean encased legs languidly twined around the legs of the adjoining chair (mine), his hands dropped off behind his own chair looking like a pair of big gloves hung up to dry. His head was cocked just-so, and occasionally he shifted his health-club type manly torso, and occasionally, without taking his large dark eyes— hot, passionate eyes—off Avery's face, he reached up to stroke his beard, as fondly as if it were a pet cat. I didn't even wonder what they were saying. Instead, I shuddered.

When I hovered over the table, feeling very much like an embarrassed guardian angel, I saw I would have to do more than just that: now, they *both* ignored me.

"Man, that's the message!" he was saying, in answer, I presume, to some faultless observation Avery had made.

"Let's go, Avery," I said roughly, as if I were rousing her from a sound sleep. But it needed more than that.

"So," she said, in the soft voice of someone drugged, "I got with it— for the first time—and I knew what Coleridge felt, what Macaulay meant, and why Modigliani started to paint the way he did."

"Say!" he exclaimed suddenly, looking up at me with those orbs of his instantly burning away my frosty objectivity. "This is a *great* girl! She knows everything. Chloe—" he grabbed my arm as if he were yanking on a stage-curtain pull. "Sit down! Listen! This girl's the *greatest!*"

And I was rung down, into my previous seat, and bent my absorption to theirs. The interest between them crackled like Fourth-of-July fireworks. But it was hard to wedge in the cold steel needle of coherence, so I sat back and took in the conversation as the words flew.

Eventually, I gathered Avery was confessing all: to wit, that she too had been "turned on" and thought marijuana great. I know that earlier in the evening, I would have found this piece of autobiography pulse-raising, but now I took it as I would have an unusual maneuver from a tennis player during an exciting match. I kept turning my head from side to side. They were both unreal and brilliant, playing a game. Soon it would all be over and we would be going home. But then, I realized, they were planning something further. Avery said fervently, or swore fervently, that she wanted to "turn on"—yes, tonight. Not in his pad—not in ours (how did "ours" get into this?)—but he knew *the* place. Not very far uptown, no, past Chelsea. Not the Puerto Rican section, either—we'd see—he didn't want to say anything, we'd see for ourselves—it was the greatest—

"We've got the car," Avery said, sounding drunk though she hadn't had a drop. "It'll be easy."

And before I could believe it, we were out of the place—Avery had taken care of the check—and this Seymour person talking, talking all the while, way above fever-pitch with intensity, was helping me toward my own automobile as if I were too inebriated to stand up and make it on my own.

I got in, feeling numb, and he told me where to go. I started the car, noticing the way he and Avery melted together, their hands interlocked in another death-do-us-part grip, their eyes having a mutual feast. And I marveled on the Seymour energy—drug inspired, or not—he was like a walking atomic pile, and all of its life force was bent on Love—love for everybody—Brotherhood of Man. He would have even picked up the Ancient Mariner, I decided. Which made his finding Avery a superb piece of serendipity indeed. About that time, he even put his arm around me; gave me a good squeeze which almost made me sideswipe a car. But his real attention was drawn to Avery, and they trained eyes upon each other as intently as those electrical ones that open doors. Or move worlds. I drove where I was told, also semi-bewitched, I suppose.

On the West Side, in the midst of all those printing companies, I found the address. All by myself, for by that time Avery and Seymour were deep in the oozing marshes and quicksands of lovemaking, and I felt embarrassed to be around at all—but sort of bewitched, as I say, their spell cast over me. Anyway, I saw, as I gave a quick nervous look, it could still sneak under the heading of necking, what they were doing, so it was all right to say, "We're here." Which is what I said.

"Briefing period," said Seymour, straightening up, swallowing hard, and trying to sound composed, though hoarse. "It's on the top floor. The password is S. K. S. and you're going to find a lot of people high on the weed, in the nude, and swinging."

I must have made some noise of incredulity, for Avery wound herself out of her clench enough to say, "Honey, stay with it," which was hardly enough of an encouragement.

However, we mounted the stairs, those two ahead, holding onto each other, clasped, like fleeing refugees, or lovers in the Dore illustrated Dante's *Inferno*. I followed, landing after landing, some bearing the names of commercial enterprises with arrows pointed toward their doors, or artists' signs, artily done, welcoming guests (invited ones, of course, as the uninvited would never find their way here) or silent landings where nothing proclaimed, except dirt and stillness, and the slanted stair-rails, ancient creaking floors, and the accumulated dirt of the industrial age. And at last we came to a violently violet-colored door initialed S. K. S., all in gold leaf and English-Gothic lettering. Seymour lurched forward and knocked.

Then the door opened.

Completely nude before us stood our host. I think the thing that shocked me most was his crew cut, and the vague impression that in his clothes I would have recognized him, at least, from somewhere else. However, he looked us up and down, and then he said, "Who are you?"

"We're looking for Shelley," Seymour cried, his voice almost piteous. "He *told* us to come."

S. K. S., or whoever he was, stared at us again; but already I had learned the signs: marijuana governed his vision—or visions—and with an almost sightless look, we were admitted, he making a slight obeisance from the waist, as if he were drunk and entertaining in Newport. Newport! That's what did it. "Isn't that Sonny Saunders?" I tried to whisper in Avery's ear, but her ear was out of earshot. Instead, I found myself confiding in the ear of our host.

He merely looked at me, his eyes were as unanimated as before, but something else had come into them as he gazed at me, as if I were a voluptuous Petty Girl, and he half-snarled, half Mae-West-insinuated, "Take off your clothes."

I looked back at this S. K. S. very sharply. "What if I don't?" I said.

"Then you leave," he pronounced tersely. "Your friends are taking off their clothes. Either you do or you leave."

"What are you besides a host, Sonny?" I asked. "Are you God?"

If he heard the "Sonny," part he didn't take note or umbrage, but the "God" reference threw him into a rage. Suddenly, I found myself in a roomful of people—where he had deliberately pushed me—seemingly to be stoned—who were all obviously his devout followers, judging by the way they looked up at him, in the most worshipful attitudes, as if he were the Heavenly Father. Their expressions while full of awe, reverence, and yes, beatitude (the Beat Generation), held something else which distinguished them from the case-book religious fanatic: the glaze in their eyes wasn't the simple transport of ecstasy, but the frozen-pupil stare of the drugged: they were all sky-high on pot, and all stark naked. They lay around that room—which was completely bare except for a hi-fi moaning out an African recording—lolling on the thick wall-to-wall carpeting looking like statues just uncrated for the Whitney collection. And it was bitter cold too, so cold that the blue of the marijuana smoke which stood in thick clouds, as still as the user's eyes, seemed an atmospheric stage effect.

I looked up at Sonny Saunders—S. K. S., and/or God—and wondered if he was going to turn his pack loose on me, bid them to tear me apart, or at least unclothe me, and saw that instead of throwing me to the wolves, he was giving them some other sign to which they gave their hushed-breath attention.

Shades of Aleister Crowley! I looked at him incredulously and for a fraction of a second felt drawn into his piercing eye like a thread drawn into a needle, powerless under his hypnotism. Then common sense whispered: this is just Sonny Saunders who once broke your tennis racket out at Glen Cove; the same Sonny Saunders with the funny crew-cut who was at what's-her-name's dinner party in Newport—only then he had on clothes, dinner clothes at that.

"Come off it, Sonny," I told him, hoping I sounded casual. "Remember me?" I went on, a little short of breath, "I knew you before you were deified." I tried to smile. But this was no time for levity, his expression clearly told me, and I felt like an Aztec sacrificial offering trying to joke the high-priest executioner out of it all.

"You will be dealt with," he promised in a trancelike sepulchral voice.

"All right, I'll leave," I answered. "I just want to collect the people I came with—at least Avery Stafford—" And suddenly I was talking to myself. He had simply disappeared, probably into a cloud of marijuana smoke.

Futilely, I looked about for a place to sit down, but there simply wasn't any except the floor, so instead I edged over by the nearest exit, and stood against the wall, my eyes beginning to sting as I scrutinized the crowd, looking for some sign of Avery and that fantastic creature who had brought us here.

Suddenly in the moiling mob, I saw Avery's albino-white shock of hair, blending with Seymour's. And with spotting Avery in this snakepit, reality came thundering down upon me like an avalanche. I turned physically sick with disgust, humming with hurt, outrage, and compassion all at once, so that I was like a dynamo of unbearable conflicting feeling, and I flung myself at the door, and tore it open.

## Chapter Fifteen

That's where Sonny Saunders took over. He was just on the other side of the door, standing by the tallest, biggest, most biceped male I've ever seen. Sonny didn't say a word, simply jerked his head in my direction. And Atlas lifted me off my feet, as if I weighed no more than his own hand, and carried me down a hall. I'm sure I screamed, and I'm sure I fought him, but it was like Fay Wray in the clutches of King Kong.

If I had visions—and I had—of being raped, brutally, voluptuously, or any which way, I was wrong; Hercules simply deposited me outside the violet-colored front door, closed it in my startled face, and left me in the crashing silence that always follows a terrible din. I guess I pounded on it for a while, then I sat down and had hysterics on the filthy, littered top step of the long staircase.

I was sobbing, talking out loud to myself, I know, giving me a scathing lecture. How-did-I-get-into-this? it probably ran. Then I heard an answer.

"How did you get into this? You asked for it," a man's voice said crisply. I looked up. I was blocking the way of one of the few unbearded, dressed (in a business suit) older men I had seen that night.

"I'm sorry," I moaned, inching over to give him room to pass. And he passed, but at the door he said, "Want to come back inside?"

I shook my head miserably.

"Well, then," he said in the same crisp voice, "adios."

And that was the end of him. I heard the door shut, and I was left again in the cold, dusty silence of the old warehouse building with only my own noises of misery to keep me company.

Finally, my own personal dawn began to come out of the pitch blackness of my hysteria. I scrambled to my feet. If Avery wanted—wanted what was back there, okay! I didn't. I began to run down the steps, and then I heard a deep, booming male voice echoing down the stairwell. "Chloe Longtree!" it sounded. "Chloe Longtree!"

I slowed down and looked up, and there was this same man who had passed me on the stairs. I waited. I could hear him rapidly coming down. "Wait!" he called again, as if he thought I wouldn't.

Clutching the stair rail where I stood, I watched him round the last landing and approach me. There was a tentative smile on his face, not eager or polite, but rather like a salesman's. "You *are* Chloe Longtree?" he asked rhetorically and added, "Incredible name. Was it changed from Grossbaum?"

"No," I said, my voice still small and slightly withered from the trauma of all this. "I don't think so."

"Lovely name anyway," he went on, but with no oily smile, thank God. Just an observation. "You think you can find your way out of this rat trap?"

"I'm sure I can," I said stonily, and started back downstairs.

But he was right behind me, as if I had said no. "Your girl friend sent me to find you," he said chattily. "I'm Shelley. Shelley Spivak."

And with that I turned on him. "Then you must be a monster! It's because of you that my 'girl friend'—as you call her—and I got into this!"

He looked at me coldly, as if I were an illogical, hot-headed fool. Then he shrugged his shoulders. "I could say that water seeks its own level."

"Please don't!" I yelled at him imperiously, and started down the stairs again, my heels pounding out my indignation. Still, in the background, I could hear him following me.

At the bottom of the stairs, he grabbed me by the elbows. "You're the most hard-bitten, peevish teenager I've ever seen," he informed me.

I slapped him in the face. "Go upstairs to your gutter!"

Then he slapped me back. "That's precisely what I intend to do after I put you in your expensive little foreign car and head you on your way, out of harm's way."

"Don't bother!" I advised him, longing to put a hand to my red, stinging face.

For an answer, he took my arm and skillfully projected me like a guided missile through the outer door. "Now where's your car?" he asked firmly.

We were on the stoop, and very carefully, I undid his fingers from my arm, as if they were a string of band-aids. "I told you," I said in a level voice, "that I don't want your help. And I'll tell you why: I have no business in a place like that. And my friend has none. We were persuaded here so your odious friend could meet you. Because of it, my friend apparently took leave of her senses. I can't help that. I'm going. I can find my way, and I prefer to find it alone. Clear?"

He had eyes as hard as, as cold as, and the color of agates. They bored into me. Rather like S. K. S.'s had, only Shelley Spivak's were like a clear winter day, full of sharpness, completely aware and keen. "Are you finished?" he asked.

But he could see by my face that I was. Completely. I hoped I would not sob; to throw myself on his sympathy was like seeking succor from the

Great Stone Face. "Now, where is your car?" he asked, his voice as quiet as a library, and as thoughtful.

We got to it. I fumbled with the keys to unlock it. He took them from my hand and expertly opened the door himself. He handed me in, and when I started to slide toward the driver's seat, he said, "Ahh-ahh," indicating that he proposed to occupy that himself. In a minute he was at the other door, and I found myself obliging him by turning up the door handle inside, unlocking it, so he could get in. He did, and we stared at each other wordlessly for a few minutes. Then he said: "Sy Marlboro is a fool."

I nodded. "And a dangerous one."

"That depends," he said thoughtfully. "But he's no judge of people. That other girl, all right, but not you."

"I guess he thought he had to take me along to get her," I said wistfully.

"He didn't think at all," he corrected me, his voice crisp to harshness again.

I studied him in the half light. He seemed to be about twenty-eight or so, older than Bart. And completely different. He had rich lustrous hair, curly and oily, or at least oiled. And in profile he looked something like a handsome bird or an extinct wild animal, or a wild man from a curious long-dead race—an Assyrian, or a Hittite. He had the long curved Semitic nose, the full sensual mouth, the high brow of the long-vanished, once proud over-civilized but savage people who had first inhabited the earth. I thought about saying so, so fascinated I was by what I saw, but one lesson I had learned tonight was CAUTION. However, he was really very beautiful in a foreign kind of way, and I was now, quietened, grateful to him for his clinical kindness to me. I had needed some human company after that experience. But then, I reminded myself, he was in some way closely connected with all that madness. I asked him, without any preface, just how.

He didn't seem surprised at my abruptness at all.

"Oh, I turn on occasionally," he said. "I like it better than alcohol for escape. Much cleaner. Actually, I prefer real hashish—pot is just for kids."

I considered this calm statement of his: its softness was like a blanket drawn over the body of a mangled corpse. Was he unaware of the corpse, how it got that way? Or was he just philosophical about it? "You shock me," I told him in a low, shaken voice.

"I do?" he turned to me swiftly. "That's not surprising. I expect you'd be rather shocked by the Easter Islanders—Maoris—or any peoples whose customs were not yours."

"That's true," I admitted, my voice smaller than ever. I was thinking how Pritch's family, and their folkways, had shocked me, and they were a tribe to be found next to my elbow, under my nose, and had been all my life. "You see, I'm not very old," I added lamely.

His laugh was instantaneous, appreciative; a pure delight. "At least you know it," he said. "That's more than most of those people up there know."

I agreed, then told him about Sonny Saunders, how I'd known him slightly all my life.

He gave a long, low whistle of surprise. "Well, I'll be damned!" he said profoundly, sounding as if he would. "I knew the kid had plenty of loot, but I didn't know he was an escapee from the Four Hundred."

"He isn't exactly," I put in uncomfortably, ready to go into a very complicated explanation of Sonny's background—how he was in, but *not* in—but face value was enough for Shelley Spivak. He chortled and glowed over this "find" like an archaeologist with a priceless treasure. Then he said to me, "If you know all this about S. K., that means *you're* one of those crazy-rich too-much-too-often dolls. You writing a book about it?"

I laughed uneasily. "The idea has crossed my mind."

"It has certainly crossed mine," he said. "As a matter of fact, I am a writer of sorts. Edited the college paper out on the Coast, got mixed up with the poetry-jazz set—that's how I know our friend Seymour—and then I worked on a newspaper here in New York. Till I got canned for goldbricking. It was a lousy job anyway."

"What are you doing now?"

"Looking for another job to goldbrick on."

"But if you want to write why don't you like such jobs?"

He laughed at me again, and told me it wasn't the same thing. "I'm a *real* writer," he explained, "not just a plodding reporter type with big ears and a sharp pencil."

"Oh. You mean you're interested in real journalism—Rebecca West, people like that," I said, pulling a name out of the air.

"Yeah, that's the pitch," he looked at me with interest. "Which brings us back to your original question: how I figure in all that stuff upstairs. I don't. I'm just a guilty bystander, one of the few His Holiness allows to stay fully clothed in that unheated marijuana den he calls the 'Sacred Sanctum,' or the 'Temple.' I first heard about him when he tried to make a case for the legalized use of narcotics by having himself committed to Bellevue. It was in all the papers. Didn't you see it?"

"No," I said. "I guess I was still in England." I wondered if I should go on to tell him that I was married too, but he just looked interested, said, "oh, really?" and went on enthusiastically giving me an account of Sonny's activities.

"He interests me," he said. "I'd like to do a story on him."

I agreed Sonny's efforts were courageous if a little outrageous.

"Outrageous? He's completely mad," Shelley corrected me. "However, you have to give the guy credit He's got a point in sticking up for pot. It should be on the open market. It's the perfect opiate for the people, so to speak. And God knows they've got to have something. Nobody can live very long in this goofed-up society without some kind of reliable anodyne."

I thought about this for a while, and was still wondering whether he was as right as he sounded, when he said, "Well, kid. You all right now? Think you can make it home?"

It rather took me aback; I don't know what I thought, but sitting there, talking to him—or hearing him talk—I'd completely lost track of the facts involved, and certainly of the obvious one that I had originally thought of him as a monster; now he was like a very close and very wise older friend. "I can make it," I told him.

He got out of my car, his long legs gracefully, skillfully avoided the hazards of the steering wheel and gear shift. He slammed the door, smiled inside and said, "So long now!"

"So long!" I called back and watched him stride up the street, back to the veritable den of iniquity where he was observer and Chief Scribe.

## Chapter Sixteen

When I heard the front door open the next morning, I was still in bed. Avery, at last, I thought to myself, and turned over, pulling one pillow up over my head, and settling another under it, making, as Avery called it, a pillow sandwich. Then the next thing I knew, Tennie was tentatively saying from the doorway of my room, "Miss Chloe? They's some man downstairs."

"What?" I asked and shot to an upright position. "Who? What is it?"

"He didn't say what he wants. Just said he'd come to see you."

"All right," I told her, my heart having dropped down like an elevator to the bottom of its shaft. And I got up and quickly threw on the first clothes I saw. Probably a plainclothesman, I thought. They'd raided that horrible place, taken Avery in, and she was now probably in the Women's Detention Home. Oh, the damned desperate fool! Why couldn't she, as Mother always said, stick with people of her own sort?

I hurried downstairs, and there in the living room, grinning up at me, as comfortably at home as a cat, was one Shelley Spivak.

"Hi!" he called genially. "I was in the neighborhood. Just thought I'd drop in."

I stopped and stared at him. "I didn't hear you knock."

"I didn't knock," he said, as if he thought me crazy for imagining he would. "I tried the door and it wasn't locked, so I just walked in."

That subject dismissed, and without further ado, he marched around the room, looking at everything. "Nice place you've got here. That fireplace work?"

I told him it did.

"Good taste too," he added. "Yours? or some decorator's?"

"Mine."

"You're a pretty bright doll to be so young," he commented, giving me a sidewise look, as if I were an *objet d'art* up for appraisal. "I thought you'd live in one of those artsy-craftsy pads, all Japanese, no individuality, somebody else's idea—but this isn't too bad at all. Family stuff?" he asked, fingering a very rare piece of Meissen.

"No," I said quite coldly. I still hadn't asked him to sit down, and had not yet decided whether or not I should. "How did you get my address?"

"Your girl friend," he said casually. "She asked me to drop around."

"Why couldn't she have come herself, or telephoned?"

He laughed at me, his humor lazy, somewhat mocking. "She's in no condition, and anyway she's shacked up with Sy and he doesn't have a telephone anymore."

At that news, *I* sat down.

"Don't get all excited," Shelley Spivak said. "It's not as bad as that, kid. She'll be all right."

I shook my head, too worried to say anything.

"Cheer up," he went on encouragingly. "Nothing's going to happen to her."

"It's all so awful," I murmured.

"Not at all," he corrected me with ease. "Sy's not a bad fellow."

I shuddered and he saw me.

"No, he's a little stupid and a little eager, which makes him reckless, but essentially he's all right."

"The whole thing is simply terrible," I said limply. "I should never have left her there."

"Probably not," he agreed, "but you didn't have much choice, now did you? Anyway, kid, I'll look after her. I made her try to remember where you lived so I could come tell you not to worry about her. She couldn't remember your phone number though. That's why I came personally."

"Thank you," I said dimly. "That was very nice of you."

"Not at all," he said heartily.

Somewhere in all this, he had sat down at the other end of the couch. Now he got up. "Well, I'll be going," he announced.

I stood up. "Why don't you stay and have some coffee? Or breakfast? I just got up and haven't had any."

"No, no thanks!" he said good-humoredly, giving me a warm fraternal-like smile. "I'm pavement pounding today—and I've got to go to the library sometime, and look up some stuff on this narcotic law that S. K. is trying to buck—I'm working with him and a couple of doctors researching this thing, to see if we can find some way to bust it—"

I thought it sounded admirable. Crude as this man obviously was, he had both gentleness and intelligence. "How can I help Avery, get her out of this?" I asked seriously.

"Leave her alone. It'll do her good," he advised. "She'll come back in a few days."

I shook my head, feeling very old-fashioned—like her grandmother— but firm. "I'm not trying to be her protector, really," I explained. "But I think she should come back—now."

"I'm afraid she won't do that," Shelley smiled. "I've already talked to her about it."

"Maybe she would listen to me—if I could just talk to her—"

"That's simple," he said as pleasant and calm as a social worker. "Got a pencil and paper handy? I'll give you the address."

I took it down—an address in the west part of the Village, a section I didn't know at all. "How do I get there?" I asked, and he gave me directions, very complicated-sounding.

He noticed my bewildered stare as I looked at my notes and said, "If you're not in any hurry I could meet you somewhere and drive you down later—say about five o'clock."

I readily agreed; I didn't relish driving down there alone in any event, and on this particular errand. "Why don't we meet at the King Cole at five?" I suggested.

"Where's that?" he asked.

Faintly surprised that he didn't know, I told him. But he shook his head. "None of your fancy joints for me," he said. "I'm a peasant, and when I go to a bar it's got to be a first cousin to an old-fashioned saloon. Anyway, I don't drink anymore, so why make it a bar? How's Macy's instead!"

*"Macy's!"* I gasped.

"Not inside," he told me. "Just at the entrance, my favorite one. You can't miss it. They've got a plaque commemorating the Straus couple who went down on the *Titanic,* and under it is this corny poem in a frame all about 'Sara' and how 'up she is holding her husband'—or something like that. Very dialectical. You can almost hear Mrs. Nussbaum reading it."

"Are you an anti-Semite?" I asked. I had heard that some Jews were and found it very strange.

"No. I'm just a Jew with a sense of humor. Don't you like jokes about old-line one hundred per cent two-headed, red-blooded Americans?"

"I never heard any."

This brought on another faint explosive blast of laughter. "You are certainly one cool nowhere doll," he informed me, but added, "however, I like it. I like you." He looked at me quite seriously. Then he made a slight bow, walked to the front door, as familiar with its location as though it were his, said, "Good morning, Miss Chloe Longtree," and was gone.

I heard Tennie coming up from the kitchen, panting as she came. She and Jess aren't young anymore. "Who in the name of the Lord was that?" she cried out at me.

"Hard to explain," I said. "Where's my breakfast?"

"Downstairs. Where'd you think it was at? And what's happened to Miss Stafford? Is she gone off and got herself into trouble with the likes of him?"

"Now, Tennie," I calmed her. "Avery's all right Just keep your shirt on."

This made her furious. "Don't you go worryin' about my shirt, Miss You! You better be worryin' about yours! You and that Miss Stafford is two of the craziest young 'uns I ever seen in my life! Miss Cornelia must of lost her mind there at the end to leave you all that money where you could jus' dip in and help yourself any old time before you was old enough too—"

"Now, hush, Tennie," I said, quite annoyed myself.

"I won't hush a-tall. I'm gonna call Mr. Bart, that's what I'm going to do!"

"I haven't done a *thing,* Tennie," I insisted. "Now look at me. Don't I look perfectly all right?"

"You looks all right, but you ain't!" Tennie said emphatically, then she went on to grumble about Pritch, and what were they making young gentlemen out of these days anyway?

I told her I certainly didn't know, couldn't care less, and would she please give me some breakfast.

She did, but she called Bart anyway.

He turned up about noon, looking like a priest come to administer extreme unction. He made me tell him all about it. I did, doing a skillful editing job on most of the night before, but admitted we had been to a rather wild party and that Avery had gone off with somebody.

I didn't reassure him at all somehow; he couldn't have looked more worried. "I don't know what to say to you, Mole." He shook his head. "Sometimes you seem so much older than you really are, but then at other times—like now—I feel you don't know what you're doing. Your sense is all right, but your experience isn't. You just don't know what you're up against with people of that sort. You've got no frame of reference. I'm sure they're interesting, intelligent, sensitive, stimulating—"

"They don't shape up all that great," I interjected, "I'm not going 'Village.'"

"You sure?"

"Positive," I said. "I find all that bit a little revolting."

He didn't look as convinced as I would have liked. "I can't tell you what to do," he said again. "But I worry plenty. By the way, any news of Pritch?"

I shook my head, that old lost, terrible feeling suddenly drowning me.

"He was all wrong for you, anyway. Very weak. Immature. Might have worked out a few years from now, but he didn't seem to know what he wanted. Kept changing his mind. A real faddist."

I perked up my ears. "Have you seen him?"

Bart shook his head. "Not once."

"You sound as if you had—or heard from him, or something."

"Indirectly, only. Ida was in to see us the other day. Seems he's been calling Lesley."

"When are they publishing the bans?" I asked bitterly.

"Now, Mole, be sensible. You don't think Lesley would go along with any reconciliation at this point, do you?"

"Of course I do!" I stormed. "Anyway, I don't care! I made a mistake, and as soon as I can get it corrected, they can do whatever they damned well please."

He eyed my wrath with wistful compassion. "You know, Mole, I wish you'd move back in with us. I'd feel much better about you all around."

I shook my head, knowing that in a minute I'd be beginning to cry. "I like my house, Bart."

"Is it all because of Joyce that you won't come back?"

"No," I lied, and dropped my head so he wouldn't see the tears that were inching down my cheeks. I couldn't tell him how desperately I longed to come home again, or how miserable and lonely I really was. Or how profoundly my estrangement from Joyce had affected my life: when our friendship cracked up, the first big fissure had come in the granite solid foundation of my short existence, and everything since had simply served to make the fissure greater.

After he left, I sat there alone in my lonely, large living room and pondered it: first Joyce and Bart marrying—thus depriving me of a brother and a best friend, as surely as if they'd teamed up on me. Oh, I know this outcome was an accident, but wasn't it also an inevitable one? It seemed so to me, considering all the factors. Joyce and I *couldn't* have remained friends, not at our unsure ages. She had to prove herself as a wife, and a girl old enough to prove it. And she was still trying.

Then there were lots of other things I had to get through: my first love affair, my first "affair," and my first "serious affair," to culminate in a broken engagement; all three of which were normal in outline, but absurd and psycho in detail. Then Mother—that was the big thing, the big wedge that had really split the fissure. If only she hadn't had to die! After that everything had been simply awful and was getting worse.

Would I make it? I doubted it. The Beautiful People did not exist; they were all ugly ones in holiday masks. And now even the holiday seemed over, and all the people I knew were going about their businesses of being narrow and tiresome, beaten—not beat—or purely vicious and corrupt, as honestly poisonous as a bottle with a label.

At fourteen, I had once remarked to our Madison Avenue druggist who met me on my bicycle on the way to the park, "Life is so futile, Mr. Smith!" He had thought it cute, and would never let me forget it.

But it seemed I had been right.

## Chapter Seventeen

"Are you as pensive as you look?" he said. "Or are you all stirred up by the tragedy of the *Titanic,* being so close to it now, as it were?"

"I saw 'A Night to Remember' on TV," I replied to Shelley Spivak, and tightened my trenchcoat belt. It had been raining when I left home, so I wore that and had tied a scarf over my head.

"You look downright Bohemian," he grinned at me, "all set for a safari into the darkest wilds of the Village."

I laughed at him weakly. Actually, he couldn't have been more accurate. I'd even left the car in the garage and had come over to Macy's by taxi.

We stood in the specified vestibule where he'd asked me to meet him, and Macy customers rushed in and out of the door, looking preoccupied and slightly worried, as all shoppers somehow do, letting down their umbrellas, brushing at their wet hair. Definitely not the Beautiful People, but just people, the inhabitants of the world I must learn to accept.

"Come, now study this memorial," Shelley said to me, his arm taking mine. We moved out of the way of the Macyites, flattened ourselves against the radiator, which was fortunately cold, and silently perused the plaque and poem together. It was my second go round, for though Shelley had arrived precisely on the dot, I had been early. I was too restless to stay at home.

"Now what do you think of it?" He cocked his head at me for an opinion, as if we were two art experts at a vernissage.

"You can't be serious," I said.

"I can be, but I'm not," he said with a fresh grin. "Come on. Where'd you park your little kiddy-car?"

"If you mean my perfectly good automobile, it's at home."

"Don't trust us, do you? And now I suppose the subway's too good for you, and you'll insist on a taxi."

"I'll insist on a bus," I told him lightly. So we went out in the very unpleasant rain, and jammed ourselves into a rush-hour bus, already packed with its full complement, headed downtown.

We were lucky enough to get two of those straps to swing onto, and as close together as we could ever get without being married or taking another rush-hour trip together via the public transportation, we grinned into each other's eyes, rather foolishly, our noses practically rubbing. "I like you, little Chloe Longtree," he said in a softened low voice.

I didn't say a word, but I felt my body responding. Not to his—it was more as if I had been standing at stiff attention for a long time, and suddenly was told to relax. I was almost happy as I held onto my bus strap, idly watching the streets flash by. By flash, I mean all the electrical heralding of the signs on the stores and buildings along the way, for it was almost dark. It was March, and spring was not yet in the air, only sort of behind it, so everything still said Winter! outside, and what was to come was not yet strong enough to make a faint whisper. But those who longed for spring, surely knew it was there. Like a crocus bulb, still brown, but a crocus bulb all the same, and a live one.

As we traveled all the nostalgia I had ever felt for this city traveled through me, as if intravenously injected, and I felt satisfied and warm with it quietly flowing through my veins, nourishing me. I thought of all the nights when Avery and I had sneaked off in Bart's car, that last summer before I was old enough to drive, and how we had toured this grand old town, up one secret street down a familiar one, each different and wonderful, as rich in treasure and terror as an unmined silver lode. And most of it I would never explore, but it was there, all there. Forever, fixed as a star. More enduring than the people who gave it its sparkling highlights. But there were always more people, and there was always New York.

"What are you so quiet for? Are you sad?" Shelley asked me.

"I'm not sad. I was thinking about—things."

"Your husband?"

I gave him a startled look. "No," I said.

"Avery told me about him."

"I gathered."

"Want to talk?"

"Not on a bus," I answered, then added, "or actually anywhere." And I didn't. I had sealed Pritch up in my mind, walled him up as surely as if I'd used mortar and trowel to do it, and only occasional chinks opened up— such as Bart's enlightening information about Pritch and Lesley this afternoon. These I closed up as quickly as possible. I didn't want or need any chinks. Pritch was buried and finished.

Shelley helped me off the bus, handing me down as if I were something precious and fragile. "We've got a long hike from here," he said. "We could take a cab."

"Let's hike," I said, even though the rain was harder than ever and I knew it would wash my face clean of every vestige of makeup, until I looked like one of those ancient Greek statues, eyeless and colorless without their polychrome. However, I didn't care. Shelley was one of those men with whom it wouldn't matter: he liked me for myself. Anyway, I found myself thinking, what did it matter to me what Shelley Spivak thought? He was just a nice, rather rough joe who was befriending me. I didn't ask myself why, but it did occur to me to inquire as to how he got the name Shelley.

"Used to write poetry—as I told you," he said with his almost shy sidewise grin—the grin that must have endeared a great many women to him; it was terribly incongruous with the rest of his rather bold personality. "My Hebrew name sounds a little like Shelley, so it was an easy transition. My family is orthodox. They live in Denver. In a section so Jewish that it's like a ghetto. Only my old man is in the jewelry business and has got lots of money. They have a big house—a cook and a maid."

"Why do you keep saying 'they'?" I asked him.

"Because it is 'they.' I don't live there. Don't care for my stepmother." He grinned again. "Don't care for the whole set-up. I haven't been to synagogue since—oh, since I was bar-mitzvahed."

Then he explained that bar-mitzvah was sort of the equivalent of Catholic confirmation, about which I didn't know too much either. He looked at me. "We're worlds apart, Chloe Longtree, but I like you. And we dig each other. As if we were long-lost relatives. Maybe you *are* from one of the lost tribes of Israel. With a name like Longtree—you sure it wasn't Grossbaum once upon a time?"

I laughed at him, but I'll have to admit I felt what he felt: I hadn't been so close to anybody for a long time. He was like Bart in another guise, and yet curiously like Pritch too, all the men I'd ever cared about, but with a difference. When he took my hand, and held it as we walked along, nothing could have been righter, more warm, more secure.

After a while he said, "What's the score with this old man of yours?"

"Who?"

"Your man," he said, laughing lightly. "This cat you're married to. Love him?"

I confessed I didn't know, was hopelessly awash and confused by everything. He listened carefully. "What you need is a good Alabama divorce. You've got to wipe the slate clean, kid. Can't afford to make too many mistakes at your age."

"I've already made them," I said, and told him more. Before I'd finished, I'd outlined my whole life's history for him.

He appeared thoughtful as we plodded through the rain. "Maybe you ought to hit bottom," he said at last. "It can't hurt a girl like you. You're the kind who has to find out how the other half lives before you can live your half."

"Sounds frightful," I tried to laugh.

"No, seriously. I mean it." He put his hand on my shoulders and turned me toward the street light to look into my wet and probably expressionless face. "A girl like you only grows up by growing."

"I'm growing," I said.

"Are you?" he asked in that crisp, challenging tone of his. "I don't think so, really. It's mostly vicarious—like wading in and lifting your friend Avery out of hot water. You only get wet, not scalded. You think you learn from that?"

"I hope so," I said.

"You afraid to get your head soaked?"

"No, not really. I just don't think its necessary."

"Then why does your instinct keep sending you back for more?"

"My instinct?" I said, truly puzzled.

"Yes. You wander from one steam bath to another. Isn't it time you sat down in one to see what it's like?"

"What do you suggest?"

Still holding me by the shoulders, he gazed at my face. "This may rock you," he said slowly, "but shack up with me—not in that fancy, self-indulgent pad of yours uptown, but down here—cold-water flat, where you learn how to cook and wait on me and do all the things a woman of mine would do. You game?"

It *did* rock me. "I'm not sure—"

"Then you're chicken. You're scared."

"It isn't that. It's just that—" How could I tell him? How could I say that I didn't think I wanted to be "his woman"? Shelley was my brother. "It would be a little like incest at this point," I said.

"Oh, I see," he said slowly, releasing my shoulders. "I've involved you in the brotherhood bit. Well, we'll see what we can do about that. How's this?"

Before I knew it, Shelley had reached up around my waist, had pulled me to him and was kissing me—a long kiss, full of love and passion. "You ever been kissed like that, kid?" he asked, his voice as husky as my own suddenly felt.

"No," I said under my breath. "I haven't."

Then we started walking on again, as naturally as if nothing had happened. But something had, and I knew as soon as we hit Seymour Marlboro's lair something more was going to happen.

If I were Avery's guardian angel, I was also a fallen one.

## Chapter Eighteen

Sy's apartment was a walk-up on a street called Greenwich Street; it was lined with other tenements, all dark and condemned looking, a few new or remodeled apartment houses which undoubtedly charged exorbitant rents and caught only the most desperate or naive of tenants intent upon having a Village residence; and then there were a lot of turn-of-the-century places of business and warehouses. An ominous locale, at best, and I was thoroughly glad I was not alone. Moreover, I was a million times better than not alone: I was with one of the most exciting—or *the* most exciting person I'd ever met. Every casual touch was like a caress; whether he brushed my arm opening the door for me, or took my hand to help me, or just looked at me; with Shelley a look was a touch, a vital physical contact.

We climbed the stairs to Seymour's "pad," I, feeling very tired and wet, yet steaming with warmth as if I sat before an open fire, and somehow sleepily immune to all the bleak awfulness of the tenement house, all because I knew Shelley was right behind me.

He knocked at the door. With a one-two, one-two-three knock that was like a password of identification. Seymour opened the door just a crack, and peered at us skeptically.

Shelley pushed open the door. "Hi, Sy. This is Chloe here. She came down to view her side-kick."

"What?" asked Seymour vaguely, not yet willing to part with his hold on the door, but he had really been brushed aside, and Shelley was striding in. That's the only word for the way he walked, entered or left a place, striding—as if it were a form of travel that could take prizes, like track-running; he did it proudly and well.

I sort of crept in behind him. There were two or three strangers in this strange room, all huddled together, frightened and hostile looking, their eyes big in sunken faces, their clothes as nondescript as a bag of rags. But then the light was bad, admittedly.

"Where's Avery?" Shelley asked with authority, looking around, his hands still in his raincoat pockets. He was rather like a private eye.

"Asleep," Sy gestured toward a closed door. "You want a stick?" he added. "We're all turned on."

"Sure," said Shelley easily. "Pack us a lunch."

"Her too?" Sy said with a gesture toward me.

"Sure," Shelley said in the same easy tone. "She's with it."

I looked at him, much as a child does toward a parent in a roomful of strange people, but by the back of his raincoat, I could tell he had thrown me into this pool on my own, sink or swim. He expected me to swim.

Very timorously, I moved over to the far side of the room, near the huddle of others, near the bookcases made out of orange crates, the only illumination coming from candles stuck in empty chianti bottles, much tallow-encrusted, with variegated colors. The furniture was equally modestly immodest; it all looked as if it had been picked up from a garbage heap—a sagging double bed on one wall with a musty, worn velvet cover, the color gone back to brown from whatever it had been, like seared winter grass; a few canvases on the wall, all very vividly violent in stroke and color, unframed, of course, still on stretchers, and in one corner a huge old upholstered chair, obviously a street relic, which done over, would have screamed for room and air even in the Allyn's old fortress uptown.

"You don't like it, I see," Seymour said in a surly way, obviously having followed my glance around his place.

"I like it fine," I said quietly, and pointedly looked toward his three pale-faced friends he hadn't bothered to introduce. He still didn't.

"I'm Marjorie," said one.

"The name's Rudy," said the male of the trio, getting to his feet in a wobbly way, "and that's Sonya, only I don't think she's up to getting up. Say hello, Sonya."

A weak hand was raised, and then let to fall like a withered blossom, or a tired flag, and Sonya's wide open eyes gazed on at me unseeingly.

I felt a cigarette being put into my hand. "Smoke deep," came Shelley's voice.

I felt myself being pushed down on the cruddy velvet bed. Shelley's arm was behind me, supporting me. He still had his coat on, as I did. "Where's Avery?" I asked after a deep puff. It tasted like burning grass.

"She's asleep inside. Like I told you," I heard Seymour saying petulantly. "If you don't believe me, go see."

"I will," I said getting to my feet, slightly staggering. I thought I was just off balance, but maybe those two puffs had had their effect. Anyway, holding the cigarette, and puffing on it, deeply, as I had been instructed, I went toward the closed door.

"Doesn't she know how much joints cost?" I heard Seymour say. "She's smoking it like a Chesterfield."

"She'll learn," was Shelley's answer. "Anyway, she's got enough to buy and sell S. K. S."

I tried to think about that, steadily, sensibly, as I pushed opened the bedroom door, but even then I knew it was a postponed topic: I'd smoked that stick of marijuana too faithfully following the laid-down rules, and I was as high as a kite; no better, no worse than the others. My mind was as blurred as a spoiled water color, and I didn't care, I didn't care. . . .

When I came to, I was obviously in bed, and the first thing I saw was the hem of the bedsheet; it was clammy and dirty, and in my face. I looked around. The one window I saw streamed dirty, mottled light, because the window was that way in addition to being cracked and uncurtained. I turned my head. There his head lay on the other dirty pillow. It was a sleeping face, very oily looking but beautiful, dark as my own was fair, and very peaceful. Then I knew what warm band encircled my waist: his arm. I stirred away from it, and it tightened. "My love," came the murmur from his sleep. "My love."

Then he was awake, and his face was upon mine, as it had been in the bus, but with all the ardor of possession, and his naked body moved to the top of mine, also naked, and he had me clamped down in a togetherness that *McCall's* talks about, but may or may not mean. . . .

And when it was all over, he said, "You are my real wife. You're the only one. Don't you feel that, Chloe? Don't you?"

And I did. The way Shelley made love to me was a fulfillment. And I belonged to him. As he had predicted, I was his woman. I knew that no matter what ever happened to us, I was his woman. "Where are we?" I finally managed to ask.

"My place," he said. "Fourth Avenue. A real dump."

"Where's Avery?" I asked, feeling as tremulous as I sounded. I had let her down. I had come to save her, and look at me.

"She's okay. Or at least she was. She's still at Sy's place. Out. Like a light. Like you were. You two were gabbing for hours and I kept bringing you sticks, then you both went. Just like that."

"It's worse than liquor," I said.

"It's better. It's clean," he corrected me. "You said a lot of very smart things—to all of us—before you passed out. Don't you remember?"

"No," I said, wanting very much, all of a sudden, to be home in my own bed. "I don't remember anything. I blacked out."

"Sounds like sauce, but it was pot, all the same. Maybe you're a doll who can't take it."

"No, I don't think I can," I said, rising to an elbow, preparatory to going home.

"Come here," he said hoarsely, drawing me back down beside him.

After awhile we lay back, watching the dawn through the cracked windows, over the moldy sheets and scratchy Army blankets, and I told him all this. I told him about Pritch and the way *he* made love; I told him about my ex-fiancée, Charles La Marr; I told him about the casual ones in

England. In fact, I told him. I filled in all of the outline I had told him earlier in the night in the rain.

And he told me: about the two wives, the four children. How responsibly unresponsible he felt. "You will marry me, Chloe," he said urgently, but quietly.

"Of course I will," I answered, feeling lightheaded, but very sure of what I was saying. "I've never met anyone like you. But you will take care of me?"

"Always," he promised. "But you know you've got to do a lot of shifting and changing to stand me."

"Such as?"

"I'm not going to be a provider. It's your money."

I shrugged. "It's there."

"And I won't 'belong' you know."

"I don't either," I whispered tiredly, tenderly. And fell asleep.

When I woke up, I looked at my watch which had obviously stopped, and looked around for Shelley. He was in the kitchen part of this strange dwelling, making coffee. Watching for it to boil. It was a strange place, even worse than Seymour's and I sat up, knowing how cold it was, that the gas stove was the only heat, clutching the blanket around my nakedness. "Where's Avery?" I said rather idiotically. And he came over, sat on the bed, tucking the blanket lovingly around my feet.

"Avery's with her man and you are with yours," he said, and then he kissed me.

I shuddered a little, cried, as he pressed me close to him. "I've never felt this way before about anybody, Chloe!" he said in my ear, and his strong arms were around me, placing me just so, and his body merged with mine, and I closed my eyes. . . .

I woke up the next time when it was dark. There was cracked light coming through the cracked window, irregular and vaguely alarming. I touched my foot to his leg. I knew it so well now, and my toe lingered caressingly. He stirred, said "hmmm?" and I asked him to tell me the time, the day, the place.

He gave a deep sigh, and flopped over on his lovely stomach. "Don't know," he breathed, and went off.

I prodded him. "I've *got* to know." I said, thinking of Tennie and Jess. "They'll be out of their minds."

"Who?" he asked sleepily.

I told him, and he sighed again, and started to go back to sleep. "Tell you later."

"No!" I exclaimed, shaking him. "I've got to go home, Pritch!"

"Pritch!" he answered, sitting straight up in bed and wide awake. He gazed at me, his face full of resentment, almost hatred. "Pritch, is it?"

"I'm sorry, darling," I made an appeal, putting my arms around him. And I was sorry and shocked, by my Freudian slip.

"Come on," he said abruptly, throwing the covers back. "I'm taking you home."

## Chapter Nineteen

Shelley refused to come in with me; in fact, he would not even walk me back to the courtyard; just stayed in the taxi. "Good-bye," he said sullenly, seeing me out. "See you around."

"Come in," I pleaded at the point of tears.

He behaved as if he hadn't heard me; and the taxi drove off, at his bidding, while I still stood there, my hand practically still on the taxi door.

There was nothing to do, but go inside. I still had my trenchcoat, thank God, which covered the fact that I had lost my skirt, and wore only my slip and sweater underneath. I felt awful. Here I was, trudging home after—how many days? Without Avery, without wits, in fact as empty as an old beer bottle up for refund. My pocketbook was, I knew, empty as far as money went, but I hopefully felt for my keys. Yes, they were still there. I put them in the lock, turned them, and let myself into the warmly lighted hall. It hadn't changed; not one bit, and when I went into the living room, there sat Avery on the couch, one foot tucked up under her, her hands scratching her hair as it always did when she read, her nose deep into an issue of *The New Yorker*. I just stood, as one returned from the grave, and when she looked up, casually at first, her expression changed to one of horrified surprise, to match my own. "Darling!" she gasped, and we were clutching each other, feeling each other to see if we were real.

About that time Tennie came into the living room, with things on a tray, and she clutched at me and cried, pushed me away and then drew me back, unable to make up her mind whether to kiss me or kill me. "You're just like your mother, Miss Chloe," she said in a truly heartrending way. "I doesn't know whether to whip you or hug you to death!" Thank God, she had the good sense, having been my Mother's watchdog, not to ask me where I'd been. I got rid of her by saying I was hungry.

When she had gone, I looked at Avery—deeply, searchingly, as if a look would tell me more than any conversation possibly could. She was examining me in the same way. Then she broke into one her peals of delighted laughter. "What fools we are! Man, what fools!"

"When did you get here?" I whispered conspiratorially, and she gave me all the data, keeping her voice as low as mine.

"I really can't stand that Sy," she said. "He's the end. Must have been the pot. He's stupid, has bad breath—*and* B.O., even after a nice bath in that lovely tub in his lovely kitchen. We both had one—together, I mean. How could I do it, Chloe? How could I?" Her eyes twinkled as if she were highly pleased about the whole thing. "Well, at least it's over. I've had my spree—and I *didn't* lose my job. Marvelous Tennie. Told them the most marvelous lie when they called up. But she was frantic, sweetie. Three days *is* a long time—"

"She didn't call Bart, did she?" I asked truly alarmed.

"I'm afraid she did, sweetie. But *I* told him a good lie . . . just now. He just called a moment ago, for the God knows how manyeth time."

"Oh, my God!" I said, sunk.

"Don't worry. The whole thing's over and done with . . . just as long as we never see those characters again. . . ."

I looked at her slowly. How could I tell her I had to see mine again, whether he wanted to see me or not? "What did you think of mine?" I asked her, for a beginning.

Avery laughed. "I wouldn't know him from mine. I was that blasted."

I regarded her gloomily. Lucky Avery! And Shelley had said I was the one who could take it or leave it, snap back.

"Well," she said, getting to her feet, yawning. "Enough of this lovemaking. I've got to get to the office. Do I look pale enough?"

"Too pale," I replied, and asked her what time it was anyway. I learned it was breakfast time.

"You don't look too red-blooded yourself," she said giving me the critical eye. "You must have really lived it up."

"I don't know what you'd call it," I said dully.

"Well, take heart in any case, darling. It really is all over."

Is it? I asked myself, watching her idly as she walked around the room, collecting her cigarettes and things and stuffing them in her purse. She picked up an old hat of mine, looked at it from a couple of angles, and said, "Not bad. Think I'll wear it," and jammed it down on her head. Oddly enough, it looked very chic. But Avery has one of those hat heads. "What are you mooning about?" she asked, giving me a sudden look. "You aren't still high, are you?"

I shook my head, heard her say good-bye, and listened for the door to slam and lock me in, closet me with my thoughts. They were running wild as horses on the range; it seemed a hopeless task to try to catch them. But I had to, and I hoped Tennie would leave me alone for a while. I didn't want any private words with her.

To forestall any, I decided to go up to my room and lie down. I felt terrible. In the physical sense I felt so awful that my mind had almost literally vacated my ruined body, like an astral spirit. But my mind was a sick thing too, trotting up and down hyena-fashion, longing, actually, to be put out of its misery. But the only way short of dying was sleep, and that was impossible.

I lay on the chaise longue and wished for the energy to get up and find some pillows. Instead I used my arms behind my head as cushions. After a while they, at least, went to sleep and when they started to tingle, I had to move them. Another terrific effort, and I doubted if they were worth it. Tennie was tapping at the door as if I were in an infirmary.

"Come on in!" I called rather harshly, and she brought in my breakfast tray, looking subdued but pleased, as if everything were all right again with the world now that I had come home. I could tell she wanted to talk, but I waved her out, saying I was sleepy.

"If you don't watch out, Miss You," she gave me one parting shot from the door, "you gonna end up in a fix."

Gimme one! was the only rejoinder I could think of, and as it was too obscure as far as Tennie was concerned, I didn't use it. But I went on thinking it.

Yes, I certainly needed something to get me out of this one. I couldn't believe it. In the first place, why had I made that silly slip and called him Pritch? Did Shelley and Pritch sound alike? No! Did they look alike, or remind me of each other in any way? No, no, no! But why had he become so infuriated? How could anybody be so contemptibly conceited as to be really upset by a little thing like that? Would I have minded if he had called me Dorothy, or Peggy, or whatever his wives' names were? No, of course not.

I got up and paced around, convincing myself what a good, kind, reasonable, lenient, understanding girl I was. And he was an oaf and a bastard. Uncouth, ugly, smug. It was a good thing it was all over. Avery was right: it had simply been a spree.

This squared away, I decided to go further with the guilt-eradicating, and went and drew myself a bath. I put out my clothes, feeling very luxurious, slightly heady with release. I was back in the scrubbed, scented, comfortable arms of Mother Normality, and no more would I stray. But even as I lowered myself in the tub, I heard the phone ringing, and my heart leaped up like a rainbow trout. I listened alertly, but could hear nothing, of course, for Tennie had taken the call in the kitchen, or wherever she was. And she wouldn't disturb me since she thought I was asleep.

I splashed through that bath as if I were drowning in it and couldn't wait to get to dry land. I dashed to my room and buzzed her on the intercom. "Who was it?" I shouted.

"The cleaners. They done lost your new slipcovers."

I rang off and wearily started to dress. Dress for what? I hadn't the faintest idea. Maybe lunch with Bart was in order, but I couldn't face him yet. And if he called up, worried as hell, to ask me, I'd put him off with some excuse. In point of fact, all I wanted to do was run back to Shelley.

Having admitted it, I dressed as though the house were on fire, thinking as I rushed into my clothes that I didn't even know his address, and would have to go by instinct in order to find his house. But I didn't care, I didn't care! I'd comb Fourth Avenue, look in every house, until I found where Shelley was. I'd find him and make him take me.

When the phone rang, I didn't bother to pick it up, even to listen in to see who it was. Something just told me it wouldn't be Shelley, and whoever it was, it didn't matter. Then I heard Tennie urgently buzz the intercom.

"Who is it?" I cried impatiently.

"It's *him*," she said significantly.

"Who?"

"Mr. Allyn."

"Mr. Allyn?" I echoed stupidly and sat down quite faint on the bed. Slowly I answered the phone.

"Hello, there," Pritch's voice came over the wire, as casual as if he'd seen me an hour before. "Doing anything for lunch?"

In a daze, I heard myself saying no, and agreeing to meet him at the Ritz in half an hour. As soon as I hung up the phone, I went downstairs and had two straight shots of Bourbon. Tennie looked at me expectantly, eagerly, and I simply closed my eyes and shook my head at her.

I also drove in something of a stupor, ran two red lights, and nearly bumped into a car ahead which made an abrupt and unforgivable stop. I said so too, leaning out of my window and yelling like a truck driver. The man appeared very startled, and I whipped around him smartly and drove away before he could recover himself.

That's how I felt—all crazy.

"You're looking well," Pritch said, giving me an admiring look as he came forward to meet me.

I murmured that he was too, but to tell the truth I was almost in a state of shock, so I hardly saw him.

"I believe our table is ready," he said, wasting no time, and we worked our way back to where our table waited for us.

He immediately set about the business of ordering, explaining to me over the top of the menu that he was very hungry and hoped I was. I said I'd like a drink.

At this, he coolly summoned the waiter and ordered two whiskey sours—what we used to drink together always. I knew life was coming back when it flashed through my wicked mind that his mother would have a fit if she knew he was lunching in this posh place, and drinking liquor to boot. But I said nothing, merely glanced demurely at the napkin in my lap and wondered why I couldn't work up any specific feeling toward him. There should have been love or hate; instead there was a sort of embalmed feeling of tiredness, such as one has when lunching with an old friend who is avoided successfully except two or three times a year. Maybe, I told myself, this will pass, and I put up a warning sign in my mind to watch out for any change.

Lunch ordered, he gave me a long, fond smile. "Well, Chloe," he said, "I'll come to the point at once: now that you have finally given me adequate and acceptable grounds for it, I want a divorce. If you don't get it, I will."

## Chapter Twenty

In the same good-natured and breezy manner, he elaborated on how he had had the good fortune to establish these grounds. "You and your pal Avery evidently forgot that Seymour Marlboro was very much in my debt," he explained.

All this news had momentarily deprived me of the powers of speech. Was he trying to say it was all a frame, that I had deliberately walked into a vice-trap Seymour—and apparently Shelley—had laid for me? But I couldn't ask him.

He, however, was continuing quite blithely on his own. Obviously, he didn't need my reply to anything, and went along as if he were giving a memorized speech, one he enjoyed very much.

"—Seymour phoned the good news this morning—that you and his pal Spivak had been couched together, shall we say, for upwards of three days. And of course I know all about that little orgy den run by that fellow Summers, or Saunders, who thinks he is practicing a new form of religion—"

"—I didn't—" I tried to protest, but he took the words out of my mouth.

"—Oh, I know you didn't. But who would believe it in court? You see, I have you coming and going for adultery. So are you going to be a nice girl and go get yourself a nice quiet divorce, or shall I get a big noisy one?"

"Suit yourself," I said coldly, starting to get up from the table. Then I looked at him. He wore the most odious grin, and the lights flashing in his eyes weren't "angry sea," but typhoon; I had never thought that blue eyes could look tawny, but they did: wild-animal tawny.

I gazed at him somewhat wistfully, as if I were looking over the edge of a precipice toward which I must go, there being no turning back. Why, why? What had changed him? What had cooled passion into pity, then pity into irritable indifference—and now this? "Why do you hate me?" I asked, falteringly.

"Hate you?" His eyes gleamed with triumph again. "I don't hate you. I despise you," his lip positively curled, movie fashion. "Why do you think I walked out on you, because I was 'influenced by my family'?" He gave a laugh like a howl. "I didn't need them to tell me what you were trying to do to me. You and your 'plans'! I was sick of the sight of you long before we even married, and I just went through with it because I thought it was the only thing to do—"

I heard him wearily. "You're very sick, Pritch," I said.

"I'm going to be a lot better from now on!" He said vehemently. "Are you going?" I was still leaning on the table. "If so, go on. All I want to see of you is your signature on divorce papers."

I changed my mind and sat down again. "Let's get this straight," I began. I wanted to hear him say—actually say—he'd never loved me; but I couldn't put it that way. It was too bare and I was too vulnerable. "You didn't really *have* to marry me, you know, Pritch."

"I know, I know," he waved this aside in annoyance. "The actual invitation was my mistake. I was confused. Lesley and I weren't getting on too well, and I thought of you back in London, and it seemed such a peaceful, pleasant—" He broke off "—But all that's over and done with. So I made a mistake—one mistake—you made all the rest!"

"Did I?" I asked. "Why didn't you tell me all this when you first felt your fad for me fading? I would have divorced you any time, and gladly."

He threw back his head and simply roared with laughter so raucous and eerie that several people nearby looked uncomfortable and were evidently interrupted in their own conversations. Then he stopped this insane humor. "You know damned well you pulled out every stop to get your way with me," he accused me.

I looked down at my untouched drink, rubbed my finger around the bottom of the glass. I wanted to say: I thought you felt the same for me. I looked up. Hadn't he? A scowl stood in his eyes. No. You can never look at a person like that if you have once loved them. He had been selling himself a bill of goods, that was all—me. He had made a manly unheartfelt effort, and so naturally now he despised me, just as he despised himself. I had been right in the first place: he couldn't love. Only maybe his awful family he pretended to hate.

I stood up again, this time for good. "All I can say, Pritch, is that you're brainwashed to tatters. When you're not busy laundering your own deformed mind, you let others have a try. Better try a prefrontal lobotomy."

This was mean, but more than the essence of truth was there: Brother Allyn was the last person on earth to know his own mind. It would be a challenge to anybody. "Good-bye," I said under my breath.

I walked away briskly, trying to feel imperious, and the speech he barked after me didn't hurt: "See to it you get that divorce and quick about it!" It simply served to inform anyone around who had failed to catch the drift earlier that we were having a final marital scene.

As I opened the phone booth, I had that deadened but composed feeling of a wronged person. His venom had acted as a cathartic; I was purified, young, blameless. Therefore, my voice was small when I called Bart and told him what had happened. He was mystified to hear of Pritch's insulting behavior, his lightning quick reappearance, his sudden insistence on a divorce. He wanted to know if I had done something to bring it about? I vigorously denied that I had—for in a way I hadn't. It had all been so indirect. The lawyer was less subtle in his suggestions that I had done something to precipitate it, or to "give him a chance to pounce, show his true colors." Both Bart and the lawyer missed the fine points involved, so it seemed to me: that I had been an innocent, trusting wife, waiting for my husband. *I* had not resorted to spying and other low tricks. It was frustrating not to be able to point this out, but I felt I had to tie my own tongue. It would not do to tell either that Pritch had gotten the "goods" on me, and had long been waiting for them. My lawyer, an old and experienced hand at the game, merely sighed, probably quite aware of my small deceit, and advised me, since I said I no longer cared to have Pritch back, to plan to divorce him as quickly as possible.

I said I would, and knew then, firmly, I really wanted to.

It was clear that Pritch had gone quite mad, so mad that all the things he had said were unbelievable. How had he been able to accumulate that fine backlog of hatred out of midair? Even granted that his family helped him assiduously, and that Joyce and possibly Lesley had done their share. Where had it come from if not from insanity? It was so unjust and untrue that it didn't touch me. All those months of fidelity, waiting for him to come back, yearning for him . . . and he was just waiting for me to fall into a trap. Or had he imagined that too? That Seymour had played hand and glove with him? If so, what had prevented Seymour from telephoning me and arranging a meeting instead of waiting for a chance encounter? It didn't make any sense at all. I was almost tempted to call Pritch's mother and have a long talk with her—if she'd let me—but that was foolish. If he'd made all this up, she wouldn't know what I was talking about, and if he hadn't, then she wouldn't talk to me in the first place.

Thoughtfully, I drove back home; Bart said he would meet me there and we would talk about everything and what the best course was. I debated telling him the whole thing. But it would have terrible repercussions if I did: he would immediately insist, for instance, that I rid myself forever of Avery; would blame it all on her bad influence. Then, also, he would probably take steps to see to it that no more Shelley Spivaks crossed my doorstep for a long time to come. And I wanted Shelley Spivak to cross my doorstep; to cross it and recross it, to camp on it, to carry me over it. I didn't believe for an instant that he had been any party to Pritch's ugly little scheme with Seymour—and I even doubted if dumb Seymour had done more than just shoot off his mouth inopportunely and after the fact. Pritch's story was all too much of a fantasy, something invented to hide hurt pride, probably, when Seymour told him about Shelley and me. But damn Seymour anyway! And Avery had said it was all over, just a harmless spree. . . .

Bart gave me what I can only describe as a lot of stern sympathy which turned out to be quite boring as he had nothing new to add, being ignorant of some of the developments. And when I tried to describe Pritch's behavior, deleting, of course, all of the salient items, such as *why* he was so insistent now on a divorce, Bart gave me a very doubtful look, and I knew he thought I was exaggerating. But his overall theme, the one that ran in and out of our conversation like a fugue, was his plea to come "back home."

But I was as determined as he was. "Come back now and fall over Lesley and Pritch too, probably?"

Bart violently insisted this wouldn't happen, but I shook my head. "You never know." And since Lesley was Joyce's sister, he had to admit there was some truth in what I said.

I guess Bart saw my impatience, though he had none himself, and stood up quite reluctantly to leave. "I have a bad feeling about all this, Mole," he lingered at the door to say. And gave me a queer look, as if he were tempted to say something more—like how he sensed I was holding out on him, or something. Then he gazed at me with a long look, as if he were trying to memorize my face.

Finally, I got rid of him by promising to come to dinner next week, a duty I'd successfully avoided for months.

As soon as he left, I left, and I found I was so nervous I could hardly drive. Every stoplight made me want to scream with impatience, and the traffic moved at the pace of a funeral march all the way downtown.

Once on Fourth Avenue, I frantically searched the buildings for some landmark. Then the old unconscious decided to stop being so selfish, and up popped the memory that his house had been vaguely in the vicinity of the secondhand-book section. This narrowed it down considerably, and I only had to drive up and down those few blocks three times before I spotted the house. I jumped out of the car, parking it illegally and not caring a bit, and rushed into the house.

I panted up the grimy old stairs, creaking as if they were in pain because of being walked on. It was up near the top, I remembered that. Maybe the fourth floor? I stopped to get my bearings and tried the door to the left. It seemed the right one.

At first my knocks were merely businesslike, then, I'm afraid, I more or less pounded, and then to my astonishment, and probably because I had been so rough with it, the old door sprang open, as if giving up before superior odds. I pushed it in a little further and gazed at the place, the late scene of my lovely crime. Quite clearly, no one was at home. I took a few trial steps, wondering as I did so how Shelley could bear to live in such filth and poverty. Then it came to me with overwhelming certainty that he didn't—maybe never had. Hurriedly, I walked around the two rooms, searching for some sign of him—books, clothes, anything. There was nothing. Either this was an apartment (if one could call it that) borrowed especially for assignations, or else he had moved, and in a great hurry too. I was reduced to a thousand shards by this realization, and walked out of the place like the sole survivor of a building just bombed.

I trudged back to the car and just sat in it, slumped over the wheel. I kept urging myself to cry, cry, but I couldn't cry, and as so often happens in times of great stress—at least with me—a crazy tune came into my head, and I found myself humming it aloud; without being able to identify it, naturally, this being my day for total frustration.

You can't sit here all night, were the words I finally managed to fit to the tune, since they were so apt, but I still sat there all the same. At last, I started the car, and drove back uptown at the funereal pace I had encountered coming down, only I set this one for myself, much to the exasperation of end-of-the-day drivers, anxious to get home. But I was oblivious to them, oblivious to such a degree that I was almost blissful, still humming to myself, daft as Ophelia. Once or twice the thought of Avery crossed my mind, but she disappeared along with other scudding clouds of thought. Maybe if I called her, she'd have some practical suggestions. But why bother?

At the garage, the man asked me if I'd be needing the car anymore that night, and I told him no in such a dim happy voice that I'm sure he thought I'd just come from the dentist where I'd been given gas. I sauntered along the street, humming still, and laughing out loud every now and then for it seemed—my entire life, I mean—such a hugely preposterous dirty joke. Lucky Chloe Longtree became my new cry, and I chanted it out loud every now and then, just for laughs. I met a few people who turned full around in the street to stare, but for the most part, this being New York, I was left to enjoy my madness in private.

It was probably after five when I let myself in the house; or if it wasn't, Avery was home early. For I heard her laughing as I walked through the hall. Then I saw her—saw him. She and Shelley were sitting together on the couch and they both looked up expectantly when I entered.

"Company!" Avery greeted me. Shelley, without getting up, lifted a hand at me and said, "Howdy."

"Howdy," I replied from a previous life, and collapsed in a chair. I guess they just thought I was tired.

## Chapter Twenty-One

The instant Avery left the room, Shelley and I were all over each other, as they say. Vulgar as it sounds, I know there is no better way to describe it.

"Darling, darling," he said incessantly as he kissed my eyes, my hair.

When Avery returned, almost inopportunely, she seemed quite amazed to see how close we were. "Well, you two certainly don't believe in letting a second go unoccupied, do you?"

"No, we don't," I told her, turning my head back to Shelley to get kissed some more.

"From now on," he said, "this is a full-time job. I've come to stay."

Avery watched us as we kissed again. "You're kidding, of course," she said after a while.

"No, I'm not," he said quite seriously. "Am I, darling?" he turned to me for corroboration. I looked at him adoringly, scarcely aware of what he wanted me to corroborate.

"But you *can't* live here," Avery said, frowning. "Chloe's lawyer wouldn't allow a man to live in the house until she's divorced."

"Is that true, sweetheart?" he asked me softly.

I considered it I wanted desperately for him to stay. "Maybe we can work it out some way," I replied. "Maybe since Avery is here, she can act as official chaperone. Then of course there are Tennie and Jess—I don't see why it couldn't be done."

"You're both simply crazy!" Avery announced in exasperation. "What if Pritch gets hold of this and wants to make something of it?"

"Pritch has already made something of it," I said carefully and gave them both a full rundown on my non-luncheon luncheon date with him.

Avery couldn't have been more surprised, but Shelley made no comment. Instead, he looked bored, as if he wished we'd hurry and get the whole discussion finished; he kept squeezing my hand, touching my hair, as if anxious to get back to the serious business of semi-private lovemaking. Consequently, the subject was dispatched in short order, leaving Avery far from satisfied with what she heard. I confess I felt a little guilty as I allowed myself to be moved back into the ecstatic circle of Shelley's arms, and I didn't blame Avery for looking on coldly. Presently, she got up and left the room.

When she did this, I broke away from him momentarily. "We really shouldn't, darling. Not in front of her." I whispered to him.

"Why not? She's a big girl. Anyway, she's a third wheel around here."

It shocked me and saddened me, this home truth. I wondered what Shelley and I should do about it.

But Avery evidently recovered her good nature and her poise, for when the three of us went to Grand Central just before dinner, she couldn't have been in better spirits. Both of us twitted Shelley for having checked his luggage in a public locker instead of bringing it directly to the house when he left his Fourth Avenue digs.

"It seemed a wee mite too presumptuous—even for me," he said with his wonderful crooked smile. "How was I to know that Chloe really meant all she said? It's one thing to hope it, and another to know it."

Both of them beamed at me as if I were in a bridal bower, and I beamed back, feeling the same way, but a bit puzzled. I had remembered that Shelley had insisted I come live with him—not the other way around, which I had been prepared to do. Admittedly, however, I found it far more comfortable for him to move uptown. For secretly I knew Pritch had been right in his evaluation of me as a housewife: if I had to rough it, I probably could never make it.

So none of us pursued this subject any further; it was tacitly understood that I had invited Shelley to share my bed and board, just as it was understood that Shelley had preferred my conveniences to his own squalor and misery, forced upon him by lack of funds. I think we all felt relieved, took deep breaths of thanksgiving, and praised providence that I could afford to foot the bills, and thus insure success to our amorous venture. In other words, it was as if I were the rich businessman who finances the brilliant young lad who discovers a gold mine but hasn't the cash to exploit it on his own.

Even Tennie and Jess went along with this to some degree, so cheered were they by the sight of my obvious happiness. At dinner that night, we all behaved like fools—at one minute young children misbehaving at table, and at the next the tender silly young couple, surrounded by doting, approving family. In a spurt of sheer *joie de vivre* at one point I was even sitting in Shelley's lap, my arm lovingly around his neck, eating from his plate, being fed like a pet bird.

After dinner, Avery discreetly said she thought she'd go to a movie. With a pang of guilt, I too readily agreed, betraying my eagerness to be alone with Shelley, but aware at the same time that we were sort of crowding her out of the place where she lived.

"Do you really like him?" I asked in an anxious whisper, seeing her out the door.

She crinkled her eyes a little, getting ready to say something sharp and funny. "He needs a little polishing. Too bad you got the job first!"

I couldn't have been more delighted.

"But," she added, "don't let him make a squaw out of you. It's not your role."

"I won't," I promised, meaning it.

She gave me a little enigmatic smile and left.

Tennie was the next to be heard from. She had brought me her approval and Jess' too, but with provisors attached. "He don't seem much like the rest of your friends," she ventured. "But he looks to be a mighty fine man. Growed up; knows what he's doing and maybe can settle you down some. But Miss You, it don't seem right he should live here—even with me and Jess and Miss Avery around. Don't you reckon you ought to see what the law says . . .?"

Reluctantly, I admitted maybe I should. After all, we could be together almost all the time if he actually slept elsewhere; and it wasn't worth it to jeopardize our future. I asked Shelley's opinion; I desperately had to know he understood before I even consulted the lawyer.

He saw it all right away because his mind worked in a flash, like a diamond drill. "Darling, of course!" he agreed. "I was so absorbed in you this afternoon that I wasn't thinking too much about consequences. But if the divorce is on the fire—and the sooner the better for me—we mustn't do anything to impede it."

He got up briskly, started toward his luggage. It nearly broke my heart; my fantasy had been so way ahead of my reason that already I felt divorced, married to him, and settled down into our life together.

"Where will you go?" I cried, as if he were leaving forever.

"A hotel," he said calmly, still smiling.

But he hasn't a sou! hasn't anything except those two pathetic old suitcases! "Wait a minute," I said hurriedly, and went to the desk and wrote a check for him. I pressed it into his hand. "Don't look at it," I begged him. "Just take it. For running expenses."

He looked at it anyway, and gave that low whistle of astonishment I'd heard from him before "You're joking," he said, handing it back. "There isn't that much money."

"There is, there is!" I insisted. "Take it and let's not discuss it at all. It's my fault, not yours, that you have to live elsewhere. Now go on and check in a hotel and come right back."

Which is what he did.

## Chapter Twenty-Two

Lingeringly, tenderly, we parted each night after a long, lovely day together, and each time he left, it nearly killed me. The days were spent going places together—hand in hand—places I would have never gone by myself, and with few other people. He was marvelously intelligent, and was as well informed as a quiz show winner about just anything, it seemed to me. There was nothing, apparently, he didn't know, for there seemed to be nothing he hadn't done. He was a gourmet chef, for instance, and Tennie even let him experiment in her kitchen and admitted he'd taught her a thing or two. And his knowledge always came up so casually, in the course of things we did—like the afternoon we went to the Cloisters and looked at the herb garden: he knew the complete culinary and medicinal history of every herb. That was when I found out he liked to cook, and had even worked for a time as a chef at the Waldorf.

He knew about things like hunting too (as well as Hemingway); 10th century music and medieval poetry, falconry, skiing, all the words to Broadway hits, the battles of the Civil War, 19th century bestsellers—*St. Elmo,* for instance—where the highest waterfalls in the world were located, their exact height, all the famous murders in history, the names of the English kings and their houses, who Brenda Frazier had married and when. Ad infinitum. And he could spell too.

We had marvelous times together, but the strain of waiting for the divorce was very hard on both of us. I was on the phone a dozen times a day with my lawyer, trying to speed him up in getting the details arranged. Finally a date was set for my departure—a whole month away.

It was during this period that Shelley began to drink again—hit the sauce, as he called it. He told me he had been on the wagon for years and years, or ever since he had discovered the joys of marijuana. Maybe I'm stuffy, but I absolutely did not want any pot-smoking going on in my house, and while there was no need to tell Shelley, he knew it, and that was why he drank. Consequently, I felt very guilty and responsible for his drinking, and wouldn't have dreamed of criticizing him for it. Avery was the one who pointed out that the liquor bills were simply tremendous; I had preferred to ignore it.

Liquor had an ulterior effect on Shelley's disposition, and I hated to be around him when he was drunk. Although he always apologized for it the next day, and often said he didn't remember anything, he was very surly, and once quite violent: he hurled a lamp at me. After that episode, I realized something had to be done. I asked him why he drank so much.

"To forget," he told me, as if it were an idiotic question, the answer being self-evident.

I didn't then go on to ask him if he was unhappy, for the answer to this indeed did seem self-evident. Something was worrying him terribly.

"Do you need money? Do you have debts?" I asked, hoping I could help.

"I don't inquire into your business," he answered coldly, and looked ready to flare into a rage.

This was all surprising to me; I had thought he had a contemplative disposition.

But the real trouble—not just danger signals—started one afternoon when I came in early, my appointment at the hairdressers' having been canceled, found the living room blue and foggy with marijuana smoke, and confronted not only Shelley very high on pot, but three other men I'd never seen before and trust I'll never have to see again.

They were lounging around, and apparently Shelley had just been reading aloud to them from his favorite poet: Shelley. He was in a dreamy, lovable mood, insisted on pulling me down beside him on the couch and continuing his reading. He didn't even notice that I was stiff as a ramrod within his embrace.

"Baby, baby," he said. "You're my baby. Somebody give little Chloe girl a joint."

I emphatically refused, eyeing the three strangers with open dislike, while they eyed me back, rather covetously. One had teeth like a lycanthrope and long unwashed hair; another was so badly pock-marked that his features themselves seemed to be just further results of his skin trouble; and the third had such shifty eyes that they ran around in his head as if he had no control over them. Maybe it was a nervous tic, but if so I have never seen anyone who more deserved to have this particular disorder.

I stayed just a few seconds, then stood up and quite pointedly announced I was going upstairs. Shelley waved me away casually enough, but less than a half hour later, he lunged into my bedroom and hotly accused me of alienating his friends. "Dirty little snob!" he shouted, then wheeled out and I saw no more of him that day.

All of which made me more and more anxious to leave, get my divorce, and come back to start life all over again. Somehow I thought by wiping the slate clean, removing all the stress, Shelley and I would be happy again. I say Shelley and I because in spite of it all I was happy; though his growing restiveness bothered me, I was still impervious to gloom, being wildly, hedonistically transported with passionate love.

Two days before my departure date, Avery came to me and said, "Do you have any idea what happened to my pearls? They're the only good thing Madre had left to leave me."

I didn't like the suspicious tone of her voice, but tactfully refrained from saying so. Instead, I helped her look for them, but they were gone. And she couldn't remember when she'd seen them last, as she seldom wore them. "Don't worry," I told her. "I'm insured."

"And a good thing too," she muttered under her breath.

"What do you mean by that?" I challenged her.

"Nothing at the moment, but everything at some future date when you're more receptive."

"I'm as receptive as I'll ever be," I informed her in cold resentment.

"Possibly," she commented in a tight-lipped way, and turned, prepared to let it go at that.

"Listen, say what you have to say now!"

"Not if you ask me in that lovely manner."

"Do say what you want to say," I said, quieter. "I really do want to hear, and I promise I won't protest—no matter what it is."

"All right," she sighed, "but let's sit down for it. This is not going to be easy."

We sat down in her room, which was very sunny and cheerful—in direct contrast to the bleak, solemn looks we exchanged. "Your little friend is a thief," she began.

I rose up in my chair, ready to murder her, but she said, "Remember your promise? Let me say all this, and then if you like, I'll go—anything you wish. I'm still very much your friend, Chloe, no matter what you think." She paused to see if she could risk going on, and though my eyes were blazing, she risked it, thank God.

"If you'll look at your jewel box, I think you'll find it nearly empty. It wasn't my business to look, of course, but when this fell out of his jacket pocket the other day—" she produced a pawn ticket and presented it to me "—I'll admit I sort of snitched it sounds like yours, doesn't it?"

I didn't look at it; I couldn't. I simply crumpled it in my hand, feeling as if I were crumpling myself. For of course I knew the ring was gone. And for days I had persuaded myself that I had misplaced it—or tried to persuade myself. Then I heard her go through the rest—all things I knew: the check forgeries (which I had honored), the strange seedy looking visitor with the scraggly beard who slunk around outside in the street every other day or so, pacing up and down furtively, obviously waiting for somebody (I pretended I didn't think he was waiting for Shelley; I pretended I didn't think he was a dope pusher and was in partnership with my love); but the thing she told me I did not know was about his extra-curricular love life. "First," she said evenly, "he made whopping passes at me. I don't know why. Maybe so I wouldn't tattle on him, for he knew from the start I was on to him. But the pay-off came yesterday when

Western Union called back to tell Mr. Spivak his message was undelivered. I simply got a copy of the message."

"How?" My voice was faint and distant.

"By telling them I was Mrs. Spivak. They seemed to find this a little odd, and I think you can see why when I read it to you; or better still, read it yourself, if you can read my writing. I took it all down over the phone."

She placed it in my dead hand, and I read it with my dead eyes:

"Mrs. Dorothy Spivak, Fargo Park, California.

Darling, am renting first-rate house for us for two months. Plenty of room for you and Sally and the baby. Will wire you the other $200 and carfare in a few days as soon as bonus check comes through."

"Bonus check," I said lifelessly.

## Chapter Twenty-Three

"People have had nervous breakdowns over less," Avery said gently.

I agreed, but didn't feel up to nodding. Instead, I stared at the sunbursts in the clouds we were passing through. It was wonderful flying weather, and aside from feeling a little weak from having been in bed for two weeks with what everyone agreed was psychosomatic pneumonia, I felt calm if not serene; very glad to be on my way to Reno at last; very glad to have Avery going with me.

There had been no trouble excising Shelley. I simply casually sat him down, with Bart, Avery, my lawyer and Tennie as witnesses, and told him what I knew. And at the end of my speech, he gave me his funny, charming little smile and said "Touché," and went to the door, saluting us as he left, grand to the end.

"You'll probably have dope addicts and pushers knocking on your door for years," Avery said conversationally.

"No, I won't," I assured her. "Somebody else may have. But I'm selling the house."

"Why didn't you tell me?"

"I just decided, just now," I told her with a grin.

"Then what?"

"The European bit again, I guess," I sighed. "After all, one Beautiful People came out of it, even if he did turn out to be a hideosity with a strong case of insanity."

"You and your damned Beautiful People!" she chided me. "Honestly, Chloe, I'd think you would have had enough by now. Can't you settle for just People? I get into scrapes—but nothing like yours. What's the matter with you, are you oversexed or something?"

"Probably," I said. "I may give myself a nice hysterectomy for Christmas."

She giggled violently. "You're the end!" she exclaimed.

And I thought to myself that I might very well be.

THE END

# Richard E. Geis
## (1927-2013)

Like Crazy, Man (Newsstand Library, 1960), reprinted as The Beatniks
    (Dollar Book, 1962; with Every Bed is Narrow by Andrew Laird)
Sex Kitten (Newsstand Library, 1960)
Honeymoon Hotel (France, 1962)
Bedroom City (France, 1962)
Champ in the Dark (Parliament, 1962)
Girlsville (France, 1963)
Slum Virgin (Saber, 1963)
The Saturday Night Party (Softcover Library, 1963)
Male Mistress (Brandon House, 1964)
Whistle Them Willing (Neva/Playtime, 1964)
Sensual Family (Novel, 1964)
Twilight Beauty (Novel, 1965)
Young Tiger (Softcover Library, 1965)
Bedroom Blacklist (Brandon House, 1966)
Bongo Bum (Brandon House, 1966)
In Bed We Lie (Brandon House, 1967)
Sex Turned On (Softcover Library, 1967)
The Punishment (Softcover Library, 1967)
The Sex Machine (Brandon House, 1967)
Eye at the Window (Brandon House, 1967)
The Endless Orgy (Brandon House, 1968)
Ravished (Essex House, 1968)
Orality '69 (Barclay House, 1969)
Orality '70 (Barclay House, 1969)
Raw Meat (Essex House, 1969)
Three Way Swap (Barclay House, 1970)
Nurses Who Seduce The Young (Barclay House, 1970) reprinted as Nurses
    and Young Men (Brighton Books, undated)
A Candid Sex Report on Young Girls Who Seduce Older Men (Barclay
    House, 1971) reprinted as Older Men and Pre-Teen Girls (Brighton,
    undated)
Women & Bestiality (Barclay House, 1971)
Revealing Case Histories of Swap Orgies (Barclay House, 1971)
Anal Husbands and Their Deviant Wives (Barclay House, 1971)
The Arena Women (Brandon House, 1972)
Reckless Living (Softcover Library, 1972)
Defense de coucher [Forbidden to Sleep] (Champs Libres, 1976)
Canned Meat (self-published, 1978)
Star Whores (self-published, 1980)

The Corporation Strikes Back (self-published, 1981)
How to Write Porno Novels for Fun and Profit (Loompanics, 1985)

**As Albina Jackson**
Dusty Dyke (Playtime/Neva, 1964)

**As Ann Radway**
Discotheque Doll (Brandon House, 1969)

**As Frederick Colson**
The Devil is Gay (Brandon House, 1965)
The Three Way Set (Brandon House, 1965)
The Passion Thing (Brandon House, 1966)
Roller Derby Gal (Brandon House, 1967)

**As Richard Elliott** (with Elton T. Elliott)
The Sword of Allah (Fawcett, 1984)
The Burnt Lands (Fawcett, 1985)
The Master File (Fawcett, 1986)
The Einstein Legacy (Fawcett, 1987)

**As Robert Owen**
Man for Hire (Brandon House, 1965) with Robert N. Owen
Drifter in Town (Brandon House, 1966) with Robert N. Owen
Off-Broadway Casanova (Brandon House, 1966) with Robert N. Owen
Sailor on the Town (Brandon House, 1966) with Robert N. Owen
A Dame in His Corner (Brandon House, 1966) with Robert N. Owen
The Carnal Trap (Brandon House, 1966) with Robert N. Owen
The Soldier (All-Star, 1967) with Robert N. Owen

**As Peggy Swenson/Swanson/Swan**
The Blonde (Midwood, 1960)
The Unloved (Midwood, 1961)
Easy (Midwood, 1962)
Pleasure Lodge (Midwood, 1962)
Call Me Nympho (France, 1962)
Sea Nymph (Midwood, 1963) reprinted as Nymph (Midwood, 1969)
Pajama Party (Midwood, 1963)
Virgin No More (France, 1963)
Lesbian Lure (Playtime/Neva, 1964) as "Peggy Swanson")
Campus Lust (Playtime/Neva, 1964 as "Peggy Swan")
Lesbian Gym (Brandon House, 1964)
Queer Beach (Brandon House, 1964)

The Three Way Apartment (Brandon House, 1964)
Suzy and Vera (Brandon House, 1964)
The Gay Partners (Brandon House, 1964)
Amateur Night (Brandon House, 1965)
Beat Nymph (Brandon House, 1965)
Pamela's Sweet Agony (Brandon House, 1965)
Rita and Marian (Brandon House, 1967)
Teen Hippie (Midwood, 1968)
Odd Couple (Midwood, 1968; with Teen Butch by Carol Caine)
The Love Tribe (Brandon House, 1968)
Devil on Her Tail (Brandon House, 1969)
Snow Bound (Dominion, 1969)
The Mouth Girl (Cameo, 1969)
Running Wild (Midwood, 1969; with Love-In by Greg Hamilton)
Time for One More (Midwood, 1969; with Gang Girl by Walter Davidson)
The Mouth Lover (Midwood, 1970)
The Mouth Girl, Vol. 2 (Cameo, 1970)
Oral Daughter (Midwood, 1971)
The Hot Kids and Their Older Lovers (Brandon House, 1971) reprinted as
    Balcony Tramps, (Brandon House, 1971)
Please Force Me (Dansk Blue, 1971)
Captive of the Lust Master (Dansk Blue, 1971)
Naked Prisoner (Dansk Blue, 1972)
Blow Hot, Blow Cold (Barclay House, 1972)
The Twins Have Mother (Barclay House, 1972)
A Girl Possessed (Brandon House, 1973)
Ghetto Whore (Brandon House, 1976)
Father-Daughter Incest, undated
The Ecstasy of Agony, undated

## As Randy Guy
Hot Wife For Hire (Liverpool Library, 1981)
Hot Twins Next Door (Patch Pockets, 1982)
The Librarian's Hot Lips (Patch Pockets, 1983)
Three Hot Granddaughters (Patch Pockets, 1984)
Horny Wild Daughter (Greenleaf Classics, 1984)

## As Sheela Kunzer
Honor Thy Parent (Bee-Line Banner, 1976)
Daddy's Harlot (Bee-Line Banner, 1976)

## As Anonymous

Lily's Secret (Red Stripe, 1990) reprinted as Sweet Sensations (Redstripe UK,
 1991)
Myra's Lightening (Red Stripe, 1993)

# William R. Coons
## (1934-2001)

**As Dell Holland**
Hellhole of Sin (Bedside, 1962)
Sin Town (Bedside, 1962)
The Wild Ones (Neva, 1963)
The Far-Out Ones (Neva, 1963)
The Drifter (Playtime, 1963)
Illusion of Lust (Playtime, 1963)

**As William R. Coons**
Attica Diary (Stein & Day, 1972)

**As John Dexter**
Sinfully Yours (Bedside, 1962)
Man for Rent (Nightstand, 1962; with Lawrence Block; reprinted as Buy
    Buy Baby, 1974, as by Jeremy Dunn)

**As Andrew Shaw/Shole**
Army Sin Girls (Nightstand, 1961; reprinted as The Brazen Corps, 1974)
Sin Devil (Nightstand, 1961; reprinted as The Devil's Maidens, 1973)
The House of 7 Sins (Nightstand, 1961; reprinted as The Obsessed, 1974)
Lust Damned (Midnight Reader, 1961; reprinted as The Violated, 1974)
Passion Slaves (Nightstand, 1961, reprinted as The Carnal Crowd, 1973)
Ponytail Tramp (Nightstand, 1961; reprinted as No Stain So Deep, 1974)
Passion C.O.D. (Midnight Reader, 1962; reprinted as Pitch Man, Lover
    Man, Nightstand, 1974)
Passion Nightmare (Midnight Reader, 1962)
Passion Madman (Leisure, 1963, as by Andrew Shole)
Sin Sultan (Leisure, 1963, as by Andrew Shole)

# Bonnie Helen Golightly
## (1919-1998)

**Fiction:**

The Wild One (Avon, 1957)

Legend of the Lost (Berkley, 1957; movie tie-in)

High Cost of Loving (Avon, 1958; movie tie-in)

Beat Girl (Avon, 1959)

Born Reckless (1959; movie tie-in as by Milton Rogers)

The Shades of Evil (Hillman, 1960; reprinted as A Talent for Loving, Belmont, 1968)

The Intimate Ones (Hillman, 1960)

A Breath of Scandal (Avon, 1960; movie tie-in)

The Integration of Maybelle Brown (Belmont, 1961)

The Wife Swappers (Lancer, 1962)

Chloe—Again (Award, 1967; combines The Wild One & Beat Girl)

In Search of Gregory (Award, 1970)

Polly Paris (Avon, 1972)

**Non-Fiction:**

Sex Without Marriage (Lancer, 1962; with Jonathan Starr)

L.S.D.—The Problem-Solving Psychedelic (with P. G. Stafford), Tandem (1967)

On the Fringe of the Para-Normal (Award, 1969)

Also Available from Stark House Press, starkhousepress.com . . .

A Trio of Beacon Books:
Marijuana Girl / Call South 3300: Ask for Molly! / The Sex Cure:
Three Hard-to-Find Beacon Classics in on volume!

Edited and Introduction by Jeff Vorzimmer
ISBN: 978-1-944520-68-7        $19.95

Made in United States
Orlando, FL
17 August 2023

36200639R00185